CW00566782

Sign up for our newsletter to hear
about new and upcoming releases.

www.ylva-publishing.com

# Nights of Silk and Sapphire

## AMBER JACOBS

Ylva

For my mom, JH, for her endless support and encouragement...
and for never so much as batting an eyelid at any of my
peculiar quirks or artistic eccentricities. Love ya. :)

# Acknowledgments

A special thanks to T. Rye, who helped me patch a lot of early cracks in my story, my editor and all the lovely folk at Ylva who helped improve and polish the story, and Cherri and Andy, for their encouragement and humor.

# Chapter 1

Heat.

It beat against her like a live thing, hungrily sapping the moisture from her body, leaving her drained and weak. Her pale skin, a stranger to such harsh exposure, was blistered and burned. Fine blonde hair, once lovingly brushed and tied into elaborate braids, now tangled about her face in sweaty snarls. Her throat was dry and parched; the few sips of water the slavers allowed her each day only teased at the thirst that plagued her, the thirst that sat in the pit of her belly like a stone. Thirst like she had never imagined could exist. Manacles of rough iron bound her wrists with a rusted length of heavy chain, opening sores where they rubbed against her soft skin and serving as a constant physical reminder of her helpless bondage. Wild, stinging winds lashed her relentlessly with whips of grit and sand, making her eyes swollen and sore. She had learned to walk with her eyes cast down. There was nothing in this godforsaken desert she wanted to see.

For the first week after the attack, Dae had cursed the slavers who slaughtered the caravan she'd been traveling with. She had begged, demanded, and pleaded with them to release her for the ransom she assured them her parents would happily pay. Her efforts were wasted, however, and she had cried herself to sleep every night. Those tears were gone now. She hadn't the energy to think, let alone feel sorry for herself. This land was strange, and to a mind accustomed to endless green pastures and placid lakes, hellishly evil. The slavers had dragged Dae and the few dozen others they had captured into this barren land, forcing them to march across the shifting sands and stretches of jagged rock. They stopped only a few hours during the hottest part of the day to rest wherever they could find shade. The captives—mostly young women and girls—were fed only enough to give them energy to move. None of them spoke of the fate that awaited them on the other side of the desert; ignorance was a blessing they had no desire to cast aside.

Dae struggled to keep pace with the others, but it was an arduous undertaking. Raised to a life of luxury and privilege, sheltered by doting parents from anything the least bit harmful, she had barely had to walk more than a mile on her own in a single stretch. Her legs felt like boiling lead had been poured into the muscles of her calves and thighs. Her feet, clad only in delicate shoes designed for beauty rather than practicality, were swollen and bloodied where the blisters had formed, cracked, and reformed. Every breath of scalding air was a trial. Yet for all her suffering, she didn't dare complain. The ugly men who had captured her held whips and carried fearsome-looking swords, and while so far the worst they'd done was threaten, Dae had no intention of raising their ire. The memory of her escort, slaughtered as they sought to protect her, was still vivid in her mind.

Stumbling along exhausted, Dae fought to place one foot in front of the other. The sun was lower on the horizon now, and she eagerly encouraged its descent, knowing that darkness would bring some measure of respite from the dizzying heat. She found the bitter chill of night far easier to bear than the fire of day. Dae licked her dry, cracked lips, tasting the salt of her sweat, and glanced about at the shimmering heat waves that played across the land. They teased at her mind with phantasmal images of trees and oceans of cool, refreshing water. Her gaze drifted away from the taunting dreamscapes, bleary and unfocused, and it took her a long while to notice the appearance of something out of place in the bleak landscape. She blinked and squinted, realizing she wasn't seeing another mirage.

Up ahead and to the right, perched on a sharp ridge of wind-carved stone, three dark, mounted figures stood silhouetted against the evening sky, watching the slave caravan make its way across the desert.

Chancing a glance behind her, Dae saw the slavers hadn't yet noticed the watchers. The idea occurred to her that perhaps she could signal the distant figures for help, for rescue, but she had no idea how to accomplish this without attracting attention from her hated captors. Anyway, from the stories her maids had told her as a child, the people of the desert were more savage even than the slavers, blood thirsty barbarians who warred among themselves and delighted in torture and plunder. Yet, against her will, a small bubble of hope bloomed in her heart, and she pulled instinctively against the chain binding her hands. How much worse could her situation be, she wondered bitterly?

Biting her lip, indecisive, Dae plodded along, keeping a furtive eye on the watchers. Under her breath, she whispered to any gods who might be listening a brief prayer for some kind of savior to rescue her.

Zafirah Al'Intisar watched the small caravan with narrowed eyes. The outlanders were moving slowly, their feet doubtless weary from trekking this far into the merciless Jaharri desert. Zafirah's great warhorse, Simhana—a beautiful white mare with solid black markings—sensed the tension in her rider and pawed anxiously at the stony ground, anticipating action and battle.

"Slavers, Scion," observed the man to Zafirah's left, running callused fingers through a wiry, dark beard that gave his face a perpetually frowning expression. Zafirah glanced at him, hearing the distaste in his voice. Rehan Al'Carin was the ruler of the Tek, one of the many tribes owing allegiance to the Scion, and Zafirah's distant cousin. His features held the worn, sandblasted ruggedness that came from living in the unforgiving, arid wilderness. His body was tough and lean, powerful as the desert made those who could brave its savage temper. Zafirah liked the old brute, as crude and hot-tempered as he could sometimes be. She nodded and looked back at the caravan.

"They choose a dangerous path, tempting the sands on foot," remarked the tall, dark-skinned woman watching from her customary place at Zafirah's right-hand side. Falak was the leader of Zafirah's elite scouts and chief military council, and the hunger in her sharp gray eyes made it clear she was eager to attack. She cradled the arch of a massive recurve bow crafted from layers of horn across her lap, and a quiver of arrows fletched with raven feathers bristled above her right shoulder. She studied the slave caravan a moment longer, her slender, powerful fingers plucking at the bowstring in a tense rhythm, then looked to Zafirah in hopeful expectation. "What shall we do, my Scion?"

One of the slaves, a young girl with pale hair and shredded clothes, slipped in the rocky sand and fell to her knees. Instantly one of the slavers was on her, dragging her to her feet and shoving her forward, gesturing with his whip in an obvious threat. Zafirah's lips pulled into a tight line, the expression hidden by the white cotton *haik* that protected her face from the wind-blown sands.

These slavers were an unwanted distraction, but one Zafirah knew she could not overlook. She had come out here leading a small army of *spahi*—the feared desert cavalry—in order to quell a simple civil dispute. The Tek tribe had been feuding with their ancient rivals, the Sakaran, a conflict Zafirah would not normally have concerned herself with. The desert tribes were made up of fierce warriors, and such blood feuds were a source of constant quarrels and skirmishes. This time, however, the Sakaran had threatened more aggressive action, and so Zafirah had left the coastal city of El'Kasari to remind those under her authority of the risk they took by proposing war. The two tribes had balefully retreated to their respective corners like chastised children, and Zafirah had been leading her men back to El'Kasari when reports came in of these strangers.

Not that strangers were uncommon in the Jaharri desert. The barren stretch of sand lay between two nations of great wealth and abundance. While the trek was perilous, crossing the desert directly was still the fastest way to trade between east and west. Sailing around the southern coastal route was safer but added months of expensive travel time to an expedition. In the past, before the city of El'Kasari had been built, the various nomadic tribes of the desert preyed mercilessly upon these traders. For hundreds of years, however, since the Scion Peace, travelers paid a tribute to the desert people and in return were left unmolested. Zafirah's people had grown wealthy from such payments, and most were satisfied. Most...though not all.

"Scion?"

"Hmm?" Zafirah glanced at Falak, her attention distracted by the pale-haired girl as she struggled along on weary feet.

"Do we attack?" The scout grinned hungrily. "Slavers have no place—"

"Slavers or no, the business of outlanders is not our concern," Zafirah interrupted softly, "provided they honor the desert and its guardians. But by the reports of your scouts, these men took water from the Kah-hari oasis without offering tribute for their passage." She frowned. "These men know not the ways of our people. They were fools to enter the desert without such wisdom." She drew a flashing, curved sword from her side and spun it quickly through the air. "A pity they shall not have a chance to learn from their folly."

Rehan and Falak grinned at one another as Zafirah wheeled her steed about and set off carefully back down the rocky rise to where the rest of the *spahi* were waiting. The people of the desert lived for battle and glory, and while this pathetic band of foreign slavers would hardly be a challenge, both were eager to enjoy the sport.

Zafirah selected two dozen riders from the army and ordered them to follow her with a gesture. The shifting sands and shimmering heat were disorienting to those unfamiliar with the desert, making it hard to judge distance or depth. Taking advantage of a shallow depression in the land, the *spahi* were able to ride to within a hundred yards of the slavers without being detected. When they were in position, Zafirah raised her hand and, tilting her head back, pierced the still air with a shattering, ululating war cry. The *spahi* answered it with calls of their own as they spurred their mounts forward. In seconds, they had fallen upon the panicked slavers, their swords painting crimson stains across the white sands.

Zafirah charged one of the terrified men. Simhana swung sideways at the last moment as she had been trained, a move which afforded the Scion the room she needed to dispatch her enemy. A single powerful stroke of her scimitar relieved the slaver of his sword, and the return stroke relieved him of his head. As Simhana wheeled about, Zafirah turned just as a second man charged her with a hoarse shout, raising a wickedly barbed spear in line for a throw. His body froze in the act, however, as three slender arrows sprouted suddenly from his chest, and after a second he fell face-first to the ground. Zafirah flicked a glance behind her, raising her sword in a salute of thanks to where Falak and her scouts were coolly notching new arrows to their bowstrings. The dark-skinned woman gave a curt nod even as she drew a bead on another target.

The fight was over in moments; the slavers could offer only pitiful resistance against the elite desert horsemen, who gave no quarter or mercy in the slaughter. In short order, the only figures left standing on the blood-soaked sands were the clustered group of terrified slave girls, who huddled together and eyed the fearsome masked figures on their prancing horses with expressions of shock and awe. Dismounting gracefully, Zafirah strode over to the cowering prisoners, immediately seeking out the young blonde she had observed from the ridge. The girl was kneeling on the ground, looking around dazedly, swooning from exhaustion and what the Scion recognized as the symptoms of exposure. Eyes the color of deep emeralds struggled to focus as Zafirah's shadow fell over her. She blinked, recoiling a little as though expecting a beating.

"Please...d-don't hurt me..." she whimpered. Then her eyelids fluttered, and she slumped forward in a dead faint.

Zafirah quickly gestured Rehan to her side. "Find some horses for the girls. We shall take them with us. They can serve your tribe to earn their freedom."

"But Scion, I cannot take this many into my tribe," Rehan protested. "I have not the means to feed more mouths!"

"El'Kasari will supplement your resources if it is required," Zafirah allowed. She knew that each tribe could only maintain positions for so many servants before the burden would drain their precious water. Still, the law of the desert was clear: those who were rescued from death or slavery owed a debt that must be repaid with service to the benefactor. In a harsh and unyielding world such as this one, nothing was ever given away freely. "And do not fear, Rehan, I do not expect you to take all the girls." Zafirah's soft smile as she studied the comatose figure lying in the sand was hidden by the folds of her *haik*. "This one, at least, will be returning with me to the city."

Rehan glanced at the wretched girl, then winked lasciviously at Zafirah. "Your tastes have altered little, I see."

"My tastes have not altered at all, Cousin," she said with a smirk. "I am certain a home for her can be found in the seraglio. Now go, get the horses." She dismissed him with a wave of her hand.

While Rehan jogged away to locate mounts for the still-quivering girls, Zafirah knelt beside the fallen blonde and studied her more closely. The girl was young—Zafirah guessed not much past her eighteenth year—and even with the ravages of wind and sun marring her perfection, her features held a rare and unique cast of beauty. The shredded rags she wore did little to hide her curvaceous figure from Zafirah's appreciative gaze. Reaching out with a gloved hand, Zafirah ran her fingers through the long, shimmering gold strands of hair that were currently matted with sweat and grit. Blonde hair was unknown among the desert tribes and was looked upon as a strange and foreign feature that was greatly prized. Zafirah had a well-known penchant for women of exotic appearance, and this girl was certainly too enticing a creature for her to overlook. Her smile grew wider as she nodded, pleased with her find, and with the day's work in general.

Zafirah stood as Falak approached, the dark archer casting the girl a knowing look before she gestured toward the butchered slavers. "What shall we do with them?"

"Detail a group of men to ride the bodies out to the Kah-hari spring," Zafirah ordered. "Have them hung from the trees as a warning of what happens if the desert is not given its rightful offerings."

"As you wish, my Scion." She relaxed a little and indicated the young blonde. "A new plaything, perhaps?" she joked.

"Perhaps"—Zafirah pulled aside the cotton *haik* and grinned rakishly at her chief scout—"if she asks nicely."

Falak laughed and shook her head. "Let us hope the other girls do not grow jealous. It has been some time since you added to the harem."

"Do not be concerned, Falak. I am quite capable of satisfying the desires of all; I do not think one more will tax my abilities overmuch."

Falak leaned closer to study the girl for herself, giving an approving nod before throwing Zafirah a wink. "With luck, the pale beauty will at least give you a chance to tempt her to your bed. These fools"—she gave a contemptuous nod to the fallen slavers—"were journeying from the eastern kingdom. It is a land rich in water but ignorant of passion. The girl may take some convincing."

Zafirah shrugged as though the issue were of no importance. "Whether she is swayed or not matters little to me," she said. "Her loveliness will be better appreciated in the palace harem than in the slave markets of the western empire. At least with me her perfection will not be marred by lashes and chains." She considered the rough iron manacles binding the girl's wrists with disapproval, not liking the open, cruel welts they had worn into her soft flesh. Zafirah looked away to the horizon and the setting sun. "We should not linger here on the open sands," she said. "The girl needs proper healing, and it is at least a day's ride back to El'Kasari. Go…attend the slain so we can be moving again."

Falak nodded, as familiar as any other Jaharri with the dangers of letting such heat sickness go untreated, and left to detail a detachment to return the bodies back to the oasis. Zafirah watched her go, then knelt beside the unconscious blonde once more.

"Such a pretty flower," she whispered, running her fingers over the girl's body as much to check for other injuries as to simply admire her perfection. She smiled, finding no whip marks or excessive bruising, and again brushed the tangled mass of pale hair away from the girl's face. "Have no fear. I will not allow the sun to wilt your petals."

Zafirah watched in silent contentment as the rest of her warriors freed the other captives. She wrapped the *haik* back over her face as the wind blew fiercely in the fading light. It was fortunate that the slavers had not possessed the common sense to pay tribute for their passage across these lands; Zafirah would have hated to see her newest prize slip from her grasp.

It had been a good day indeed.

# Chapter 2

DAE STRUGGLED TO SHAKE OFF the fog that clouded her mind, cracking open her eyes and blinking several times before she was able to make out anything of her surroundings. For a moment what she saw made her think that her ordeal had been blessedly no more than a night terror and she was back in her own room at home. Richly embroidered cushions lay everywhere, and the walls of the lavishly furnished room were decorated with expensive tapestries and hangings. The air was heavy with the sweet scent of perfume—jasmine, she identified fuzzily—and cool satin sheets caressed her skin. The wonderful illusion lasted only a moment, however, before Dae felt again the terrible thirst as she tried to swallow and the burning in her cracked skin. Confused, she tried to sit up and was overcome by a wave of dizziness.

A cool hand pressed against her forehead soothingly. "Easy now, little one," said a feminine voice tinged with a heavy, exotic accent. "The desert did not take kindly to you. It will be some time before your full strength returns." Something rough and cold was pressed against her lips, and Dae recoiled. "Drink," said the voice gently. "You must replenish what the sun took from your body."

Feeling sudden moisture lap against her parched lips, Dae quickly opened her mouth and reached up to clutch at what she now recognized as a ceramic jug. She struggled to swallow as much as she could, choking and spluttering in her haste to accept the offering before it was revoked. Hands like silk eased her efforts.

"Slowly," instructed the voice. "Take smaller sips, or your stomach will cramp and reject the water."

Dae did as she was told, sipping slowly until the jug was taken away, her thirst only moderately slackened. Whimpering, she lay back and tried to look up at her savior.

"Wh-who are you?" she asked, her voice raspy.

"My name is Inaya." Delicate hands caressed Dae's face tenderly. "*Tsharraafna*—I am honored to make your acquaintance."

Blinking painfully, Dae finally brought the features of her benefactor into focus. Inaya looked to be not much older than herself, and she was quite possibly the most beautiful girl Dae had ever laid eyes upon. Her olive-toned features were framed by hair blacker than midnight, so dark that the highlights shimmering in it shone blue in the soft light. Her deep, liquid brown eyes held a sense of mystery and seductive promise complemented by full, sensuous lips that smiled far too easily.

Inaya was dressed in an outfit comprised as much from jewelry as it was from cloth, exposing most of her firm, dusky body while covering just enough to maintain some semblance of modesty. Dae had never in her life imagined such a scandalous wardrobe, and she couldn't help but stare. When her gaze slipped helplessly down over Inaya's body, she immediately noticed another oddity: a bejeweled metal stud pierced the skin of the girl's navel, its shiny gleam contrasting against her sun-darkened skin. *How barbaric!* Realizing her unblinking reaction might be bordering on offensive, Dae quickly returned her attention to Inaya's face.

"Where am I?" She looked around the strange, exotically decorated room in bewilderment, remembering only the dark, shadowed figure standing over her as she knelt on the blazing sands, surrounded by bloodcurdling screams. "How did I get here?"

"You are in the harem of the Scion Zafirah Al'Intisar, in the great city of El'Kasari," Inaya explained slowly. "You have been unconscious for a day and a night. From what I understand, the Scion rescued you from slavers in the desert. You were brought here by the guards, and I have seen to your recovery."

"The slavers?" Dae asked in confusion. "What happened to them?"

"The Scion dispatched them for failing to pay tribute on their passage across the sands. I heard that none survived the slaughter."

*Dead.* Dae breathed a sigh of relief. *I'm safe.* Then, she suddenly recalled Inaya's words more clearly. "Wh-where did you say I was?"

"In the harem of the Scion Zafir—"

"Harem?" Her eyes flew open in stark terror. Dae had heard terrible stories of what happened in such places. Harems were said to be havens of debauchery and hedonistic sin. Panic engulfed her and she struggled to sit up, but Inaya had little trouble pressing her gently back down again. "What... Why am I here?" Dae asked.

"The Scion was extremely taken with you," Inaya explained. "I can understand why. Your beauty is of rare quality. You are to remain here as a servant."

"But I...I want to go home!" Dae pleaded.

"The Scion rescued you. According to our laws, since she saved your life, it is her right to take control of your destiny. If she wishes you to stay here, then it shall be so. There can be no argument against it."

Dae felt a fresh surge of depression and loss well up inside her. "Are you a slave here as well?"

"Not exactly." Inaya smiled softly. "I am one of the harem girls, a pleasure-servant of the Scion."

It took Dae several moments to process that information, and when she did, her jaw dropped in horror. "You're a...a whore?"

Inaya's expression stiffened instantly. "No," she corrected a little coldly. "A pleasure-servant is very different to a whore. I provide for the desires of the Scion, whatever they may be, and I do so willingly and with great pride and joy! It is an honor that I should be chosen for such a position in the palace." She gave Dae a hard look. "You would do well to remember that, since it is a position, and an honor, that you yourself now hold."

Dae shrank back from Inaya's displeasure. "I-I'm sorry," she stammered quickly, not wanting to alienate someone who was being so nice to her. "I just... This is all so strange to me. I don't understand."

"Understanding will come with time." Inaya's features softened quickly. It seemed almost as though the stern expression had difficulty holding its place on the beautiful girl's face. She reached into a bowl that rested on a small table nearby and retrieved a moist towel. "Here," she said, placing the cloth on Dae's burned face. "This will help soothe your skin."

Dae accepted the ministrations shyly, still trying to come to terms with the sudden and inexplicable changes in her life. "So...you're expected to..." She hesitated. "To...bed with this Scion?"

"You can put it that way if you like," Inaya said, her tone of voice suggesting she found Dae's innocent phrasing amusing. "It is not so bad as you might be imagining."

Dae shivered fearfully despite the consolations. "I've never...done such things before," she admitted quietly.

Inaya nodded. "I had guessed as much."

"What's he like?"

"He?" Inaya looked confused. "*He* who?"

"Well...the Scion, of course. Is he gentle?"

Inaya laughed lightly, a pleasant lilting laugh that sounded almost childlike. "Oh, my child, have you not listened? Scion Zafirah is no man. She is a woman!"

"What?" Dae sat up in surprise, confused by this revelation she had somehow missed. "But I thought you said—"

"I did indeed," Inaya agreed cheerfully, watching the expression on Dae's face with interest. "Zafirah is an extremely talented and generous lover, a woman of great passions."

Dae shrank back in horror. "You mean you...you sleep with... another *woman*?"

"There is precious little sleep involved, I assure you!" Inaya laughed. "Of course I take pleasure with other women. It is a common practice among the Jaharri people." She tilted her head to the side curiously. "I have heard that such things are forbidden in your land, that to even speak of them is not permitted. Is this true?"

"Of course it's true!" Dae's nose wrinkled in fearful distaste. "It's an unnatural and disgusting perversion!"

Inaya stopped her gentle ministrations and lifted a delicately plucked eyebrow haughtily. "You are very quick to condemn an act of which you have neither knowledge nor experience," she scolded quietly. "Perhaps when you come to understand the beauty that can be found within such a taking of pleasure, you will not be so harsh in your judgment."

"I-I didn't mean—"

"Yes, you did," Inaya interrupted. "But have no fear, child, I am not offended. It is natural for you to carry with you the same intolerances and foolish propriety that I have heard are so common among the people of your land."

Dae considered this new information and felt renewed despair and terror. "I could never do such a thing," she whispered almost to herself. "I couldn't ever do...*that*...with a woman!"

Inaya smiled mysteriously and gave Dae a reassuring pat on the shoulder, her fingers caressing lightly. "Do not concern yourself. The Scion has no need to force her attentions on the unwilling. There are more than enough women who will go to her most joyfully. If you do not wish to take pleasure with her, she will not take you against your will."

"Are you certain?" Dae's features lit up with a tremulous hope.

"Of course. Zafirah would never wish to taint the beauty of such an act with force. There can be no pleasure for her if her partner does not take equal joy as she herself."

"Then why would she keep me in the harem?"

Inaya shrugged. "It is her wish," she said simply. "You should consider yourself most fortunate, child. The position of pleasure-servant is held in high regard within the palace. We have respect and honor from others, and we are provided a life of great freedom and luxury. We want for nothing—water, fruit, entertainment... We are permitted to indulge in whatever activity we so desire. When you have properly recovered from your ordeal, I will introduce you to the other girls and take you to see the rest of the seraglio. The gardens and pools are quite lovely, I promise, and a rare sight you will find nowhere else in the desert lands. For now, lie back and relax. You must allow your body to heal itself, so be calm in the knowledge that you are safe. I am sure the Scion will wish to see you when you are well again."

Feeling exhaustion rise suddenly to reclaim her, Dae did as Inaya suggested, lying back into the silken caress of cool sheets and pillows, letting the soothing ministrations of her new friend ease away her pains. In a few moments, her eyes had drifted shut and she fell into a healing sleep.

Wetting the face towel in the bowl beside her, Inaya smiled softly to herself and enjoyed the task of providing for the sleeping girl. The other inhabitants of the harem were all intensely curious about the Scion's latest find, and Inaya knew they were envious that she had received the privilege of tending to the needs of the foreigner. Gently letting her fingers comb through the last few tangles that remained in the silken locks, Inaya hummed a soft, lilting melody to herself, watching the lines of tension ease from Dae's face. She was already looking forward to getting to know the refreshingly innocent and naïve girl better in the coming weeks.

Over the next few weeks, Dae slowly regained her strength and equilibrium as she recovered from her harsh experience in the desert. Her blistered and cracked skin soon flaked off and was then soothed with scented healing oils until it was healthy once more. Calluses had formed around her wrists where the rough iron manacles had bitten into her skin, and she knew these final marks of bondage would be a long time fading. Eating strange but delicious fruits and drinking water sweetened with wine soon gave her back her strength. But as Dae's health returned, the initial surge of relief she had felt at being rescued from a life of slavery gave way to despondence at the new fate the Gods had set before her. Dae had never been away from the embrace of her parents for more than a few days, and her sense of loss was overwhelming. Many mornings, her pillows were stained with tears of grief and homesickness.

Inaya remained by her side almost constantly during this time, always ready to serve. The desert girl did all she could to help Dae adjust to her new life, easing her fears and melancholy with empathy and understanding. She was extremely considerate of her charge's well-being, slowly drawing Dae away from depression with her happy chatter. During her visits, she spent a lot of time explaining the way of life in the palace harem. Dae wondered why her new friend seemed so eager to serve her, but she accepted being waited on easily; it was something she had grown used to at home, and the attention was reassuring. Sometimes Inaya spoke of the Scion, but Dae was determined not to think about anything involving the woman who, in her opinion, must surely be a savage and lustful demon to indulge in such terrible sins as were hinted at by the darkly enchanting girl.

During this time, Dae was provided with a new wardrobe made from fine silks, exotic and brightly colored. Inaya also brought her new jewellery—gifts of welcome, she said, from the other pleasure-servants Dae had yet to meet. The worth of the jewels must have been considerable—they sparkled brilliantly with diamonds, emeralds, and other precious stones—but when Dae protested this generosity, Inaya insisted she accept them. She also overrode any objection regarding the new clothing that was offered.

Although Inaya assured her painfully self-conscious ward that her outfit was the most modest and reserved one she could find, Dae was still embarrassed by how much of her body it revealed. Her entire stomach was left bare, and the embroidered green silk that covered her firm, ample breasts seemed designed to enhance her cleavage rather than conceal it. Loose gossamer pants shimmered about her legs in almost transparent waves, and gold bracelets and chains adorned her lithe figure. With her hair brushed by the ever-attentive Inaya till it shone in the lamplight and her eyelids dusted with a faint indigo powder, Dae barely recognized herself in the mirror's reflection. She fidgeted often, uncomfortable with what seemed an immodest display of flesh.

Dae did not venture from the room during her recovery, and Inaya informed her that the chamber would be her own private quarters from now on. As her depression faded, Dae's curiosity about her new home grew, and eventually Inaya agreed to show her the rest of the seraglio where the other girls usually spent their time.

Following her new friend—guiltily mesmerized by the way Inaya's hips swayed enticingly beneath the thin beaded chains that hung about her waist and how the motion constantly revealed vast planes of smooth olive skin—Dae found herself walking down a long, expansive corridor with rooms evenly spaced on either side. There were no doors, she noted, and looking into the rooms, she found each to be similar in design to her own. From that, Dae concluded these were the quarters of the other harem girls.

"Um...how many other slav—Um, I mean, 'pleasure-servants' does the Scion have?" she asked Inaya.

"Not including you and me, there are twenty-two other girls in the harem," Inaya said over her shoulder. "Of course, the Scion sometimes takes a lover from outside the seraglio...and those she takes to her bed are honored to be chosen. We..." she gestured to the other rooms, "are those more dedicated to her service. Though every girl in the seraglio came here by a different path, we are all special...each of us chosen by Zafirah as more than a simple tryst. We are her companions as well as her lovers."

"Oh." Dae tried hard not to dwell on the terrible images her imagination conjured of what the poor girls must endure. "Does she only ever take other women as lovers?"

Inaya nodded, her earrings jangling musically as she did so. "She has no desire to bed with men. Zafirah's passion runs strongest for young women of great and exotic beauty," she flicked an admiring glance at Dae, "just like you."

Dae swallowed hard, praying that the terrible Scion would be as unwilling to rape her as Inaya had promised.

The corridor led the two young women to an enormous hexagonal-shaped room with intricately carved walls and a vaulted ceiling. The center of the floor dropped into a large sunken area filled with plush cushions and lounging chairs, and around the perimeter were tables laden with platters of fruits, breads, sweetmeats, and other delicacies Dae could not identify. Three young women lay sleepily among the cushions, all dressed in a similarly-provocative manner as Inaya. The three looked up as Dae and Inaya entered, their eyes widening a little when they fell upon the fidgeting visitor. In a moment, they had crowded around the uneasy girl, reaching out to touch her skin and hair excitedly, exclaiming over her exquisite beauty.

Inaya shooed them away and stood protectively in front of Dae. "Enough," she said sternly. "The poor girl has been through a great deal already. She does not need you all fawning over her right now."

"But Inaya," one of the girls protested with a deep pout, "you've been keeping her hidden away for too long. It's not fair."

Inaya sighed. "Very well." She gestured for Dae to step forward. "Dae, this is Shadiya, Firyaal, and Husn." Each girl bowed in turn, and Dae nodded shyly.

"It's nice to meet you all," she said politely, feeling very self-conscious among these people. Dae considered herself quite attractive, but each of these women was absolutely stunning! Shadiya and Husn both had similar features to Inaya, with dark hair and olive skin, while Firyaal had pale skin and thick, lustrous hair the color of flame. Next to them, Dae couldn't help but feel like an ugly duckling.

The girls of the harem didn't seem to think so, however, and they were soon reaching out to touch her again in wonder. Inaya let them "ooh" and "ahh" for a few minutes before she rescued Dae from their admiration and guided her around the sunken area to a doorway on the other side. The three women followed, asking questions of Dae's homeland and her life, and of how she came to be in the desert when the Scion rescued her. A little overwhelmed by the attention, Dae didn't have time to answer before she found herself being led through the door and into sunlight and laughter.

Blinking in the sudden light, Dae found herself in a great garden surrounded by trees and plants she had never seen before in her life. The air was heavy with the scent of water, and she smiled as she looked around. The sight of the garden was comforting to her, being a similar environment to the homeland she'd been stolen from. A short waterfall nearby cascaded into a deep pool of crystal clear water, around which grew ferns and palms of every description. Several laughing nymph-like figures splashed about in the pool, their carefree play stopping the moment they noticed Dae. Other girls were lying around happily, eating or dozing in the sun. Though they were all of different heights and coloring, the women were all young and extraordinarily beautiful…and they all instantly stopped what they were doing when they saw Dae and rushed over excitedly.

Before Inaya could offer a protest, the girls had flocked around an embarrassed and shy Dae, seemingly amazed by her hair and skin, exclaiming over the color of her eyes and her remarkable beauty. Uncertain what to do, not wanting to insult anyone, Dae stood still as wondering hands reached out to caress her face and body, the touches curious and gentle. Though the intimacy of their admiration made her uncomfortable, she had the impression it was a natural custom among these strange desert people. They seemed to express themselves with such touches and physical contact; she had seen that much from her dealings with Inaya. In Dae's homeland, such behavior would have been looked upon as barbaric and uncivilized. Cultured people expressed themselves with words, not actions. Still, she accepted the fascinated touches as calmly as she could, trying to ignore the display of so much bare skin surrounding her.

Before Inaya could free her charge from the avid admirers, the sharp sound of steel ringing against steel brought an instant hush to the garden. The girls immediately stopped their fawning and, pouting a little, returned to their previous activities, most casting curious looks back at the confused girl. Suddenly left alone, except for Inaya, Dae looked around to find the source of the noise.

Two female guards stood on either side of one of the doorways leading into the garden, drawn swords pressed against their wrist-shields. They watched the harem girls retreat, then brusquely sheathed their weapons. Dae watched as a new figure emerged from the doorway, her breath catching a little in her throat at the magnificent sight.

The woman was tall and slender, yet she carried with her a quiet air of assurance and power that revealed her true strength. She wore a fringed and slitted skirt which revealed the smooth expanse of her bare legs with every stride and a single length of cloth which wrapped around the back of her neck, crossed diagonally over her breasts, and circled around her waist like a sash. Long, ink-black hair was tied into a thick braid over her left shoulder, and eyes the color of burning sapphires looked around the seraglio garden briefly before they settled on Dae. Her hard features softened into a pleased smile, and Dae could only gasp at her incredible beauty—a beauty which seemed almost to outshine that of the other girls.

Glancing at Inaya curiously, Dae saw a playful light in the girl's eyes. "Who is she?" she asked quietly as the magnificent woman approached.

"She is the Scion, of course."

Dae's mouth hung open in shock. "*That's* the Scion?"

"Indeed."

This was not the twisted, perverted demoness Dae had been picturing in her mind. This woman was radiant and glorious; the look about her was regal and commanding, yet at the same time, alluring and playful.

As she neared the two, the woman's dazzling gaze wandered over Dae's pleasantly displayed body and her smile grew a fraction wider. Inaya bowed deeply as the Scion stopped in front of her, and Dae clumsily did the same, wishing she possessed a fraction of her companion's grace.

"My Scion," Inaya greeted.

"Inaya." Zafirah accepted the homage that was her due before turning her attention back to Dae. "I trust your charge is recovered from her ordeal?"

"She is, Scion. I was just now introducing her to the other girls for the first time." Inaya grinned a little. "They have been anxious to meet her."

"So I would imagine." Zafirah cast her eyes over the rest of the garden, seeing the other girls still watching their new friend curiously. She knew they must be eager to learn more of their new playmate... and she also knew that their ideas of "play" often included activities of a nature she was certain the painfully innocent blonde would not understand or enjoy. Zafirah encouraged her pleasure-servants to engage equally with each other as with herself, but she could tell that it would take the young girl time to come to terms with the strange new world in which she found herself. That taken into consideration, Zafirah decided it was time to have a little talk with the latest addition to her harem. She faced Dae and addressed the trembling girl directly.

"You are feeling well, child?"

Eyes the color of wet emeralds stared blankly at her for a long moment, the girl appearing nervous and almost on the verge of fainting, before she managed to stammer, "I-I am, S...Scion."

"Excellent. I wish to see you in my chamber in the *aseau*, after meals." She glanced at Inaya. "See to it."

"As you wish, Scion."

"Thank you." Zafirah allowed her eyes to wander over the contours of Dae's body for a few lingering moments, then turned and departed the garden, her two guards trailing behind her.

Dae breathed a sigh of relief once the tall figure was out of sight. Inaya—casting a warning glare at the other girls, who looked ready to flock forward once more—gathered Dae into her arms and led her back into the now empty hexagonal room, where she settled her on one of the lounges.

"Not quite as you expected her to be, is she?"

Dae shook her head. "She was…" She struggled to find an appropriate descriptive for the woman. "Amazing." Suddenly, she considered the reason why the Scion must have summoned her, and her muscles tensed with alarm. "She wants to see me alone in her chambers! She must want to bed me, I know it! She—"

Inaya placed a delicate finger over Dae's mouth to forestall her growing panic. "She wants to talk. You may believe me, Dae, Zafirah means you no harm. If you tell her you do not wish to take pleasure with her, she will respect your decision. Never has she forced herself upon another woman, and never shall she. It is not her way."

"But she will be angered if—"

"She will not harm you," Inaya insisted. "Now, put the matter out of your mind. The others will not leave me be until I have allowed them to see more of you. Do you feel ready to face the jackals?"

Dae took a deep, calming breath, wanting badly to believe Inaya's reassurances but still uneasy about what would be expected of her. She needed a distraction from what might lie ahead, so she forced herself to focus on the more immediate—and less intimidating—situation. "I suppose so."

"Excellent. They will not hurt you, so you need not be fearful. Do not let their curiosity overwhelm you. It has been some time since another girl was welcomed into the harem, and they are naturally excited and anxious to know you better."

So saying, Inaya led her charge back into the garden and the impatiently waiting flock who quickly gathered around once more. The flood of questions and introductions that followed effectively stole Dae's attention from her fears.

Later that evening, after a meal she'd been too fretful to eat, Dae was escorted through the palace to the bedchamber of the Scion. She was far too consumed by her dread to notice the beauty of the palace architecture, though she did note absently that it was constructed mostly from white marble that was pleasantly cool in contrast to the heat of the seraglio gardens. The guards escorting her led her into the expansive room, which, like all the others, had no door, and announced her to the woman waiting therein.

Zafirah turned from the window she was looking out of and smiled in welcome to her guest. "Leave us," she ordered the two guards, who saluted and returned to their duties. Zafirah slowly approached the trembling girl, her eyes warm and curious. She studied the freshly-healed skin and radiant hair, pleased to see the outlander girl restored to full health.

"It seems Inaya's efforts have been well rewarded," she said softly, her voice deep but still feminine. "You have recovered from your ordeal with the slavers with little lasting damage."

Dae found herself captivated by the seductive pull of the burning eyes that held her, and though she sensed no threat or malice from the tall, dark-haired woman, her mind still conjured nightmarish images of what she might be forced to do in this chamber. She swallowed hard, wishing she were home in the safety of her parents' arms.

Zafirah ran her eyes over Dae's body. "I trust you are pleased with your quarters?" she asked. "Is everything to your satisfaction?"

"Um…everything's fine, m-my Scion."

"And the other girls? They have treated you well?"

Dae nodded, remembering the somewhat overwhelmingly enthusiastic welcome she'd received. "They were very nice, yes."

"Excellent." Zafirah gazed with fascination at Dae's blonde hair, then at her shy green eyes. "What is your name, child?"

It took Dae a long moment before she managed to open her mouth. "Dae. Dae of Everdeen."

Zafirah clapped her hands in delight. "As the night is to the day?"

"Um…no, it's not spelled the same."

"Spelled?"

"Yes…you know, the letters are different."

Zafirah shrugged. "We of the desert have no written words," she said dismissively. "Our customs, laws, and history are passed down from generation to generation by oration. We do not trust dead words written on dead parchment, as do your people. Such words can lie without guilt or shame."

Dae didn't know what she should say to that, and so remained silent.

"You are from the eastern lands, are you not?"

Dae nodded. "From the Heartland, yes."

"'The Heartland,' is it?" Zafirah's expression turned faintly contemptuous. "The eastern kingdom changes its name every time a new king usurps power from the old. It has failed to hold the same title for more than a few generations, as each man in power seeks to glorify his rule by renaming it. Given that changeable tendency, we Jaharri have always referred to your homeland simply as the eastern kingdom." When Dae made no comment, Zafirah continued. "Based on your demeanor and health, I cannot imagine you had been in bondage long. How is it you came to be captured by the men I rescued you from?"

"I was traveling to the monastery in the city," Dae explained. "It was a few days after my birthday, and my parents told me I needed to be blessed by the priests. The men…" She shuddered at the awful memory. "They attacked my escort…I don't know if any survived. Then they grabbed me and took me away."

Zafirah nodded her understanding. "And how old are you, child?"

"I just saw my nineteenth summer," Dae said softly, fidgeting nervously.

"Nineteen?" Zafirah's dark brows rose in surprise. "I would not have guessed so many years by the youth of your face. You have been treated kindly by the Fates to be blessed with such beauty." She reached out a hand to caress Dae's face, stopping when the girl recoiled, her eyes wide. Zafirah's features softened. "I mean you no harm, child. Surely Inaya told you as much?"

"She did, but…"

"You were uncertain whether or not she spoke the truth?"

Dae nodded.

"I understand." Zafirah moved closer, settling her hands lightly on Dae's shoulders and urging her to relax. "Does it make you uncomfortable that another woman would look on you with desirous eyes?" she asked, her voice low and seductive. "Does it repulse you that I would wish to bed you?"

Dae shuddered, the warmth of the taller woman's hands and the hypnotic tone of her voice having a strange and disturbing effect on her body, as though a fever ran through her blood. "I do not like... such things," she said hesitantly, not wanting to incur this powerful woman's wrath, but fearing more the uncertain terror of giving in to her seduction.

But the Scion only nodded a calm acceptance. "I have learned from ambassadors that it is forbidden in your land for women to share pleasure with other women, and for men to share pleasure with men. Indeed, many ambassadors from the eastern kingdom have been shocked to hear that such things are accepted in the desert—shocked and disgusted, for some reason. One such man refused to agree to a treaty and then demanded I pay him restitution simply for offering him hospitality in my home." Zafirah's smile grew cold, and her eyes flared dangerously. "I could forgive his ignorance, but the insult cost him his head."

Dae did not doubt for a moment that this commanding woman was entirely capable of carrying out such a punishment personally. Zafirah stood very close to her now, close enough that she could smell the scent of incense and perfume that clung to her like a vaporous robe. Close enough that she could feel the heat radiating from her, a heat that felt almost enticing. Dae drew away a little. "I don't mean to be rude, but..." She hesitated, glancing to the enormous bed that seemed to dominate the bedchamber. "I...cannot..."

The sapphire eyes darkened to an almost purple shade, Zafirah's lashes lowered not in anger but desire. "You do not wish to take pleasure with me?"

Dae studied her feet intently, but shook her head.

"Because I am a woman, or because you do not find me attractive?"

"Well..." Dae was confused for a moment, wondering how to answer that question. "I-I think you're quite attractive," she stammered, looking up now. "In fact, you're probably the most beautiful woman I've ever seen, but..." Zafirah brightened at the praise. "I'm just... I don't like..." She trailed off.

Zafirah lifted a hand and ran a single finger down along Dae's face, from her temple to her chin. Her glittering eyes flickered down over the young girl's well-displayed body, appreciating the generous curves and exotic coloring. "You are very beautiful, Dae," she whispered, her voice a caress. "I do not deny that nothing would give me greater pleasure than to tear the clothes from your body, throw you onto my bed, and spend the rest of the night introducing you to the joys of another woman's body." Dae's eyes widened in terror, but Zafirah's expression was more reassuring than predatory. "Yet I cannot force you to enjoy something against your will, and there would be no pleasure for me unless you were a willing participant. I shall not ask you to warm my bed if you do not wish to do so."

The panic in Dae's eyes dissipated a little. "You really mean that?"

"Of course."

"Then…" Dae's brow furrowed. "What do you want with me?"

Zafirah shrugged and drew away a step. "You will remain in the seraglio," she said simply. "It is a good life. You will be well cared for, provided every luxury I can offer. I wish for you to be my pleasure-servant."

"But I cannot serve you as the other girls do."

Zafirah laughed—a rich, throaty laugh that was quite pleasant and which had the effect of dissipating much of the tension in the room. "My dear child, there are more pleasures in life beyond the sharing of one's body." Her eyes slid lingeringly over Dae. "It is a great pleasure for me simply to look upon the radiance of your form, even if you will not permit me to sample your delights more intimately."

Dae squirmed. The way Zafirah looked at her was so uninhibited— so unreservedly sexual—she wasn't certain how to respond. Though her mind recoiled in horror and disgust at the notion that this strange woman desired her, for some reason her body wasn't inclined to follow the same path. She was uncomfortable with the strange warmth that flowed through her belly as Zafirah studied her with obvious admiration.

"If there is anything at all you require to make your life in the palace more enjoyable," the Scion continued, "do not hesitate to tell the guards. They will do all they can to accommodate your needs. I want you to be happy here."

"So you won't let me go home?"

Zafirah shook her head. "Though it was not by your will, you entered the land of my people. Had I not intervened, your fate would have been one of misery and great suffering as a slave. According to the laws of the Jaharri, you owe a debt of service to me for saving you from that fate."

"But if you contacted my parents, I'm sure they could pay any ransom." Dae folded her hands pleadingly. "They are wealthy and—"

Zafirah raised a hand to calm her pleas. "Wealth holds little interest to me...and your debt can not be purchased with coin or jewels. The laws of the desert have served my people for centuries, and by those laws your fate is now bound to me."

Dae's expression shifted from fearful to helpless and finally to sad resignation, the knowledge that she would likely never again see her parents or her homeland clutching at her heart painfully. She felt her eyes misting with tears and turned from the Scion to stifle a quiet sob.

"Do not be upset, little one." Zafirah took a step closer, her tone no longer seductive but compassionate. "Your life here will be one of ease, and you will be accorded every honor by my people. I understand that this world is strange to you. I know our ways are not the same as those of your people. It will take time for you to become comfortable with the customs of the desert and with the way of life here in the palace." Tender fingers lifted Dae's head. "Perhaps, with time, you may come to accept and appreciate those things that you have been taught to revile."

Dae saw something like hope in Zafirah's expression and realized what the Scion was referring to. She shook her head, moving quickly past any despair at her situation. "No matter how long I stay here, I will never bed with you or any other woman so long as I have any choice in the matter."

Zafirah smiled a little dejectedly, then shrugged. "If that is true, then so be it," she accepted. "However, if you change your mind—"

"I won't."

"Well, the offer stands nonetheless. And I would still like very much to be your friend, Dae, even if you will not permit me to be your lover."

For a moment, Dae wondered if Zafirah was joking with her. Having been born to a noble family, she knew that rulers did not spend time with their servants in a social capacity, and they certainly didn't become friends with their slaves. But studying the Scion's sculptured features carefully, she found no trace of guile or jest. "You want us to be friends? But...you're the Scion..."

"So? I am friends with all the girls in my harem. They are more to me than simply lovers and servants. They are treasured companions."

Zafirah's sincerity seemed honest enough, and Dae was even more confused than before. Still, thinking it would be best not to offend this strange woman with hostility, she offered a faint nod. "I suppose that would be okay."

"Excellent." Zafirah clapped her hands, apparently satisfied. Placing a hand on Dae's shoulder, she gently guided her past the bed and onto an expansive balcony that opened beyond. "Come, you may look upon your new home from here."

Dae fought the impulse to draw away, knowing she would have to get used to such physical contact if she was going to be living among these people, and looked out from the balcony without any real interest. The view, however, drew an involuntary gasp from her, and she stared in awe at the magnificent sight below. Seeing her reaction, Zafirah smiled with pride and pleasure.

"You look upon the majesty of El'Kasari, first and last city of the Jaharri," she said softly. "It is a sight few from the watered lands have ever seen."

The city spread out before Dae like an intricate mosaic, perfectly symmetrical, its design resembling a blossoming lotus flower, with the palace forming a jeweled bud at the center. Dae was surprised to see shimmering water in the distance and realized the city was built on the coast of the northern sea. Throughout the streets, glimmering in the last rays of the setting sun, hundreds of artificial ponds—or *hauzes*—sparkled like dewdrops on the petals of a flower. The buildings were all constructed along similar lines, with walls and towers carved from white marble and strange, tiled roofs that looked to Dae like giant onions. Everything was alive with exotic colors: blue and orange silks, the green and brown of the desert plants, and the rainbow of the many market stalls below as the traders sought to hawk their wares on the last customers of the day. To Dae's eyes, the city and the palace grounds were amazing—a fanciful, beautiful design unlike anything she'd ever seen before.

"It's magnificent," she breathed, wondering if she would ever be allowed to explore the wondrous city on her own.

"It is the jewel of the desert…our greatest treasure." Zafirah spoke of the city with the same loving pride a parent might use to praise a child. "Many centuries ago, the people of the desert lived in tribes, banding together to fight over the meager water supplies. Bloody wars were fought over the few oases and springs that gave us life. Then one day, one of my ancestors discovered the secret of purifying the waters of the great sea. He joined many of the strongest clans together, offering an alliance in exchange for sharing this secret. El'Kasari was built in the spirit of that alliance, its purpose to protect the water we are now able to make drinkable, and to defend those tribes who joined under the Scion banner."

"Defend against whom?"

"Many of the tribes refused to help with the building of the city," Zafirah said. "Ancient blood feuds and arguments ran too deep, too bitter, for them to let go. At first, they sought to destroy El'Kasari, but the task proved impossible. Now, they content themselves with raiding the weaker tribes, and then retreating before the army can retaliate. Since the Scion Peace, the Jaharri people have made treaties with those inhabiting the lands to the east and west and even those across the northern sea. Most of my people still dwell in the sands; they feel trapped and stifled within the city. But still, they often journey here to trade with the merchants or to collect water when times grow hard. Here, and nowhere else in the desert, water is freely given." She pointed to the *hauzes*. "The great sea provides us with limitless bounty, and the method of purifying its water is still our most closely guarded secret."

Dae smiled genuinely, amazed by the sight of the desert city. "There are no walls," she noted.

"El'Kasari knows better than to defy the desert with walls. We embrace the sands, and the freedom of the horizon. There is no need for us to make our city a cage."

Dae found such thinking difficult to comprehend, differing as it did from what she was accustomed to. "I've never seen anything like this before."

"Your people do not build such cities?"

Dae shook her head. "Not like this." She'd only seen the city that lay several days' ride from her parents' estate a few times in her life, and there were few similarities between it and the sight before her. Dark, foreboding walls surrounded the whole city, and the streets were filled with beggars and thieves waiting to prey on the unwary. It was a dangerous and dirty place, especially for an innocent young maiden like Dae, who had been carried around the entire duration of her visit in a covered palanquin surrounded by a retinue of armed guards. Compared to the magnificent spectacle of the open desert city, the memory of that place seemed cold and ugly. "It's beautiful."

"If you would like, perhaps one day you would allow me to show you more of the city. Its beauty does not fade as one draws nearer."

Dae glanced at the tall woman uncertainly. "You would let me out of the palace?"

"Of course. You are not a prisoner here. Put such thoughts out of your mind. I want for you to be happy in your new home, child, and if you wish to see more of El'Kasari, I would be greatly pleased to take you."

"Oh." Dae was doubtful if the offer was truly genuine, but she nodded anyway. "I would like that…someday."

"Excellent." Zafirah turned away from the window and back into the lavishly appointed bedroom. "Now, since you do not desire any more personal pleasures with me this night…" She paused and raised an eyebrow at Dae, inviting her to change her mind. Dae quickly shook her head, blushing again at the hungry look in the Scion's sapphire eyes. "I suppose you should be returning to your quarters in the harem. Do you have any questions of your own before we part?"

Dae was about to shake her head again when she suddenly stopped and cocked her head curiously. "How old are you?" she asked, half expecting her question to anger the Scion.

Zafirah, however, just smiled and answered honestly. "I have seen the desert rains come twenty-six times, once for every year of my life."

"Twenty-six?" Dae's jaw dropped in surprise. "But isn't that young for…"

"I was barely twenty when I first took the reins of power and became Scion. The desert nourishes the strong and kills the weak. Wisdom is granted to the elderly, power to the young; thus it is that the young rule while the aged advise. It is the way of things in the desert."

"Oh."

"Anything else?"

"No, thank you."

"Most welcome." Zafirah clapped her hands, and instantly two guards materialized at the doorway. The Scion addressed them. "Escort the girl back to the harem and then return to your duties."

They bowed and gestured for Dae to precede them into the corridor. With a few backward glances, Dae led the way out of the bedroom and back to her own quarters. Once again, her mind was too preoccupied to enjoy the stunning architecture of the palace halls, although no longer was it filled with expectant terror. Now, Dae was silent and thoughtful as she contemplated her meeting with the Scion. While her fears of rape and mysterious tortures had been largely alleviated, she was now faced with concerns of a far more subtle—yet even more disturbing—nature, as she struggled to understand the way her body had responded to Zafirah's overtures.

The deep desert was a deadly and merciless region, as many a foreign traveler had discovered to his great regret. Centuries of blistering winds had carved the outcroppings of rock into lethal sharp ridges that sprang up out of the barren white sands like knives thrust into an unsuspecting back. There was little shelter from the glare of the sun; heat killed quickly out here, and a fallen body never sat long before it was found by the scavenger birds and mangy jackals that called this land their home. Water was scarce and fiercely guarded by those nomadic tribes who had refused to let ancient blood-feuds die so they could join the Scion Peace. Those few merchants and explorers who were brave or foolish enough to venture into the deep desert, and were graced with such luck as to return alive, brought with them stories of the ugly, inhospitable land and warned others never to test the murderous sands themselves.

But to Shakir Al'Jadin, the Jaharri desert was home, and its many perils and hardships were a comfort to him that he wouldn't have traded for the wealth of a thousand kingdoms.

Shakir breathed in the vastness of the ocean of sand and stone around him. He loved the nights out here; the half-moon and the brilliant sparkle of a million stars filled the heavens with silver light, and the air was cool and silent except for the faint clip-clop of hooves passing over stone. The desert at night had its own particular beauty, its own peace that could be found nowhere else in the world. Scanning the surrounding wilderness, he searched among the many granite and sandstone escarpments, eventually finding what he sought: a faint crimson glow at the base of a not-too distant cliff. Shakir grunted, and turned his horse toward his destination.

Shakir Al'Jadin was Calif of the Deharn tribe, a small but tough group of nomads who made their home far from the structure and order of El'Kasari and the Scion Whore. For hundreds of years before the Peace, the Deharn had lived well, plundering the trade routes between the western and eastern lands without mercy. They had been feared as cunning and vicious warriors, and as such had earned the enmity of many of the most powerful tribes. When the first Scion had forged the Peace, however, things had changed. The Deharn refused to ally with its ancient rivals and had led many charges against the then-weak city on the northern coast. All their attacks had been rebuffed, and now Shakir was the leader of a tribe forced to rely on speed and stealth to attack its enemies. He was a handsome and charismatic leader, skilled in the arts of warfare his people prized so greatly. In his younger years, he had learned how the power of words could fan the flames of hostility into a roaring blaze, and over time, he had mastered the skills of oration and used them to garner a fanatical devotion among his people.

Shakir was also a leader constantly seeking a way to restore his tribe to their ancient position of strength...and who believed he had finally found it.

Crossing the stretch of desert before him, Shakir arrived at his destination: a shallow-mouthed cave carved by the wind into the rock wall of an escarpment. Dismounting, he strode purposefully into the cave, waving aside the two guards he was pleased to note were standing outside the entrance with drawn scimitars. The men were loyal and disciplined warriors of his tribe, and he had sent them ahead to mind his path and prepare the scene for his coming demonstration.

Inside, a gathering of fifteen men and women sat around a flickering fire in various positions. They all looked up as he entered their ring, some smiling and offering respectful nods, others greeting his arrival with glum disinterest or suspicious caution. Though he was young, having seen the rains come only twenty-three times in his life, Shakir had earned a reputation for his brutality and quick temper. His hatred of the Scion and the city ran deep, as it ran deep in all those who were gathered here.

Shakir met the eyes of each person in turn and nodded in satisfaction. "My brothers and sisters, thank you all for coming," he said, opening his arms in welcome. "Some of you have traveled a long way to be here this night, and I hope to make your journey worth your while."

"How?" demanded Brak, a grizzled, scarred elder whose tribe lived closest to the great salt desert in the south. "Will you offer food or water for our troubles? Or only more talk of useless war?"

Shakir eyed the older man steadily. "War against the Scion or El'Kasari is never useless."

"Bah!" Brak spat on the ground, the reason for this assembly now clear. "For centuries we have spilled our blood for the sands, trying to break the back of the Scion Peace, and have gained nothing for our efforts! We could not defeat the city when it was but an unstable alliance. What has changed, except that they have grown stronger, and we have weakened? Tell me this!"

Shakir offered a smug, enigmatic smile. "Much, which I will reveal to you if you would allow me." Brak was critical to the Calif's plans; his tribe bred the finest *merharis* in the whole of the desert, and those swift camels would be invaluable to Shakir in the coming months.

The old warrior snorted but settled himself once more and glowered at the assembly.

"Brak is right," Shakir stated more loudly, letting his presence fill the cave. "We throw ourselves against the might of El'Kasari and the Scion Whore, only to perish to her forces time and time again. Our raids against those who dare trespass into the desert glean fewer rewards each year, and the other tribes grow fat and strong while we starve like jackals on the rocks! We cannot continue on this path, my friends. We will destroy ourselves, and our enemies will laugh at our extinction. Would you have this?"

"No!" One of the women stood and gestured fiercely. "But pretty words and tired rhetoric will not avail you here, Shakir. What can we do? I have seen young men like you before, filled with anger and arrogance. I have seen them lead others to an early grave! Do you offer any more than they did? Can you bring down the *spahi*? How? They have training and weapons beyond our means! A single rider of the Scion is worth five of our own men!"

"Perhaps this was true...once," Shakir said. "But I have come across a means by which we might at last strike back against the Whore and her forces—a means I would share with you if you would agree to my plans."

The woman studied Shakir a moment, her head cocked. "What means?"

Shakir clapped his hands once, and immediately the two guards at the cave mouth hurried in, bearing between them a heavy wooden chest, the design of which was obviously not of the desert. They placed the chest on the ground before Shakir, bowed, then left.

Shakir spread his arms wide in joy. Kneeling almost reverently, he lifted the lid on the chest and proudly displayed its contents to the gathering. The people moved closer, curious, as Shakir reached in and pulled out a strange device.

It was a long pole of dark cast iron set into a wooden brace with several intricate-looking levers attached. Although none of them had ever seen such a device, every man and woman in the cave recognized a weapon when they saw one...though its method was beyond their comprehension.

"This," grinned Shakir, shouldering the weapon, "was traded to me by a traveler from the far west. My people attacked his caravan when it crossed into our lands, and he offered us his help if we would spare his life. After seeing this marvelous weapon in action, I could not help but agree to his parlay."

"What is it?" demanded Brak. "I do not think you will defeat the Scion with an iron club! Her army wields swords crafted by the weapon masters from across the seas. Her scouts are armed with powerful bows that would cut you down before you could strike!"

"This is no club," Shakir corrected in a dangerously soft tone. "It is the power of the storm made flesh! It is thunder and lightning! In our hands, this great weapon can bring that bitch who calls herself Scion to heel! Come, my friends, and I shall demonstrate what power I offer."

Leading his fellows outside, Shakir made his way out onto the rocky sands a short distance before he stopped. His two guards had made the arrangements he asked for: perhaps a hundred paces from his position, they had planted a stake into the ground, bound to which was the skinny, weakly struggling figure of what had once been a man. Slaves of the Deharn typically lived brief, tormented lives, and this one had grown too weak to serve much usefulness any longer. He had been dressed in the uniform and armor of a *spahi* rider of El'Kasari for this occasion, the captured garb hanging loose on his shrunken frame. As the others looked on, whispering among themselves doubtfully, Shakir hooked the wooden butt of the weapon into his shoulder and sighted along the length of the iron rod. "Watch the slave, my friends," he instructed. "Watch carefully as I strike him down."

The group observed through narrowed, speculative eyes. A moment later, the sound of a thunderclap boomed across the desert, shocking them all. They cried out in fear and confusion, searching the empty skies for signs of a storm, only to be met with laughter from the young Calif.

"Relax, friends. The noise was not that of a storm approaching… it was the weapon. See what power it unleashes." Shakir pointed to the bound slave, now hanging limp against the stake, and when the gathered tribespeople moved forward to investigate, they gasped in unison at the sight.

A wide hole, about the size of a man's fist, had been blasted through the wretch's chest, leaving a bloody mess beneath the ruined, torn armor.

"What magic is this?" breathed Brak in awe, now eyeing the strange weapon with more respect.

"No magic," Shakir assured him easily. "This weapon works as a bow, striking an enemy from afar…however, with far greater accuracy and from a good deal further distance. It fires these"—he held out his hand, showing the people a collection of small lead projectiles—"with sufficient force to penetrate armor, steel, and flesh with ease."

"How?"

"It uses a powder of unique ability, whose formula I will share with you if you will but agree to help me strike back against the Scion Whore!"

There was much muttering at this, but Shakir let it go. Most were excited by his demonstration, as he expected—the nomads needed little incentive to want to war—but others were still cautious, and he respected that. It was no small thing to propose an attack against the mighty Scion.

"How many of these weapons have you managed to steal?" asked Brak.

"A hundred…but with more to come, and enough projectiles and powder to inflict tremendous harm." Shakir eyed his fellows smugly, unconcerned by the accusation of theft. Unlike the tribes aligned under the Scion Peace, the renegades still survived largely by raiding merchant caravans or the camps of their rivals. All those assembled understood that the only style of "trade" Shakir would ever engage in with an outlander would be tribute given in exchange for mercy. Watching their faces, it was clear to Shakir they were impressed by the spoils he had won. "With these, we can strike with great speed against the *spahi* and the scouts, and disappear back into the desert before the Scion has time to retaliate. We will chip away at the mountain until it is weakened, slaughter the tribes of the alliance one by one so their support is empty…then we shall ride against the city itself and cut down the citizens who have allowed themselves to grow soft and complacent under the Whore's rule." He held up the weapon proudly. "This is our destiny, brothers and sisters! It is time for us to take back our strength and honor, and cast our enemies to the jackals!"

Again the murmurings began, but this time with a more excited edge. Brak came forward and asked that he might test the weapon for himself, and Shakir graciously showed him how it was used. Smiling as he watched the elder fumble awkwardly with the foreign weapon, the Calif felt warm pleasure course through his blood.

The winds of change were blowing…and he meant to whip them into a storm that would crush El'Kasari into dust!

# Chapter 3

Life in the palace harem, Dae soon discovered, was a curious affair. On the one hand, she found the long days seemed to drift by tediously, and during the fierce midday heat it was often difficult to muster any energy at all. During the early mornings and late evenings, however, when the sun wasn't quite so intent on baking the earth beneath its withering gaze, the girls would play like children through the seraglio gardens and the maze of rooms appointed for their use. Everything was provided for their comfort: fruits and meats to nourish their bodies, puzzling board games to challenge their minds, and a beautiful environment to soothe their senses. Musicians and scholars would often come to entertain or enlighten them, and most of the girls would dance provocatively to the tune of reed pipes, hypnotic drums, and intricate stringed instruments. It was only during the long hours when the sun was at its hottest that the girls tended to shelter beneath the branches of the garden trees, lounging sleepily on silk cushions or frolicking in the cool waters of the great pool.

The pleasure-servants proved to be polite and humorous companions for Dae, and she found herself quite liking their ever-cheerful presence. They treated her kindly, offering to do anything they could to make her more comfortable in her new home. Dae was fascinated by their strange, exotic accents and manner of speech; they were eloquent and articulate, rarely abbreviating their words as most people did in the eastern lands. Where she had expected to find ignorance and barbarity, instead she found intelligence and insight, compassion and beauty. Although few of the girls could read or write, Dae found that their skill as storytellers more than compensated for their lack of literary education. As Zafirah had said, oration was clearly an important and valued skill among the Jaharri. The telling and retelling of traditional fables and legends was an almost daily activity for the pleasure-servants, and Dae enjoyed the adventurous, often bawdy tales very much. At times, she wished she could have access to some of the books she had grown up with in her homeland; she sensed the other girls would have enjoyed hearing tales not native to the desert, and it might have offered a forum for her to engage with them in a meaningful way. Still, for the most part, she kept to herself, feeling out of place and awkward around the more worldly pleasure-servants. As the weeks became months, Dae found herself spending most of her time with Inaya, who seemed to take the greatest interest in her. The two gradually settled into a solid friendship, the edges of their vastly different personalities and backgrounds somehow fitting against each other with gentle ease.

The life of a pleasure-servant was one of great decadence and luxury. The harem was spacious and airy, but the pleasure-servants were not permitted to roam freely about the palace—much to Dae's disappointment. Female guards—the most trusted in the Scion's army and chosen for the fact that they had no interest in bedding with other women—guarded the entrance to the seraglio at all times and escorted the pleasure-servants whenever they were required to venture into the palace proper. These guards were also polite and courteous, despite their stern profession, and treated the women with great respect.

In truth, Dae found the culture of the desert people to be quite interesting and pleasing...as long as she didn't dwell too long on certain of their practices. Everything here seemed so much more intense than in her homeland; the colors were brighter, the foods more delicious and spicy, and the environment more active and physical. The air was filled with the scents of gardenia, jasmine, and wild rose. At times it was almost overwhelming; she could feel her senses struggling to take it all in. Dae's parents had always been very protective toward her, particularly as she grew older, and she had never experienced this type of intense communal living. So little was forbidden here: there were few rules, few restrictions. The girls of the harem were utterly carefree and insouciant...and, Dae noted bashfully, extremely affectionate. They expressed themselves in a very physical way, their hands seeming to gravitate toward skin-on-skin contact whenever they were near each other...or near to Dae herself. She tried her best to be polite about the constant caresses and lingering touches, not wanting to offend anyone over what she believed was a cultural habit, but at times it was a struggle. And as the weeks passed and she grew to understand more of this strange new world, Dae found her mind constantly straying back to ponder on a single point of focus—that of the enigmatic Scion, Zafirah Al'Intisar.

Zafirah was unlike anyone Dae had ever associated with, and certainly different from any ruler she had ever heard of before. As the daughter of a noble family in her homeland, Dae had some measure of experience when it came to the ruling class. She had been taught that it was unseemly for a ruler to interact with a subject as an equal. To actually socialize with the servants would be vulgar; it undermined the ability of the noble class to rule their underlings, made them more human and thus more capable of human error. While Dae knew without question her father was greatly respected and deeply loved by his people—she had seen as much in the devotion shown to him by the commoners and the soldiers—it was very different from what she saw in Zafirah. In the eastern kingdom, nobility equaled superiority.

In stark contrast to this ideal, Zafirah spent every spare moment she could in the harem with her pleasure-servants, mostly just talking and laughing, but occasionally joining in their play with childish abandon. While she always carried with her the quiet air of regal power and command that Dae found so strangely mesmerizing, Zafirah seemed to enjoy relaxing in the seraglio gardens with her harem, often just watching the girls as they splashed in the pool or chased each other across the sweet grasses, a slight, contented smile curving her sensuous lips.

Of course, her presence would inevitably lead to a seduction of one or more of the girls as soon as night began to fall. Many times, Dae watched with wide eyes as Zafirah wove a spell of temptation on a pleasure-servant, whispering enticingly into a delicate ear and running a persuasive hand along smooth thighs, eliciting giggles and chaste blushes that were, in truth, far from innocent. The chosen girl—or, on some occasions, girls—would be led away from the seraglio shortly after, and

Dae had noted that their expressions the next morning always spoke of great satisfaction and languid bliss. Her mind had trouble rationalizing this phenomenon, and she found herself puzzling more and more on what exactly went on during the mysterious dark of the night.

Sitting under the shady branches of a fig tree, Dae watched Zafirah and the other girls as they laughed and played by the pool. Tonight it seemed the Scion had set her sights on Inaya; the raven-haired pleasure-servant reclined against the taller woman, eating slices of persimmon from Zafirah's hand. This was the first time Dae had witnessed her friend in such a situation, although Inaya certainly seemed to enjoy flirting with the Scion whenever she visited. Just watching the subtle, intense display of seduction in so public a forum made her feel like she was intruding upon a private moment, but it was impossible to look away. Only when Zafirah turned in her direction and an alluring smile flashed across painted lips did Dae hastily turn her attention to the girls who were dancing suggestively to the pulsing rhythm of drum music on the clipped lawn. When she noticed movement before her, she glanced up and cursed silently, seeing Zafirah rise from her place at Inaya's side and start to wander over.

"Why do you sit over here all alone, little one?" inquired the Scion, kneeling beside Dae. "Do you not care for company this night?"

Dae shook her head. "No, I just… I wanted a little space, that's all." In truth, she felt ill at ease being around the other girls when they were dancing like this. Invariably they would encourage her to join in, and while she could admit to herself privately that the provocative moves were strangely fascinating, she was far too shy and modest to ever think of attempting them herself.

Zafirah accepted her explanation without comment, however. "There will be a full moon tonight," she observed, looking at the brilliant orb hanging low in the skies. "I always enjoy such nights. When I was but a girl, my mother would take me out into the city and we would wander the *souks* for hours, watching the street performers practice through the dark." She sighed. "There is something about a full moon that fills me with energy and joy." Her eyes darkened noticeably as she let them slide along Dae's ill-concealed figure, lingering over the swell of her breasts and the curve of her hips. "These nights should be filled with reckless passion, not squandered in idle solitude."

Dae felt her cheeks glow with a sudden rush of blood. In the last few days she'd found herself unable to control her body's reaction to Zafirah's continued overtures, and the feelings that washed over her were deeply disturbing. "I prefer the peace of my own company."

"Perhaps tonight I could entice you to try something different?"

Dae swallowed nervously, wishing she could control her racing heart. "L-like what?"

"Inaya and I were about to retire for the evening. I wondered if perhaps you would care to join us?"

Surprised, Dae stared wide-eyed at the Scion, then over to where Inaya was watching their exchange with interest. "I-I-I..." She struggled to form a response, caught completely off guard by the offer. "I don't... don't think so, my Scion," she managed to get out after a moment, letting her hair fall forward to hide her face. "I don't like such things." Those words had become her creed in this new world.

"So you have said." The tall woman shifted closer, and the conversation became suddenly more intimate. "You would not have to join our pleasure if you do not wish to. I thought perhaps you might simply deign to...watch?" Zafirah raised an eyebrow. "It may prove to be an educational experience."

Dae very nearly swallowed her own tongue. Images of naked flesh and tangled limbs flashed unbidden across her mind, and she hoped fervently for their dismissal. Seeing Zafirah watching for a response, she shook her head firmly. "I have no interest in such an education," she insisted, wondering if tonight would be the night the Scion would abandon her sense of honor.

But Zafirah merely smiled mysteriously. "As you wish, my little Tahirah." Leaning in close, she ran a single finger along Dae's collarbone, her breath a caress against her skin. "But I could promise you the lessons would be most thoroughly enjoyable."

Rising again, giving Dae a last lingering once-over, Zafirah returned to her place beside Inaya, who regarded Dae with a curious expression for a long moment before turning her attention back to the Scion.

Left alone once more, Dae tried to reclaim her former peace of mind but found it had been shattered beyond repair. For some reason, every time Zafirah so much as glanced in her direction, she felt her stomach churn excitedly, her palms begin to sweat, and her blood grow warmer in her veins. Struggling to bring her body back under control, Dae considered the request carefully, wondering whether Inaya had known it was being offered. What did the pleasure-servant think about the idea? Watching Zafirah lead Inaya from the seraglio, Dae wondered for half a heartbeat what things she might have witnessed had she accepted the invitation. As soon as the thought entered her head, she stomped it to death immediately.

Gnawing her lower lip thoughtfully, Dae consigned herself to what she knew would be another restless night of troubling considerations.

"*Salaam aleikum*, little one," greeted a lilting, feminine voice cheerfully. "Such a serious face you wear for such an early hour."

"Huh?" Dae glanced up from her work to find Inaya studying her from a few feet away. She raised a delicately plucked eyebrow at the sheaf of parchment spread over Dae's lap.

"What are you doing that has you so focused?"

"This?" Dae shrugged. "Just some drawings. It helps to pass the time."

Inaya immediately settled herself on the lawn beside Dae and leaned over to get a better view. Her arrival brought with it the strong scent of rose, jasmine, and wild musk, and the musical jangle of jewelry. "May I see?"

"Um...sure, if you like." Dae offered her friend the papers. She had asked the guards for the materials yesterday and spent all morning carefully sketching out remembered images from her homeland with a sharpened stick of lead that served as a pencil. Somehow, it helped her feel more at ease in this alien environment to maintain those memories of a world that was green and alive, where water was plentiful and life was structured and orderly.

Inaya flicked through the many pictures curiously, pausing often to study them in greater detail. "You have great talent."

Dae looked away modestly. "They're not really that good."

"Oh, but they are!" Inaya held up a scene depicting a tranquil lake surrounded by enormous, ancient trees. The detail was indeed very good; Dae's knowledgeable hand had perfectly captured the motion of a gentle breeze as it whispered through the variegated leaves, and the rippling waves that disturbed the still waters of the lake. "This is your homeland, yes?"

"Uh huh."

Inaya stared at the picture, fascinated. "I have never seen such a place," she whispered. "What is this?"

"Well…it's a lake, of course."

"And what is a lake?"

The question was so unexpected that it caught Dae off guard. "A lake is…well. It's like a pool of water that lies over a vast area of land… sort of like a small ocean."

"Ooh." Inaya studied the drawing with fresh understanding. "Sometimes when the rains come in the springtime, the water flows so fiercely down the dunes that the sand cannot drink it all, and it pools in the valleys and chasms. That is like a lake, no?"

"Sort of. But a lake is always filled with water. It never drains away completely."

Inaya smiled wistfully at the thought. "I think the people of your land are very lucky to have such bounty. I do not think they realize just how fortunate they are to be so blessed."

Considering how much she had taken for granted in her homeland, Dae nodded. "I think you're probably right." She watched her friend peruse each of her drawings in turn. When she reached the last picture, Inaya's expression became teasingly playful.

"I see not all your thoughts find focus on your homeland." Holding up the parchment, she presented Dae with the image of a familiar face.

Dae grabbed the drawing away from the grinning girl. "It's not what you're thinking," she said, studying the elegant lines and shadings that had perfectly captured the fierce yet enticing features of the Scion. "Her face lends itself well to paper, that's all."

"I see." Inaya's grin told Dae she wasn't convinced.

"Shouldn't you be sleeping after last night's activities?"

41

Inaya sighed languidly and lay back on the soft grass, closing her eyes and letting her long fingers toy idly with the jeweled stud in her navel. "Perhaps. But I want to enjoy this feeling for as long as possible before I allow sleep to diminish the memory."

Dae noted the contented, satisfied air about Inaya and, despite her best efforts, could not help but be curious. "So you enjoyed yourself?"

"Mm, indeed." Inaya purred. "I am most thoroughly sated. Zafirah was in an unusually vigorous mood last night; her passion was quite voracious." Her dark gaze rolled in Dae's direction. "You should have joined us."

Dae averted her eyes immediately. "How many times must I say I have no interest in such affairs before you will believe me?"

"I know not. How many times will it take before you believe yourself?"

The gentle challenge in Inaya's question made Dae look up in surprise. "What?"

Inaya propped herself up on her elbows and regarded her frankly. "I have eyes, Dae," she said. "I have seen the way you watch Zafirah when she comes here. I have seen how you respond whenever she glances in your direction."

"I...You...That's not true!"

Inaya shook her head. "You may deny it all you wish, little one. Your tongue may speak lies, but your eyes tell the truth. I have seen the signs of arousal and interest enough times to recognize them when they are so evident. You reject your own heart because you are uncertain and afraid. You have been taught that such desires are wrong, and because you know no better, you believe those teachings. One day, however, you will have to accept that you are curious about what it is Zafirah offers so readily." She paused and then added softly, "That is why I say you should have joined us last night. At least then you would understand better what it is you deny yourself." She smiled at the hesitant, wary expression her words elicited. "We have a saying in the desert: 'It is better to see the truth than to imagine it.'"

Dae stared hard at her friend, but Inaya just smiled back at her. Eventually she shook her head and turned away. "I would rather remain ignorant," she said primly. "The only thing I feel for Zafirah is a gratitude for saving my life from the slavers. Whatever you *think* you've seen exists only in your mind."

Inaya sighed. "As you wish." Sitting up fully, she crossed her legs and watched a group of the other girls playing among the spreading branches of an aspen tree nearby. "There is nothing wrong with being curious," she continued in conversational tones. "Zafirah seems quite enchanted by you. Her eyes always manage to find you immediately whenever she comes here."

Dae remained silent, determined not to be drawn into making any further comment. Inaya watched her a moment longer with quiet, undaunted certainty, only looking away when movement drew her attention to activity high in the aspen tree. She grinned and pointed.

"Look. Johara and Hayam have found themselves a new place to enjoy one another's company."

Dae looked where her friend indicated, and her jaw dropped in paralyzed shock at the sight. Perched high in the branches of the tree, two of the harem girls were entwined in a tangle of arms and legs, engaged in a passionate kiss that seemed likely to last forever. Even from a distance, their ardor was unmistakable, and Dae stared unblinking at the couple. This was the first time she had witnessed such an intimate act between two women, and she couldn't tear her eyes away. It had not occurred to her that the pleasure-servants would willingly engage in such a fashion with one another.

Inaya studied Dae's shocked reaction. "You see? It is a beautiful thing to share passion with another woman, not something to be feared or reviled. They do not lock their desires away as I have heard people do in your land; they express them, give them life and power."

Dae had never seen such an open display of love and desire. Certainly her parents, who she knew loved each other a great deal, had never kissed with such carnal hunger. "They seem so unaware of anything around them," she whispered almost to herself. "It's like they're in love."

"Well, of course they are." Inaya laughed merrily at her. "Johara and Hayam have been lovers for three years now. They are very much committed to one another."

"They are?" Dae glanced around to check the entrance to the harem, wondering what the guards would do if they saw the two women trysting. "What about Zafirah?"

43

"What about her?"

"Wouldn't she be angry if she knew?"

Inaya shook her head, chuckling, and Dae knew her innocence and naïveté were once again showing. "Of course not, little one. She presided over their joining ceremony just last year!"

"Joining ceremony? You mean..." Dae struggled to understand this latest twist to harem life. "A marriage?"

Inaya shrugged, clearly never having heard the word before. "They exchanged vows of devotion and love, and tokens to symbolize that they were now one in the eyes of the great Goddess Inshal. The Scion was most honored to play a role in the consecration of their love."

"So they don't bed with the Scion then?"

"I said no such thing," Inaya waggled her eyebrows saucily. "Their union makes them one being, inseparable. When Zafirah takes pleasure with one, she knows to include the other as well." Nimble fingers toyed absentmindedly with a silky lock of blue-black hair as she regarded the two lovers. "Johara and Hayam are quite a couple. Their love only brightens the flame of their passion, and they eagerly share that passion with others."

Dae's mind struggled to comprehend this notion of such freely offered sexual favor, the idea making her almost dizzy. "And Zafirah doesn't mind that her pleasure-servants sleep together?"

"Why would she? The Scion would never wish to deprive any of her people of pleasure. In fact, she encourages us to share our bodies equally with each other as with herself. As I have said, she is a most generous lover." She paused and regarded Dae with a coy expression the young girl had learned to dread. "It may interest you to know that Zafirah's loins are not the only ones to have stirred at your arrival. The other pleasure-servants take an equal measure of interest in your presence."

Dae's eyes finally tore themselves from the ardent couple in the trees as she jerked her head around. "What?"

Inaya's smile was perfectly innocent, but her dark eyes were sparkling mischievously. "You had not noticed the attention they pay you?"

"Well, yes, but I thought..." Dae's voice trailed off as she suddenly realized that all those lingering touches she had interpreted as simple expressions of friendship might not have been entirely based on cultural norms. She stared nervously at the other pleasure-servants climbing through the aspen. "You mean they...?"

"Wish to bed you?" Inaya laughed. "Why does that seem so strange to you? You are young, Dae, and strikingly beautiful...and your innocence serves only to add to their interest, makes you even more attractive to them. There is not a woman in this harem who would not crawl through a pit of scorpions for the chance to lie between your thighs."

Dae's jaw worked up and down for several moments in silence before she managed to form words. "B-but I don't... They can't..."

"These women have never met anyone like you before, Dae. They have never known a person who does not live for the pursuit of pleasure. A person who, seemingly, avoids pleasure. Here in the desert, where life is so often harsh and brief, such people simply do not exist. Here, every moment in precious. To squander what time we have in this world by denying our own passions and desires is unheard of." She paused, regarding Dae with a gentle but serious expression. "They do not understand your chastity, but from the whisperings I have heard, it seems they find it every bit as arousing as does Zafirah. For a single night in your bed...for the chance to be the first to introduce you to the pleasures your body has never known... Ah." She sighed in longing at the thought. "You do not understand how tempting a creature you are, little one."

Recalling the invitation of last night, Dae narrowed her eyes curiously at her friend. "Do you feel the same way?" she asked timidly, unsure if she wanted to know the answer.

Inaya shrugged, her eyes sincere and honest. "I like you, Dae. I feel that we have formed a bond since you came here and hope that we will be companions for many years to come. But I will not deny that I find you attractive. And though I respect your wishes to remain untouched by the hands of another woman, I would consider it a great honor if you were ever to allow me to warm your bed." Her full lips tweaked into a slightly sad smile at the confused, almost wounded look that crept over Dae's face. "I am sorry if you do not understand."

"No." Dae held up her hand. "It's okay, really." She sat up a little straighter and shook her head to clear it. "I can handle this. It's no different than dealing with Zafirah, right?"

Inaya's smile brightened a little. "I have no wish to lose you as a friend, Dae."

"I know." Dae returned the smile shyly. "It's just…" She considered carefully, the revelations of this morning only adding to the jumble of thoughts and feelings that seemed to bombard her since she'd come to the harem. A lifetime of indoctrination came to the fore, speaking the words for her. "I mean no offense, but…I can't be with another woman. Not like that."

Brown eyes glanced again at the detailed drawing of Zafirah, and Dae could see Inaya was reading every careful line of her sketch, every subtle shift of shading and focus, with unnerving interest. She didn't like the quiet, knowing smile that twitched at the corners of Inaya's lips, and for a second Dae worried her drawing had revealed something to her friend it shouldn't have… But then Inaya returned her gaze to Dae's face and said nothing more than, "As you wish."

Dae was silent for long moments, half wondering if she should offer further protest and defense, when she suddenly recalled something from last night. "Inaya? Have you ever heard the word 'tahirah' before?"

"Certainly. It is a name meaning pure…chaste. Why, where did you hear it?"

"It was just something Zafirah called me last night."

Inaya raised an eyebrow at her friend. "I think the Scion names you well."

Dae rolled her eyes and, smiling a little to herself, returned to her artwork while Inaya watched with avid interest over her shoulder.

Whooping wildly, Zafirah leaned over the neck of her horse and cast a quick glance behind her, grinning when she saw she had outpaced the other riders by several lengths. Racing across a stretch of desert sand just in sight of the city's first buildings, the Scion and a group of twenty hand-picked *spahi* churned great clouds of dust into the air as they sped between two markers planted several hundred feet apart. Zafirah's mare, Simhana, possessed a spirit every bit as wild and competitive as that of her mistress and needed no urging to increase her pace. When she reached the marker, Zafirah pressed against Simhana's right flank with her leg, and the well-trained war horse executed a sudden turn that would have thrown a lesser rider to the ground. Expecting the move, however, Zafirah twisted her body in the light saddle and then watched as the rest of the riders crossed the finish in a tightly packed group.

"An excellent race, my Scion," said one of the riders, pulling away his *haik* and grinning broadly at her. "You ride swifter than the *sirocco* winds!"

"Bah!" Zafirah returned the grin wryly. "You only say that to ease your pride. I have seen outlanders ride faster than you!"

The men and women all laughed, trading jibes back and forth while they readied themselves for another set of exercises. Zafirah joined in their camaraderie, enjoying the time spent among her troops. The exercise was particularly welcome this day; she was feeling the need to work off some energy.

Since the start of her rule as Scion, Zafirah routinely set aside a few hours every day in the morning to be spent training with the men and women of her army. Sometimes she would ride with the *spahi* out in the desert, other times she would train with the weapon masters who helped perfect her skill with scimitar and spear. The ritual not only kept Zafirah in prime fighting condition, it also served to endear her to the soldiers of the army, engendering a loyalty among them that was almost holy in its power. By demonstrating that she was every bit as willing to fight in defense of her home and her people as she expected them to be, the charismatic Scion had molded an army of fanatical warriors who were feared by all who dared to oppose the Scion Peace.

Watching each man in turn spur his mount through a dazzling series of equine acrobatics, Zafirah suddenly noticed a dust cloud on the horizon. Squinting, she made out a dark, shimmering patch that she knew indicated a group of riders was approaching. Halting the exercises, she called her troops to order, and they waited till the strangers drew close enough to identify. When she saw the flash of green and red that marked the banner held aloft by a forerunner, Zafirah relaxed. As the group drew closer, she rode out to greet them, grinning at the short, grizzled man riding at their head.

"What is the matter, Cousin? Did you come to miss my company so greatly in but a few weeks that you decided to pay me a visit?"

Rehan Al'Carin snorted, wiping his sand-blasted forehead with the back of his arm. "Hardly! I would be a happier man to see less of your face in my life than more." He gestured behind him to a number of pack camels weighed down with sacks and carved wooden chests. "A caravan of merchants traveling east paid well for its use of the Kah-hari oasis. So great a tribute as this called for a personal delivery."

Zafirah's grin widened a fraction, knowing Rehan could have entrusted the delivery to one of his many sons. But she bowed her head in a show of thanks. "I am most grateful to you, then. Will you be staying in the city during your visit? I would be honored to offer you a room in the palace if you wish."

"My thanks, Cousin, but my men would prefer to camp in the desert. However, I would gratefully accept an invitation for dinner. It has been some time since I feasted in the great palace."

"Of course." Zafirah understood well the way of the tribal people—walls and ceilings made them feel caged and edgy—so she was not offended that Rehan declined her offer. "I will see that you are supplied before you return...and rest assured I have not forgotten your favor of taking in the other girls we rescued. You will be compensated."

Rehan bowed his thanks; his dislike of those who dealt in the slave trade was well known. In fact, it was a point of contention between the Tek and several of their neighboring tribes. Slavery was not universally outlawed among the Jaharri, and practices varied between the tribes depending on their individual traditions. Indentured servitude, however, was widely regarded as an acceptable and honorable means by which a person could repay a debt to another; the girls would be released in a few years and given the means to resume a life where they chose.

"How have they fared?" Zafirah asked, joining the older man at the head of the procession as it made its way toward the city.

Rehan grunted. "As well as can be expected, I suppose, given the trauma they suffered. A few have adjusted well and may even decide to remain among us, but it will take time for the others to recover from their ordeal." He raised a bushy eyebrow at her, his smile slightly lecherous. "And what of the flower you plucked from the pack? I wager you have been most solicitous after her experiences, eh?"

Zafirah's face was impassive as she replied. "She is well, to be sure... though she is not so easily wooed to the pleasures of my bed."

"Indeed?" Rehan smirked. He knew as well as any the power of the Scion's seductive lure and seemed impressed that the girl had withstood her charms. "Perhaps then, if you have no use for her, she could be persuaded to join with my tribe? One of my older sons will soon be of age to take a wife. If the girl holds no interest in entertaining your affections, she might find such a union preferable to remaining in the city."

Zafirah regarded him with amusement. "You know me better than that, Rehan, to think I would part so easily with a flower of such rare and wondrous beauty. Though she denies me the chance to sample her delights personally, that does not mean I am not pleased with her company." She laughed at the disappointed look on Rehan's face. "She will remain in the palace with the rest of my harem."

In truth, Dae's presence in the palace had been causing Zafirah some discomfort recently. She was not accustomed to having her advances rejected, and the young girl's exquisite beauty and innocence only served to add fuel to the already impressive blaze of Zafirah's sexual appetite.

"Hmph." The grizzled nomad scowled a little but didn't press his hopeful suggestion further. "You will be pleased with the tribute given by the foreigners."

"Truly? I have seen enough gold and jewels in my lifetime that their sparkle does not easily impress me anymore."

"As have I, Cousin. As have I." Rehan leaned closer to Zafirah conspiratorially. "These merchants were doubtless wise about our ways. They offered items of lesser value, but far greater worth."

A dark brow lifted interestedly. Usually, travelers crossing the desert gave riches like gems and gold and fine cloth in exchange for their passage—items that were of limited use in the harsh Jaharri desert. Zafirah regarded the grizzled nomad chief with curiosity. "Such as?"

"Spices and coffee from across the seas, steel weapons crafted by the masters in the far west. They even left a sack of *brehani* leaf among the offerings...proof enough that they knew exactly how to win the support of the desert guardians."

Zafirah's brilliant eyes widened with delight. This was indeed a treat! *Brehani* leaf—the Breath of Inshal—grew only in the dangerous, barren salt flats that bordered the Jaharri desert to the south. Difficult to collect, the herb was prized among the desert people for its intoxicating qualities that could—so the priests claimed—sometimes provide visions from the Goddess herself. Zafirah had not enjoyed the herb for a long time now, and she gave Rehan a broad smile. "This is a great tribute indeed," she agreed, knowing the weapons and other useful items would be a welcome gift to her people. "I will be sure to see you receive a just share before you return to your tribe."

Rehan bowed in the saddle, obviously not doubting she would be more than fair in distributing the wealth. "Thank you, my Scion. Your generosity is greatly appreciated."

Zafirah rejoined her *spahi*, and the two groups marched into El'Kasari together, their entrance met with much delight by the citizens who flocked to greet them. Leading the procession, thinking happily about the rich tribute, Zafirah was all smiles as she touched the hands of the people who reached out to her. Already her quick mind was deciding how best to distribute the new wealth...and she concluded that it was past time she gave her pleasure-servants a gift they would truly appreciate.

# Chapter 4

DAE WOKE RELUCTANTLY, FOGGY MEMORIES of a wonderful dream still tugging gently at the edges of her consciousness. She opened her eyes and looked around her room, smiling sleepily. She'd grown accustomed to waking in her new surroundings, the initial strangeness of the exotic furnishings and decorations now becoming familiar and comforting to her.

The other pleasure-servants continued to offer her little gifts and trinkets they thought she might like—another custom that seemed common among the Jaharri—and Dae had added to and altered the room according to her personal tastes. It was starting to feel more like home to her. After stretching her arms above her head and groaning as tired muscles protested the strain, Dae rose from the luxurious pile of cushions and silk sheets that made up her bed, performed her waking ablutions, then went in search of the other girls.

Living in the desert had forced Dae to make changes to her normal sleeping cycle. After observing her fellow pleasure-servants over several weeks, she decided to take her rest during the hottest parts of the day, when the sun was too intense for any activity. Then, during the *dohar*—mid-afternoon—she would get up and remain awake until close to midnight, when the chill air would force her back to her room where she would nap till early sunrise. This meant she slept twice each day, and it had taken her a while to adjust to the new conditions. The routine had finally become familiar to her now, the rhythms of sleep and waking no longer jarred. Likewise, her stomach had adjusted to the changes in her diet, and Dae was happy to feel well again after weeks of intermittent nausea.

Strolling through the corridor and out into the seraglio gardens, Dae greeted the end of another perfect—though scorching hot—day. It was early in the evening, the sun just beginning its descent in earnest, and the air was still heavy with heat. Dae couldn't see anyone else around, which surprised her. Usually there were at least a few girls watching the long sunset together. After a brief search, she found the entire harem gathered in a group behind one of the stone arrangements nearby, sitting in a circle.

"Hey," she called as she approached cautiously, wondering if this were some sort of desert ritual she wouldn't be welcomed at...or which she might not want to be included in. "What's going on?"

The girls glanced up at her, smiling welcoming smiles that made it clear they were happy to see her. Inaya in particular appeared in high spirits, her whole face lighting up at Dae's arrival. "*Salaam aleikum*, little one! You are just in time. Come sit." She gestured for Dae to join their circle.

Settling herself beside her friend, Dae saw that the girls were all gathered around an odd looking device constructed from delicate glass and shining metal. To Dae, it looked almost like an oil lamp, except there were several strange tube-like arms sprouting from the base, and the main body was filled partly with water. Nasheta—a girl only a year or two older than Dae and the only other pleasure-servant in the harem possessing blonde hair and pale features—was kneeling beside the contraption and working at something with studious concentration.

Dae frowned at the device, puzzled. "In time for what?"

"The Scion has sent us a gift!" Inaya laughed, holding up a small pouch. She reached in and pulled out several dried leaves with her fingertips, displaying them proudly to the young girl.

Dae studied the leaves curiously, wondering why Inaya was so enthused about them. They looked a little like sage to her. "What is it?"

"They are *brehani* leaves...the Breath of Inshal!" When Dae blinked questioning eyes in apparent confusion, Inaya shook her head. "You have never heard of the Breath of Inshal?"

Dae shook her head.

A slow, mischievous smile spread across Inaya's face. "Then you are in for a treat, little one, for this is a pleasure you may indulge in without fear of corrupting your virtue."

The other girls laughed merrily. Dae colored instantly, feeling naïve and immature beside the more worldly pleasure-servants. Inaya hushed the others with a glance and hastened to explain.

"*Brehani* is an herb that grows deep in the salt plains far to the south. Few merchants will brave the perilous land to reach it, but those who do find the rewards well worth their efforts. Once dried, the *brehani* leaf can be smoked much like tobacco…only with far greater effect. It fills the senses with wonderful feelings, enhances the colors of the world, and makes everything dance and shine!" Inaya gestured enthusiastically, her jewelry creating a musical jangling sound. "It is a rare treat for us to be blessed with, one normally reserved for religious rituals. Zafirah must be in an especially good mood!"

Dae regarded the slender leaves suspiciously. "This is a drug?"

"A perfectly safe one, I assure you. Its effects last but a night and do no harm. In fact, they instill a sense of peace and relaxation for many days thereafter."

Dae's eyes narrowed skeptically; her father had warned her sternly about partaking of such things, telling her of the evils of alcohol and the terrible poisons produced by certain plants…poisons that caused a mind to conjure devilish images and living nightmares and that could drive a man completely insane if ingested. She recoiled a little from the herb. "I-I don't think I'd like it."

Inaya's joyous expression turned tragic at once. "What? Of course you will like it! Please, at least try it before you pass judgment."

The other girls nodded encouragingly, and Dae frowned. She didn't want to seem like a child to these people, but her natural caution made her reluctant. "I don't think so."

The girls pouted and began pleading with her to reconsider and share their pleasure. Dae's will began to falter.

"Well…maybe I could just watch and see first?"

Somewhat mollified, the other girls smiled and waited for Nasheta to finish her preparations. Several of the leaves were crushed and sprinkled into a small bowl at the top of the pipe, which was then covered by a fine mesh of steel. One of the girls produced a pair of tongs and used them to pluck a small lump of glowing coal from a metal box, carefully placing the ember over the steel mesh. When all was ready, a few girls took up the strange tube-like devices which Dae now saw were each fitted with a brass mouthpiece. She watched as each girl took a turn breathing from the tube and was fascinated to observe the water held in the glass body of the device beginning to bubble and churn furiously. A moment later, the glass chamber filled with a dense white smoke, which was inhaled through the tubes. Each girl held the smoke from the burned herb in her lungs for several seconds before exhaling and then passed the mouthpiece on to the next waiting person. Inaya took her turn at the pipe, breathing deep and then smiling brilliantly at Dae as she blew smoke rings into the air.

"You see? Nothing to fear from a little smoke." She closed her eyes and sighed peacefully. "It is wonderful, Dae. You will enjoy it, I promise." Inaya offered the mouthpiece and batted long eyelashes persuasively. "Please?"

Dae shifted, uncertain. A few of the girls had run off to summon musicians, and several others were diving into the still waters of the great pool with loud squeals. Soon, the sounds of laughter and splashing filled the air. Watching them carefully, Dae admitted the smoke didn't seem to be doing any harm, and she regarded the ornate brass pipe dubiously.

"What exactly will it do?"

Inaya smiled, sensing victory. "Nothing bad," she insisted. "It will relax your mind and your body, will send sparkles through your blood, and will let you see the world and yourself more clearly. The Jaharri people have used this herb for centuries without injury. It is held as a sacrament by the followers of Inshal. You may trust me, Dae, I am your friend. I would never willingly urge you to do something that might bring you harm."

Dae frowned. "It won't…you know…make me do anything foolish, will it?" *Like succumb to any amorous advances?*

The knowing sparkle in Inaya's eyes told Dae her friend had heard the unspoken question all too clearly. "It cannot make you do anything that is not already in your heart," she promised, the very hint of a dare in her voice.

Considering one last time, Dae gave a mental sigh of resignation and accepted the mouthpiece from her friend. As she brought the warm metal to her lips, Dae glowered at Inaya sternly. "If I regret this, I'll make certain you do too."

Inaya laughed and swatted her playfully. "Have no fear, little one. Tonight you shall enjoy the magic of the herb, and tomorrow you will heap blessings upon my head for convincing you to try it."

Dae grunted and cautiously set her lips to the brass. She took a shallow breath, still wary of the drug, and was surprised when the white smoke filled her lungs. Its taste was sweet, almost like honeysuckle, and Dae followed the example of the others and held the smoke in her lungs for a moment before exhaling. She concentrated hard, but felt nothing bad happen. Inaya was watching her with a sensuous smile, apparently waiting for a reaction. After a few seconds, Dae felt reassured she wasn't about to keel over and took another deeper breath from the pipe before passing the mouthpiece on to the next girl.

Sitting cross-legged on the ground, Dae looked around curiously and waited for some kind of terrible hallucination to jump out at her. She was a little disappointed when no such phantasm manifested itself, feeling cheated that her father's warning had not been justified. Instead, a subtle, rather interesting tingling sensation began to crawl across her body, tickling her nerve endings. It started at her fingertips and spread up her arms and over her skin, creating a strange sense of self-awareness that seemed to sharpen her senses to a finer point. A few moments later, Dae began to notice other subtle effects; the colors of the setting sun became brighter, more vivid. The leaves on the garden trees seemed to jump out at her, each in sharp definition against the others. Sounds became clearer, more distinct. It felt like she could hear the very whisper of the earth itself breathing, and Dae shivered as a little rush sparkled down her spine and made her toes tingle.

"You see?" Inaya smiled at her, a smile that was warm and comforting. "Not so horrible, is it?"

Dae felt her lips pull helplessly into a grin and allowed herself to relax. "I guess not." Her body seemed indecisive, unable to figure out if it was feeling sleepy or energetic. A sudden giggle escaped her, and she regarded the smoky pipe with new appreciation. "This is actually kind of nice."

"I told you. Here." Inaya held out the mouthpiece again. "Have some more."

"Okay." Dae accepted readily this time, no longer fearing the herb. After taking another deep breath of the white smoke, nearly choking, she struggled to hold it in her lungs a few moments before blowing it out onto her hands. She watched the curious smoke as it drifted away, momentarily fascinated by its writhing movements. Over near the palace walls, lively music began to play, and Dae's body suddenly reached the conclusion that it did feel energetic. Getting shakily to her feet, she grabbed Inaya by the arm and started tugging her up.

"Come on, let's go listen."

"As you wish." Inaya happily allowed herself to be dragged along behind Dae, who couldn't help but notice the way her eyes, bright and alive with playful hunger, roamed daringly over every inch of skin left exposed by her outfit. But for the first time since coming to the harem, Dae managed not to blush in the face of her obvious carnal interest.

Joining a group of girls gathered around five musicians playing a variety of instruments, Dae sat on the sweet-smelling grass and happily began clapping along with the drumbeat. Several girls were dancing to the lively rhythm, and Dae watched their hypnotic movements avidly. The dancing here was, of course, unlike anything she had ever seen in her homeland. It was physical and alluring, hinting at a sexual pulse Dae didn't fully understand but which she couldn't help but find mesmerizing. The dancers gyrated and swayed their hips in a wild, exotic style, twirling their arms in sensuous waves about their bodies and tossing long hair about crazily. Dae's attention fixed on Asalah, a tall, willowy girl who wore her long auburn hair in a mass of beaded braids. A colorful tattoo of two exotic-looking birds with extraordinarily long and beautiful tail feathers ran from her neck, around her left breast, and down her body, reaching low on her left thigh. Dae admired the way Asalah—arguably the finest dancer among the harem girls—seemed able to bring the birds to life with her movements and found herself wishing she could move with such graceful eroticism.

By now, the intoxicated girls were spread out all through the sprawling seraglio gardens. Some were playing and splashing about in the pool or diving from the top of the small waterfall; others were climbing through the branches of the giant aspen. A few simply sat and watched the sun paint the clear blue sky with fantastic stains of crimson and purple, the colors reflecting off the tiled palace domes like an iridescent rainbow. At the foot of an enormous bronze statue of a nearly naked woman, Johara and her mate Hayam were engaged in a passionate embrace, their mouths exploring one another passionately. Dae glanced at the other activities going on around her, but decided she wanted to stay here and watch the dancing for now. She could feel the music in the air, like a benevolent spirit that wanted her to join its band of merry revelers. Still clapping, Dae grinned as she enjoyed the sparkly, magical rushes that played over her body in time to the drumbeat.

Inaya leaned against her and gave her a gentle nudge with her shoulder. "Would you like to join them?"

Dae lowered her eyes and shook her head. "I-I can't dance like that," she said quietly.

"Why not?"

"I just…can't."

"They could teach you if you wish to learn."

Dae studied the suggestive motions thoughtfully. The herb had lowered her inhibitions, and she considered the idea of joining the dancers seriously for the first time.

*Why shouldn't I join in? They always ask me to, and I'm sure they wouldn't make fun of me if I'm a bit clumsy.* The music was tempting her to move with it, and Dae didn't much feel like fighting it. *It'd be nice to be a part of the group…to be able to move like that.*

"You know," Inaya whispered persuasively, "Zafirah has always found the dancers to be particularly arousing…"

Dae blushed instantly, but didn't bother making any comment. Still, the information was enough to tip the scales of her mind quickly, and after a long moment, she shyly stood up and moved to join the others.

Seeing her move into their circle, the girls all smiled delightedly and sidled alongside her. Asalah held out her hand invitingly, and Dae hesitated only a moment before accepting it. The auburn-haired dancer moved behind her and rested a hand on Dae's exposed stomach. She leaned forward to whisper directions into her ear.

"Feel the muscles beneath my hand?"

Dae nodded. The *brehani* made her skin extremely sensitive, and she was aware of every muscle in her body...of the warmth of Asalah's breasts pressing against her back...her breath tickling the nape of her neck.

"Draw the lower part of your belly in, as though you are taking a deep breath."

Dae did as instructed, contracting her abdominal muscles. Asalah's fingers moved higher in a slow caress.

"Now, push it out...and at the same time draw in the upper muscles."

After a few minutes' practice Dae was able to make her belly ripple in fluid waves, and she laughed in pure delight. The other dancers praised her efforts and started showing her how to sway her hips and move her arms. At first uncertain, Dae quickly abandoned her modesty and began to join in, giggling at her own mistakes and slowly improving her style. The music was powerful and addictive; for some reason, her body responded readily to its directions. Twirling happily among the other girls, relaxed and at ease, Dae wondered why she had ever been apprehensive about accepting the invitations to dance. Even when she caught Inaya staring at her with open lust, she felt no shame or embarrassment...just a guilty thrill of pleasure that raced down her spine and seemed to settle low in her belly, urging her to explore more provocative movements. The other girls watching whistled and clapped, their own appreciation no less evident than Inaya's.

Thoroughly enjoying the confidence inspired by the *brehani*, Dae didn't offer protest when another of the dancers moved behind her and ran a hand over her abdomen to the curve of her hip in a light caress. The contact was sensuous and undemanding, and Dae slowed her movements to more fully enjoy it, letting the touches linger a long while before drawing away.

In the back of her mind, unburdened by maidenly modesty, Dae entertained a brief, illicit fantasy of dancing like this for Zafirah. The thought of those stunning sapphire eyes consuming every inch of her skin sent another wash of tingles across her nerve endings...and for the first time, Dae found the sensation exciting rather than disconcerting. When she caught Inaya's smoky gaze again, she grinned happily, only blushing a little at the promising, inviting heat in her regard.

That heat seemed more appealing now than ever before.

Inaya wasn't the only one watching the dancing with avid interest. From a terrace jutting out from the palace wall thirty feet above the seraglio gardens, a sapphire gaze darkened hungrily at the sight of Dae's provocative movements.

Zafirah felt heat flood through her lower body and licked suddenly dry lips, hardly daring to blink for fear of missing a moment of the girl's dance. Her position on the balcony afforded Zafirah a wonderful view; when Dae bent forward, her impressive cleavage was splendidly revealed for attentive study. The Scion had always had a weakness for such erotic displays, but she had never imagined the shy and modest blonde would be so willing to join the other girls. This was an unexpected and welcome bonus, and Zafirah was pleased she'd shared some of the *brehani* leaves with her harem.

In the course of her life, Zafirah had shared pleasure with many women. Her appetite was legendary, and deservedly so. Though the girls of her harem were talented and inventive lovers, Zafirah often seduced a bedmate from among the ranks of her army and even—when she was in the mood for something a little wilder—from among the nomad tribes. Yet in all the years of her rule, the charismatic Scion had never felt herself so completely drawn to another woman as she did now. For some reason, Dae seemed able to inflame Zafirah's lust with no more than a simple timid smile.

It was something Zafirah found increasingly frustrating. While outwardly she gave little indication of her turmoil, inside the Scion was growing more and more confused. She had a whole harem filled with girls whose greatest joy in life was to offer her sexual satisfaction, yet she couldn't seem to rid herself of the image of those sparkling emerald eyes that called to her incessantly. And of course, the knowledge that her hunger would not be sated only made it that much more intense.

It was, Zafirah thought as she watched Dae with hooded eyes, the most delicious of tortures.

Entranced by the vision below, groaning audibly when a particularly enthusiastic chest thrust almost strained Dae's brief top past its bursting point, Zafirah didn't hear the sound of light footsteps approaching from behind. Only when she caught sight of a dark shape in her peripheral vision did she spin around, hands raised defensively, to confront the intruder.

Pearly teeth flashed against ebony skin. Falak stepped from the shadows into the low lamplight, smiling at her momentary alarm. "You startle easily, Scion. Perhaps you should seek an outlet for this tension."

"And you should be more careful when skulking about another woman's bedchamber," Zafirah scolded, relaxing as she turned back to her study of the activity below and gesturing her friend to join her.

"The council has just now been concluded," Falak reported.

"And?"

"There are stirrings among the renegade tribes in the south. They gather in greater numbers, seemingly around the banner of the Deharn."

"It will mean war, then," Zafirah predicted without much interest. "Shakir is a hothead; soon enough he will need to be dealt with. But I will not venture out to meet him. Let him march his men across the sands. They will be stunned with exhaustion by the time they are within sight of the city."

"Still, I have sent my scouts to keep an eye on their movements. We will know the moment the young jackal decides to test his teeth."

Zafirah grunted. "What else?"

"There was general displeasure over the amount of tribute you offered to the Tek."

The faint scowl that turned the corners of Zafirah's lips was more of resignation than true ire. The city council was a thorn in her side, as it had been a thorn in the side of every Scion before her. Comprised of elder representatives from all the most powerful tribes owing allegiance to El'Kasari and the Scion Peace, the council bickered over every trivial thing Zafirah did. Though ultimately their power was more symbolic than real, their infighting and rivalries often made things more difficult then they needed to be.

"Rehan was given nothing his people did not earn," Zafirah told her chief scout. "He serves us well and is rewarded for that service. If the other tribes worked as hard as his to defend the Peace, perhaps they would find themselves similarly rewarded."

"That is a truth they do not care to see, my Scion."

Zafirah glanced at her head scout, rolled her eyes pointedly, and then went back to watching the scene below. She was in no mood to discuss politics right now, and Falak knew her well enough not to press the matter further. Instead she joined Zafirah in studying the harem girls, her attention easily drawn to the blonde hair amidst all the dark.

"She dances well."

Zafirah lips twitched into a fond smile. "Yes, she does."

"It is good to see her settling in so readily. This cannot be an easy adjustment for her to make."

"I suppose not." Zafirah's fingers ran absently along the intricate railing, tracing the details with a long, painted nail. "Still, the people of her homeland have instilled their ignorance in her mind. I doubt she will ever truly accept the way of life in the desert."

Falak's teeth flashed in the low light as she turned to study her ruler and friend knowingly. "I think there is one particular aspect of our way of life that you would wish for her to accept above all others," she said wryly. "You watch her with the eyes of a hawk about to dive upon its prey."

"She is very beautiful. Of course I desire her." Zafirah was careful to keep her tone of voice indifferent.

"And yet you have barely glanced at the other girls. Surely they are equally beautiful...equally desirable."

The sound of lilting laughter rose from the girls as Dae made a silly mistake and burst into a fit of giggles. Zafirah sighed longingly and shook her head. "Nothing is as desirable as she is."

That remark earned the Scion a raised eyebrow. "Indeed?" Falak's gaze shifted between the dancing girl and Zafirah, visibly intrigued. Zafirah could feel Falak reading her face intently, but she ignored her and continued watching Dae. Absorbed in her study of the foreign girl, lips drawn in a soft, unguarded smile of utter fascination, she almost didn't register when Falak's voice, equally amazed and amused, broke the silence. "By Inshal! I never thought I would live to see this!"

Zafirah's concentration didn't waver for a moment. "See what?"

"You...falling in love."

"*What?*" That got Zafirah's attention. She pinned her head scout with a startled, defensive look. "What are you talking about?"

Falak didn't flinch. "With all due respect, my Scion, I cannot remember you ever being so captivated by a single girl, much less a single girl whom you have not even bedded! The way your eyes follow her so avidly...the way you smile when she smiles... You have never looked so lost to this world as you did just now."

Zafirah waved her hand dismissively. "So what? I have shared love with many women in my life, Falak."

"You have shared your body, Scion...not your heart," Falak corrected gently.

Zafirah paused at that. "I have cared for all those who ever warmed my bed," she said a little defensively. "Every last one."

"That girl has completely bewitched you, Zafirah," Falak insisted in a quiet voice. "It is nothing to be ashamed of—"

"I am not ashamed."

"—or scared of."

"I am not afraid!"

"Then why do you deny what you know to be true?" Falak's expression was calm and certain, and Zafirah found herself uncharacteristically unable to meet her steady gaze. "Desire that feeds from the heart cannot be so easily sated as desire that feeds from the eye," Falak offered quietly.

Her mouth opened and closed a few times, but as much as Zafirah wanted to reject the notion, she was unable to form any words of denial. She felt suddenly vulnerable, exposed, her emotions too near the surface for them to be hidden. In the gardens below, the girls had paused in their dancing to watch the sunset, gathering by the far wall where they could better see the lengthening shadows slowly conquer the streets of El'Kasari. Resting her elbows on the terrace, Zafirah easily picked out Dae's figure among the group. "Wanting her, even with my heart, will not make her mine," she whispered almost to herself. "She has made it clear she has no interest in warming my bed. That is something I cannot contend against."

Falak considered her words and the audible resignation in her tone. "She is young. Perhaps when she has grown to better understand the ways of pleasure and passion, she will be able to accept your desire for her."

"And how is she to gain such wisdom?"

Falak chuckled and gestured to the pleasure-servants. "Living with those girls? I should think her education has already begun!"

Deep in the far reaches of the Jaharri desert, beyond the rule of Zafirah and her fierce army of *spahi*, Shakir watched with exultant eyes as his own troops went through their motions across a broad expanse of flat, empty wilderness.

These last few months had been busy ones for Shakir. His alliance of the tribes had started on shaky ground, but soon enough most were swayed to join his cause, awed by the marvelous foreign weapons he had procured from the western empire. Old rivalries were set aside to support a common purpose, for though their ancient feuds ran deep, if there was one thing that could possibly unite the fractious renegade tribes, it was their hunger to see the Scion and her legions humbled in battle.

From among the ranks of the nomad warriors, Shakir had chosen seventy-five men and women to arm with his great weapons—which had come to be known as thunder-bows by the desert people—and he had added that number to the twenty-five elite soldiers from his own tribe. He had spent the last few months training those hundred until they were competent with the strange devices, teaching them how to aim, fire, and then swiftly retreat and reload. It had not been easy for some. The nomads were a proud and independent people, and they did not take kindly to their many stumbles when it came to learning new skills. Still, Shakir was smart; he knew well the competitive spirit of his people. With a little encouragement, the warriors were soon striving to perfect their skills, each tribe seeking to outdo the others in mastering the new weapons.

Now, finally, Shakir could see his plans for the downfall of El'Kasari taking form in reality. The time he had dreamed of since childhood was fast approaching, when he would march triumphant into the torn city and strike down the Whore who kept his people from achieving their rightful place in the world.

"Calif?"

The call attracted Shakir's attention from his troops, and he turned to see a young man riding swiftly toward him on the back of a great *mehari*—a gift from Brak and his tribe. When he got closer, Shakir saw the man was a scout, and he raised a dark eyebrow.

"What news?"

The scout took a moment to catch his breath; his ride had obviously been one of haste. When he had composed himself, the man pointed to the north. "Scouts, *Effendi*," he reported. "Scouts of the Scion, riding across the escarpments on the northern ridge."

"Hmm." Shakir's lips pursed as he absorbed this news. "They saw us?"

"Only our outriders, Calif, not the camp. They dared not ride further into the deep desert." Seeing Shakir make no response, the man waited a moment before asking, "What shall we do?"

"Leave them be," Shakir said, looking back to his troops on the field.

"But *Effendi*, they—" The man started to protest but stopped at a sharp glance from the Calif.

"Leave them be," Shakir repeated, and though his tone was soft, he carefully set his expression into a coldly wrathful mask. The scout swallowed nervously. "Let the Scion bitch see what fate awaits her. She is too arrogant to lead her army out to face us, and by the time she realizes the danger, it shall be too late." He smiled cruelly, envisioning his victory already. "Soon enough it will be time to test the troops. Until then, let the scouts wander as they please. They will be the first to taste our power."

Visibly unsettled, the scout saluted and went to relay the instructions to his fellows still watching on the ridge.

# Chapter 5

IT WAS MIDDAY BEFORE DAE finally pulled herself from the grip of a deep, restful sleep and looked around lazily. She was back in her room, though her memory was a little sketchy about the details of how she'd gotten there. Her body was relaxed and still pleasantly tingly from the *brehani*, and she actually felt quite good. Groaning mildly at an unfamiliar stiffness in her muscles as she sat up, Dae closed her eyes again and recalled the events of last night.

She had stayed up late with the rest of the harem; none of them had felt the least bit tired by midnight, and even the chill air seemed comfortable for a change. Dozens of torches and lamps were always lit through the night to keep the darkness from ever encroaching too far into the seraglio, since a few of the pleasure-servants preferred to be more nocturnal than the others, so they had danced and sang and laughed long past Dae's usual nap time. The girls had even managed to teach Dae to sing a few traditional songs of the desert nomads, laughing every time she mangled their words with her foreign accent. Reflecting back on the evening, Dae couldn't help but smile a little. It had been the first time she'd truly felt at ease among the other pleasure-servants since arriving here, the first time she hadn't felt awkward in their company. The sense of belonging to a group, of being a part of something larger than herself, had felt very nice.

But there was more to it than just a sense of belonging, Dae realized. Something had changed in her head last night…something subtle but important. Joining the other girls, sharing their pleasures, Dae had accepted her fate—accepted that this palace, this desert world with its strange customs and scandalous morals, was now her home. The people she shared it with would likely be her companions for life. For the first time, Dae had put all thoughts of her homeland and family aside and had simply enjoyed the companionship that was offered. Enjoyed the knowledge that she was free from the judgment of others, that no one would glare at her if she acted unladylike or giggled foolishly. There was something liberating about this world that Dae was finding more and more to her liking as time passed.

Dae's thoughts were interrupted by a throaty, feminine voice from her doorway. "Dae? Are you awake?"

"Yes," she called, waving languidly when Inaya poked her head into the room. "Come in."

"Thank you." As Inaya crossed the room, Dae's gaze drifted lazily down over her curves, admiring the sensuous flow of her stride. When she realized what she was doing, Dae immediately returned her focus to her friend's face. She shifted a little when Inaya joined her on the bed, certain her friend had not missed the lingering look. Inaya studied her a moment, her dark eyes amused. "How are you feeling?"

"Okay, I suppose. What time is it?"

"Nearly midday." Inaya gave a pretty scowl of distaste. "The sun is too hot to go outside yet. I fear we have slept through the cooler morning."

"Mm." Dae had suspected as much. "It was a late night."

"But a pleasant one, no?" A slender brow arched in a definite "I-told-you-so" fashion. "The *brehani* destroyed neither your mind nor your virtue, did it?"

Dae rolled her eyes a little. "No. You were right, it was…very nice."

"As are many other things in life of which you choose not to partake." Inaya ran her eyes over Dae's body for a moment before returning to her face. "Last night was good for you, I think. It was a joy to see you relax, to see you release your concerns, if only for a few hours. You enjoyed the dancing, did you not?"

"Well…it was okay." Dae shifted uncomfortably. "I've never done anything like that before."

"You were very good."

"I was clumsy as a one-legged ox."

Inaya laughed and shook her head. "Why is it so difficult for you to accept your own talents?" she asked, pulling her long legs under her. "I thought you were wonderful for one who has never danced before."

"It was strange," Dae confided quietly. "I felt so exposed. These clothes…" She plucked at the transparent fabric of her loose pants and the top that barely contained her full breasts. "They don't cover much."

"And nor should they. You are too beautiful to hide away from those who would admire you. It would be a waste to conceal such a body as yours, and an insult to the Gods who created your beauty!" She patted Dae on the arm. "Do not be afraid to enjoy your body, Dae. If you like dancing, you should dance."

"I think I will," Dae agreed quietly. "It was fun, and I'll get better if I practice." She winced as she sat up. "I'm a little sore, though. I used muscles I never even knew I had!"

Inaya's eyes hooded sensuously. "I am certain we could show you many other muscles you have never used before either," she purred.

"Um…n-no, thank you." Dae immediately looked away from the amorous heat in her friend's regard, wondering if she would ever get used to being an object of lust for every female in the palace seraglio.

"As you wish. But do not be afraid to change your mind," Inaya said. "Who knows, you might enjoy discovering other such pleasant feelings as those you experienced last night."

A question suddenly occurred to Dae, and she fidgeted nervously before summoning the courage to ask. "Is that…is that what it feels like when you're with Zafirah?"

"The *brehani*? Not really." Inaya studied her expression a long while in silence, and Dae guessed she had never needed to find words to describe an act she thought of as universally understood. "Physical pleasure is difficult to describe, Dae, especially to someone such as yourself who has not the slightest comprehension of what it entails."

Dae lowered her eyes, feeling embarrassed that she'd even asked. "I-I just wondered, that's all."

"It is good to be curious," Inaya quickly assured her. "My words were not intended as a disparagement, so do not feel shame for your interest. You are a young woman; your body is awakening and beginning to want new things. This is perfectly natural."

Dae remained silent.

"Sexual pleasure is about intimacy and passion," Inaya explained slowly. "It is a hunger for the body of your lover that grows so great it consumes your every thought. A hunger so powerful it can never be fully satisfied...only calmed for a time. And the pleasure it brings..." Inaya closed her eyes and sighed. "Zafirah's talents are such that she can drive a lover to the brink of madness simply with her touch alone!"

"But..." Dae twisted her fingers nervously. "What does it *feel* like?"

"There is no comparison to anything you have experienced," Inaya said softly. "Of course, I could show you...?" Dae blushed and shook her head. Inaya sighed. "It is like heat in your belly," she offered after a moment of consideration. "A fire that spreads through the blood until every part of you burns with need. A pressure that builds inside until the ecstasy grows to such a point that it seems it could tear you asunder! And in a way...that is exactly what it does."

Dae knit her brows thoughtfully as she processed this explanation. She was slightly disappointed that Inaya's words hadn't really helped her at all. Her body certainly responded to Zafirah's presence when she was around, and the feelings, though strange and new, weren't exactly unpleasant. But given the sexualized atmosphere that so permeated the harem, Dae couldn't help but be curious about exactly what all the fuss was about. She looked awkwardly away from Inaya's frank appraisal. "It doesn't sound all that nice to me."

"Certain things in life must be experienced before they can be understood and appreciated."

"But I can't—"

Inaya raised a hand to silence her protest. "You need raise no arguments, little one. I have heard the words before and I accept them, as do Zafirah and the others." She leaned closer, her voice taking on a deeper tone, her eye contact suddenly intense. "But your body was created to desire pleasure and stimulation, Dae, to seek out a lover and share itself. That is the nature of all people, not just the Jaharri, and you cannot fight against it. In time, the will of your body will grow stronger than your resistance, and you will have to decide how to deal with your appetites." Inaya gave a sultry grin and a quick wink. "Zafirah is an excellent teacher of the erotic arts. I am certain she would be most willing to instruct you."

The warmth that flooded through Dae's belly indicated her body was entirely in favor of the idea. Still, she pushed the thought down as hard as she could, determined not to let herself be swayed by the temptations her new home offered so constantly. "Speaking of appetites, I'm kind of hungry. Are there any of those purple fruits left? You know, the ones with the big dark seeds in them? Those were nice."

Inaya smiled at the sudden change of topic, but thankfully made no comment at Dae's obvious retreat from the uncomfortable discussion. "I think a few may have escaped the notice of the other girls. Come, let us find out." Still, when she rose from the bed and offered a delicate hand to help Dae up, that mischievous, slightly amused expression still sparkled in the depths of her dark, seductive eyes.

Together, the two friends left Dae's room and headed down the corridor to the hexagonal chamber where their food was most often laid out. As she walked, Dae couldn't help but dwell on Inaya's words, wondering how true they would prove to be. Was her body starting to want physical pleasure? Sexual pleasure? Why? Was it simply because she had suddenly been plunged into this desert harem where such lusts were so prevalent and unrestrained, or was it a natural phenomenon as Inaya claimed? What would she do if it got worse?

And in the back of her mind, she wondered what might happen if she accepted the mysterious delights Zafirah and the other girls continued to offer. What might they do to her? Would she like it?

Dae's body responded quickly to the silent questions, and she worried at the tingling heat that raced through her blood so delightfully. Yes, she thought, something was happening to her...and although the strange longings troubled her deeply, it was impossible to fight against them. The thoughts of another woman touching her, kissing her, running fingers through her hair and moaning with passion... Dae couldn't deny that a hunger was indeed awakening inside her.

And at the heart of all these alien desires, Dae knew, lay a pair of burning sapphire eyes, haunting her dreams and calling to her seductively from the darkness.

# Chapter 6

THE NEXT EVENING, ZAFIRAH SAT beneath the weeping branches of a willow tree in the seraglio, her eyes wandering back and forth between two different points of focus. The first was a group of girls dancing and laughing on the lawn nearby, the second was a solitary figure who watched the proceedings from a comfortable spot beside the waterfall, surrounded by several pieces of parchment on which she scribbled absently. Zafirah had been observing Dae for over an hour now, trying to will her to get up and join in the dancing, but to no effect. The sun was now starting to set, and Zafirah's hopes of seeing the captivating girl whirl and gyrate again were slowly dying.

*Why does she not dance?* Zafirah frowned sulkily and began stripping the flesh from a pomegranate. *She did it the night before last without care or concern. Why not now? Is it me? Does she avoid joining the others for fear of my eyes watching her?*

Sighing, feeling a strange melancholy settle over her like a depressing cloud, Zafirah wondered at her feelings for Dae. Since her conversation with Falak, her thoughts had dwelled more and more on the young blonde. Dae's stunning features and deliciously unexplored body taunted Zafirah, and she found her want growing stronger by the hour. For the first time that she could remember, the Scion felt her normally ravenous sexual appetite oddly dulled. Though the girls all flirted and tried to catch her fancy, hoping to win their way into her bed for the evening, their touches and smiles couldn't rouse the flames of Zafirah's passion. Their whispered words of seduction and suggestions of nightly delights elicited no response. The music sounded too spirited for her despondent mood, and she glared at the way everyone else seemed so happy.

Only when she turned her attention to Dae, who was sitting apart from the group, did Zafirah's blood stir. She watched every subtle motion the girl made as she scribbled away, entranced by each simple gesture and movement. When she began sucking absentmindedly on a strand of her golden hair, Zafirah almost swooned with longing. And as she stared hungrily at her, Zafirah realized she would find no satisfaction in the arms of another lover this night.

And so, when she left the seraglio gardens some hours later, Zafirah was alone.

Such occurrences were not terribly rare, however. No one seemed to pay much mind to Zafirah's strange distance or lack of interest, likely assuming she would take a lover from among the army barracks for the night as she often did.

However, when the same behavior was repeated every night for a week, and then another, puzzled murmurings began to stir like an ill wind through the harem.

Dae was still a stranger to most desert customs, so it took her some time to realize anything was amiss. But eventually she noticed the peculiar tension that marked the faces of the other pleasure-servants and the way they whispered conspiratorially in groups from time to time. When Inaya approached her one morning with an unusually somber frown, Dae raised an eyebrow curiously.

"What's wrong? Why is everyone acting so strangely?"

Inaya settled herself beside her friend and fiddled with the beads of her outfit. "They are troubled," she explained in a concerned tone. "Zafirah's behavior these last weeks is not normal for her."

"Oh?" Dae cocked her head thoughtfully. "I hadn't really noticed anything."

"She has not taken a lover for a fortnight!" Inaya said, her eyes wide with terrible dread.

"Two weeks?" Dae couldn't help but giggle. "So what? Surely she's gone that long before without..." She trailed off as Inaya shook her head ominously. Her eyes widened in surprise. "You mean—"

Inaya nodded. "As I have told you, Zafirah is a woman of great passion. She has never abstained before without serious cause. This is not like her at all."

Dae absorbed this, then shrugged. "Maybe she's just taking a lover from somewhere else. You said she does that sometimes, right?"

"Indeed. But we have spoken with the guards. They say Zafirah has slept alone this past half-moon. Her sleep is troubled and sporadic. And there are other things." Inaya leaned closer, her tone more conspiratorial. "She has been training with the soldiers for hours on end, even during the heat of the midday sun! She rides alone across the dunes and returns near exhaustion. The guards are afraid to approach her, but they are deeply concerned."

Dae wanted to shrug away any concern for the Scion's strange behavior, but she could see plainly that Inaya shared the guards' concern. "She seems okay whenever she comes here," she observed thoughtfully. "She doesn't seem to stay in the *seraglio* with us as long as she used to, but I just figured she was busy with affairs of state. I'm sure it's nothing to worry about."

"You do not understand," Inaya persisted. "Even during times when raiders attacked the outlying tribes, Zafirah rarely slept alone. Whatever troubles her must be a powerful influence indeed to keep her from seeking pleasure."

"So what do you think is wrong?"

Inaya's limpid brown eyes studied Dae's face cautiously. "I have my suspicions," she said. "But that is all they are—suspicions. For now, all that is certain is that Zafirah's behavior is not healthy for either her mind or her body. If she does not settle with her troubles soon, I fear the damage done will be far more severe."

Zafirah sat cross-legged in the Temple of Inshal, taking long, deep breaths of the incense-soaked air, trying desperately to quell with the peace of meditation the energy that thrummed though her body. The priests of Inshal who watched from the darker shadows of the temple pillars were starting to grow nervous; she had been sitting here like this for over three hours, and the time no longer seemed to stretch into eternity. But still, Zafirah could find no respite from the urges of her body.

Abstinence, in any form, was not in Zafirah's nature. The two greatest pleasures in her life were the pursuits of battle and sexual gratification, and she had never felt the need to restrain herself from either…until now.

Two weeks. Fourteen long, frustrating nights. Zafirah's low-burning arousal was reaching a critical level, the strain of holding back now almost physically painful. But though she had a harem filled with gorgeous women who would have enjoyed nothing more than to relieve her of her ache, Zafirah knew none of them could satisfy her now.

None, that was, save Dae.

In the back of her mind, Zafirah knew she needed a solution quickly. If she allowed this hunger to grow for much longer, the temptation might prove overwhelming and Dae could be hurt. Zafirah was wracking her brain to come up with a way to avoid this fate, but so far nothing had presented itself. Initially she had thought to exhaust her sexual appetite with physical exercise, hoping to distract herself with endless martial drills and long desert rides. And at first, the plan had seemed to work. But now, nothing could stop the force of her desire for the girl. Sleep came only with great reluctance, and the Scion's dreams were filled with erotic images of Dae's untouched body writhing beneath her own. Each day, it got a little worse. Without release, Zafirah knew, this passion could become a detriment to her rule.

And then, suddenly, the solution sprung fully formed into her mind.

Zafirah's eyes opened for the first time since she had entered the sacred temple. She took a moment to consider her idea more thoroughly and then nodded to herself, pleased. Rising stiffly from her meditation, the Scion rubbed her cramped legs to restore their circulation, then strode swiftly down the hallowed hallways till she located one of her guards. Gesturing the armored woman to her side, she issued a single concise instruction.

"Go to the seraglio and request Nasheta's presence in my chamber at once."

The guard saluted and hurried off toward the seraglio gardens to fulfill her mission.

Nasheta entered the Scion's bedroom and looked around curiously, not certain exactly what to expect. Though she had served Zafirah for three years as a pleasure-servant, Nasheta had learned never to underestimate the woman's creativity or motivations. And since her beloved ruler had been acting so strangely this last fortnight, she wasn't about to make any assumptions about why she'd been summoned here, nor what the Scion might ask of her. Nevertheless, Nasheta had prepared for the evening as she normally would have done, anticipating that like any such meeting, this one would likely turn carnal sooner or later. Her hair had been thoroughly brushed and styled, drawn over her left shoulder so that it spilled down her chest like a flow of honey. She wore her favorite outfit, gossamer sheer pantaloons and a revealing top, both dyed in shifting shades of blue green that complimented her fair hair and pale complexion. Her skin had been oiled and perfumed, and despite her uncertainty, Nasheta could feel the warmth of arousal already kindling in her belly.

The chamber glowed in the soft light of several dozen small *shamedan*, their flames casting secretive shadows over the corners of the room. Smoke from a bundle of glowing incense sticks resting on a table curled up to the ceiling in serpentine spirals, twisting and writhing into the air and filling the room with the rich scent of vanilla and hyacinth. Nasheta gave a coy smile when her eyes came to rest on the enormous bed that dominated the chamber, and it was returned by the woman who lay there like a tiger in repose.

"Enter, Nasheta," invited the familiar husky voice in a tone that sent shivers down her spine. "I have been waiting."

Nasheta stepped closer, letting her hips sway in a conscious display she could tell was instantly noted. "How may I be of service, my Scion?" she asked in a heavy whisper. The heat in Zafirah's eyes had immediately cleared away any doubts as to why she had been summoned here. Nasheta decided these past weeks of abstinence must have simply been a one-time occurrence—strange, perhaps, but not nearly as ominous as Inaya and the others had feared.

Zafirah sat up and studied her intently, her eyes lingering over her blonde hair and full breasts before they dropped lower and passed over slender hips and toned thighs. Her smile grew wider. "Come closer."

Nasheta did as instructed, moving slowly to ensure her audience had ample opportunity to properly appreciate every languid stride. She stopped just a few inches in front of Zafirah and deliberately thrust her breasts forward, inviting the dark-haired woman to sample her flesh intimately.

But Zafirah ignored the tempting offer and rose slowly from the bed. Nasheta watched the sheer robe she was wearing slip from her shoulders, revealing the barest of undergarments, and felt her pulse quicken. Zafirah circled behind her, moving with the intense grace of a stalking panther, and Nasheta's breathing grew heavier under the intensity of her gaze. When a single finger combed through her fine blonde hair and traced over her shoulder, she couldn't suppress a low shiver of anticipation. Zafirah's voice, low and husky with desire, whispered two words that almost caused Nasheta's legs to buckle.

"I hunger."

Zafirah stepped away again, deliberately prolonging the moment. Nasheta whimpered, her body awash with desire. She knew from experience that the Scion would only make this torment last longer if she made any move to hasten the proceedings, and so remained silent and still as she waited for Zafirah's next move. Warm breath blew against her neck, raising gooseflesh and causing her to tilt her head in open invitation. But no lips pressed against her heated flesh. Instead, a silken voice whispered into her ear. "Nasheta?"

"Mmmm?" she moaned, eyes closed in anticipation of the pleasure to come.

"Would you like to play a game?"

Nasheta's eyes flashed open and looked back over her shoulder. She knew that when Zafirah wanted to "play," it inevitably portended a night of blistering ecstasy for her chosen partner. Zafirah smiled expectantly down at her, one dark brow raised, and Nasheta batted her eyelids with practiced innocence. "What kind of game, Scion?"

Zafirah's smile became an anticipatory grin as she resumed running her fingertips lightly over Nasheta's skin. "Oh, I think you will find it to your liking," she promised softly. "It is the kind of game where you shall scream your passion to the night until you grow hoarse."

Nasheta trembled. "What would you have me do?"

Zafirah was quiet for several moments, her hands never ceasing their teasing caresses. "I was hoping..." She swallowed, looking away as though unable to meet Nasheta's gaze. It took a long moment for Nasheta to realize, with considerable surprise, that the Scion was nervous. "I was hoping perhaps you might be willing to...entertain a fantasy I have."

In the course of her service to the Scion, Nasheta had been involved in bringing many of the Scion's fantasies to life. Zafirah had never shown even the slightest hint of apprehension when sharing her desires and dreams, some of which had shocked even the more experienced pleasure-servants. The Scion was bold and adventurous with her lovers, confident in her desires and unafraid of expressing them. Remembering some of the things Inaya and the guards had been whispering about recently, it suddenly dawned on Nasheta why she was here. Why she had been summoned, and not one of the other girls.

Blonde hair and pale features. A slight frame with full breasts. Green eyes. Nasheta and Dae were the only two girls in the harem to possess such attributes...

...and Dae was untouchable.

Comprehension brought a slow, seductive smile to Nasheta's lips. She turned to face the Scion directly, stepping away from her wandering hands. "I believe I understand your desires, Zafirah," she said, using the more familiar name with complete confidence. In the bedroom, Zafirah was no longer Scion of a mighty desert nation; she was simply a woman. As she backed away Nasheta began to touch herself slowly, firmly tracing the contours of her own body. She cupped the smooth outer curve of each breast in turn, then ran her palms down over her hips and thighs. Zafirah's nostrils flared, her avid eyes following the wandering hands over every inch of their journey. "I understand why I am here."

"You do?"

"Oh yes." Nasheta backed up to the bed and laid herself among the plush cushions, writhing erotically against the silk and enjoying the way Zafirah was staring at her. "Close your eyes."

Zafirah's eyes widened for a moment in surprise at the command, then obediently slid shut.

"Picture in your mind what you wish to do to me," Nasheta instructed in a low whisper. "Picture *her* body as you have seen it in the seraglio."

Zafirah's breathing stopped, her posture uncertain for a heartbeat before she shivered and relaxed.

"She is beautiful, is she not? So pure. So innocent. She has never known the touch of another woman. Never felt her body explode with fiery release." Nasheta was pleased to see her words have their intended effect: Zafirah's expression softened, her breathing grew shallow. "Open your eyes."

Sapphire eyes flashed open, their depths darkened to midnight blue.

Nasheta sat up, kneeling with her hands folded neatly in front of her. She allowed her posture to shift from alluring to something more maidenly. "Tonight, my body shall be her body," she whispered. "Tonight, you may love her without fear of rejection, without fear of consequence. I am yours to command, my Scion."

Zafirah stared at her, mesmerized, her whole body quivering with the visible effort it took to rein in her passion. "You are certain you...do not mind?" Her tone was almost shy, and though her trepidation seemed needless to Nasheta, it was understandable; in all the years she had ruled the Jaharri, Zafirah had never felt the need to play a game such as this with any of her lovers...had never asked a woman sharing her bed to be anyone other than who she was. Having once served as a body-slave among the nomads, Nasheta was hardly offended by the request. On the contrary, in fact, she was only too happy to accept her role this evening and to provide Zafirah with an outlet for her passion.

Nasheta smiled and lowered her head, letting her hair fall forward to cover her face as she had seen Dae do so many times. "I am honored," she said, making a conscious effort to soften her accent so her voice might better mimic Dae's. "I ask only one thing."

Zafirah swallowed hard, the simple, familiar gesture clearly bringing her blood to the boil. "Wh-what?"

Nasheta glanced up through a curtain of pale hair, adopting an expression she hoped didn't reveal the true depth of her excitement. "Be gentle." A pause. "I've never done anything like this before."

Before Nasheta had time to applaud her own excellent imitation of Dae's voice, she found herself pressed hard against the cushions by the full weight of Zafirah's ardent body. Desperate hands roamed everywhere, shaking with need but remaining gentle. Nasheta groaned when Zafirah claimed her lips with a forceful kiss, eagerly surrendering to the hot tongue that invaded her mouth and began to battle with her own. The flimsy outfit she wore proved no match against Zafirah's passion and was quickly torn from her body and flung across the room. Once naked, Nasheta lay back upon the cushions and prepared to be devoured.

Zafirah was dizzy with lust, completely consumed by her fantasy. In her mind, it was Dae's body she had pinned to the bed, writhing so deliciously on the silk sheets. Her fingers ran over burning skin and through fine blonde hair, and she suckled strongly at her lover's neck, leaving marks. Zafirah hadn't gone this long without sexual release since she was eighteen years old, and the scent of sex and sweat made her almost frenzied with desire. Two weeks of unspent passion erupted from within, and she felt a minor climax seize her just from the sound of a low, rumbling moan that escaped the woman beneath her. With trembling fingers she sought out hardened nipples and began to excite them with an expert touch.

"You like this?" she gasped.

Nasheta was struggling to hold her focus against the sensuous assault. "I-It feels wonderful, Scion!" Her hips were rocking forward in an instinctive rhythm that seemed a little too practiced for the virginal maiden she was trying to portray, but Zafirah was so drunk with lust she barely noticed. "Please, show me more. I want you to show me everything!"

The words were oil thrown on an already blazing inferno. Zafirah growled low in her throat and abandoned the breasts she was working on so she could move closer to the slick golden treasure that had haunted her dreams this past moon. Her hands worshiped briefly over the firm stomach and spreading thighs before they journeyed inwards, quickly finding velvet heat that almost drove her over the edge again. Struggling for breath, Zafirah let her fingers play through damp blonde ringlets and then lower, teasing the hardened nub that crowned her lover's center before quickly sliding between the slick folds. She was pleased when the younger girl's hips began to thrust even more desperately against her.

"Easy, my little Tahirah," she soothed, planting wet kisses possessively over her lover's chest and up her neckline. "Be patient...we have all night."

Nasheta clawed at the silk sheets, struggling for control. Aching to feel as much of the girl's bare skin against her as possible, Zafirah straddled her left thigh and began grinding her dripping center hard against the firm muscle. Nasheta responded with a rocking motion that caused Zafirah's head to loll forward in ecstasy. Zafirah's long fingers stilled a moment as she concentrated on her own pleasure, but after a second they resumed their delightful fondling.

"You are sooo wet, little one," Zafirah groaned, lost in her fantasy and overjoyed at how responsive her lover was to her touch. "Can you feel me touching you?"

"Gods, yes!" The rest of Nasheta's response dissolved into a series of short whimpers and high-pitched squeals as Zafirah brought her quickly to the brink of orgasm and held her there with expert skill. "I've never... felt anything...like this!" she gasped. "Please, Zafirah, don't stop! I want to feel you doing this forever!"

That was all it took for Zafirah. A powerful wave of orgasm crashed over her body, stiffening her limbs and drawing a loud cry from her throat. She continued thrusting against her lover's slippery thigh with passionate force, feeling her own juices create a tantalizing friction against her pulsing core. Just before her climax reached its zenith, Zafirah managed to spear two fingers deep into the body beneath her, and with a few steady thrusts, she felt and heard the young blonde scream out her own joyous release. There was a moment of pleasure so intense that it was almost painful, and for a second her vision went white and barren as the desert sands. Then, shuddering with the last pulses of ecstasy, Zafirah collapsed against her partner, sobbing gratefully.

"Thank you!" she gasped, dizzy and spent, feeling cool sweat drip down her naked back. "Thank you so much!"

They lay like this for several minutes, Zafirah momentarily overwhelmed by the intensity of her climax and, as her breathing steadied and her senses returned to reality, feeling a little exposed and awkward at how completely she had lost herself in the fantasy of ravishing Dae. But when she tried to withdraw, Nasheta immediately wrapped her arms around her and held her close, fingers threading through her mane of sweat-dampened hair as she whispered sweet words softly against her neck. Zafirah relaxed, allowing herself to be comforted and enjoying the moment of peace and calm after weeks of building tension.

It wasn't long, however, before the mingled scents of their arousal and the sensation of Nasheta's hands caressing over her skin blew the spark of Zafirah's passion back to a flame. When she lifted herself away from the disheveled girl, she smiled down into her sea-green eyes and cupped her cheek affectionately. "Many thanks, 'Tahirah'," she said softly, her tone slightly teasing. "How fortunate I am to welcome such enthusiastic innocence to my bed. But the night is young, little one, and I trust you realize I am far from finished with you."

Nasheta smiled lazily, and though she managed to shift her voice back to a reasonable approximation of Dae's accent, she could not keep the eager gleam from her eyes. "Oh, I hope not, Scion. There are so many things I have yet to experience…and I would trust no other hand but yours to teach me."

Zafirah chuckled at her words. She leaned down and gave Nasheta a quick kiss before rising from the bed and regarding the expectant girl hungrily.

"On your knees," she ordered, the command softened by her gentle tone. Nasheta moved hastily to comply, kneeling before her and assuming an air of coquettish innocence.

Zafirah circled the bed, studying her prey from all angles. She felt much more in control of her emotions already, and Nasheta's coy, excited expression made it clear the girl was only too happy to play along with her fantasy. "Turn around and lean forward," she instructed after completing her inspection. "Rest your weight on your elbows."

Nasheta again did as she was told, adopting the familiar position and setting her knees far apart so that her dripping center was temptingly displayed. Zafirah grinned at the sight, amused by Nasheta's unmaidenly eagerness and wondering if Dae might not behave similarly if only she could be tempted to indulge in such passion play. She spent a few moments caressing Nasheta and watching her squirm in breathless anticipation, then turned and made her way across the room. Her bare feet created hardly any sound against the ornate rugs covering the marble floor as she walked over to the intricately carved wooden cabinet placed innocuously against the far wall of the bedchamber. The hinges creaked when she opened the cabinet's doors, and behind her Zafirah heard Nasheta's breathing catch loudly in her throat. She grinned. This particular cabinet was only ever opened on such occasions as this, and every girl in her harem was intimately familiar with its contents. Zafirah spared a brief glance back to ensure Nasheta wasn't peeking, then ran her eyes over the items displayed within.

Zafirah's collection of erotic devices and toys was surpassed only by her knowledge of their applications and included items gathered from the mysterious lands that lay across the northern seas. She spent a moment studying the various treasures, considering her choices before selecting a phallus carved from horn, beautifully polished and following a natural, gentle curve. Zafirah turned back to Nasheta, toying with her selection and waiting until the girl's curiosity finally outweighed her patience and she snuck a furtive glance behind her.

Sea-green eyes widened instantly when she saw what Zafirah had selected for her. Zafirah grinned roguishly at her reaction, having no trouble at all envisioning Nasheta as Dae and reveling in how perfectly the scene matched her fantasies. "You are about to be educated," she promised, approaching the bed and taking a position behind the prone girl. She spread Nasheta's buttocks firmly with her palms, admiring the way her vulnerable center glistened in the flickering lamplight. Nasheta flexed her body rapturously in anticipation that was hardly virginal.

Very slowly, Zafirah drew the full length of the phallus along Nasheta's sex, teasing her, enjoying the way she moved her hips to gain firmer contact against her sensitized flesh. Only when the shaft of carved horn had been thoroughly slicked in her abundant essence did Zafirah set the tip against Nasheta's core and press forward lightly. Nasheta buried her face in a cushion to muffle her sounds of pleasure, her fingers clawing at the rumpled silk sheets beneath her. The high-pitched scream that escaped her throat a moment later was muffled but filled with desperate need.

Zafirah grinned as she slowly pushed deeper into her blonde lover, reveling in the tight resistance that met her thrust. "Do not scream too hard, my Tahirah," she counseled. "You shall have need of your energy for the night ahead."

Nasheta, however, appeared to be too far gone to heed her advice. Screams of ecstasy soon echoed unrestrained through the palace halls, raising the eyebrow of more than one amused guard.

Things, it seemed, were back to normal.

# Chapter 7

WHEN DAE EMERGED FROM HER room early the next morning and wandered out into the cool air of the seraglio gardens, it took her only a moment to sense the tension that crackled around her. Most of the other girls were already awake, and Dae glanced about curiously, seeing the worried looks on their faces and hearing their nervous whisperings.

"What's going on now?" she mumbled to herself and went looking for Inaya. She found her friend over near the entrance to the seraglio, speaking in hushed tones with one of the two guards stationed there. "Hey. Why is everyone so tense? Is something wrong?"

Inaya glanced up at Dae, her expression grave, lips drawn in an unusually somber frown. "Zafirah ended her abstinence last night."

"So? Isn't that a good thing?"

"Perhaps." Inaya abandoned her conversation with the guard and stepped closer to Dae. "She summoned Nasheta in the *dohar*. But Zafirah has always preferred to sleep alone once her passion is spent. It is a habit of hers she has kept all the years of her rule."

"So what?"

"So Nasheta has not yet returned from the Scion's bedchamber. We grow worried."

"Why?" Dae suddenly became concerned. "I thought you said Zafirah wouldn't ever hurt a lover."

"She would not, but this behavior is unlike her." Inaya took Dae by the shoulder and guided her off to the side. "You must understand that in a world such as ours, where we live in such intimate an arrangement, any change at all gives us cause for concern. That Nasheta has not returned is unusual and therefore gives rise to ill whisperings."

Dae considered this thoughtfully, then nodded. She had seen the importance of routine in the harem and how easily it could be disturbed. "I understand." Still, she thought it seemed the other girls were making too much of this. So Zafirah had abstained for a few days? It didn't seem like any cause for alarm to Dae. And so she had decided to keep Nasheta with her through the night? Perhaps she had simply fallen asleep and desired company until morning.

A sudden commotion from the hallway leading into the palace proper caused the guards to immediately snap to attention, their eyes hardening with professional intent. The pleasure-servants quickly abandoned their tense whisperings and gathered closer. Even Dae was curious, and her eyes widened when two new guards entered the gardens, bearing between them a litter on which lay Nasheta's pale form.

The girls flocked closer, their concern making them oblivious of the guards who were trying to clear the way. Dae hung back, feeling a sense of dread foreboding fill her senses. Her imagination, which had lately been investing its energy in vaguely tantalizing contemplations of untasted erotic delights, now changed course and began to conjure images of terrible sexual tortures that might have been inflicted upon poor Nasheta. She watched the tangle of bodies before her, seeing the guards trying without success to get the pleasure-servants to give them room.

Eventually, Inaya stepped forward and began to clear the way. Though young and of a typically gentle nature, the enchanting girl seemed to hold a place of high esteem within the harem, and her fellow pleasure-servants respected her instructions to move aside.

"Come, give them some room!" Inaya parted the clustered girls with seemingly magical grace. "We shall learn nothing by scrabbling about like turkeys in the dust! Let them through."

The guards flashed Inaya looks of extreme gratitude and carefully shouldered their burden. Inaya gave the prone Nasheta a quick once-over, her face impassive, then gestured to the guards. "This way." She turned and led them through the seraglio, back toward the sleeping quarters. The other girls trailed behind at a discreet distance, wary of raising Inaya's ire and chattering excitedly among themselves.

As they passed by, Dae managed to catch a quick glimpse of Nasheta, and she covered her mouth in shock. Nasheta's skin was deeply flushed as though from a fever, and her eyes were closed as though she slept peacefully. Her beautiful face was streaked with sweat, and her hair lay matted and wild about her shoulders. Purplish bruises marred her neck and breasts, and her clothes had been torn at and ripped in many places, leaving them barely sufficient to maintain even the smallest shred of modest decency. Dae's nostrils twitched as Nasheta was carried past her, detecting a strange scent—something musky and animal. Dae stared a moment at the comatose girl, hypnotized by the terrible sight. Yet, just before she managed to look away, she noticed something strange, something extremely out of place. Even in her unconscious state, Nasheta's lips were bowed in a slight, lingering smile of utter contentment.

Dae followed the other girls back to the sleeping quarters, where they all crowded around the doorway to Nasheta's room. Dae had noticed that while there were no actual doors or barriers of any kind among these desert people, the boundaries they represented were always respected. No one ever entered the personal domain of another without invitation. And so she watched now as Inaya directed the two guards to lift Nasheta onto her pallet, noting the scarlet marks of fingernails that had been raked down the poor girl's inner thighs and buttocks.

Satisfied that their charge had been safely deposited, the two guards left the seraglio, ignoring the questions thrown at them by the pleasure-servants. Curious despite herself, Dae managed to shoulder her way to a good spot just outside the doorway and watched as Inaya knelt beside the now-stirring Nasheta.

Inaya poured water from a nearby jug into a tin cup and held it to her lips. Nasheta drank thankfully, then lay back against the cushions of her bed. From her place in the doorway, Dae watched her friend ask Nasheta a question. The words were so low they didn't travel across the room, and Inaya had to lean down so she could hear Nasheta's reply. The two exchanged a few words, and Dae studied Inaya's face carefully, hoping to read some kind of explanation in her expression. Inaya smiled a little, a soft, tender smile that seemed reassured, and Dae wondered what Nasheta had said. Rising from her place, Inaya stroked Nasheta's cheek tenderly and offered some final words, then headed over to where Dae and the others were waiting.

"She is well," Inaya said. "Let us leave her in peace for now. Nasheta will need much rest before she is recovered."

"What happened?" asked Johara. "Was she hurt?"

The other girls erupted with their own questions but quieted instantly when Inaya held up her hand. "She is fine. No harm befell her. It was simply…a long night, that is all." Her dark eyes sparkled with something like playful amusement, a look that puzzled Dae but which apparently communicated something to the other girls, for they smiled in understanding and began wandering back to the seraglio in small groups, conversing in low tones. When they were alone in the hallway, Inaya sighed and wiped her hands daintily together, studying Dae with a strange expression. Still concerned, Dae peered into the room where Nasheta lay sleeping.

"Will she really be okay?"

"Given a day and a night to sleep, she will be fine," Inaya said.

"What about the bruises? What happened to her?"

"Nothing."

Dae stared at her friend for a moment. "Nothing? She was unconscious! Something must have happened to her!"

Inaya regarded Dae seriously, then took her arm and guided her back down the hallway. "Come. We shall talk."

She took Dae back to her own room and sat her down on the sleeping pallet, then knelt beside her. Her dark eyes studied Dae a long time before Inaya sighed and looked away.

"Nasheta was not harmed," she stated, and it was obvious she was choosing her words with care. "She is simply exhausted, that is all."

Dae's face was blank for a moment as she processed Inaya's meaning, then her eyes widened in shocked comprehension. "You mean—"

"Yes." Inaya looked Dae squarely in the eyes. "She has been ravished." A pause, then she added wryly, "Quite thoroughly ravished."

Dae sat still, trying to figure this out. She had never seen a pleasure-servant return from a night in the Scion's bed in such a condition as

Nasheta, yet she recalled again that strange smile on the comatose girl's lips and wondered. "So…" She gave her friend a probing look. "This is…normal?"

"Not exactly, but it is understandable."

"The bruises? The scratches?"

"Marks of passion Zafirah inflicted during their coupling, yes." Inaya shook her head at the face Dae made. "Do not wear such a mask of horror, child. Nasheta will be the object of great envy in the coming days, in that the Scion chose her as the vessel through which she would relieve two weeks of unspent passion."

Dae was utterly mystified, unable to comprehend that anyone would want to be so injured. "She's hurt."

"No, little one. She is tired and doubtless a little sore from her experience, but the pleasure of Zafirah's ministrations will more than overshadow such earthly discomforts for her. When she recovers, I predict Nasheta will be in a most joyous spirit."

Dae's brows contracted in puzzlement. "She liked it? How could anyone enjoy being bruised like that?"

"The line between pleasure and pain is a thin one," Inaya explained. "In the heat of the moment, when one's body is consumed by desire, all extremes of sensation tell the same tale—a tale of pleasure. Zafirah is an intense woman and an intense lover. The marks are not as bad as they might seem, little one."

Dae studied Inaya curiously. "Has she ever done that to you?"

Inaya smiled seductively, her eyes growing hooded. "That, and much more."

"Like what?"

Inaya shook her head. "My descriptions would only confuse you, child," she said. "Such pleasures cannot be meaningfully conveyed with mere words; they exist only as sensation."

"But…you liked it?"

"Of course." Inaya reached out to pet her thigh reassuringly, obviously not wanting Dae's imagination to lead her to dark thoughts. "It is a strange world, the world of pleasure. It compels us all to experience it, yet few will ever come to understand its mysteries completely, even those who pursue it their entire lives. Do not let yourself be mired by confusion, Dae."

Dae listened to her friend, then nodded firmly as she cast aside her ponderings. "You're right. I'm not interested in such matters anyway."

"Exactly."

"I have no desire to warm Zafirah's bed."

"So you have said."

"And as long as Nasheta is unharmed, all is well once more." Dae gave a determined smile. "Just as I told you, Inaya, there was nothing amiss with Zafirah's behavior. Her abstinence didn't herald any doom as you were certain it would. Things are back to normal."

Inaya cocked her head to the side and gave Dae a sly look. "Oh, I would not be so certain of that, little one."

"Why not?"

Inaya lay back on the cushions of Dae's bed, a single graceful eyebrow arched in muted contemplation. "Because Zafirah has not yet claimed what she desires. And what she desires…is you."

"Me? But—"

"You are the cause of her strange behavior of late," Inaya continued in confident tones. "I have known Zafirah since before her rule began, and in that time she has taken many lovers. But never have I seen her so affected as she has been since you arrived. You have captured more than the Scion's eye, Dae, and I believe she is just now beginning to realize the effects of her fascination for you."

Dae sat up straighter, interested in Inaya's words despite herself. "She lusts for me," she refuted, "but that's all."

"If it were only lust she felt, then why did she not simply spend her passion with one of us? That kind of physical need is nothing new for Zafirah. She has known it since she was younger than you; it is an intrinsic part of who she is. No, child, she abstained from taking pleasure because she felt only your touch could satisfy her. And she would never force you to submit to her against your will."

Dae waved a hand dismissively. "She took Nasheta, didn't she?"

"Ah, yes. But she did not choose her at random." Inaya's eyes were intense as she gazed back at an uncertain Dae. "Do you not find it coincidental that Zafirah chose as her lover the only other girl in her harem possessed of blonde hair and pale skin? You and Nasheta resemble one another in form and figure, right down to the green eyes. Zafirah could not contain her hunger any longer, so she claimed a substitute for the lover she truly wanted: you."

"That's ridiculous!"

"Is it?"

"Yes!" Dae shook her head. Inaya's smile and expression were unnervingly calm. "How can you be so certain?"

Inaya didn't even blink. "Because Nasheta told me so herself."

That stopped Dae's defense instantly. She stared at Inaya, unsure that she'd heard correctly. "What?"

"She told me so herself," Inaya repeated quietly. "Zafirah even asked her permission." Sitting up on her elbows, she studied Dae's reaction carefully. "Though she took Nasheta's body, in Zafirah's mind, it was you she loved through the night."

Dae's mouth opened and closed a few times, her brain struggling to process the truth of Inaya's claim even as her body was warmed again by that strange, forbidden heat. "She wanted to do…that…to me?"

"Wanted it with such zeal that she asked Nasheta to mimic your behavior and mannerisms that she might more fully lose herself to that fantasy." Inaya shifted closer to her. "Does this news disturb you?"

"I-I don't…" Dae shrugged a little helplessly, not comfortable with the emotions and physical sensations rushing through her. "I don't know."

"If it is of any comfort, I can assure you that you are perfectly safe," Inaya offered in a gentle tone, clearly not wanting to add fear to her obvious confusion. "No matter how powerful her desires, Zafirah would never force herself upon you. It is not her way."

Dae nodded absently, images of what Nasheta might have experienced in the night filling her mind, images of what joys or terrors that could cause the kind of great pleasure Inaya hinted at.

"And of course," Inaya continued with an innocent face, "you have made it quite clear that you have no interest in sampling the delights of Zafirah's bed, so…"

"Yes, that's true," Dae murmured, though some deep part of her she didn't fully understand seemed not so certain.

"I suggest you put all thoughts of this matter aside," Inaya said with an earnestly sweet smile. "So long as your opinions remain as pure and chaste as they are, it is not an issue of consequence for you." A long, slightly challenging, pause. "Is it?"

Dae shook her head. "Of course not."

"Well then…" Inaya clapped her hands and rose gracefully to her feet. "Shall we see what food we can find for morning meal?"

"Y-Yes, that sounds…fine." Dae joined her friend, and together they walked back down the hallway to the sitting room beyond, where they found the tables laden with fresh fruits and other delicacies prepared by the palace kitchen.

Dae picked through the food without her usual enthusiasm, distracted by the revelations of Nasheta's night with Zafirah and finding it difficult to summon her appetite. She could feel Inaya watching her with that same slightly teasing, amused expression that made it clear she wasn't fooled by her protestations of disinterest.

Dae could feel a hunger growing, yes….but the exotic fruits and sweetmeats couldn't satisfy this craving. This hunger was sharp and aching; it seemed to live in every part of her, a deep, esurient need long dormant, now stirring with relentless strength. She silently repeated in her mind the teachings of morality and self-restraint her parents had instilled in her years ago, but nothing seemed to quell the yet-unformed imaginings of what Nasheta must have experienced at Zafirah's hand.

Light from the rising sun bled slowly across the floor in Zafirah's bedchamber, bringing with it the first subtle rise in temperature that heralded the arrival of yet another sweltering day. The room was quiet and peaceful now, and the Scion lay naked on her bed, one arm draped over her face to shield her eyes from the dawning light. Her body still tingled with the aftermath of spent passion and the languid bliss of pure satisfaction. With every breath she took Zafirah inhaled the sweet perfume of incense, and the stirring scent of Nasheta's desire still lingered in the air.

But although the Scion's sexual appetite had been appeased—if only for the moment—she felt an emptiness pervade her senses that spoiled the perfection of this moment. Now that she had quieted the screams of her libido, Zafirah felt oddly vacant, and her drifting thoughts concluded somewhat bitterly that while her night with Nasheta had settled her immediate needs quite effectively, it was at best a temporary solution to a far larger and less easily solved dilemma.

*Desire that feeds from the heart cannot be so easily sated as desire that feeds from the eye.*

Falak's words rang through Zafirah's mind, and they sang to a tune that was starting to make sense to her.

Zafirah felt very confused. She had never experienced these kinds of emotions that struck her heart every time she was around Dae. They defied logic and reason. After all, she was the Scion of a vast and powerful desert nation. She had legions of women under her rule who would have considered it the greatest honor to provide for her every desire. The girls in her harem were all gifted with extraordinary beauty and grace, and they were all extremely talented lovers. Why, then, did their faces no longer interest her? Why was it she had become so fascinated by the innocent, naïve young blonde?

Through the years of her rule as Scion, and even before, Zafirah's appetite for pleasure had led her to the embrace of many lovers. Though in some cases she had spent but a single night in their bed, if she concentrated, Zafirah knew she could recall the faces and names of every one of those women she had taken. Many had been friends. Many, like Falak, still were. Zafirah took pride in the fact that she did not seek her pleasure as blindly as some others; as she had told Falak, she had cared for every woman with whom she shared her body. A sharing of pleasure was mutually satisfying and enjoyable. But for Zafirah, that was as far as her desires had ever ranged. Though she believed that true love existed—had seen it in the depth of connection that bound her father and mother together—Zafirah had decided long ago it wasn't something that held any interest for her. She was far too much in love with passion and lust to devote all her energies to a single person...or so she had believed. Now, with these alien feelings surfacing, Zafirah was growing less certain of her own heart.

Scowling, Zafirah lifted her arm and looked around, seeking a distraction, anything to take her mind away from these longings. Rising from her bed, she quickly dressed herself in a pair of white cotton trousers, a loose-sleeved shirt, and a soft leather vest and headed out to the stables in the army barracks located to the east of the palace. Perhaps, she thought, a long ride out among the expansive dunes would help to soothe her restless spirit.

The heat of the Jaharri desert was intense this day, and Zafirah was careful not to push Simhana past her limits. She rode alone along the coastline of the great sea that bordered El'Kasari to the north, feeling the coolness of the coastal wind catch the blistering heat from the sands as it rolled inland. Zafirah smiled to herself beneath her *haik* as she paused a moment to savor the desert air—dry and wild, with a slight tang of salt. She welcomed the emptiness of the desert, willing her mind to follow the example of the barren environment. But the teasing memories of Dae's laughter as she had danced with the other harem girls to the beat of pulsing drum music refused to be diverted, and Zafirah shook her head, irritated.

*You cannot have her!* she scolded herself silently. *You can never have her! Accept it now, or she will drive you to madness and misery.*

For a moment, it crossed Zafirah's mind to offer Dae to Rehan after all. Certainly the girl would be well cared for among the Tek, though her life would be harder living with the nomads than in the palace harem.

*Could removing the temptation help to cure this strange attraction?* Zafirah wondered. But then she scowled, wheeling Simhana around and beginning her ride back toward the city. No. She knew Dae would haunt her dreams forever, no matter how much distance she set between them.

It was just past midday by the time Zafirah finished washing down Simhana and returned her to the stables. The sun was stunningly hot, making the streets of El'Kasari shimmer with heat waves. The palace was far cooler than the streets outside, and Zafirah breathed a sigh of relief as she entered her chambers, stripping out of her sweat-stained clothes with a casual lack of modesty. Filling a wide bowl with rose-scented water from a pitcher, she took a few moments to scrub her body clean before slipping into the comforting caress of a silk robe. Glancing to her bed, Zafirah was pleased to note her servants had changed the sheets during her ride and straightened everything up after her night with Nasheta. She contemplated taking a nap, but her body was still too awake with uncertainty for rest, so Zafirah wandered back out into the hallways of the palace, nodding absently to the guards who passed her by.

With her mind preoccupied with thoughts of Dae, it was unsurprising that Zafirah's rambling footsteps led her to the harem. She paused a moment before entering the seraglio gardens, her thoughts a tangled mess. A part of her wanted desperately to see the young outlander girl, but what could she say to woo Dae now that had not been said before? Accustomed to being an assertive conqueror in the game of seduction, Zafirah didn't much like the feeling of being so out of control. Still, her thoughts led her on before her brain managed to convince her to retreat, and she entered the gardens of her harem.

Few of the pleasure-servants were about, the midday sun too stifling for any kind of activity. Those who were splashing about in the relatively cool waters of the great pool didn't notice Zafirah as she slipped past them into the rooms beyond the garden. The Scion strode quietly along the hallways that led to the sleeping quarters of her pleasure-servants, pausing when she came to Dae's room.

Peering in, she smiled at the sight of the young girl sprawled across the cushions of her bed, eyes closed in sleep and a vague smile curving the edges of her lips. The vision of such simple, graceless beauty shot like an arrow to Zafirah's heart, causing her to clutch her chest at the physical ache that spread through her body. For half a second the Scion felt herself stepping into Dae's room, thoughts of waking the girl with a sweet caress dancing through her mind. Then she shook herself clear of the erotic notion, knowing she would ruin even the tenuous respect Dae had for her.

Zafirah stood a while longer in the doorway, just letting her eyes roam at will over the inspiring curves of Dae's ill-concealed form. Then, sighing heavily, she turned away and headed further down the hallway, her thoughts turning to another of her pleasure-servants. One who might be able to offer some solace or advice to ease her suffering.

She found Inaya in her room, awake as she had hoped, sitting on her sleeping pallet and working diligently on an intricate necklace of colorful glass beads. Zafirah hesitated, then cleared her throat. "Inaya?"

Inaya glanced up, smiling instantly as she rose to her feet. "My Scion."

"Are you busy?" Zafirah gestured to the necklace. "I do not wish to disturb you."

"Of course not, Scion. My time is yours to command." Inaya laid her beadwork on a table nearby. "Come in. How may I be of service to you?"

Zafirah stepped into Inaya's room, swallowing nervously. She caught a seductive glint in the girl's eyes and realized what Inaya was thinking. "I was hoping we might...talk."

The wicked glint shimmered for a moment, then vanished. Inaya raised an eyebrow, obviously intrigued. "As you wish. Please, will you sit?"

"Thank you."

"Would you like something to drink, perhaps? Some sweetened water?"

Zafirah nodded, though she wasn't thirsty. "Yes, please." Among the desert people, it was considered rude to reject such simple offerings, so she accepted the small cup Inaya handed her. "Thank you."

Inaya inclined her head. "Most welcome, my Scion."

There was a moment of awkward silence after that, Zafirah wondering how best to broach the subject of her attraction without being too obvious. Inaya watched her in curious silence while she collected her thoughts, but Zafirah didn't doubt that the girl had already guessed the reason for this visit. She had known Inaya since the days her father ruled the city and was well aware how skilled she was in reading the emotions and desires of other women. Indeed, it was this very ability that had made Inaya such a successful seductress in her youth and earned her a place of honor in the palace harem soon after Zafirah assumed power. Realizing there was little point in being anything other than direct, Zafirah eventually met Inaya's steady gaze and said, "I wanted to speak with you...about the young foreign girl, Dae."

"Ah." Inaya nodded knowingly.

"I understand you have grown close to her," Zafirah continued. "She seems most comfortable in your presence. I have seen the bond grow between you, and I...I hoped perhaps you might have some insight into her mind."

"I see." Inaya spread her hands and cocked her head. "And what insight would you have me impart, my Scion?"

Zafirah sat up a little, her eyes alive and intense. "*Everything.*"

"Everything?"

"Yes. I want to know everything about her. Omit no detail, however irrelevant it may seem."

Inaya studied Zafirah for a long moment in silence. "You like her very much, do you not?"

Zafirah's eyes shifted, then looked away. She sighed longingly. "May I speak with you as a friend, Inaya?" Her voice was soft and held a rare note of vulnerability. "Not as your ruler, but just...as a woman?"

"Of course." Inaya smiled warmly. "You have no need to ask such a question, Zafirah, of any of your servants."

Zafirah returned the smile, grateful at least that she had such people as Inaya in her life—people who could look beyond her title and see the person beneath. She was still a minute, considering her words carefully before she gave them voice. "I have found my thoughts of late dwelling more and more upon her," she said at last. "She confuses me, makes me feel things I have never felt before."

"She is very beautiful. It is only natural for you to desire her."

"Perhaps, but..." Zafirah threw her arms up and scowled. "There is more than simple desire to this! She fascinates me, compels my every waking thought and rules my dreams each night! And yet I barely know her, have barely spoken with her." She looked at Inaya with eyes that hungered for things beyond erotic delights. "That is why I come here, to better understand her, that I might better understand how it is that she can inspire such feelings in me."

Inaya listened carefully, hearing the stark desperation in Zafirah's tone. "You think perhaps you love her?" she asked bluntly.

Zafirah instantly looked away. "I do not know."

"Mm." Inaya tilted her head in consideration. "She has a certain quality about her, does she not? Something rare and special. You are not the only one to feel it."

The Scion glanced up. "Really?"

"Of course. It would be a cold heart indeed that would not beat faster in her presence, though I think her charm has struck you harder than it has others."

Zafirah sighed. "And yet I am the one most distanced from her."

"The heart is often wiser than the head, Zafirah; it can see things deeper than our eyes. Yet, all too often we ignore its teaching in favor of a more sensible form of reason." The slender girl lay back against the cushions of her bed and regarded Zafirah with a slightly playful look. "Yes, Dae and I have grown close. I value her companionship a great deal, as I value her trust. But you will find my words a poor substitute for what you truly desire, Zafirah."

Zafirah shook her head. "Then what am I to do?" she demanded, her tone harsher than intended for her frustration. "Her body stiffens whenever I draw near! She can barely bring herself to look at me, knowing how I desire her."

"And therein lies the problem."

"What?"

"Dae does not fear you, Zafirah. She fears the unknown. She recoils from your hunger because it unsettles her. She does not understand it. But if you were to put aside all thoughts of carnal gratification, I think you might find her nature may change."

"So you think she would talk with me? As a friend, if not a lover?"

"There is but one way to find out." Inaya fingered a strand of her blue-black hair thoughtfully. "Dae has mentioned on occasion her admiration for the city and her desire to see more of it. She said you offered to show it to her when first you spoke with her…"

As intended, the suggestion took root in Zafirah's mind, formed quickly into a plan. "You think she would like me to take her outside the palace?"

"I think she would find you less intimidating if she could see more to you than simple lust." Inaya hesitated, obviously cautious of betraying Dae's trust but still wanting to give Zafirah comfort and hope. "Dae has been settling in well," she said at last, her tone careful. "She is young and adapts readily to change. Lately, I have seen her growing more confused by the urgings of her body." Zafirah's eyes widened with interest, and Inaya held up a hand. "She has not spoken of desire," she stated firmly, "only of a curiosity quite natural in one her age. If you do not wish to frighten her away, Zafirah, you would be wise to tread cautiously, lest you crush what hope you have beneath a careless heel."

Zafirah absorbed this advice gratefully. "Yes, you are right." She thought for a long moment in silence, then bowed to Inaya with a smile.

"I thank you for your counsel, Inaya," she said, rising from her place on the bed. "It has helped me greatly."

Inaya bowed in return. "I am always glad to serve, my Scion." Her eyes twinkled daringly with hooded fires. "Would that I could offer solace beyond mere words."

Zafirah grinned fully at the blatant invitation and winked. "Perhaps another time."

"I shall look forward to it."

Zafirah turned to leave, but just as she reached the doorway, Inaya called out. "Zafirah?"

"Mmm?" She glanced back.

Dark eyes regarded her seriously. "Dae may be innocent, but she is also intelligent and gifted with natural intuition. If you can show her a part of yourself outside the bedroom, she will see it and respect you more for sharing it. Do not try to be more than who you are for her; such deception would only win you her contempt."

Zafirah nodded. "Thank you."

"Most welcome."

She left Inaya to her beadwork and made her way back down the corridor to the seraglio gardens, her stride buoyant and intent. One of the girls splashing about in the pool called out to her as she passed, tempting her to come play in the cooler waters. Zafirah politely declined the invitation, not letting the girl's dismayed—and very sexy—pout of disappointment sway her.

She had a more romantic rendezvous to plan.

Inaya watched the Scion leave her room. Things, it seemed, were moving nicely. Zafirah was out of her element playing the pursuer, but she was smart enough to realize it and not pretend a confidence she didn't have.

It was strange, actually, to see how effortlessly Dae had captured the Scion's attention despite neither woman intending it. Though Inaya could neither read nor write, she was perfectly fluent in the language of sexual attraction, able to interpret the flow of energy and desire between people as though it were as tangible a thing as words scrawled on parchment. She had never believed Zafirah could be so ensnared by love, had thought the charismatic Scion more akin to herself—a creature born to revel in excesses of ecstasy, for whom pleasure and intimacy could deepen bonds of friendship and affection yet rarely touch the soul. Inaya loved Zafirah as she loved all her companions in the harem, but it was becoming clear to her that Dae was more than a simple passing fancy for the Scion.

Not that she was jealous. Indeed, the emotion was as foreign and incomprehensible to Inaya as Dae's depictions of her homeland had been, utterly beyond her experience. True, a large part of her wished she might one day earn the honor of introducing her friend to new pleasures, but Inaya was patient enough to bide her time. Besides, she reminded herself with a smile, she was a pleasure-servant, and as such her duty was to serve the Scion's desires. Right now, Dae was clearly front and center in Zafirah's heart's eye.

Of course, the poor girl still believed her pretense of disinterest was fooling all those around her. Inaya shook her head as she picked up the beaded necklace from the table beside her and set it on her lap. It seemed so silly to her, such a waste of time and energy, but like the other pleasure-servants, Inaya didn't press Dae to accept more than she felt ready for. Besides, it was highly entertaining to watch Dae's expression of dawning lust every time her gorgeous emerald eyes wandered where she felt they shouldn't be wandering. The girl seemed to be coming to terms with the way she reacted to Zafirah, cracks forming deep and wide in her defenses. She might not know exactly what she wanted...but in spite of her innocence, it was clear that Dae had realized she wanted *something*.

As Inaya saw it, her responsibility would be to ensure Dae's ignorance was properly illuminated when the time was right...and she allowed herself a little lapse into fantasy as she considered various scenarios that might achieve that goal.

Finding her place once more in the intricate necklace, Inaya's deft fingers continued with her project. She hummed a quiet lullaby to herself as she worked, looking forward to seeing how Dae would respond to Zafirah's more gentle overtures.

# Chapter 8

THE NEXT EVENING FOUND A nervous Dae walking through the palace hallways, flanked on either side by an escort. She had been surprised when the guards informed her that morning that Zafirah had summoned her to her chambers and had been trying for over an hour to quell the butterflies stirring in her stomach. A part of her feared the Scion had finally succumbed to her lust, but another part was humming with excited anticipation, almost hoping that she would be subjected to the same mysterious delights as Nasheta. Dae's hands were clammy and her heart was beating fast in her chest. When they reached the entrance to Zafirah's bedchamber, Dae hesitated, and one of her escorts gave her a gentle nudge and an encouraging smile.

"Do not fear, little one," the guard said kindly. "You are safe."

Taking a deep breath, struggling with a body that seemed uncertain of what it wanted, Dae stepped into the chamber and looked around.

As soon as she saw Zafirah, a large part of Dae's fears were set aside. The tall woman was dressed in loose cotton trousers and a leather shirt. She wore sturdy boots, and an open *haik* was wrapped around her head. From that attire, Dae concluded Zafirah's thoughts were running to destinations other than seduction.

She wasn't sure whether she felt relief or disappointment.

Zafirah turned when she heard Dae enter, her smile so brilliant it almost stopped the young girl's heart. "Dae! Enter, please." The Scion waved her guards away with a simple gesture.

Dae took a few nervous steps into the room, her eyes unconsciously wandering to the great bed. Her mouth was dry and she swallowed hard before remembering to bow to the Scion. "Y-you sent for me?"

"Yes, but…" Zafirah grinned rakishly at the obvious trepidation in Dae's eyes. "I had plans other than carnal pleasures for this night."

Dae smiled hesitantly.

"I thought perhaps you might deign to join me for a walk," Zafirah continued. "You wished to see more of the city, did you not?"

Dae's expression brightened instantly. "You would show me?"

"If you like. However," Zafirah took a moment to cast her eyes appreciatively over Dae's figure, still clad in almost transparent silk pantaloons and a top that barely managed to contain her full breasts, "I think perhaps a change of wardrobe is in order first. Walking the streets in harem clothes would attract far too many admirers, and I would prefer to be your only one this night." She gestured toward the bed, and Dae saw a pile of neatly folded clothes laid out on the sheets, topped off with a pair of simple, practical boots. "Please, change. I will not watch if it makes you uncomfortable." Zafirah turned away to offer her a measure of privacy, taking a few strides toward the far balcony.

Dae fidgeted a moment, considering the offer. Indeed, she wanted very much to see the streets of El'Kasari up close, having looked upon them from the seraglio gardens all this time with wondering eyes. But she was ever cautious around Zafirah and sensed a ploy. "What if I don't want to go?"

Zafirah glanced back at her. "That is your decision, and of course I will respect it." Her eyes softened a moment, and Dae was caught for a moment by the uncertain, fearful longing that lay beneath those stunning sapphires. "I just hoped we might talk. Without consideration of desire or sex. You have been in my harem for some time now, yet we are still nearly strangers. I had thought…perhaps we might learn more of each other."

Dae's eyes narrowed skeptically. "You won't try to seduce me?"

Zafirah cocked her head to the side, a playful half-smile forming on her lips. "The temptation may prove stronger than my resolve, but I shall endeavor to resist my baser urges for the night."

Dae couldn't help it. She giggled. "I guess that'll have to do." She gestured to Zafirah. "Please turn around."

Zafirah grinned and did as bade.

Studying the clothing that had been arranged for her, Dae hesitated only a moment before she stripped off her harem clothes and began to dress in the far more concealing shirt and skirt. The boots fit her feet snugly, and Dae grimaced a little in discomfit; she had grown accustomed to walking barefoot these last few months in the seraglio. When she was fully dressed again, she turned back to Zafirah, smoothing down her new outfit nervously. "Okay, you can look now."

Zafirah, who had been fighting valiantly against the desire to steal a quick peek at the beauty unfolding behind her, turned. Her eyes ran up and down Dae's figure. "I think I prefer the harem clothes."

Dae shuffled her feet self-consciously. "They don't cover much."

"They cover enough that I am driven to the brink of madness for want of what lies beneath," Zafirah assured her. "You are far too magnificent a creature to be covered in swaths of cloth. But I would prefer our walk be as inconspicuous as possible, so…"

Dae smiled. In truth, she felt a lot safer and more comfortable with Zafirah now that she wasn't so exposed. While she had grown accustomed to wearing the revealing outfit and to being in the presence of so much bare flesh in the seraglio, Dae couldn't help but feel especially vulnerable when she was around the enigmatic Scion. Zafirah had a way of looking at her that made her feel very strange—a tense, warm sensation that wasn't entirely unpleasant and which sent confusing shivers over her skin. Wearing these new clothes went a long way toward settling her nerves.

Zafirah held up an arm in invitation. "Shall we?"

Dae nodded and preceded the Scion out into the corridor.

When she'd first been brought into El'Kasari, Dae had been unconscious, so she had never seen the palace from outside. Looking around her at the magnificent architecture of gold-laced marble and amazing bas-relief carvings, she soon forgot all about any concerns regarding her chastity. A stunning archway marked the entrance to the palace proper, standing over thirty feet high with walls studded with a mosaic of silver and dazzling semi-precious stones. Rays of sunlight caught in their facets flashed rainbow colors across the cool marble floor. With a trembling hand, Dae reached out to touch the arch, her eyes roaming upwards in awe. "It's so beautiful!"

Zafirah watched, pleased with her reaction. "The wealth of a thousand kings, all in a single wall of my palace," she said. "The people from your land and the lands to the west pay us tribute to cross the desert safely. They have done so for many generations, since the time of my ancestors. Most often, they give jewels or gold or rich cloth, things they consider to be of tremendous value. But in the desert, such riches mean little compared to food or water. They sparkle prettily in the sunlight, but that is their only true worth to us."

Dae let her gaze trace along the patterns of the wall, wonder still shining bright in her eyes at the treasure so casually displayed. She gave Zafirah a shy smile. "I still think it's beautiful."

"Then come. Let me show you more pretty things."

The two walked out of the palace and along a shining marble bridge. The streets of El'Kasari spread out before them in carefully planned lines, busy with people going about their errands in the cool of dusk. From outside, Dae realized for the first time just how enormous the palace truly was; it perched at the heart of the city at the highest point, serving as a focal point for all those living under the Scion's rule.

Merchants hawked their wares from wide, open windows in their shops or from the convenience of a sheltered cart. Dae saw only a few horses among the commoners; most seemed to prefer using camels to move around. She had heard stories of the humped desert creatures, and they seemed wonderfully exotic. The city itself was clamorous with the sounds of merchants crying out for buyers, and there was an interesting smell to it—something like the desert itself, but with a subtle hint of many people all living and breathing together in close proximity. Certainly the air wasn't as fresh here as it was in the gardens of the seraglio, but Dae had vivid memories of the stench of the open sewers that ran through the cities in her homeland and decided this was comparatively pleasant. Wandering along the streets, wide-eyed with excitement at the unfamiliar sights all around her, Dae grinned easily at her companion as she walked.

"Is it safe for you to be out here without your guards?" she asked, noting the absence of any escort.

"Of course. I have walked these streets since I was but a child; there is no need for me to fear my own people. Besides, I am a skilled fighter.

Any thief or bandit foolish enough to attack me would soon regret his error."

Dae turned her attention back to the streets, considering this. She wouldn't have expected a ruler to act in such a manner as Zafirah. In her homeland, no personage of the ruling class ever went anywhere without a small army of bodyguards. It struck her again just how different this desert world was from the world she once knew. Only now, the differences did not seem so distasteful as they once had.

El'Kasari was a riot of color and movement. Everywhere Dae looked, she saw amazing things that shocked and intrigued her. On a raised platform, scantily-clad women with jewels in their navels danced to the tune of wailing reed pipes. On a dusty street corner, a man with a monkey on his shoulder begged for coins, the small animal aiding his master by turning back-flips and chattering at potential donors. Dae caught sight of a street performer on a small stage, and she stared in fascination as the skinny man somehow managed to swallow the blade of a slender, straight sword all the way down his throat, to the applause of onlookers.

"How did he do that?" She moved closer, amazed.

Zafirah watched a moment, then shrugged. "I have no idea. It is not a skill I have ever had cause to pursue." The Scion was enjoying just observing Dae as they moved from one wonder to the next, the girl's attention easily caught by one thing and just as easily stolen by another. Her exuberance was refreshing, and Zafirah felt some of her inner tension ease just being in the presence of Dae's youthful energy. She also noted, with some amusement, the way Dae managed to attract the eyes of many men and women from among the crowd, her face and figure drawing more interest even than Zafirah herself. Yet Dae seemed blissfully ignorant of the attention, and the Scion grinned at her naïveté...even as she warned away the would-be suitors with an occasional glower.

She watched as Dae strolled past the vendors, pausing every now and again when something caught her fancy. She stopped at the stand of a jeweler to admire his assortment of necklaces, reaching out to caress an elegant silver chain whose design struck a familiar chord.

"I remember the jewelry my mother gave me just before I left home for the last time," she said, tracing the lines of the necklace fondly. "There was a garnet ring, a bracelet of gold with a ruby set in it, and a necklace that looked just like this one."

Zafirah heard the hint of sadness in Dae's voice and immediately sought to ease it. She plucked the necklace from its place and held it out. "Here, take it."

"Oh, no…I couldn't."

"I insist." Zafirah tossed a small pouch of coins to the merchant, who hefted it briefly, then bowed in gratitude. "It is a gift. And among my people, it is considered bad manners to deny such an offering."

"But—"

"Please." Zafirah held the necklace out earnestly. "I want you to have it."

"Well I…I suppose. If you insist."

"I do." Zafirah smiled as Dae turned and allowed her to clasp the slender silver chain about her neck. As she caressed the necklace to settle it, she let her fingers linger a moment longer than was necessary among the silken tendrils of blonde hair that curled about Dae's neck. Her breath caught in her throat and her body began to thrum with desperate longing.

Dae must have sensed the lingering touch, for her body tensed slightly and her breath seemed to catch in her throat. Turning, she gave Zafirah a wary, shy look. "I thought you said you wouldn't try to seduce me." Her tone was slightly reproaching.

Zafirah took an unsteady breath and looked away. "Forgive my lapse," she said hoarsely, withdrawing her hands and firmly setting them at her sides. "It is difficult."

Dae looked up at her with an unreadable expression, then nodded after a moment. "That's okay," she said quietly after a long moment, and Zafirah mentally chastised herself for letting her desire momentarily get the better of her. As they continued strolling along the street, Dae's eyes continued to glance at her curiously. "You're not used to women saying no to you, are you?" she observed in a casual tone.

Zafirah met the emerald gaze cautiously, wondering at the question. Seeing only genuine interest in Dae's eyes, she shrugged slightly. "It is not often a problem for me, no."

"And there are a great many women who would be happy to lie with you." Dae fingered her new necklace absently as she watched Zafirah. "Why do you care so much about winning me over?"

Again, Zafirah shrugged. "You are different," she said quietly. "Something in you calls to me, and I cannot ignore it, no matter how I distract myself." It was difficult for her to find the words that might help Dae understand her feelings, but after Inaya's advice, she was determined to at least try. "I am not ashamed of my desire for you, Tahirah, but my interest goes deeper than the flesh. I want to understand you, be near you. I hunger for it beyond reason." She turned away and continued walking. "I would never try to force myself upon you, but neither will I fight against my own nature by denying the attraction I feel."

Dae listened, her expression puzzled but not offended. "Are you trying to say that...you're in love with me?"

"Perhaps," Zafirah said, no longer certain of her own heart but unable to offer more fitting words to describe these emotions. "I have never been in love before, and I have never felt so powerful an attraction to another person before. It is possible the two are cause and consequence of one another." She regarded Dae curiously. "Would it offend you greatly if I were in love with you?"

Dae flushed, but shook her head. "I-I guess not. I mean, it's even a little flattering, in a strange way."

Zafirah grinned at her small victory. "Perhaps I could court you," she suggested playfully. "An unrequited courtship of course, if you would prefer."

Dae giggled. "Let's just enjoy the walk, shall we?"

The Scion gave a martyred moan. "As you wish, my Tahirah."

Dae raised an eyebrow. "Why do you keep calling me that?"

"What?"

"'Tahirah.' You use it more often than my true name."

"Oh." Zafirah shrugged. "I do not know. It just seems to slip from my tongue more easily. If it bothers you, I will try to stop."

"No, it's okay. I like it." Dae hesitated. "It means 'chaste', doesn't it? The name 'Tahirah'?"

"It does, but I mean no insult by terming you thus. It is a term of affection, nothing more."

"Well, I *am* chaste," Dae admitted, "at least by Jaharri standards. I'm not ashamed of that fact, even if it is seen as out of place here."

Zafirah considered that a moment, then shook her head. "Chastity for a purpose is respected among my people," she said. "Like the priests of Inshal, who abstain from pleasure for periods so that they might better understand the Goddess. But when that chastity stems from ignorance, or from fear of the unknown, then I would consider it a wasted resolve." She saw Dae color a little and held up a hand. "Again, I mean no insult against you. It is simply an opinion I have."

Dae remained conspicuously silent, but watching her closely, Zafirah realized the girl was every bit as conscious as she was of the magnetic force that seemed to exist between them…and seemed to find it just as confusing and difficult to define. When it became clear that her companion wasn't going to offer a response, Zafirah continued. "Of course, such matters are highly personal in nature, and I think it a good thing that not everyone views things in the same light as myself. Take my father, for instance: he governed the Scion Peace for five years without knowing the touch of a woman. He waited all that time to fall in love, and after he met my mother, he stayed true and devoted to her until his death."

"Really?" Dae said with interest at hearing the Scion speak of her family.

"Yes. During his reign, the harem grounds were unoccupied."

"How did he die?"

"A sickness claimed him. Though I was young at the time, both the priests and the council accepted me as the new Scion. My mother is of the desert, born to the Herak tribe. When she fell in love with my father, she moved to El'Kasari to be with him, but I think a part of her never truly parted with the dunes. After he died, she returned to her people to mourn."

"Is she still alive?"

"Yes, though I do not see her often. Her people are very proud; they do not often journey to the city for water or food, preferring to accept only what the desert offers." She regarded Dae intently. "So you see, I do understand the concept of devoted love like that. I respect it a great deal, as I respected my father."

"But you don't subscribe to it?"

"No. I believe more strongly in pleasure and freedom. In my way, I have loved all those with whom I have lain in passion, but not to the exclusion of all others. To my mind, it seems selfish to place boundaries on something as beautiful and sacred as sexual pleasure. It is a gift to be shared with the world, experienced by all, not just bestowed upon a single lover." She raised an eyebrow at Dae. "You have seen Johara and Hayam, have you not? You have seen the strength of their passion?"

"They're not exactly shy about displaying it," Dae observed wryly.

"Nor should they be. They love one another very much, enough that they sanctified their union in the Goddess' name. Yet their connection is such that they are able to invite others to share in their love, to partake of their passion and join with them in ecstasy." Zafirah sighed. "Theirs is a love I can understand and admire—a love that is devoted without being caged or controlled."

Dae seemed to absorb this explanation thoughtfully, as if she appreciated Zafirah's honesty. "And have you ever thought about being with a man?"

"Why would I? I do not find men appealing in a sexual way, either physically or mentally." Zafirah gave Dae a rakish grin. "A beautiful woman, however, can set my blood afire."

Dae blushed prettily and turned away...but Zafirah could see she was suppressing a smile. "But what about children? Who will be Scion when you die?"

"I am young. My death will not come for many years, I hope. But when it does, a young man named Kadin is destined to be my successor."

"Who's he?"

"He is a child of the Bharinah tribe, a nomad. He is but a boy now, barely past his twelfth year, but with luck, he will have opportunity to grow into a man before his time comes to rule El'Kasari."

"Is he a relative?"

"A distant cousin, yes."

"So why him? Don't you have any closer kin?"

"I do, but succession to the Line of Scions is not hereditary like it is among the nomadic tribes. The final decision is in the hands of the High Priestess of Inshal, and I do not dispute her wisdom in this matter.

I have met Kadin many times in his life. He is a strong boy, brave and honorable. Though he is young, he already hunts with the men of his tribe, and he is an excellent rider and archer. The desert will teach him patience, wisdom…and when he is ready, I have little doubt he will enforce the Scion Peace with a firm but just hand."

"Why doesn't he live here in the city?"

"Because he prefers to remain in the desert with his tribe." A group of rowdy children armed with wooden swords came racing down the street toward them, and Zafirah took Dae's arm and guided her gently out of their way. "In my youth, I also spent most of my time outside the city, with my mother and her people. It is important to understand the nomads and earn their respect, for without them the Peace would crumble into chaos."

"I can't imagine why anyone would want to live out in the sands," Dae said with a slight shudder, no doubt recalling memories of her ordeal with the slavers. "It's so hot, and there's no food or water or shelter."

"It is a hard life," Zafirah agreed, "and it breeds a hard people. But there is a certain savage beauty to the desert that takes time to appreciate. Once it is in your blood, however, that beauty is never forgotten."

"Hmm."

Zafirah clapped her hands. "But enough of this. Tell me about yourself, my Tahirah. I wish to learn more of you."

"Well…" Dae shrugged. "What would you like to know?"

"Anything! What things make you smile? What do you enjoy doing? Perhaps you could tell me more of your homeland, your family."

"I…I guess I could do that." Dae chewed her lower lip a moment. "Uh…well, my father is Lord Richard of Everdeen, one of the nobles serving under King Gerald. His marriage to my mother was arranged to ratify a treaty between his family and a trading rival. They came to respect and love one another a great deal, and their union helped to increase my father's holdings and land." Zafirah raised an eyebrow, and Dae rushed on. "I suppose you must know something of the system of government in my homeland, right?"

"I have learned about it from ambassadors, yes. In truth, it is not so different from the ways of my own people. Your lords and the armies they govern are much akin to the tribes who owe allegiance to El'Kasari and the Line of Scions. Of course, among the nomads, ancient rivalries and blood-feuds run deep…far deeper than a simple joining ceremony could heal."

"Well, that happens sometimes in my homeland, too. Thankfully not for my parents."

"Have you siblings?"

Dae shook her head. "My mother had complications giving birth to me, so she couldn't bear any more children afterward. I know they would have wished for a large family, but my parents never let it burden them. Instead they poured all their affections on me; they gave me almost everything I could have wanted. My father waited a long time before he would allow any man to court me. That was why I was traveling to the city when the slavers attacked my escort and abducted me…so that the priests could confirm my purity for my future husband and offer their blessings before we were introduced."

"And who was your husband to be?" asked Zafirah.

"I don't know. My parents were handling all the negotiations privately. I never actually got the chance to meet any of the suitors."

"So you would have joined with a man whom you did not even love? Did not even know?" Zafirah's eyebrows rose in astonishment. "Are such practices common among your people?"

"Certainly, at least among the wealthier families."

"I think, then, that your lands must be populated with much discontent and little true pleasure," Zafirah concluded stoutly. "Not to mention a great deal of stupidity."

Dae grinned. "Perhaps." Zafirah saw the merriment fade from her face, however, and Dae sighed. "My parents must think I'm dead by now. I wish they could at least know that I'm safe. It would ease their grief."

Zafirah saw the wisp of loss in the young girl's face. "I am sorry to stir up such memories that sadden you."

"No, it's okay." Dae squared her shoulders, visibly setting the memories aside. "I don't really think about it much anymore. The palace is a wonderful place to live, Scion, really. I'm grateful to you for saving me from the slavers…and for taking me into your home, knowing that I can't repay you as you wish me to."

Zafirah's eyes sparkled. "So your new life here pleases you?"

Dae considered the question seriously. "Yes…actually, it does." She sounded surprised, as though this fact had come as a revelation to her.

"Then I have reward enough simply in the smile that curves your lips. What more could I ask for than to see you happy?"

Dae regarded her knowingly, a slightly teasing edge creeping into her voice. "You could ask for my body. I know it's what you want, and I appreciate the fact that you haven't just taken me."

"Yes, well…" Zafirah smiled modestly. "You have made your thoughts on such matters quite clear, little one. Still, my desire shall not wane with your refusal, and if ever you find your curiosity grows, I would be most honored to entertain and enlighten it." The Scion's tone was light and playful, but Dae's face was perfectly serious as she returned the playful gaze steadily.

"I'll be sure to keep that in mind," she said softly, not trying to stop the corners of her lips from forming a smile.

Zafirah stared wide-eyed at the girl as Dae deliberately turned her attention back to the street, thinking perhaps her ears had fabricated the response her heart most longed to hear. But from the awkward silence that followed and the way Dae let her hair fall forward to hide her face, she realized she had heard true. Warmth flooded through her loins in a familiar tide, and she swallowed hard. Suddenly, Zafirah saw that something had indeed changed in Dae since her arrival, just as Inaya had hinted at. Where the young girl had once recoiled from any flirtations in disgust, she now seemed almost interested and shyly responsive.

*Take things slow*, she remonstrated silently. *Do nothing that might frighten her. If she perceives a threat, she will retreat and all will be lost. Let her come to you in her own time.*

Zafirah had seen dormant desire awakening enough times in her life that she recognized Dae's body language now. The girl was still shy and nervous, and probably not a little frightened, but she was also giving definite signs of interest. Zafirah ordered herself to be patient. This evening had already gone better than she had dared to hope, giving her a chance to interact with the foreign girl as a friend and as an equal, and Dae seemed comfortable in her presence for the first time since she had arrived. Possibilities began to whirl through Zafirah's mind in an exciting, confusing tumble.

*Inaya was right. The flower is beginning to bloom.*

Dae concentrated on the sights around her, conscious of the effect her words had had on Zafirah and fighting the urge to giggle. She was pleased with the response, sensing the Scion struggling to process the unexpected statement, and rather proud at having taken the confident woman so completely by surprise. Dae wasn't sure what had prompted her to say the words out loud, but she couldn't help but enjoy the delightful tension that now pulled low in her gut or the shivers that ran across her skin.

By now, the sun had diminished on the horizon to little more than a distant glow. The streets were lit by hundreds of torches that burned from sconces all over the place and which cast shadows into the alleyways and hollow windows. Glancing at her companion, Dae was mesmerized by the way Zafirah's eyes glowed in the flickering firelight and by the elegant, strong lines of her face. The Scion was, without question, an incredibly beautiful woman...and for the first time, Dae allowed herself to more intimately appreciate that fact.

The two walked in silence for several minutes before Dae decided to continue their conversation as though nothing had happened. "I like to draw. My mother taught me to paint and such from when I was a child, so it comes easily to me." She looked around at the city with eyes filled with wonder. "There are so many amazing things to see here and in the gardens. I used to just sketch things I remembered from my homeland, but then I realized how much beauty I was overlooking all around me."

Zafirah cleared her throat. "Perhaps," she said softly, "you might allow me the pleasure of viewing your pictures the next time I visit the harem? I would very much like to see them."

"Sure." Dae brushed her hair back behind her ear and looked up at the taller woman. "That'd be nice."

"And what of the dancing?" Zafirah probed with a teasing smile. "I watched you from a balcony that night you joined the others. It seemed you enjoyed yourself very much."

"You saw that, huh?" Dae covered her face with a hand. "I wasn't very good."

"You were amazing," Zafirah protested. "My dreams since that night have been filled with your image, so greatly did you inspire them."

"Really?"

"Indeed. Did you not enjoy the dancing?"

"No, it was nice. I liked it."

"Yet you have not joined in since that night," Zafirah observed, offering a slight pout that gave Dae's uncertain body an extra tingle. "Was it because I was there? Did you not participate for fear that I would see you?"

Dae shrugged. "It wasn't you. I was just a little nervous about it, that's all." She took a deep breath, wondering how to explain. "It's hard for me to do that kind of stuff, I guess the same way as it's hard for you to go against your nature by restraining your, um…urges." She felt her cheeks warming and tried to control the blush. "But I did like it, and I do intend to do it some more, so…" She offered what she hoped was a demure look. "I don't mind if you want to watch me next time, okay?"

Zafirah grinned fully. "I would like that very much."

They walked along the streets in silence, casting one another secretive, sidelong glances. There were still many people moving about the city, taking advantage of the cooler night air to conduct their business, and Dae watched the reactions of the few who recognized Zafirah. Many who passed them by gave slight bows of homage to the Scion, which she returned without thought. Those few with courage enough to reach out to her were rewarded with light touches, and Dae saw in their eyes such looks of devotion and rapture that she couldn't help but be impressed. These people clearly loved Zafirah deeply; their respect was more than simply a facade to hide contempt or envy, as it so often was in Dae's homeland. Looking at the Scion as she accepted their gestures with graceful courtesy, Dae felt her admiration for Zafirah rise a few notches more.

The streets eventually circled back to the palace, and before long the two women found themselves passing back into the cool marble embrace of the great halls. Their footsteps slowed, neither wanting to hurry the end of their night.

"I should let you get some rest," Zafirah whispered, her tone reflecting Dae's own reluctance to bring their evening to a close.

"Mm."

"May I walk you back to the seraglio?"

"Sure. I'd like that."

Zafirah smiled charmingly, and Dae felt her heartbeat quicken. They walked side by side back through the palace hallways, pausing outside the entrance to the seraglio gardens. Dae looked up at Zafirah shyly, shuffling her feet. "Well...thank you," she said quietly. "I, ah...had a really nice time tonight. The city is truly amazing."

"If you would like, perhaps I could show you more of it another time," Zafirah said. "We could walk along the docks and watch the ships set sail. Or perhaps you would like to see more of the palace grounds?"

Dae lowered her eyes but nodded. "Okay...I'd like that." Glancing up, she was caught and held by the dark sapphire eyes watching her—eyes that were filled with an intense hunger that carried an almost physical strength. Dae's legs felt suddenly weak. Her mouth became dry as heat pulsed through her stomach and groin. She forced herself to look away, confused more by the reaction of her body than by Zafirah's evident desire. The scent of spicy incense and exotic oils reached her nostrils as Zafirah stepped closer, then a hand gently cupped her chin and drew her eyes back up. Dae swallowed nervously as she found herself in close proximity to the powerful, dark-haired woman—so close she could feel the heat radiating from her body.

Zafirah dipped her head nearer still, and Dae's eyes darted to her lips, then back to her eyes nervously. The blonde felt suddenly unable to control her breathing. She sensed what was coming, ached for it beyond reason, but Zafirah paused when only an inch of space separated them. Her voice was a caress. "May I?"

Dae shivered, dazed by both the closeness of the tall woman and by the strength of her body's response. And in that moment, all the old-fashioned rhetoric of her homeland...all the teaching of what was right and moral and good...everything she had ever been taught by her father and the priests and the tutors...it all fled from Dae's mind, overwhelmed by a need to experience the touch of those lips that breathed so close against her own. She nodded very slightly and whispered in a voice that sounded barely like her own, "Yes."

Given permission, Zafirah completed her descent and brushed her lips lightly against Dae's. The kiss was brief—almost chaste compared to those Dae normally saw the Scion bestow upon her lovers—but it caused a sighing whimper to escape her throat. Dae's eyes closed as she accepted the kiss, completely fixated on the light caress of Zafirah's lips against hers. She had never in her life been so conscious of every nerve ending in her body, of the way her skin seemed to come alive in the taller woman's presence. When Zafirah withdrew a fraction, Dae followed the movement instinctively, not wanting the contact to end. As though sensing this, Zafirah's lips met hers in a second kiss, this one not so modest. Zafirah's tongue traced intimately along the edge of her lower lip, gently sensuous and filled with promise.

When she felt the soft tongue slide across her lips, Dae almost swooned at the realization of what Zafirah was doing to her. But just before her body and mind had the chance to open more fully to this wonderful experience, Zafirah withdrew and retreated back a pace. Dizzy from the brief but frighteningly erotic exchange, Dae opened her eyes slowly and looked up at the Scion, her lips still pursed.

Zafirah smiled at Dae fondly and ran a single finger along her cheek and across her lips. "Thank you, Tahirah," she whispered in a husky timbre. "Just that single kiss is worth the thousand sleepless nights it will cost me." Her finger withdrew, leaving Dae staring at her with glassy eyes. "I shall leave you to your rest, little one. May your dreams be sweet." And releasing her magnetic hold, Zafirah turned and walked slowly away, her hips swaying suggestively the whole way down the passage for Dae's eyes alone.

Only when Zafirah turned the corner and passed out of sight was Dae able to pull herself out of the languid bliss wrought by the kiss. Shaking herself, Dae struggled to understand what had just happened. Her body was still aflame with that strange burning, and her lips still tingled from the touch of Zafirah's tongue. She took a long moment to calm her racing heartbeat before heading back into the seraglio gardens, glad to see that no one had witnessed her moment of intimacy with the Scion. Striding quickly past the other pleasure-servants, conscious of the curious, wondering glances that followed her, Dae retreated back to her room where she cast herself upon the pillows and cushions of her bed. Staring up at the ornate, carved ceiling, she let her thoughts rush through her head in a helpless tumble, aware that something had changed in her this night...

...and wondering how to satisfy the cries of a ravenous, dawning appetite.

## Chapter 9

AT DAWN THE FOLLOWING MORNING, as the sun painted the desert skies with majestic tones of purple and crimson, Dae sat in the seraglio gardens with her back propped against one of the many statues arranged about the harem grounds. Across her lap lay a sheet of coarse parchment, and she traced idle scribbles over it with a sharpened stick of lead. She had been trying since the darkness first began to recede to summon some kind of interest in her work, to draw inspiration from the natural beauty around her, but her mind was far too preoccupied with thoughts of everything that had transpired the previous evening.

Zafirah had flirted with her.

And she had not been offended.

Zafirah had kissed her.

And she had allowed it.

No. Dae flicked at a blade of grass absently. She had not simply allowed the kiss, she had enjoyed it. Enjoyed it so much that she longed for another, longed to rekindle the flames that had sparked so deliciously through her at the touch of Zafirah's lips. The memory of the Scion's body, with its powerful curves and intoxicating scent, had kept Dae up most of the night, struggling to adjust the perceptions she had carried with her all her life.

It was wrong for a woman to have carnal knowledge of another woman. It was perverse to even harbor such depraved thoughts! That was a truth Dae had been taught since she was old enough to understand such matters. And yet now, she was faced with the bitter realization that this cornerstone of morality she had believed in with such conviction was flawed.

Looking around her at the dozen or so other girls who were enjoying the sunrise, Dae smiled. These people were not evil. They were fun and loving and caring. She had been told of the barbaric customs of the desert people all her life but found the reality vastly different to all those stories she'd heard from her tutors and handmaidens. These people spoke eloquently, in precise tones, and their manners were a good deal more civilized than those displayed by many people in the east. Yes, they were also licentious and possessed some rather quaint notions of morality, but the lives they lived were fulfilling in a strange way. They indulged so freely in their passions, with no fear of consequence or chastisement. There was, Dae had come to understand, a certain innocence to the pleasure-servants that had nothing to do with their sexual escapades. An innocence that stemmed from having lived their lives without ever being judged or condemned. And having lived among these people for only a few months, Dae found herself envying their carefree existence for the first time.

A giggle and a low, throaty moan called her attention to the far wall of the seraglio. There, beneath the sprawling mass of a creeping honeysuckle vine that flowed across the stone, Hayam and Johara were engaged in a gentle yet passionate embrace. Johara, the taller of the two, had wrapped her long legs around the shorter frame of her mate, and Dae watched with studious interest as she ran her hands up Hayam's body to cup her breasts over her top.

Remembering the sensation of Zafirah's tongue as it skated against her lips, Dae tried to imagine what it might feel like to kiss the Scion as Johara was kissing Hayam. The two were avidly exploring one another's mouths in a sensuous display that Dae couldn't help but find stirring. She allowed her musings to roam further, wondering what else Zafirah might do to her, if only she were granted permission. Would she touch her breasts? Dae considered that a moment, studying her own full chest curiously. Yes, she decided. Zafirah always paused to admire her cleavage and breasts whenever she let her eyes wander. But would she herself enjoy such a touch? Would she find pleasure in reciprocating? Closing her eyes, Dae called to mind an image of the Scion's body, letting her focus shift to Zafirah's chest. She imagined her hands reaching out to touch the offered flesh...fondling, stroking, feeling the heat rise in Zafirah's skin as her excitement grew—

Dae's eyes snapped open and she pulled in a sharp breath, somewhat surprised by how quickly her body responded to the image. Yes, she admitted. The idea of touching the Scion like that was pleasing to her.

But what else might happen if she were to give in to Zafirah's seduction?

Trying to imagine anything further was futile. Dae hadn't the vaguest notion how two women might make love. She had, in truth, only a child's comprehension of how a man and a woman would couple—enough to understand the basic mechanics, but little idea of any practical realities. She watched Hayam and Johara as they basked in their love and desire, wondering what it was her body wanted that could satisfy these feelings of emptiness and hunger that plagued her more and more with the passing of each day.

Her thoughts were interrupted by a lilting, playful voice. "*Salaam aleikum*, little Dae. May I sit and enjoy the sunrise with you?"

Dae glanced up at Inaya as she approached. She shrugged. "If you like."

"Thank you."

As Inaya sat beside her, Dae forced her attention back to her drawing, marking a few lines on the parchment without much interest. Inaya watched, amused. "You seem distracted this morning. Did you not enjoy your walk with the Scion?"

Dae looked up, startled. "How did you know about that?"

"I wondered where you were last night and asked one of the guards. She told me you had been invited by Zafirah to see the city." Inaya blinked at her in a display of utter innocence. "Why? Did something happen?"

Dae shook her head and returned to her drawing. "No. I-I'm sorry, I just..." She sighed. "Never mind."

Without much enthusiasm, Dae continued sketching idle shapes on the parchment, but she could feel Inaya studying her with knowing interest. Recently the focus of much of Dae's art had shifted; where once she had only drawn pictures of her remembered homeland, she now focused on the things around her. She sketched the gardens, the desert, the other girls—no longer feeling the need to cling to her homesickness and enjoying the exotic beauty of her new environment. Still, with the memory of last night preoccupying her thoughts and Inaya's dark eyes reading every line of her posture and expression, Dae was too distracted to care about her drawing. When Inaya's gaze lowered to her neck, she reached out to finger the delicate silver chain that hung there.

"This is a pretty thing," she admired. "A gift from the Scion, perhaps?"

Dae ignored the wicked glint in the girl's dark eyes. "She insisted."

"Of course." Inaya continued watching her with that same steady gaze, her expression inviting further comment that Dae didn't care to make. After a moment of silence, she waved a delicate hand to Johara and Hayam, whose amorous antics were gaining intensity. "I could not help but notice you no longer seem so repulsed by the sight of such an ardent display as you once were," she commented. "Perhaps last evening's walk stirred questions in your heart you have avoided confronting before now?"

Dae's cheeks burned, and she returned her attention back to her drawing immediately. "I-I just...I wasn't really...doing anything..."

"Do not be defensive, my friend." Inaya cut off her stammering. "You look upon a union of great beauty. It is only right and proper that such beauty be appreciated. And," Inaya's eyes sparkled mischievously as she continued, "you certainly seemed quite able to appreciate it. You have changed much since you first arrived here."

Dae opened her mouth to offer a reflexive protest but closed it after a second. She lowered her head a fraction, looking up at Inaya through a curtain of pale hair. "Maybe I have," she admitted softly.

Inaya beamed a smile at her. "And is it such a terrible thing to see the world through more mature eyes? Through eyes that have gained a greater depth of understanding, and from that, a greater wisdom?" She reached out and patted Dae on the shoulder. "The people of your homeland do not understand us because our customs differ so greatly from their own. Therefore, they distrust us, brand us as barbaric and uncivilized, as living in sin and debauchery. What they fail to realize is that desire and lust come to us naturally." She gave Dae a little wink and added, "There is freedom and joy to be found in surrendering to the delights of sensation."

Dae listened as she watched Hayam whisper into Johara's ear, raising a devilish grin that was apparent even from across the garden. Hayam rose and pulled Johara up after her. Together they headed back toward their sleeping quarters at a brisk pace, their hands wrapping around one another, impatient with need. Dae's eyes narrowed thoughtfully for a moment, then widened in understanding as she turned to study Inaya. Her companion sported a broad smile, and her eyes danced as she watched the departing lovers.

"They're going to...?" Dae left the sentence hanging.

"Passion that burns with such intensity as theirs requires little incentive to burst into flames."

Dae considered this, her lips pursed. She recalled again the sensations evoked by Zafirah's kiss, remembered the feeling of powerful desire that the Scion had restrained. And the need to better understand what Zafirah wanted from her became suddenly more urgent.

"Can I tell you something?" she asked Inaya, her fingers twisting together nervously around the lead pencil. "Something in confidence?"

"Of course."

Dae hesitated, knowing that in the palace harem, little stayed secret for long. "You can't tell anyone else. I mean it, Inaya...*no one*, or I'll never speak to you again."

Inaya nodded sincerely. "As you wish, little one. I would never betray a trust."

Dae studied her friend sternly until she was satisfied Inaya understood and was serious in her statement. She glanced away, chewing her lower lip nervously before she leaned conspiratorially closer. "Last night..." She took a long pause to organize her thoughts. "Last night...Zafirah kissed me."

Inaya's brown eyes widened a fraction, and the very edges of her lips pulled tighter, though whether in a frown or a smile, Dae couldn't tell. "You allowed her?"

Dae flushed and nodded. "I liked it," she admitted in a shy whisper. "It felt..." She struggled for a moment to find words to express how the touch of Zafirah's lips against her own had made her feel, then shook her head in frustration. "My body got all hot, as though a fever ran through me. And I felt sort of sick too. But not in a bad way. My stomach felt like I'd eaten something disagreeable, but it was nice. And I got all dizzy, and I could feel the heat of her right next to me."

Now, Inaya did smile. "Then what happened?"

Dae shrugged. "She drew away, just when I was about to..." She felt a deep blush rise in her cheeks when she recalled the wet sensation of the Scion's tongue tracing her lips. "I was about to..."

"About to what?"

Unable to hold her friend's gaze, Dae looked away to study the sunrise intently. "She was...using her tongue, and I wanted to...open my mouth..."

"Ah." Inaya's smile turned into a mischievous grin. "You wished to deepen the kiss?"

Dae nodded, thoroughly embarrassed, but Inaya's laughter at her response was not mocking or harsh. "You color so prettily, little one, yet there is no need to feel shame or abashment. It is natural to hunger for such greater contact from one you desire." Dark eyes narrowed with interest. "You *do* desire her, do you not?"

Dae hesitated a long while, still fidgeting. "I don't know," she said at last. "All I know is I liked what she did last night. She was so open and honest with me, and she made me feel very special."

"I think Zafirah cares for you a great deal. More, perhaps, than she yet realizes."

Dae smiled fractionally. "As soon as she pulled away, I wanted her to continue. I was dizzy and excited, but for a second there, I wanted so much more from her."

"More?" Inaya shifted closer still. "What more would you have liked?"

Dae shrugged. "I have no idea. I don't know what she might have done if I'd allowed her the freedom to do as she pleases." Restless fingers set aside the lead pencil and parchment now, and Dae turned her full attention on her friend. "But you could tell me. What would... How do two women make love?"

"I have told you before, little one, it is difficult to explain—"

"You couldn't explain how it *felt*," Dae interjected. "Surely you can tell me what happens. Would she touch me? Where? What would she want me to do? How would I—"

Inaya held up a delicate hand to stop her questions. "It is not so simple."

"Why not?"

"Because pleasure is a jewel of many facets; one cannot see them all in a single glance. What one person enjoys, another might shy away from. Such matters are of a highly personal nature. I cannot describe what you might find to your liking."

"Well, what does she do when you're with her?"

Inaya's olive skin hid her blush somewhat, but the bashful response was so surprising and unusual that Dae couldn't help but notice it and wonder. "That is…somewhat difficult to explain."

Dae scowled, irritated by how burdensome her innocence now seemed. "How am I supposed to know whether or not I could be with her if you won't at least give me some information?"

A light popped into Inaya's eyes. "You wish to better understand the expression of desire?"

"Yes."

"Then you would surely be better served learning from the act itself, and not from empty words. I believe I know a most perfect way for you to gain such wisdom. Come." Inaya grabbed Dae's hand and pulled her to her feet, then started tugging her back toward the sleeping quarters. "It is past time your eyes were opened to such matters."

Dae suddenly saw where this might be going and offered a faint protest. "Inaya, look, you're my friend and I like you very much, but….I-I don't think this is such a good idea. Can't you just give me a few academic descriptions?"

"Relax, child. I do not intend to bed you," Inaya assured Dae, who was only offering weak resistance to being dragged back to bed. "Unless, of course, you wish it…?" A raised eyebrow was cast back.

Dae shook her head, embarrassed by the part of herself that was disappointed. "N-no, thank you."

"Do not be afraid to change your mind."

Dae's fear turned to puzzlement as Inaya led her past her own room and further down the corridor. "Where are we going?"

"Somewhere you may find answers to your questions." Inaya stopped them outside the furthest room of the hall. Her dark eyes sought and held Dae's focus with their intense gaze. "Better to see the truth than to imagine it," she said simply before pushing Dae into the chamber entrance.

Dae's mouth opened to pose yet another question, but she lost the power of speech at the sight before her. Sprawled among a pile of pillows and satin sheets, Johara and Hayam were in the midst of removing the last of one another's clothing, their lips and hands exploring every new area of skin as it was revealed. The light from several oil lamps lit the scene splendidly, gleaming off the couple's skin as they entwined.

Inaya cleared her throat. Two sets of eyes blinked and lazily turned to regard them. Dae fully expected an outburst of some kind—anger sparked over the intrusion—but to her surprise, the two lovers grinned in obvious delight.

Johara, tall and lean with long brown hair and the deeply tanned body of a huntress, lifted herself slightly from where she had her shorter mate pinned. "Inaya! Please, enter and most welcome." Her hooded gaze shifted to Dae. "And the little one! What occasion brings you to our chamber?"

Inaya stepped into the room, pulling an uncertain Dae along with her. "A mission of enlightenment brings us here."

Hayam, who was about as tall as Dae and possessed the golden skin, midnight-black hair, and almond eyes of the lands across the northern sea, grinned happily. Her voice carried a light, musical accent. "You wish to join our pleasure? We would be most honored to—"

Inaya shook her head. "Not today, I fear, though I should be overjoyed to accept another time. No, I hoped perhaps you might be willing to allow Dae to observe you...and perhaps offer her some instruction." She smiled benignly at Dae's startled expression. "She wishes to learn how a woman might please another woman."

Johara nipped playfully at Hayam's neck, earning a muffled giggle. "Then you have indeed come to the right place," she said, "for we possess such knowledge in great abundance!"

"Oh, that's not necessary, thank you." Dae recovered control of her jaw and managed to glare at Inaya. "I-I don't think—"

"Thinking is often overrated," Inaya interrupted, pushing her over to a chair and firmly seating her so she could watch the couple on the pallet. "You have questions? What better way for them to be answered?"

Dae glanced at the lovers, who were watching her with interest and some amusement. "I can't—"

"Yes, you can." Inaya leaned close to Dae's ear and whispered, "They will not harm you, my friend. Indeed, they will not even touch you unless you invite them to do so."

"But—"

A finger pressed against her lips, quieting her protests. "Do not argue," Inaya stated firmly. "Sit. Watch. Learn. You will be better able to understand your own longings when you have witnessed something of what Zafirah offers to share with you." Inaya turned back to Johara and Hayam, winking saucily. "Play nice."

"We will." Johara ran her gaze up and down Dae's figure, her hands exploring the body of her lover as she did so. Feeling the heat of her appraisal, Dae shifted in her seat uncomfortably, her eyes searching the room for anything to look at other than the nearly naked bodies that lay not five feet from where she sat.

Inaya chuckled at her friend's discomfort, then, offering a last reassuring pat on the head, she turned and exited the chamber.

Left alone, Dae offered the couple on the bed a weak smile. "I'm really sorry about this," she said. "You probably want your privacy right now, so I can just go back to my own room for a while—" She started to rise from the chair.

"Nonsense, little one," Hayam responded quickly. "We are always glad of company and would consider it a tremendous honor to be a part of your introduction into the world of earthly delights." Her hazel eyes flashed to her lover playfully. "Johara is quite a show-off; she appreciates an audience."

"And you do not?" Johara teased back, her fingers seeking out her lover's small breasts. She glanced at Dae, who was watching with a strange mix of fascination and absolute terror. "Please, Dae, do not leave," she pleaded sincerely. "It is right that you learn more of the pleasures you deny your own body."

Dae stared at Johara's fingers as they sought out a hardened nipple and began to manipulate it with knowing skill. She swallowed hard at the sight. Her mouth felt too dry to offer a reply, but she did sit back down again and set her restless hands firmly on the arms of the chair—a precaution against them deciding to wander off on their own accord. Johara and Hayam both smiled approvingly at her surrender, and Dae felt their eyes crawl over her body even as they shifted on the bed to afford her a better view.

"So." Johara positioned herself behind her lover and began caressing Hayam with long strokes that ran the full length of her body. "What things do you wish to learn?" Dae remained silent, and Johara raised an eyebrow playfully. "Would you like to know how Zafirah might touch you…or how she might like to be touched?"

Dae's gulp was audible even over Hayam's increasingly ragged breaths as Johara drove her arousal to a deeper level. But after a moment, Dae steeled her resolve and offered a faint nod.

"I…I want to know what she wants from me." Her gaze drifted helplessly down Hayam's exposed body to the juncture of her thighs. The northerner was slight of frame, with lean muscles and slender legs, but every inch of her skin glowed in the lamplight like burnished brass. She was, Dae allowed herself to appreciate, an incredibly beautiful woman. It was impossible to keep her eyes from taking it all in, and she watched in fascination as Johara continued to touch and caress her mate. Dae felt a tightening in her own groin, and a strange sensation of wet heat begin to flow through her loins. She shifted in her seat, somewhat uncomfortable with the strength of her body's reaction.

Johara ran a line of slow kisses from Hayam's shoulder to her neck, her gray gaze fixed on Dae the entire time. "Do you think you might be willing to give the Scion what she desires, if you find what you see here to your liking?"

Dae was finding it hard to think straight with the erotic display being played out before her, so her response was automatic. "I might."

Even that simple admission inspired a twisting jolt of guilt, but Dae was helpless to stop the aching need she felt stirring within her as her eyes feasted on what had been for so long a forbidden fruit. With her fingers dancing over her lover's body in a teasing exploration, Johara grinned at her knowingly. "You have affected Zafirah strongly, little one. I have seen her watch you from afar when she visits, and her eyes are filled with more than simple lust. There is much affection and true care in her regard. I recognize it well, for I saw the same look in Hayam's eyes when we first fell in love."

Hayam whimpered softly and arched her back to gain a firmer touch from Johara's hands on her chest.

Johara was clearly delighting in the effect of her performance, and Dae found herself breathing faster, her fingers twitching, when her gaze drifted from her face down her neckline to her breasts. "You are a creature of rare beauty, Dae," Johara said in a husky voice. "If you would like to join us, do not be afraid. It is one thing to simply watch an act of passion, but it is something far more fulfilling to experience the sensations themselves."

A small part of Dae was sorely tempted to accept, itching to know the feel of that silken skin beneath her touch, but the stronger part of her nature was still ruled by uncertainty and fear. She shook her head. "I don't think I should."

"As you wish." Johara's left hand slid lower down her partner's body. Hayam's stomach contracted as fingertips roamed across her abdomen and began to scrape tantalizingly along her inner thighs. She spread her legs wider, and Dae stared at the treasures laid bare before her. Johara ran a single finger through the sparse black curls that crowned her lover's center, watching her reaction with interest. "Have you ever looked upon another woman before?"

Dae shook her head, transfixed by the sight of Hayam's swollen petals gleaming with slick moisture in the lamplight. In some lucid part of her mind, she wondered whether Zafirah would look the same.

"Then let me show you." Johara's fingers split over Hayam's sex and parted her folds, revealing the coral-pink flesh beyond. She stroked her lover slowly, and Hayam bit her lower lip in delight at the sensuous torture. Dae could only stare in amazement, feeling her body tremble with a powerful, erotic rush. Johara noticed and smiled slyly. "Hayam is quite aroused," she observed as she continued to caress her lover slowly. "You see how wet she becomes?"

Dae nodded, licking her lips unconsciously.

"That is a sign of how much her body wishes for deeper contact. She wants to feel me inside her…touching her most intimate places." Hayam cried out as Johara grazed her clitoris, and Dae's eyes widened with concern.

"You're hurting her!"

"No, child." Johara repeated her actions, eliciting another drawn out moan. Hayam leaned back against her, needing more support as she abandoned herself to sensation. "The sounds she makes are sounds of pleasure, not pain. Do not let them deter you. Hayam likes to make a lot of noise during our lovemaking. She will be screaming before we are done."

Dae's eyes narrowed now in academic curiosity. "How can you be sure?"

"We can test her if you wish." Johara withdrew her fingers slightly from the velvet of her lover's core. "Hayam? Dae here is concerned for you. She fears you find my touch unpleasant. Shall I stop?"

"NO!" Hayam's eyes flew open instantly, pulled back to awareness by the suggestion. She desperately grabbed Johara's wrist with a trembling hand and urged it back to her center. "Please, keep going! Never stop!"

"As you wish, *aziza.*" Johara returned to her ministrations immediately, smiling at the wide-eyed Dae. "You see, little one. Hayam feels only pleasure from my touch, pleasure so intense it shall soon grow overwhelming and rob her of all reason." She lifted her fingers for a moment and displayed them to Dae; they glistened with moisture in the flickering light. "Her body reacts strongly. Hayam is very sensitive right now."

Dae leaned a little closer, interested in the proceedings despite her innocence. She could smell the same wild animal musk that had lingered around Nasheta after her night in the Scion's bed and realized it was caused by this arousal. Indeed, she could feel her own sex beginning to tingle with heat, and squeezed her thighs together to ease the strange sensation…an act which seemed only to sharpen her growing ache.

Johara gently laid her lover on the bed and settled beside her, watching her own fingers dance through the slick heat of her core. Hayam writhed on the silk sheets, cupping her breasts and tugging hard on her nipples. "There are many ways to bring pleasure to a woman," Johara explained in a casual tone. "Ways that do not require the aspects of a man. My touch alone could bring Hayam to fulfillment, and I would find great joy in the act of providing her this pleasure." With her free hand, Johara pulled Hayam's legs further apart, displaying her sex more openly for Dae's rapt attention. "A woman's sex is a highly sensitive realm," she continued. "It is a matter of individual preference what will bring the highest form of pleasure. Some like to be touched gently…slow caresses that build the tension and linger long on simpler delights. Others prefer something a little firmer…" Two fingers slid into Hayam and began to thrust solidly in and out, drawing a high-pitched squeal. Dae gasped, her imaginings never having dared consider such a thing. "…to be taken hard and fast, with a climax that stuns the mind with shocking ecstasy, and as quickly moves on to further delectations."

Dae's breath was much shallower now and her body flushed with heat at the sight of Hayam writhing under the assault of her lover. She couldn't believe what she was seeing, but her imagination was absorbing the sight and busily applying it to a new and more detailed notion of what Zafirah might do to her.

Johara pulled her fingers from Hayam's dripping sex and dragged them up to pull the hood from her hard clitoris. "This," she explained, "is the center of a woman's desire, the heart of all ecstasies. It is called the clitoris, and a wise lover will treat it gently and with the utmost devotion and love, for it is very sensitive. Rough treatment will kill sensation after a time and can cause pain that rivals the pleasure. You see…" She circled the hard little bud with a wet fingertip, and Hayam's hips surged upwards, instinctively seeking more. Hayam growled. Johara giggled. "Too much too soon will end our play," she reminded her lover before returning her eyes to Dae. "She is like liquid velvet, soft and hot. Would you like to touch her?"

"I-I don't…" Dae shook her head, even as she noticed Hayam regarding her with a fierce animal hunger. "No, thank you."

Johara frowned. "As you wish." She circled the bundle of nerves once more, enjoying the responses of her mate before continuing the lesson. "Of course, this is not the only way to touch a woman. It is a good way to begin lovemaking, but all too often the hunger of lust must be appeased with a more…oral…form of expression."

Hayam's eyes lit up and she panted anxiously. "Please, Johara! Yes! Do it!"

"Patience, love," Johara soothed, petting Hayam calmly. Dae was puzzled, and Johara continued her explanation. "Fingers are wonderful," she purred. "They are firm and long and can touch places deep inside the body. But a tongue can provide a far more sensuous means of contact— wet and powerful, a tactile, intense muscle that can more fully mold itself to every fold and crevice. Not to mention"—she flashed a quick grin as her mouth descended—"the delight of tasting your partner's essence."

Dae watched in disbelief as Johara's long tongue swept the full length of Hayam's sex. Hayam gasped and abandoned her breasts to clutch at her lover's mane of long hair, pulling her closer. Johara made certain her audience had a clear and unobstructed view of her attentions, then began to suck and lick at her partner's wetness with avid devotion. Dae felt her inner temperature rise a few notches, and the heat between her own legs became noticeably warmer. And, she realized with a deep blush, wetter. The amative acts she was witnessing easily sparked the first signs of arousal in a body that had never known such feelings. Dae's hands gripped the armrests hard as she stared, unblinking, at the things Johara was doing.

Pausing in her ministrations, Johara glanced up at Dae, lips wet with the nectar of Hayam's pleasure. "The sensation of a tongue against one's sex is truly exquisite," she offered with a grin. "Zafirah is much gifted in the art of oral service. Perhaps you would like me to show you something of what she could make you feel?"

Dae's somewhat addled brain took a moment to figure out what Johara was offering, and when she did, she lowered her head instantly. "I can't." Her body, however, had awoken with a hunger that was frightening in its strength and screamed out its approval at the suggestion. This was fueled further by a vivid imagination that considered how Johara's supple, wet tongue might feel pressed against her own most sensitive and private places.

Johara licked her lips, and Dae knew she had not missed how very weak her refusal sounded. "Are you certain?" she asked. "Hayam moves quickly to the breaking point of ecstasy; doubtless she is driven there by the added joy of your innocent eyes upon her." Though lacking experience, Dae recognized the truth of Johara's words. Hayam's eyes were ablaze with raw lust and carnal appreciation as they stared back at her. Her breathing came in heavy panting, and her hips continued their rocking undulations despite the fact her lover had paused in her oral play. "She would surely find the touch of your fingers even more satisfying."

Dae remained frozen, warring within herself, and she swallowed nervously when Johara held out her left hand and offered it to her. "Come," Johara invited. Dae didn't move, and she wriggled her fingers coaxingly. "Please, come closer."

Dae's eyes flicked about the room anxiously, and she shook her head. "I can't."

"Do not fear, little one," Johara soothed. "I only wish for you to be a part of our love, not the focus of it. Please?" Dae's will began to falter, and Johara hurried to reassure her. "You are quite safe, child. Do not let yourself be ruled by fear and doubt. I can see in your eyes that you find us pleasing. Why deny yourself the opportunity to better learn the ways of passion and desire?" Johara wriggled her fingers again. "Please? Will you at least come closer?"

Dae hesitated a moment longer, feeling her modesty and the indoctrination of her childhood war against the newly discovered hunger that surged with ferocious strength at the erotic sight of the two lovers on the bed. But eventually, her desire overwhelmed her innocence, and she reached out to accept the offered hand.

Johara smiled warmly and gently pulled her onto the pillows beside Hayam. Still holding her hand, she spent several moments simply stroking her fingers soothingly over her palm and around her wrist, the touches undemanding and reassuring. Her senses awash in the mingled scents of wild rose perfume and feminine arousal, Dae managed a timid smile when Johara's gaze caught and held her own. When Dae had relaxed enough to go further, Johara lowered both their hands to Hayam's thigh. Dae gasped, feeling the warmth in the glistening skin under her fingers and an answering heat that bloomed between her own legs. She eyed Hayam with a touch of uncertainty, worried she might not appreciate her presence during such an intimate moment. But Hayam's eyes were filled only with raw craving, and when Dae's fingers caressed her unconsciously, she moaned and bucked her hips.

Dae's expression changed from fearful to wondering and then to curious as she let her touch wander along the sensitive leg next to her. "You see?" Johara purred approvingly, leaning closer to her. "She finds great joy in your touch. It is not so difficult to pleasure a lover, is it?" Johara ducked her head and sucked at Hayam's stiff nipples. Dae watched her in open-mouthed wonder.

"But of course, pleasure takes on many guises." Johara pulled away from the hardened little buds and continued sliding a hand down Hayam's belly to play briefly with Dae's fingers before she sought out the slick heat of her lover's twitching sex. "Far more than we could show you in a day. A woman like Zafirah, who has engaged with so many and so often, learns many skills in the art of ecstasy. Many positions..." Her fingers quested inwards, drawing a sharp intake of breath from her writhing lover. "Many ways to prolong the moment..." Hayam's eyes were locked on Dae, who was staring at her in awe. "And many ways to guide her to the peak."

"Please!" Hayam panted, every muscle in her slight frame held taut as a drawn bowstring as Johara's knowing caresses held her at the very edge of something beyond Dae's understanding. "Just a little more, I beg you!"

Johara appeared to consider the plea. "What say you, Dae? Shall we finish this?"

Dae, not entirely understanding the question but reading the stark desperation in Hayam's voice, nodded.

"Here..." Johara withdrew her fingers from their tight nest and reached for Dae's hand. "You shall help me." Dae was totally enthralled by the look of intense rapture in Hayam's eyes and couldn't offer any resistance. Johara guided her fingers along a journey of a few inches across skin that grew hotter and wetter. Then, she slid their entwined fingers over and around the hard nub of Hayam's engorged clit.

The result of this direct stimulation was immediate and spectacular. Hayam's hips surged upwards and her body stiffened even further. Her mouth opened, but she seemed unable to draw breath to scream. Straining and struggling in the throes of a passion greater and more consuming than Dae's innocence could comprehend, Hayam still managed to keep her eyes open and locked with hers, sharing her enjoyment.

Though uncertain exactly what was happening, Dae understood on some primitive level that whatever this rapture was, it was overwhelming and pleasurable for Hayam. Looking deep into Hayam's eyes, she saw the anticipation build like gathering thunderclouds on the horizon. The storm grew, then crested, held for one long breathless heartbeat before it erupted in an explosion of dazed wonder that rolled through Hayam's shaking body. It lasted a few seconds before Hayam gasped, strained, and cried out in joy, her sweat-slicked body quaking as though caught in the grip of an earth-tremor. When the shudders finally passed, she melted back on the bed and lay there, breathless and writhing weakly against the damp sheets, her smile sanguine and sated.

It was, Dae thought, the most beautiful thing she had ever witnessed.

Only after Hayam had collapsed, drained from her climax, did Dae finally realize where her fingers were resting. Feeling soft, slick flesh under her touch, she stared transfixed at her glistening fingers, not quite believing they were her own, before she blushed furiously and tried to pull them away.

"Be calm, little Dae," Johara said, maintaining her hold. "You did nothing wrong. You have brought only pleasure to us both. Relax." Lifting Dae's fingers to her lips, she proceeded to lick and suck the clear honey from them.

Dae shuddered at the sensation of Johara's tongue as it wrapped around her fingers, her body craving something more, but her mind still uncertain how to attain any satisfaction. The carnal look in Johara's expression struck her like a fiery arrow, and she felt her body shiver with longing. When Johara released her hand, Dae could only stare at it uncertainly, wondering what to do with it now. At length, she returned it to her lap and regarded Hayam curiously. "Wh-what happened to her?"

"She climaxed," Johara said simply. Then, seeing her explanation met with only a blank look, she shook her head. "Gods above, girl! Did your parents tell you nothing of such matters?"

Dae looked away, her blonde hair falling forward to hide her embarrassment. "They told me about how babies are made," she said softly. "And about giving birth...but nothing about..." She gestured vaguely between Hayam and Johara. "...this stuff."

"Then they neglected your education much, I think, and cruelly kept you ignorant of pleasures no one should be denied." Johara sat up a little straighter on the bed, and though Dae felt embarrassed by how complete her naïveté seemed in contrast to this display of sexual experience, there was no trace of mockery or condescension in Johara's voice, only earnest compassion. "When one is touched by a lover," Johara explained after a long moment of consideration, "one experiences a building sensation of pleasure. That pleasure grows in intensity until it reaches a peak, a climax. It is like an explosion inside the body that results in a great wave of ecstasy. When we touched Hayam just now, that is what she experienced."

Dae considered this explanation as she returned to her seat, putting some distance between herself and the two lovers. She remembered what Inaya had told her of physical pleasure, of the heat which consumed and embraced. She looked at Hayam, who seemed to be slowly recovering her wits, and in a very quiet voice, she said softly, "It was beautiful."

Johara smiled sweetly. "Yes, it is." She regarded Dae with a countenance both friendly and amorous. "Are you certain you do not wish to experience such beauty for yourself? Hayam and I would be very gentle, and we would stop if you found our ministrations not to your liking."

Dae looked away, uncomfortable and confused by the part of her that wanted to accept Johara's offer. "I-I can't ask you to..."

Johara's pout of disappointment did nothing to cool the fire sparking in every nerve ending of Dae's body.

"Inaya brought you to us to see your curiosity appeased, little one," Johara said. "I would consider myself negligent if you left our bedchamber still ignorant of the delights you might experience under the Scion's touch."

"Perhaps there might be another way," Hayam offered, propping herself up on her elbows and eyeing Dae with a look of anticipatory hunger.

Johara raised a dark brow curiously. "Indeed?"

Hayam gave her lover a suggestive smile. "Perhaps we might offer instruction on another form of pleasure—one that might serve young Dae's desire to learn, but still remain untouched by the hands of another woman."

Dae wasn't sure what new "instruction" was being suggested here, but Johara grinned immediately. She planted a quick kiss on Hayam's lips. "Yes, *aziza*. Perhaps we might."

Dae regarded the two lovers warily, uncertain how to read their playful expressions. "What are you talking about?"

"Well…" Johara shifted on the satin sheets, positioning herself between the spread thighs of her still-reposed mate. "There is a way we could show you that would enable you to bring pleasure to your own body." Her slate-gray eyes were hooded sensuously. "We could instruct you how to touch yourself in ways that would simulate the caress of a lover. Ways that might offer you a glimpse of the many joys you have never known."

Dae's eyes narrowed in confusion, but widened in sudden, shocked comprehension as Johara's hands began a slow, thorough exploration of her own body. "You mean…" Her tongue locked in her mouth, for a moment unable to complete the words. "I could make love to myself?"

"Indeed." Hayam had shifted slightly around her mate so she could watch and enjoy the show as well.

"Would such instruction be of interest to you?" Johara inquired, splaying her hands over her own breasts and toying with her nipples slowly. "It would be but a simulation of a true act of pleasure, but it might at least provide some level of illumination."

Dae stared at the way Johara was touching herself, still struggling to accept what she was seeing. She tried to picture herself doing such things and found it impossible. And yet her body wasn't about to let this hunger go unattended, so she nodded. "I-I guess so."

"Then watch," Johara said, arching her back to present Dae with a better view of her thrusting chest, "and learn."

Johara continued to fondle herself before Dae, her hands and fingers bringing her stiffening nipples to attention and building the heat between her legs. Obviously incapable of leaving her lover untouched, Hayam lightly stroked Johara's back and shoulders, occasionally running the tip of her tongue erotically along a shoulder blade. Johara shivered at the extra stimulation but kept eye contact with Dae. "If you choose to employ this new knowledge," she said, "do not feel shame for it. You are young, Dae, and the passions of youth flow quick and hot. It is natural for you to want to learn more of your body as it awakens, to fully explore the limits of sensation. This is an excellent way in which to discover what feels nice, what pleases you and what does not."

Dae let the words flow over her, absorbing them but keeping the greater part of her focus fixed on what Johara was doing. She could feel her own breasts tingle in longing, jealous of the attention Johara's were being paid. Her fingers itched to satisfy this craving, but she prudently kept them clutching at the arms of the chair.

Johara seemed all too aware that the cause of Dae's tension had shifted from apprehension to arousal. "You are very beautiful," she said somewhat breathlessly. "More so than you yet realize, for innocence is a quality that carries a potent and carnal edge. If you wish to touch yourself now, do not be shy. I would find it greatly arousing to look upon you more intimately."

Dae shifted uncertainly in her seat. She saw Hayam pause in her gentle caresses and regard her with a hopeful look. She imagined herself removing her top, exposing her full breasts to those admiring eyes, then covering them with her hands. The ache in her center was more acute now, more desperate…yet not so much that it could overcome a lifetime of modesty. She shook her head, but did offer, "Perhaps another time. I just…want to…"

"You need not explain, little one," Johara shushed. "These matters should not be rushed or forced, they should be allowed to happen in their own time." She smiled a quietly desirous smile. "If in the future you wish to share yourself with us, however, we would be most honored to welcome you back to our bed."

Dae was pleased and started feeling a little more comfortable. This was all very new for her, and slightly frightening, but it was reassuring to know that she was safe. As Johara began to run her fingertips along her sides, Dae watched her tanned skin shift and flex over the ridges of her ribcage. She licked her lips and enjoyed the sight. When Johara spread her knees wider and exposed her center, Dae gasped aloud at what was revealed: Johara's sex was bare except for a slender, elegantly shaved arrow of dark pubic hair above her mound. Such an intimate level of grooming had never crossed Dae's mind, but she found the sight of the smooth, exposed lips extremely exciting.

Johara heard her surprised gasp and languidly split two fingers up the length of her naked sex, further exposing her most intimate, glistening flesh for Dae's consideration. "You like it? It is a common practice among pleasure-servants and body-slaves to shave our bodies smooth. Bare flesh can heighten one's enjoyment of certain sexual acts."

Dae continued to stare, unable to form words.

"When one has the opportunity," Johara continued, her hands moving up over her belly, tracing the contours of her abdominal muscles, "it is often nice to take time to fully ignite one's body. I would suggest you move slowly, for while it is often tempting to answer the call of certain lower longings, the destination is far more satisfying if it is attained by the longer route."

Hayam leaned closer to her lover's ear and began whispering words Dae couldn't hear. Whatever she said, however, had a definite effect. Johara's breathing grew even more ragged and sweat glistened over her lithe frame. She groaned as she stared at Dae lustfully. Dae had never been looked at in such a blatantly sexual manner—not even by Zafirah, who was far from chaste in her regard. She leaned closer, wondering what Hayam was saying, but the few words she managed to make out made no sense to her. Hayam was speaking her native tongue, the language of the people from across the northern sea.

"What's she saying?"

Johara, who was now openly fondling her swollen sex with both hands, panted for breath. "She is describing…in great detail…exactly what she would do to you…if only she were given your consent."

Hayam shot Dae a wicked grin, her eyes roving over every pale curve of her body, leaving a burning trail in their wake. Dae swallowed hard, unsettled more by the way her body reacted to Hayam's expression than by the expression itself. "What would she do?" The words were past her lips before she could stop them.

Johara pressed two fingers into herself, shifting her thighs further apart to enable Dae to see clearly every move she made. "Can you not imagine for yourself?" she asked coyly. "I am certain she would make you feel wonderful sampling the untasted delights of your body." Johara's excitement was mounting visibly at the whispered descriptions her lover continued to offer, the muscles in her upper thighs trembling and her eyes growing glassy and unfocused. When she finally withdrew her fingers from their ministrations, it was obvious to Dae she was doing so with the greatest reluctance. Johara flashed her a toothy smile, and Dae looked bashfully away for a moment, knowing the more worldly pleasure-servant recognised how intriguing and stimulating she found this intimate exhibition.

"There are many places that bring pleasure to a woman if touched properly," Johara continued, and Dae was grateful she chose not to comment on her evident excitement. "Do not limit yourself to the most obvious and intense, or you will miss out on many things." Dae watched Johara slowly scrape her blunt nails up along her inner thighs, her lean muscles shivering at the sensations she caused. Although it seemed like Johara intended to prolong her self-pleasuring, the wicked glint in Hayam's eyes suggested she wasn't possessed of the same inclination. She moved behind her lover and began running her hands eagerly over her sweat-slicked shoulders. Dae stared, lips parting in a silent gasp as Hayam ran her right hand over Johara's hips to her buttocks...then slipped lower still. Johara's eyes squeezed shut and she arched her back sharply, entirely at the mercy of this new sensation. She drew in a deep breath and released it as a sighing, "Yessss!" then turned her face to the side so she could accept a long and passionate kiss.

Dae watched the women with wide eyes, seeing only beauty and love in an act which would have repulsed her but a few short months ago. Though she couldn't see Hayam's hand, Dae knew something was going on by the way Johara had reacted...and she had a pretty good idea of what that something might be just from the position of Hayam's arm. Her blush returned full force at the notion of what Hayam was doing, and she wondered if anything was considered taboo to these people.

Despite her valiant efforts to draw out her demonstration, it was clear Johara's self-control was failing in the wake of Hayam's pleasurable assault, and soon enough her hands returned helplessly to her slick core. Gasping for air, Johara broke the kiss and arched her body.

"Gods, please! I...I cannot endure!" she panted, and when Hayam lowered her lips to her neck and bit firmly at the pulse point there, she all but collapsed back against her. Johara's eyes squeezed shut, and she gave a high-pitched scream that ended in a strangled sob. Her hips thrust hard, desperate to hold the pinnacle of pleasure as long as possible before she fell back. Hayam wrapped her in her arms and held her for the long moments it took to recover, murmuring words of love and devotion in her strange, musical language.

Dae watched in awe, considering Johara's release to be even more spectacular than Hayam's. The scream startled her, but she realized instantly that it was one of pleasure, not pain, and wondered what feelings could be so intense as to draw such a cry. She imagined herself bringing Zafirah such pleasure, and comforting her afterward, finding the image to be actually quite appealing. That the mighty Scion would offer herself so intimately, would let Dae see her in such an open and vulnerable state, and would share such great beauty with her. For the first time, Dae began to understand what an honor it was that Zafirah paid her such devoted attention.

And she began to wonder whether she might actually enjoy sharing such moments of emotional closeness with the Scion.

When Johara finally regained her composure, she pushed her disheveled hair from her face and sat up straighter on the pillows, flashing a smile to Dae. "I apologize for not restraining myself that you might gain better insight," she said in a charmingly husky tone. "Hayam takes great delight in my pleasure and cannot keep her hands from wandering."

Hayam grinned unrepentantly and nipped at Johara's shoulder playfully. "I think Dae saw enough to understand how things work." She lifted a jet-black eyebrow curiously. "Did you not?"

Dae nodded dazedly. "I think so." Was the "lesson" at an end then? Apparently not.

"Besides," Hayam continued, "there are many other delights to explore, other paths of pleasure that might be of interest to the little one. Positions and methods that we might demonstrate..." She poked at her lover teasingly. "...if you possess the endurance to do so?"

Johara gave an indignant scowl and twisted about, pinning Hayam to the bed with a growl. "Endurance? We shall see who begs for rest first, then, shall we?" Hayam only giggled and bared her teeth, trying to nip at the arms holding her down.

Amused at the obvious playful streak that underlined the sincere love and desire in Johara and Hayam's interactions, Dae settled herself in her seat and looked on as the two began another passionate coupling... wondering as she did so who was enjoying these "lessons" more: herself, or her instructors?

# Chapter 10

IT WAS SOME TIME LATER when Dae returned to her room, having watched Hayam and Johara bring each other pleasure in a variety of styles they thought might be of interest to her. Her mind was reeling from the demonstration. Her body thrummed with electric tingles, and in certain places—places she had never properly appreciated before this very hour—she felt a throbbing ache that beat in rhythm with her heart. Dae needed time to collect herself, to process the new wisdom she had gained before she returned to the seraglio and faced Inaya.

Breathing deeply, trying to calm her racing heart, Dae paced a few times around her room, eyes closed. She wanted to take her mind off the tension in her groin, but of course, this was not easily accomplished.

"Well," she lectured herself, "you wanted to know how two women make love. Now you know, and now you have to deal with it."

It took several minutes of deep breathing before Dae regained control of her body, but there was one image that stubbornly refused to be shaken from her mind—the image of Johara as she stroked herself with a lover's caress, bringing pleasure to her own body. She recalled Johara's parting words to her as she placed a soft kiss on her cheek. "New worlds are often frightening, little one, and it is understandable to be wary or nervous. But there is no need to let that fear dictate your actions. Do not let the ignorance of your people and your homeland keep you from exploring what could be a beautiful and wondrous thing."

Almost of their own accord, Dae's hands ran slowly, lightly along her hips, teasing her highly sensitive skin. The touch sparked an instant reward; pleasure zinged through her, running straight to her center. Dae was surprised by the sensations and curiously let her touches roam a few moments longer. In a gilt-framed mirror that stood against the far wall she observed her reflection in a new, knowing light. Cocking her head to the side, Dae studied her body critically, standing up a little straighter and squaring her shoulders.

These months in the desert had had an effect, she admitted, narrowing her eyes in contemplation. The image reflected back by the mirror was that of a young woman, not the grown child she had been before her abduction. Her body was all feminine curves and smooth, ivory skin, accentuated and highlighted by the harem clothes she wore now without concern for modesty. Her lips were stained with berry juice, her eyelids shadowed with crushed indigo powder. What little baby fat had once softened her frame was gone, for though water was plentiful in El'Kasari, one never truly forgot the grim specter of the desert just outside, and Dae's new diet reflected that fact. Her blonde hair hung low down her back, the tips brushing just above her buttocks, and her emerald green eyes flashed from beneath her lengthening bangs.

All in all, Dae thought, the mirror presented a pleasing enough picture—certainly pleasing enough to warrant the attention she was paid by Zafirah and the other pleasure-servants.

Looking at herself, Dae slowly let her hands move where they would. She watched them trace the outer curve of each firm breast in turn, her lips parting at the approval of her tingling body. Dae closed her eyes and summoned to mind an image of Zafirah: the tall, powerful body that was so often veiled beneath the folds of a *chador*...the alluring, playful half-smile that bowed those sensuous lips...and of course, the sapphire eyes that burned with an intensity so deep that sometimes it seemed their flames could reduce a woman's soul to cinders.

The image lent courage to her hands, and Dae's touch became firmer. A soft whimper escaped her throat, snapping her out of her daydream just as she'd been about to let her hands drift lower, to where the ache seemed strongest. Dae stared at herself, light color rising in her cheeks, then turned from the mirror and tried once more to settle her raging desires.

Throwing herself onto her bed, she growled in frustration. She felt the two halves of her nature warring and was perceptive enough to realize that this newer half—the half that wanted to explore and experience what Johara and Hayam had shown her—was far stronger than its rival. The idea of touching herself so intimately was exciting, all the more so because she was certain it would have been forbidden in her homeland. Her fingers were itching to roam, and after several long minutes of restraint, Dae heaved a dramatic groan. *You know you're going to try it sooner or later*, she admitted silently. *Might as well do it now and get it over with.*

Sitting up, Dae turned again to the mirror. Her hands fluttered for a final moment with indecision, then slowly reached for the laces that held her top closed. Slipping the jeweled cloth from her shoulders, she shook out her hair and regarded her reflection seriously. Her hands followed the path of her eyes, very lightly running across her full, firm breasts, the touches causing her nipples to harden enticingly. Dae's expression was earnest as she let her fingers drift lower, and she stood to slip off her gauzy trousers and brief undergarments. Curiosity outweighed her natural self-consciousness as she looked frankly at her naked form, her eyes exploring every secret inch for long minutes before she lay back on the bed and took a steadying breath. A carnal tide surged through her blood, its song incessant. Dae closed her eyes and let her fingers begin their first timid explorations over sensitive flesh.

Silence reigned in the dim light of the room for the space of several breaths. Then suddenly, Dae gave a quiet, squeaky gasp. Her eyes shot wide open and she sat up, an almost comical look of surprise on her face reflected back at her from the mirror. She stared in mute astonishment at where her hands had paused in their explorations. Then a slow, very sexy smile pulled gently at the edges of her lips—the kind of smile that might be worn by a child who has suddenly discovered a forgotten stash of sugar-cookies…and who plans an instant feast.

Dae closed her eyes once more, lay back, and continued her explorations a little more boldly, humming at the brilliant flashes of sensation that rewarded her pioneer spirit.

The feelings evoked by these touches were far more powerful than Dae had imagined, and she began to appreciate a bit better why Hayam and Johara had been swept along by them so completely. It seemed odd to her; after all, she had touched herself plenty of times before in complete innocence, but had never experienced such things as this. She was aware of the throbbing that rose between her legs, its beat keeping time with her racing pulse. She was aware of the liquid heat that now slicked her core. She squirmed on the sheets of her bed, her breathing growing harsher. Dae continued to fondle her left breast while allowing her right hand to venture lower, teasing the crease of her rib cage and on, down over her belly to where she sensed the center of her need now lay.

When her fingertips encountered the swollen nub of her clitoris as it peeked shyly from its hood, Dae froze, stunned by the blue-white bolt of pure pleasure that arced through her body and sizzled her brain. She gasped, then curiously ran a single finger along the upper folds of her sex. Sure enough, the sensation was repeated, and her smile grew a fraction wider. Remembering what Johara had told her about prolonging the act, Dae resisted the temptation to explore this delightful treasure for the time being. There were, she reminded herself, other pleasures to explore. Her hand moved reluctantly past the slick petals of her center and began to comb along her inner thighs.

In some deeply entrenched part of her conscience, Dae felt the slightest pangs of guilt and shame over what she was doing. But Johara's seductive voice was more than compelling enough to drown out the cries of her modesty. *She was right.* Dae returned both hands to her breasts. *This feels nice. Why shouldn't I want to feel like this? I'm young. I suppose I'm beautiful. And everyone here says it's natural for my body to want to feel these things.* Still, the sliver of shame remained, and Dae supposed it would be a long time before it would disappear completely.

As she continued her journey of self-discovery, Dae felt the subtle changes begin to rise. The tension in her lower belly, at first a bare tingle, built itself into a steady and potent throbbing. Sweat beaded on her forehead, and her skin felt alive with excitement over every new pleasure she discovered. And, she found, there were *a lot* of pleasures to be discovered. Eventually, though, her hands were drawn inexorably back to the burning heat that pulsed from her now-dripping core, and Dae spread her legs unabashedly in order to get the most access possible for her questing fingers. There was an emptiness she'd never felt before, but as much as she wanted to attain complete fulfillment, Dae was mindful of her virginity. She'd been told enough stories of pain and blood by her mother that even her current state of dazed ecstasy couldn't entice her to penetrate that mysterious place between her legs. But thankfully, she found such a thing to be unnecessary anyway. The sensations elicited as she explored every fold of her slick sex were more than enough to keep the waves of blinding pleasure coursing along quite nicely, and Dae felt her senses climbing higher, spiraling upwards to dizzying heights.

The climax to this symphony of pleasure struck so suddenly it caught Dae completely unprepared. The first teasing ripples washed through her in a gentle roll, but they were swallowed almost instantly by a tidal wave of ecstasy that surged with ragged strength, stealing the air from her lungs. Dae's limbs shook and stiffened; her fingers pressed firmly into the velvet heat of her spasming center. The pleasure almost deafened her, but Dae could make out the high-pitched, breathless little screams that she managed to gasp out as her vision was stunned into blindness broken only by spots of rainbow colors. There was a sensation of falling from a great height... No, rather, it seemed she was floating. Dae's hips thrust urgently twice, as sensations of heat and raw pleasure ran through her that were so overwhelming, she thought they might well burst her heart.

But then, just as she was beginning to sob for breath, Dae felt the ecstasy crest, then mellow back into a low, sensuous burn. Her limbs began to obey her orders once more, and she relaxed with a grateful sigh. A sudden wave of sleepy contentment stole over her, and Dae dragged air into her aching lungs in deep, hitching breaths. Her fingers still played in the silken petals of her sex, the sensations enjoyable but not nearly so urgent as before. She became aware of the sweat cooling her skin and laughed a little shakily.

"Well..." Dae looked around her room in wonder, her eyes bright with the aftermath of passion. "I guess that's what all the fuss is about, huh?"

She laughed into the silence that answered her question, looking at herself in the mirror. The flushed and disheveled reflection surprised her, but Dae was past feeling awkward. She blew her damp bangs from her eyes.

"Maybe I could see my way to being a little more open to Zafirah. I mean, this is my home now, after all." She gave herself a surprisingly wicked little grin. "It couldn't hurt to embrace the culture, could it?"

Lying back on her pallet, Dae closed her eyes and let her wet fingers continue caressing her sensitive flesh, feeling languid and blissful in the wake of her spent pleasure.

# Chapter 11

EMERGING FROM THE INNER SANCTUM of the harem some time later, Dae struggled to keep her expression from revealing too much about what she'd been doing this last hour. Inaya, sitting nearby with her legs folded under her, glanced up when she noticed her return. Dae couldn't stop the blush from rising hotly in her face and upper chest when she ran her gaze slowly down the full length of her body. Dae had combed her fingers through her tousled hair and redressed hurriedly before leaving her room, but she knew from the playful grin on her face that Inaya—so astute at reading the passions of other women—wasn't fooled by her attempt at nonchalance.

"Ahhh…" Inaya clapped her hands as Dae approached her. "Truly nothing is quite so beautiful as a young woman in those first moments after she has tasted satisfaction!"

Dae's eyes darted about nervously, and she waved a warning hand. "Shush!" she hissed.

"Why?" Inaya gestured about her at the mostly empty gardens. Those few pleasure-servants who were outside were busy about their own affairs and paid no mind to Dae's arrival. "They would not condemn you for taking pleasure. You forget where you are, little one."

Dae looked around again and was relieved to see Inaya was correct. No one seemed to be watching her with greater interest than normal. Still, she sat down very quickly beside her friend, feeling as though every single girl in the seraglio knew exactly what she had been doing these last few candle marks. She fidgeted nervously with the glass beads that dangled about the waist of her trousers, certain her efforts to remove the scent of her passion hadn't been entirely successful. The knowing, mischievous smirk plastered across Inaya's pretty face seemed to confirm this.

"So did you find your experience with Johara and Hayam to be enlightening?"

Dae studied her own hands intently. "I suppose so."

"Mm." Inaya looked her up and down, one eyebrow lifted curiously. "I have seen that look in the eyes of many women during my life," she observed after a long period of silence. "You were persuaded to join their pleasure, no?"

Dae shook her head, eyes still downcast.

"It is nothing to be ashamed of, Dae. You are past the age that such things should remain a mystery to you."

Dae swallowed hard, but managed to meet Inaya's gaze without looking away. "They wanted me to join them but...I couldn't do it." She felt her cheeks burn with a deep blush, but pressed on. "So they... showed me how to do things to myself..."

Inaya's eyes widened a fraction in understanding. "I see." A pause. "And you exercised this new wisdom."

Dae nodded, though she knew the question had been less a question than a statement.

"So?" Inaya's tone was gentle, since it was obvious in her body language and expression that Dae was still uncertain about this new world she had discovered. "Did you find it to your liking?"

Dae's fingers were twisting knots in the string of beads at her waist, but she nodded. "It was...really good, I guess."

Inaya reached out and petted Dae lightly on the shoulder. "And not half so terrible and sinful as you were led to believe in your homeland, no?"

Dae shook her head. She lifted her eyes now with more courage. "Is it always like that?" she asked in a low whisper.

"Like what?"

"Like, so powerful and..." Dae struggled to find an appropriate word to describe how her body had felt. "And...nice." It was woefully inadequate, but her brain was still a bit frazzled.

"You are unpracticed in the arts of pleasure," Inaya said after a moment of consideration. "Skill comes with time and further instruction. And of course, sensations are usually more intense when they are shared with an actual lover. However nice it felt when you touched yourself, it was but a pale shadow of what Zafirah could make you feel."

Dae's eyes widened in awe. "Really?"

"Of course."

Dae considered this, then gave a silly smile. "I don't think my heart could handle that."

Inaya laughed delightedly. "Oh, child, you would be surprised by what the heart can handle if the body is willing."

Dae giggled and shifted closer to her friend. "I guess I can understand a bit better now why everyone was so eager to show me that stuff."

"And would be willing to instruct you further in such affairs," Inaya added. "But I think Johara and Hayam are good teachers. Perhaps when you are more comfortable with your own body, you will be able to join them in their passion."

Remembering the way the two lovers had embraced and entwined— and remembering how her body ached with desire at the sight—Dae felt again a tingle in her lower belly. "They were beautiful together," she said almost without conscious thought.

"You found their demonstration pleasing?" Inaya asked, looking rather pleased with herself.

"Yes."

"Did it arouse you?"

Dae shrugged. "I guess." Her brows knit suddenly in a stern line, and she frowned. "But why?"

Inaya saw the troubled expression suddenly steal across Dae's face. "What do you mean, 'why'?"

Dae looked up at her friend seriously. "I've never had such thoughts of being intimate with another woman before in my life," she stated. "I've never looked on another woman with desire. Before I came here, such issues never even crossed my mind! But now..."

"Now?"

Dae sighed. "Since I came here, since I met Zafirah, it seems like that's all I've been able to think about. Now when I look at Zafirah, or when she's near me, I can feel the way my body reacts to her. Watching Johara and Hayam would have seemed an appalling notion to me just a few months ago! But now I found it...exciting."

"Desire is not something to be rejected or wrestled down," Inaya argued. "And you do feel desire for the Scion. Why is it so hard for you to accept this?"

"Because I don't understand why!" Dae said firmly, shaking her head in frustration. Taking a deep breath, still unsettled by her experiences this morning and last night, Dae sighed. "If I'd never been abducted by those slavers, would I still be feeling these things? Or is this just something that's happening now because I'm living in a harem with a dozen girls constantly propositioning me?"

"Oh, I think there are more than a dozen."

Dae gave Inaya a dirty look. "You know what I mean." She turned away, staring at nothing in particular but seeing in her mind that curiously arousing half-smile Zafirah had worn last night. "Is this something that's a part of me...or is it just something I'm picking up because of where I am?"

Inaya considered her with an expression of frank curiosity. "Does it matter?"

"Yes, of course it matters!"

"Why?"

"Well, because..." Dae's hands fluttered about her like two lost birds. "Because it just does, that's why."

Inaya caught Dae's hands in her own and brought them to her lap. "I have a story you should listen to," she said softly after looking at Dae a moment in silence. "Some generations ago, a man came to El'Kasari from the western lands. He was a learned man, a man of great wisdom, who had done great things for his people. He claimed to have made maps of the stars and to have discovered how their movements changed with the passing of the seasons. Anyway, he came before the Scion at the time and requested permission to study the great spring that forms the Kah-hari oasis. I understand you saw the oasis during your time with the slavers, no?"

"We only stayed there a few hours during the midday, but yes." Though most of her ordeal in the desert had faded to a blur, the way a night terror will vanish almost as soon as one awakens, Dae still clearly remembered the beautiful, lush oasis that had appeared as if by magic in the middle of all that sand and rock. Completely out of place in the harsh Jaharri desert, the oasis was supported by a bountiful spring of fresh water that had flowed since time immemorial, and Dae had heard tales from her handmaidens that it was regarded as a true wonder of the natural world.

"Though there are many springs and oases in the desert, none are so plentiful nor well-known as the Kah-hari," Inaya continued. "This man said he wished to learn how it was that the water came to flow into the sands, and how it supported life in so barren a land. The Scion was amused by the man's request, but since the foreigner was respectful and polite, he granted permission and an escort.

"Well, the man went out to the oasis and he spent nearly two years there, struggling to solve the mystery of the spring. When at last he returned to El'Kasari, he was frustrated and weary, for the answers he sought had eluded him utterly. The Scion listened to his bafflement and could not help but laugh.

"'What is so funny?' the man asked. 'Why do you laugh? I have invested two years of my life in this matter and have learned nothing!'

"The Scion shook his head, still smiling. 'Forgive my humor, friend,' he said, 'but I cannot help but find it amusing that a man of such wisdom would journey all this way and struggle for so long, trying to find answers that do not matter, to a question only a fool would ask.'"

Dae stared at her friend warily. "What's your point?"

"My point, little one, is that some answers are unimportant," Inaya explained slowly. "When an answer changes nothing, what purpose does the question serve? That man tried to understand the spring, but would his knowledge have been useful? Would such wisdom cause the desert to erupt into a jungle? No. The Kah-hari spring has flowed since as far back as my people have lived in the desert; it is as consistent and reliable a thing as the waves that break upon the shore. No one has ever fully understood it, but their ignorance has not caused the spring to stop."

Dae scowled. "That's somewhat hypocritical coming from someone who keeps telling me I shouldn't let ignorance stop me from learning new things," she said.

"Perhaps," Inaya admitted. "Or perhaps it is simply that one should learn when an answer is of worth. The lone eagle flying high above the desert who spies the carcass of a sheep lying on the sands does not pause to wonder how that sheep came to stray from his flock. The why simply does not matter. It is enough that he will return to his nest that night with a full belly." She shifted on the lawn, regarding Dae earnestly. "You are attracted to the Scion, Dae. You feel desire for another woman. And this day you have tasted pleasure, and enjoyed it. Would knowing 'why' change anything for you? Would it cause these feelings to shimmer and fade like a mirage?"

Dae considered this, suddenly understanding what Inaya was getting at. She shook her head. "I guess not."

"Then why ask why?" Inaya twined her fingers with Dae's affectionately. "Perhaps these feelings have always been a part of you but were stifled by the prejudices of your people. Had you never been abducted and brought into this land, it may be that you would have discovered them on your own. But in your homeland, do you think they would have found the strength to grow?"

Dae shook her head. She had heard rumors of what happened to those who indulged in forbidden acts, and knew she would never have had the courage to let such emotions have free rein.

"Or perhaps these feelings have only emerged because you are here, in the harem, where you can understand and appreciate them in a way you never could have before. The result is the same; you have discovered a treasure that holds value to you now. Do not dissect your feelings, little one, for they are better left intact and unspoiled. Let them hold their mystery. Enjoy them for what they give, and do not look for answers to questions that change nothing."

Dae could feel her mind still struggling to adjust to all these new things, but she couldn't dispute Inaya's logic—a logic she knew would have been considered barbaric in her homeland, where science and order ruled supreme. "It's still a lot to get used to," she said.

"Do not let your head be burdened by confusing thoughts," Inaya advised, still hearing a lost tone in Dae's voice. "You have all the time in the world to sort through your emotions, and to accept the leanings of your heart and body. And as strange as all this is for you, you must realize it is every bit as difficult and confusing for Zafirah as well. She is learning a gentler form of love than that to which she is accustomed, just as you are learning a more passionate one. But if you are patient with one another, and allow the roots of your connection the chance to grow strong, I am confident you will be rewarded."

"But what should I do when she comes here tonight? I mean, I let her kiss me last night. Perhaps she'll expect more from me now."

Inaya's playful smile returned, her dark eyes laughing merrily. "Zafirah is as frightened of making a wrong step as you are, little one. Talk with her. Let her see you for who you are, without the walls. Show her how you feel: nervous, excited, afraid. She will understand."

"Will she?"

"Of course. Though she was born to glory on the battlefield, Zafirah is a compassionate woman, even though she is often ruled by her more carnal appetites. Her body desires you, yes, but her heart desires you more."

Dae heard a strange, almost reverent tone in Inaya's voice, and saw the faint shimmer in her large eyes, something akin to adoration. "You love her very much, don't you?"

Inaya shrugged. "We all love her, little one," she said. "She makes it impossible to do otherwise. But such love as ours is born in the bedroom, not the heart, and its pleasures take a different flavor to what she feels for you."

Dae shook her head, confused. "I don't understand."

"With time, you will," Inaya assured her. She looked up at the sun high overhead and wiped her glistening brow. "For now, however, I fear the heat is growing uncomfortable. Shall we see what we can find to eat inside? I have not had a chance to break bread this morning."

"Sure." Dae's stomach chose that moment to voice a loud approval of this suggestion, and she giggled as she stood up. "I think that might be a good idea."

"Mm." Inaya petted her on her pale, smooth belly soothingly, and Dae laughed and slapped her hand away lightly. "You must keep up your strength, little one," Inaya advised with a grin. "After all, sexual pleasures tax the body a great deal, and I would think you should have need of your strength in the coming days, if you are to more fully explore the world of carnal delights."

Dae might have offered a protest of modesty, but with the memory of those stunning sensations still fresh in her mind, she figured it couldn't hurt to follow Inaya's suggestion and satisfy her growling stomach as quickly as possible. Dae had already accepted the fact that, as soon as she had the opportunity, she would lead her hands and fingers on another long expedition into the mysterious pleasures her body longed to sample again already.

She was definitely going to need her strength.

# Chapter 12

ZAFIRAH CAME TO THE SERAGLIO just as the sun was lowering itself onto the cradle of the horizon, a time when most of the pleasure-servants liked to play and roam through the gardens as the air cooled. Dae, who had been sketching images of the other girls from beneath the shade of the giant aspen tree, sensed an almost palpable shift in the air and glanced up to find the Scion's glittering eyes watching her. She felt instant heat shoot through her loins, but this time the sensation wasn't so much a stranger to her. She understood it better and welcomed the honey-sweet burn that crept along her skin like a slow caress. Dae offered Zafirah a slight smile and went back to her drawing.

Beneath the aspen, Dae let her fingers continue tracing idle lines on the parchment spread across her lap, but in truth she had lost interest in drawing. Zafirah had joined a group of girls by the waterfall, accepting their gentle flirtations while continuing to steal furtive glances at her. She watched Zafirah interact with the other pleasure-servants, noting the relaxed energy that surrounded her, the crooked smile and occasional flash of pearl-white teeth when the Scion grinned…the soft, uninhibited touches she exchanged with the flirting harem girls. Dae's eyes narrowed a fraction as she observed the subtle battle being waged for Zafirah's attentions, a war fought with lingering caresses and intimate suggestions of nightly delights whispered into the Scion's ear. For the first time, Dae felt something other than curious dread watching the seduction—something like…jealousy? No, that wasn't it. It was more like envy. Envy at the easy way the girls flirted with Zafirah. It came so naturally to them, was so intrinsic to their nature, while she was forced to wrestle desperately with every new desire that occurred to her. For the first time, Dae wished she could behave with such carefree abandon, could flirt and touch and giggle and blush with assumed—rather than actual—innocence, as the others could. For a moment, the urge to get up and join them by the waterfall was so strong, the muscles in her calves and thighs tensed, ready to start walking.

But then those sapphire eyes caught and pinned her with a look of such devotion mixed with utter lust that Dae felt her breath catch painfully in her throat. The look was enough to settle any feelings of envy Dae had. She didn't need to vie for the Scion's attention. She had it already.

Smiling, Dae focused back on her drawing, surprised to find her hands had been working during her distraction. A nice image of Zafirah's angular, beautiful face had been sketched without her even knowing it, each line perfectly shaded and keeping the correct proportion of the Scion's features. It was a moment of true insight for Dae. *I know her face so well I can draw it with my eyes closed*, she realized, marveling at the way her attraction toward Zafirah had grown so powerful without her consent. She was still staring at the picture when a familiar, throaty voice spoke.

"You have much talent."

"Huh?" Dae looked up to find the subject of her art standing a few paces away, one dark eyebrow cocked, her full lips pulled into an amused smile. Those astonishing eyes regarded the picture on her lap with interest, and Dae shifted shyly. "Oh, I was just...um. Practicing."

"Mmm." Zafirah gestured to the grass beside her. "May I sit?"

"Of course." Dae made to roll up her sheaf of parchment-drawn pictures, but Zafirah stopped her.

"Please? May I see?"

"If you'd like. Some of them aren't very good, but..."

Zafirah took the drawings from her, letting their hands brush together in the exchange, and began looking through them. Dae watched her expressive eyes study each image in turn; some of the sketches were only basic, but Zafirah seemed to find them all intriguing, particularly the older ones which portrayed images of her homeland in the east. Dae knew these landscapes would have been better depicted in color, but since such art was not commonly practiced among the Jaharri, the guards attending the harem had not been able to acquire the necessary paints for her. Zafirah paused a long while when she came across the portraits Dae had made of her, before glancing up with a playful smile. "I am flattered you find me a worthy subject."

Dae shrugged, extremely conscious of the way her body was reacting to the Scion's proximity. "You're very beautiful," she observed calmly. "Your face is easy to draw."

"I see." Zafirah finished looking through the drawings, then carefully handed them back to her. "Perhaps one night, I might pose for you," she said. "I would be honored if you would draw something especially for me."

Dae swallowed the lump forming in her throat at the intense regard in those deep sapphire orbs watching her. "I suppose, maybe. If you'd like—"

"I would," Zafirah assured her in a low voice. "Very much."

"Okay. Tomorrow, maybe?"

"I shall look forward to it."

Dae nodded and pretended to go back to watching the girls who were busy gathering together a group of musicians to play for them.

Sitting back against the trunk of the aspen, Zafirah set herself so she could look at Dae's profile without being too obvious. The lively sound of drums mixed with the jangle of finger-cymbals rose from the other side of the lawn, and the Scion watched a few of the pleasure-servants begin dancing. "Will you join them?" she asked her companion hopefully.

Dae glanced back at her, a coy expression on her face. "Would you like me to?"

"Of course, Tahirah, though the sight may add to the burden of my restraint."

"I think it's probably worth the risk," Dae said wryly. "Besides, you could use a little extra practice in that department."

"Oh, Tahirah, I am practiced in the art of restraint far more than you could realize." Dae blinked at her, clearly not understanding, and Zafirah chuckled at her innocent confusion. A fantasy scenario involving lots of rope and a naked, squirming blonde tied to her bed sprang to life in Zafirah's imagination, and though it seemed a wonderful way to clarify her reference, she set the thought aside for another day. Zafirah cleared her throat and continued. "But regardless, there is no reason to deprive us both of the pleasure of your dancing…is there?"

Dae cocked her head to the side, considering a moment, then shrugged. "It's too hot right now. When the sun goes down properly, I'll join in."

"Then I shall wait with great impatience for the dark," Zafirah said, leaning back again so she could study the young blonde thoughtfully.

The Scion was skilled at reading women, a talent honed after years spent practicing their seduction. It didn't take her long to realize that something had changed in the girl since last night—something subtle, yet distinct. A part of her wanted to attribute the change to the kiss they had shared, but Zafirah recognized that this was simply the voice of ego. Her lips pursed in consideration, trying to pinpoint what this enticing difference was exactly.

*Her eyes are open.*

The thought occurred of its own volition, and she gnawed at it mentally for a moment. *Yes*, she thought, *her eyes are open. She no longer draws away from my presence or flinches at my touch. She did not even react when I looked at her with lust.* And there was more. Zafirah could detect a new scent about Dae, something so low and delicate that it seemed less a physical presence than an aura surrounding the girl: the scent of a dawning sexual maturity, an understanding that had not been present last night. Zafirah had wondered if kissing Dae had been too forward, too aggressive, if she might have scared her away. But now she saw that perhaps it had prompted her to seek out new knowledge, to accept her own needs and wants.

*Her eyes are open*, she thought again. *I wonder who is responsible for opening them?*

Across the lawn she saw Inaya watching her with stealthy interest. The slight smile on the girl's face was answer enough for Zafirah. *Of course.* Zafirah gave Inaya a quick, devilish grin. *I shall have to thank her later for this gift of enlightenment.*

The two women sat beneath the aspen, exchanging furtive glances and a few words now and again. The dancers moved out onto the lawn as the sun disappeared and torches were lit around the seraglio grounds, the girls swirling and swaying in a display intended to catch Zafirah's fancy. Those not dancing gathered around Dae and the Scion, clapping along to the beat of the drums and urging their fellows on. Zafirah watched with an expression that was half amusement, half appreciative desire, but her attention always returned to Dae. She gave the girl her most plaintive, pleading looks, making her laugh and turn away, until finally Dae took pity on her and rose to join the circle of dancers.

As soon as she stood up, the other girls cheered their approval and encouragement. Dae blushed profusely at the attention, but shyly accepted a hand from one of the dancers. When she looked up, she found Johara's laughing eyes gazing back at her. The slender brunette flashed a wicked grin and pulled her into the circle of dancers, twirling her about and guiding her first awkward movements with casual grace.

Though the *brehani* had lowered her inhibitions the last time she tried this, Dae found it easier to pick up the rhythm than she'd expected. Johara helped ease her initial tensions, and she soon relaxed and allowed her body to dictate the way she moved in time to the spirited music. Filled with joy, laughing as she struggled to emulate the fluid motions of the other girls, Dae began to enjoy herself.

And while she danced and laughed, she watched Zafirah watching her with eyes of blue flame.

A pleasant little shiver thrilled along her spine, but Dae didn't find the Scion's attention now to be in any way uncomfortable. In fact she welcomed it, and began shedding her natural modesty in favor of more provocative movements suggestive of new, primal rhythms she didn't yet fully understand. When Johara caught Dae's eye for a moment, the two exchanged secret, knowing smiles...acknowledging the bond of intimacy that had been forged between them that morning. Johara took an opportunity to run her hands along Dae's rippling belly, leaning close and whispering into her ear. "Attentive, is she not?"

Dae flashed the Scion a quick grin, nodding.

"She is even more so in the bedroom," Johara added, letting her hands explore a heartbeat longer before drawing away and returning to Hayam's side.

Dae felt wild as she whirled about to the tune of exotic music, exhilarated by a sudden sense of absolute freedom and delight. The night air felt cool against her hot skin, and she was breathless and giddy from the active dance. A fresh breeze blew in from the desert, bringing with it the scent of vast, open places and the distinct perfume of sand and stone. She liked the way Zafirah's gaze never left her body. She liked knowing she affected the dark-haired woman in this way. An image from her experience with Johara and Hayam that morning blazed suddenly to life in her mind, and she pictured what it might be like to share such delicious intimacies with the powerful, seductive Scion.

Dae danced until she grew too tired, then returned to Zafirah's side, begging off the pleas of the other girls who tried to persuade her to continue. "I need a rest," she insisted. "Maybe later."

Zafirah smiled and waved a hand, signaling the musicians to play again. As the dance began once more she let her eyes roam over Dae's figure, appreciating the way her pale skin shone under a fine layer of sweat. Dae was breathing heavily, her long, golden hair charmingly ruffled. To Zafirah's eyes, dazzled by pangs of sweet affection, she looked absolutely gorgeous.

"You were magnificent!" she complimented.

Dae lowered her head modestly. "Thanks. It was fun."

"You seemed to enjoy it." Zafirah could smell the musk of Dae's sweat, and it made her dizzy, made her want to rub up against the girl... feel the friction between their bodies...breathe the same air and let the tension build until it burst. With an effort, she resisted the powerful temptation to reach out and touch that glistening skin, but she shivered slightly at the vivid images that skipped through her mind like a teasing itch, daring her to give in and scratch them.

Dae noticed the shiver. "Are you cold? I could get a cloak from my room if you are."

"No, child." Zafirah shook her head. "In truth, I am warmer than I might care to be, and that is something I thought never to feel."

The answer confused Dae a moment, and she almost opened her mouth to ask a question. But then she noticed the smoldering heat in Zafirah's eyes, a heat that made her pause, uncertain how to respond.

She dropped her eyes and plucked at her trousers with nervous fingers. "Oh."

"I lost many hours of sleep last night," Zafirah admitted with a quiet smile. "The memory of your lips against mine would not subside, even in my dreams. But I consider it an experience worth the sacrifice of slumber."

Dae licked her lips unconsciously, remembering every detail of the kiss all too clearly. "You must have kissed hundreds of women."

"But none like you." Zafirah shifted closer so her low voice could be heard over the music, and Dae found herself leaning in as well. Her whole body was tingling as it always seemed to do whenever she found herself in close proximity with the Scion, but the sensation was more familiar to her now. She understood it better. The other girls, sensing the two wanted some privacy, turned their attention to matters other than winning their way into the Scion's bed, giving them some extra space. "None like you."

Dae felt shy but couldn't help feeling flattered at the same time. A small part of her mind argued that Zafirah was only saying these things to seduce her into parting with her virtue, but that voice was silenced by the honest sincerity in the older woman's piercing eyes. There was no lie in those sapphire gems, no trace of guile or deceit. They were as open as the desert itself, and Dae felt a spark of courage burst from inside her just seeing how Zafirah was willing to lay herself so bare in this way. *If she can be honest with me*, she thought, *how can I be anything less with her?*

"The kiss?" She sat up a little straighter. "I didn't hate it."

Zafirah considered that statement, one eyebrow raised in cautious hope. "Indeed?"

A nod. "In fact..." Dae chewed her lower lip, but she managed to meet Zafirah's gaze steadily. "...I kind of liked it."

Zafirah's smile at her words was so filled with longing joy that Dae feared it would melt her heart. "Indeed?"

Another nod. "A lot."

"Mm." Zafirah moved closer again—close enough that Dae could detect the scent of rose perfume mixed with the faintest traces of leather and horse, a smell that seemed enticingly feminine. "Enough that you might wish to experience another?"

"Maybe." Dae stifled a grin as she appeared to give the matter the most serious of deliberation. "If I could find someone willing to give me a second try."

"I think I could be persuaded," Zafirah said with becoming gravity.

Dae looked away quickly before she could be snared by the Scion's devastating eyes; she knew if that happened, nothing short of death would stop her from sending her tongue on a mission of conquest into the older woman's mouth. "Maybe one day," she said very softly, "you could show me how to do it properly. You know...the way Hayam and Johara kiss."

Something had indeed changed in the girl, Zafirah thought, and it had been more significant than even she had dared to hope. Still, her feelings for Dae were too compelling for her to allow any baser urges the chance to ruin this moment. "Are you certain? I do not wish to lead you down a path you have no desire to tread."

"I thought it was something you wanted."

"I do, but not if you feel even the most minor of unease." Zafirah reached out and laid her hand on Dae's thigh, not attempting a seduction, but simply needing a physical connection to the girl. "I remember all too clearly what you told me when we first spoke of such matters. You said you would never wish to seek pleasure with another woman, no matter how long you stayed here."

"Well..." Dae gingerly set her own hand on top of the Scion's, and though her touch was hesitant, Zafirah sensed an acceptance and understanding in it that had grown stronger since last night. "Words spoken in fear or haste are never set in stone. Perhaps they could be... negotiable."

Zafirah looked deep into Dae's timorous emerald eyes, searching. "You have much fear in your eyes," she whispered after a long moment.

Dae lowered her head momentarily. "Maybe I do," she admitted calmly. "But not as much as when I first came here."

"Mm." Zafirah considered this statement and the message that lay beneath it. "Perhaps in time, that fear might fade to nothingness?"

"I think it might, yes. Perhaps until then, we could just take things… slowly?"

Zafirah lifted her free hand and ran a single finger along Dae's lower lip, then up her cheek. "I am, if nothing else, a patient woman, Tahirah. Until you are ready, I shall do no more than long for you."

"Well, I don't think it'd be fair of me to give you nothing but longing." Dae leaned forward, her expression nervous but excited. "Patience deserves some reward, after all."

Zafirah shivered as Dae closed the distance between them and kissed her softly, a kiss of youthful innocence tempered with a fierce edge of excitement. As much as she wanted to deepen their contact, she waited breathlessly as Dae relaxed against her. When she felt the first timid touch of the girl's tongue against her lips, Zafirah almost choked with the force of her restraint. The inquisitive, wet muscle explored along her lips, then, with more assertiveness than she would have expected from the foreign blonde, swiftly demanded entrance to her mouth. Zafirah complied and allowed Dae to lead the kiss, dueling softly with her own tongue and feeling the wonder in the body held so close to her own.

When they parted, both were breathing heavily. The seraglio had fallen silent, but in their mutual distraction, it took them both a moment to realize that fact. When they eventually managed to tear their eyes away from one another, puzzled by the lack of music, they found several dozen grinning faces watching them with great amusement. A moment later, a loud cheer went up among the gathered pleasure-servants, many of whom whistled and cried out for more.

Dae turned crimson in an instant and buried her face in the crook of Zafirah's arm. The Scion merely smiled indulgently at her harem.

"Music!" she commanded. "Come now, let us not make poor Dae a spectacle. More music! More dance! Play on!"

The musicians did as ordered, and several girls began to dance again. The others went back to their conversations, still laughing and smiling at the couple.

Zafirah chuckled. "Come now, little one. They are happy to see you indulge your desire. Do not be embarrassed."

Dae peeked up at her, her face still a brilliant scarlet. "Easy for you to say."

Zafirah licked her lips and waggled her eyebrows. "We could give them something more to watch," she suggested half-jokingly, half-hopefully. "No? Perhaps another time."

Dae gave her a bashful smile, then shifted herself around a little so she could lay back against Zafirah's body. "Definitely. Only next time, maybe we'll try somewhere a bit more private."

Zafirah froze when she felt Dae settle against her, hardly breathing for fear of ruining this dream. Their two bodies fit together so splendidly, so naturally, she could not recall ever feeling so at peace with any woman she had lain with before. Dae's breath tickled against her skin as she gave a contented sigh. After a moment, Dae pulled Zafirah's smooth, powerful arms around her waist, and the Scion happily let their fingers tangle together.

"Whatever you desire, my Tahirah," she said, leaning forward a few inches so she could press her lips against Dae's forehead. "Whatever you desire."

Under the light of a full moon, the group of mounted figures moved across the shifting sands, riding single file to hide their numbers. They kept to the shallow ground, skirting the higher dunes to avoid offering any watching eyes the opportunity to spot their silhouettes against the starry sky. Their rear guard trailed a lightly weighted skid behind his horse to obscure any trace of their passing in the rocky sands.

Bahira, a young woman who had served as a scout of the Scion for almost a third of her life, listened to the echoing silence of the desert at night. Her eyes, trained over the years to be ever-watchful, skipped along the expanses of rock and dune, never idle, always attentive. This assignment was important to her. Falak, the leader of the scouts and Bahira's sometime lover, had entrusted to her the task of keeping watch on the stirrings among the renegade tribes being led by Shakir Al'Jadin. It was a promotion she did not intend Falak to regret giving her.

Glancing over her shoulder, around the raven-fletched arrows that were the trademark of the Scion's elite scouts, Bahira nodded to the line of troops behind her. These were all skilled and able soldiers. They had been her family since she first left behind her nomadic tribe to seek her fortune in the city of El'Kasari. Nasir, the slender, hard-muscled man riding directly behind her, was her second in command and had fought beside her through many battles. She gestured for him to ride at the front with her.

Nasir gave his commander and friend a smile, his eyes remaining watchful; this was, after all, the wild-land. The land of their enemies. "The night seems quiet," he said in a low tone, one practiced so the sound would not carry more than a few feet. "Shakir and his dogs would be fools to move about under the light of a full moon."

"We must be vigilant still. I do not flatter myself to think that our presence here has gone entirely undetected. Shakir knows the Scion will be watching him. It is possible he may try to blind her eyes."

"True enough. Yet we have been here some time now, and they have made no move to attack us."

"Our mission is too important to leave to chance," Bahira reiterated. "The Scion needs to know when Shakir decides to strike."

Nasir was silent for a long while before he asked gravely, "And what of the thunder? Have you reported it to Falak?"

Bahira frowned. Everything, it seemed, came down to the thunder. Her fellow scouts were edgy and concerned. Through the weeks they had been here, their efforts to watch Shakir's actual camp had been foiled by geography. The camp was nestled in a wide canyon, surrounded on three sides by towering, sharp-toothed cliffs, impossible to climb, even for the adept scouts. The position afforded Shakir great protection from spies; his men patrolled a wide perimeter, and Bahira had been unable to penetrate their ring of steel. But by monitoring the supply wagons and the number of guards, she had gained at least an idea of how many troops the renegade Calif commanded, and of their general condition. What remained of concern, however, was the thunder.

Most evenings it cracked across the desert plains, a series of loud, sudden bolts of sound that seemed to herald a coming storm. But of course, the season when the rains would come was still many months away, and the skies remained a clear and brilliant cobalt blue. No lightning ever accompanied the strange, ominous thunder. No rain or clouds ever darkened the horizon. The mystery was disconcerting, and it caused Bahira a measure of fear. What strange power did Shakir command that he would go to such lengths to hide it from the Scion and that it could make such noises as these?

"I have kept Falak apprised of all we have seen and heard," she told Nasir now. "She knows as much—and as little—as we do. We must learn more before the knowledge becomes useful."

Nasir studied her a moment, reading the lines of her face carefully. "You are worried though, are you not?"

"I do not like the uncertainty," she said, one hand holding the reins of her horse loosely while the other stroked the horn grip of her recurve bow. "Whatever power he has found, Shakir should not be given time enough to master."

"The Scion is no fool. Her tactics have been successful time and time again. The *spahi* cannot maneuver so well in the canyon passes. Let Shakir bring his dogs into the open, where their advantage will be lost."

"Mmm. Perhaps." Bahira sighed. "Still, I do not like the not knowing of all this."

"Perhaps they will move soon," Nasir suggested hopefully. "They cannot remain overlong in the deep des—"

A sudden sound like the cracking of stout wood shot across the open desert at that moment, silencing Nasir. The horses shied, but having been trained to stay calm under battle conditions, they quieted almost immediately. Bahira and the other scouts lifted their bows, arrows nocked in a heartbeat, eyes scanning the horizon for their enemy. The sound had been close, and Bahira realized with sudden, sinking surprise that her party was under attack.

"Where are they?" she demanded, her eyes finding nothing. "Nasir, can you see them?" There was no reply. "Nasir?"

Bahira glanced at her second, and her eyes widened in horrified disbelief. Nasir was staring down at his chest, his hands covering his ribcage, a look of shock and pain etched on his face. In the light of the full moon, Bahira could see the blood welling out from between his fingers, not crimson, but a rusted black color in the silver light.

"Nasir?"

Nasir looked up at his commander and friend a final time, then his hands dropped limply to his sides and he toppled from his horse. Unable to believe this was happening, Bahira saw a gaping hole had been torn from his chest. She took a moment to gather her energies, then turned back to her remaining scouts. She signaled them to form a circle with their backs to one another. Even as they moved to obey, a second booming *k-raaack* rang out, and another scout fell to the sands. This time, however, Bahira caught sight of movement on the dune line, and she pointed. "There!"

Five arrows were loosed simultaneously, but the target was gone while they were still in the air. Another rider appeared, his figure silhouetted against the night sky, and Bahira fired again. Her shot fell short; the enemy was out of range, even for the powerful bow.

But apparently, whatever weapon he was armed with was still effective. A third explosion, and a third scout was slain.

Bahira felt a moment of panic grip her. It was only for a second, but it chased up her spine like the cold fingers of death. She didn't know what she was up against, but the facts she did understand were clear enough: she and her scouts couldn't strike the enemy, but the enemy could pick her whole party off at their leisure. Trained to be adaptable, Bahira decided on the only possible course of action that might save at least some of their lives. Lifting her head, she cried out, "Take them! Ride them down!"

Ululating war cries split the night air as the scouts spurred their horses to attack. Arrows were nocked at a gallop as they charged the unknown numbers beyond the dune ridge, all of them determined to close the distance so they might at least fight back effectively.

Leading her fellows on, Bahira was the first to crest the rise, an act of leadership which very nearly cost her her life. A line of fifteen or so figures mounted on swift *mehari* were ranged against her, no more than a few dozen paces away. She had barely enough time to sight a target and let loose an arrow before an explosive boom blasted against her, the sound deafening her. Flashes and smoke sparked in the darkness, and the acrid stench of sulfur stung Bahira's nostrils a moment later. Startled by the noise, her horse reared up, and it was all Bahira could do to keep her seat. Behind her she heard screams as her brothers and sisters were felled by these mysterious weapons, but she didn't have time to grieve. Not yet. In a fluid motion practiced since she was five years old, Bahira drew another arrow, nocked and sighted in one move, and let loose. A feral grin spread across her lips as she saw her aim hold true; one of the mounted enemy cried out and clutched uselessly at the shaft embedded in his lung. The surviving scouts shot arrows of their own, and for a moment, Bahira thought perhaps they might overcome their enemy yet.

Another clap of strange thunder dismissed this hope, however. Bahira's eyes squeezed shut at the sound, fully expecting to feel the punch of whatever magic these men were using, expecting agony and blood and final darkness. But miraculously, she remained untouched by the deadly hand of the thunder. In the confusion of shouts and screams all around her, Bahira saw more of her party fall and realized the fight was as good as lost. They could never hope to defeat this ambush. And if none survived, the Scion would remain ignorant of the enormity of this threat.

Retreat, then, was the only option.

Glancing about quickly, expecting at any moment to hear that thunder again, Bahira searched for an escape. Running back into the dunes was useless; she had seen at how great a range the thunder could kill. Scowling, her eyes glinting like chips of steel in the moonlight, Bahira considered a moment, then charged straight toward the edge of the enemy line. Her only chance was to break through and hope she could lose any pursuit in the rocks that lay beyond the sand.

Charging at a gallop toward the man, screaming the war cry that had struck fear into the hearts of bandits for over a hundred years, Bahira saw the man fumbling with the weapon he held. A sudden realization dawned on her: he was trying to reload, just as she would have done with her bow. She grinned and pulled another arrow from the quiver at her back. Nocking it, she sighted carefully, letting herself fall into the rhythm of her horse's gait. As she drew closer, she saw panic in the man's eyes and loosed the arrow. It buried itself soundlessly in his throat, and he struggled to pull it free even as he toppled from his camel.

Bahira, never slowing her stead's galloping stride, flipped her bow over her shoulder and slipped her right foot from the stirrup. Bracing her thigh muscles, she leaned over precariously in the saddle, feeling the subtle shift as her horse recognized what she was doing and tensed to adjust to the redistribution of her weight. Eyes locked on the strange metal staff the man clutched in his hand, Bahira held herself almost parallel to the ground in a maneuver that foreigners from the east and west had marveled over for years. With her left hand hanging limp, seemingly relaxed, Bahira grabbed up the weapon from the ground as she passed at a full gallop, then swung herself back up into the saddle with a grunt of effort.

Sudden thunder boomed from behind her, and her horse whinnied and bolted. Bahira chanced a quick look back, her heart aching when she saw the rest of her scouts being butchered. She also noticed blood on the rump of her horse, and realized he'd been hit. Offering a calming pat, she twisted in the saddle to examine the wound. It was deep, had torn through muscle, but she judged that the injury would not lame her horse for some time. She said a silent prayer of thanks to the Goddess. The nearest tribe allied with El'Kasari was some distance away, and Bahira knew she would never make it on foot.

Slowing her steed to a canter, confident she could lose any pursuit in the rocks, Bahira scowled darkly at the weapon clutched in her hand. She would see that her fellows did not die for nothing. Falak and the Scion needed to know what power Shakir had somehow discovered. Then, she could begin the task of avenging her fallen comrades.

# Chapter 13

THE NEXT DAY WAS HOT. Of course, most every day in the Jaharri desert was hot, but today the heat lingered long into the afternoon, forcing the pleasure-servants to remain indoors where the marble walls deflected most of the sun's rays. Even when the shadows lengthened into evening, the temperature outside in the seraglio was such that many chose to sleep through until full dark.

Since coming here, Dae had found herself adjusting well to the desert climate. She still tried to stay out of direct sunlight since her pale skin burned easily, but she was now quite comfortable living with temperatures that were unheard of in her homeland, even during the summer months. But when she stepped outside today, the heat was like a physical wall, and she winced as sweat beaded instantly on her forehead.

"Gods above!" Even breathing seemed difficult in the heavy air. Dae looked about the seraglio, expecting to see every plant and blade of grass withered to dust beneath the glare of the sun's irate gaze. But the garden was still impossibly green and lush, and there were even a few other girls about, mostly lounging in the shade of the taller trees or splashing about in the pool beneath the waterfall. For a moment Dae wondered whether she should just go back to her room and wait for nightfall, but after being inside all day, she wanted to stretch her legs a bit. Plus, she recalled that Zafirah had offered to pose for her tonight, and she wanted to be here when the Scion arrived.

The thought of being alone with Zafirah caused an instant jolt of eager anticipation to shoot through her lower body. Last night, Dae knew she had crossed a line. She had accepted that she was attracted to the Scion and had gone so far as to admit her feelings in a physical way. The kiss she had shared with Zafirah had been exciting and carnal, and Dae had lain awake late into the night, remembering every detail of how it had felt to have her tongue in the older woman's mouth. The memories had guided her hands and fingers across her body until she was quaking under the fury of climax for the second time that day. The thoughts and fantasies of what might happen when she eventually gave herself to the Scion were as frightening as they were thrilling. Dae was acutely aware of the delayed anticipation slowly building within her, as it had surely been building since she'd first come to El'Kasari.

"Dae!"

A voice calling her name broke Dae from her licentious ponderings, and she glanced over to the pool where Nasheta and a few other girls were splashing about in the cooler waters. The blonde pleasure-servant waved her over. "Come join us, little one. The water is wonderful!"

Dae hesitated but wandered over after a moment. Sitting on one of the boulders that broke the water's edge, she eyed the pool uncertainly. "I'd rather just stay up here." Dae had only been in the pool once; after realizing how the water made her clothing transparent—and realizing further how appreciative the other girls were of that fact—she made a point of staying on dry land.

Nasheta pouted up at her. "Please?" she begged, batting wet eyelashes persuasively and managing to look quite forlorn at Dae's rejection. "The sun is too hot for any comfort. Surely you would rather be cool in here with us than remain in the scalding air." Her hands caressed the surface of the water. "We promise to play nice…"

Dae detected a distinctly mischievous edge in Nasheta's tone and recognized that the older girl was trying to draw her into a flirtation. Sea-green eyes almost the same shade as her own emerald ones skipped down her figure for half a second, and Dae felt her body respond helplessly to the attention. She wrestled a moment with her modesty, and with the new pleasures she had been experiencing recently adding strength to her internal debate, she actually managed to win quite easily. After all, it *was* hot, and the cool water *did* look rather inviting.

"Well…" Dae gave the matter consideration, then she smiled. "I guess it couldn't hurt."

Nasheta clapped her hands and squealed in delight. "Excellent!"

Dae dipped her hand in the pool, testing the temperature of the water. It was rather pleasant: not too cold, and much nicer than the stifling air. Standing up, she took a deep breath before jumping into the pool with a big splash. She stayed underwater for a moment, shaking her head to get her hair wet as she sorted through the folds of her outfit, then she found her feet once more and stood up. Her head broke the surface. The water lapped just above her breasts, and she grinned at the other girls.

"This is nice."

Nasheta giggled and splashed her playfully. Of all the pleasure-servants, she was without question the most aquatic loving of them all, spending almost all her waking hours either in the water or sunning herself beside it. "You should join us more often. I believe no treasure in the seraglio can compare to the decadence of this pool. Come, it is even better under the fall."

The two swam over to the waterfall, Dae looking up at the cascade with interest. The water was far shallower here, leaving most of her upper body exposed. From this angle, the spray cast the last rays of the sun into iridescent rainbow arcs, and Dae laughed delightedly. "I bet this is the only place in the whole desert where you can see a proper rainbow."

When she looked back at Nasheta, Dae saw that the other girl appeared far more interested in appreciating the way her minimal clothing now clung to her every curve in transparent folds than she was in admiring the rainbow. When she caught her staring, however, Nasheta dutifully turned her attention to the fall with a tempting grin. "Such things are common in your land then?"

"Oh yes. Sometimes when there's a fine rain, you can see giant ones that stretch across whole fields. My handmaidens used to tell me that if I ever found the foot of a rainbow, there'd be a pot of gold waiting there for me."

Nasheta grinned and immediately dove toward the colorful arc. Dae laughed at her antics as she pretended to look confused when the rainbow eluded her efforts to catch it. "I must have run after a hundred of these things as a child," she remembered. "I never stopped trying to catch up to them when they disappeared."

"I think it is a wonderful dream," Nasheta sighed, leaving off her chase. "In the desert, children are taught never to follow such mirages. It is dangerous to believe in their reality." Finding a smooth rock shelf to the side of the fall, she pulled her lithe body from the water and sat on the slick seat. "I was born in the west," she explained as Dae joined her. "My village was attacked when I was a little girl, and the bandits carried me across the seas to the far north. I cannot recall much about my homeland, but I sometimes wish I could see it again, see lands that are fat with water and green life."

Dae listened, curious. It hadn't really occurred to her that Nasheta must have been born outside the Jaharri, though with her blonde hair and pale skin it seemed obvious now. "How did you come to be living here?" she asked, shifting closer so she could hear better over the noise of the waterfall. "You have a desert accent."

"And I speak their language fluently," Nasheta added. "The men who took me traded me to the desert people as soon as I grew old enough to be appealing as a body-slave. Pale hair and green eyes are qualities highly prized among the Jaharri nomads. I lived in the deep desert for a year or so before Zafirah saw me. She purchased me for a king's ransom, and I have been happily in her service for some years now." Nasheta paused and gave Dae a probing look. "I think you are very lucky to have been rescued so quickly from your fate at the hands of those slavers," she said. "I have seen the slave markets in the western empire with my own eyes, and they are home to great cruelty and despair. I doubt whoever purchased you would have possessed the same sense of honor as the Scion."

"You're right," Dae said, not wanting to imagine what might have happened to her had her abductors been given a little more time. "I try not to think about it too much."

"As well you should not. Why dwell on such negative thoughts? You live in a beautiful palace, accorded every respect and granted every luxury you could wish for. And," she added with a wink, "you have captured the heart of a very beautiful, very passionate woman, who would lavish much pleasure upon your body if given permission to do so."

Dae looked away, though her smile remained. "I wouldn't say it was her heart that seems most interested in me," she protested shyly.

"Oh?" Nasheta gave her a look filled with secret knowledge. "If you truly believed only lust motivated Zafirah's attentions, would you have kissed her so ardently last night?"

Dae's silence was answer enough.

"I thought not. You may believe me when I say Zafirah feels much love for you, little one. I have experienced at least a taste of her passion for you, and know better than most how strong her feelings are in this matter."

Dae looked up at Nasheta then, feeling inquisitive but also a little awkward. After all, Zafirah had used this woman to vent passions which were aimed at her. Nasheta hadn't spoken about her night with the Scion, but Dae felt again that stab of wonder lance through her, and the thought that she had tried to keep silent for so long now crept back into her mind: the thought that Nasheta knew exactly what Zafirah wanted to do to her and that she might be willing to share that information. She moved closer to the other blonde, uncertain how to broach such a delicate subject. Finding a half-submerged seat in the pool, Dae puzzled on the matter silently for a moment while Nasheta watched her with an amused smile. Just as she was about to abandon the subject for lack of courage, Nasheta's laughter broke the tension and she splashed Dae playfully with her fingers.

"Forgive my mirth, little one, but your expression is too adorable to describe." Nasheta grinned. "You have the look of a woman dying to share in a secret she is not yet privy to. If you wish to discuss what the Scion did to me that night, you need not tear yourself apart searching for your tongue. Just ask me. I am most willing to entertain your curiosity."

Dae hastily looked away, embarrassed her thoughts were so obvious. "I-I wasn't...I mean, that wasn't what I was...I couldn't—"

Nasheta held up her hand. "You are curious, Dae, and after last night, it is no longer a secret that you feel desire for Zafirah."

"Well, I don't—"

Nasheta immediately cut off her instinctive protest. "Can you look me in the eye and deny that it is no longer a question of 'if' you will warm the Scion's bed, but rather, 'when'?"

The cool water wasn't enough to stop the blood rushing to Dae's face…and other, lower, parts of her body. "I-I guess, maybe."

"You wish to know what she did to me? What things she would do to you when the time comes?"

Dae nodded. "I saw the scratches."

Nasheta grinned. "And the bite marks?"

Dae nodded again. "And your clothes were all…torn…"

"Zafirah was gripped by a deep arousal," Nasheta said. "She needed to vent her lust completely. Do not be afraid; I did not mind the little pain, and I am certain she would be gentler with you than she was with me."

"So…" Dae hesitated. "You liked what she did?"

"Of course. She seemed determined that I should feel as much pleasure as my body could stand, and perhaps more. Such generosity and desire to please are excellent qualities in a lover. Although," Nasheta pouted, "she barely allowed me to touch her at all, so intent was her focus on my absolute satisfaction."

"What did she do to you?" Dae's eyes were as wide as those of a child who waits impatiently for a story to be told.

Nasheta leaned forward. "She kissed me. Everywhere. Long and deep." She spoke softly, her tone smoky and seductive. "And she touched me. At first she was almost frenzied with desire, and I think in her delirium she was caught up completely in her fantasy of ravishing you. But after a time, she calmed somewhat and became more thorough in her ministrations." Nasheta sighed theatrically. "I fear my memory of exact details is a little unreliable; my body and mind were overwhelmed with sensation. The pleasure was quite extraordinary, and I am certain I passed out a few times during the night."

Dae remembered the state Nasheta had been in when the guards returned her to the seraglio, and the way she had looked during the days after. "You seemed…in pain…when they brought you back."

"I was sore," Nasheta admitted. "Particular—highly sensitive—areas of my body had received more attention than they are accustomed to. Even pleasure-servants have their limits. But a little tenderness and a few days rest are small prices to pay for the gift of such intense bliss as I experienced." Nasheta paused and studied Dae's face seriously, gauging her reaction. "I have lain with Zafirah many times, child," she said after a moment. "I know her well and consider her a friend as well as a lover. Believe me when I tell you that she loves you."

Dae looked away, uncomfortable. "How can you tell?"

"Because I have seen her naked and exposed during a moment of intimacy that she wished to share with you. I heard the emotion in her voice and I felt it in her touch. Had you been in my place—in the place you were meant to be—you would have no doubts as to the depth of her affection for you."

"But..." Dae frowned, unable to accept Nasheta's insistence. "Why would she love me? She's like a queen. She could have anyone she wants."

"And she wants you." Nasheta shook her head and grinned, obviously amused by Dae's continued resistance. "Is it really so difficult to understand? People fall in love all the time, and you are as deserving of such attention as any other. You are beautiful, kindhearted, and warm natured. Zafirah may be a ruler, but that does not make her any less a human being. Her heart is not as armored to the arrows of love as she might have believed it to be."

"But she still beds with others," Dae countered. "Even last night, she didn't sleep alone."

Nasheta shrugged, obviously not considering this fact relevant to her argument. "Would you wish for her to stop?" she asked seriously. "For her to give up pleasure?"

Dae shrugged. "I-I don't know. In my land—"

"You are no longer in your land, little one. Is it fair for you to set boundaries and borders on her love?"

"Well, she'd probably expect me to be...faithful...to her..." Dae trailed off as Nasheta shook her head.

"Do you honestly believe Zafirah would be angered if you shared pleasure with another? If so, than you still have much to learn of her."

Dae paused to consider this. She remembered her conversation with the Scion regarding love and realized Nasheta was right. Zafirah didn't expect fidelity or monogamy from any lover. She believed pleasure was too pure a thing to be bound by rules.

Nasheta smiled and gave a little nod as understanding dawned in Dae's eyes. "I think you will find that if you promised her your heart, Zafirah would be more than satisfied. Perhaps, like Johara and Hayam, she would want to include others in her pleasure-taking, but jealousy is something completely foreign to her nature." Nasheta slipped closer to Dae and ran a single finger along her left shoulder blade, flashing her a toothy smile when she turned in surprise at the lingering touch. Sea-green eyes darkened, and Nasheta's voice grew huskier. "She would want you to be free to explore *all* pleasures that present themselves."

"Umm." Dae became suddenly aware of her companion's proximity and intentions. Nasheta's eyes roamed over her chest, and Dae froze, completely uncertain as to what she should do. She started to fold her arms across her breasts but was stopped by a voice in her head—a voice she'd never heard before, but which spoke with a confident and commanding sense of authority. *Let her look*, the voice suggested calmly. *She likes your body. What harm is there in letting her see you? She'll probably think of you tonight when she's alone, and the memory will excite her. Perhaps she'll touch herself while thinking of you...or seek pleasure in the arms of another.*

Dae's hands remained at her sides, but her eyes were still wide.

Nasheta shifted closer still, settling the full length of her thigh against Dae's frozen body and leaning into her lightly. When Dae made no move to cover herself, she seemed to accept this as an invitation to let her eyes linger where they would. "Mm...so many delectations yet to be sampled," she whispered, almost purring. "So much flesh untasted by lips that would lavish such attentions upon you as cannot be imagined." The tip of a pink tongue darted out to lick her lips and Dae shivered as the sight stirred the memory of Johara and Hayam's demonstration of oral pleasures. "Your nipples grow hard, little one, and I doubt they are affected by the cool of the water. Perhaps you find the thought of my mouth pressed against your flesh appealing...?"

Dae's breathing had grown shallow. Her pupils dilated and she felt telltale heat flood through her loins. Under Nasheta's ravening gaze, she felt positively naked. In her peripheral vision she was conscious that the other girls in the pool had paused their playful splashing to watch them, doubtless curious to see if she would succumb to Nasheta's seduction. Dae had withstood every such proposition previously made... but it wasn't so easy now that she had gained a greater insight into the pleasures being offered.

Nasheta ran her right hand up the length of her own body, smiling when Dae's eyes obediently followed its path from her hip, along her flat, exposed stomach all the way to her cleavage and around the swell of her breasts. "I could teach you many things that would be of great use when you decide you are ready to be with Zafirah," she coaxed, heat rising between them where their bodies were pressed together. "I could show you pleasure without even risking your virtue." Nasheta stared longingly at Dae's breasts. "Shall we make a game of it? See if I can make you come just from suckling your breasts...?"

"No!" Dae dragged herself out of an erotic daze, stopping Nasheta just as her lips were about to descend. "Um...th-thank you, but...I don't think I'm quite ready for that. It's a lovely offer, really, but I just...I can't—"

Nasheta halted, eyes still hooded, before backing off a little. "You are afraid to feel pleasure?"

"No, it's not that, I just..." Dae trailed off, unable to find the words to explain her continued resistance. She knew that if Nasheta's lips had touched her aching flesh, all would have been lost. She would have allowed the other woman to do whatever she pleased, to take her right here beneath the waterfall, in full view of the other girls. As it was, her blood was still roaring through her veins in a tide of lust; when she went to bed later, Dae knew she would have to satisfy the ache between her legs with her own fingers.

"I can see the desire is in you," Nasheta said, her expression honestly puzzled. "Why do you fight against it? Because of Zafirah? She would be pleased to know that you are exploring the pleasures of the flesh."

"It's not Zafirah, it's me," Dae said. "I just..." She shrugged helplessly.

Nasheta nodded, and some of the fire faded from her eyes as she withdrew a fraction further. "I understand. You do not feel ready." Nasheta laid a hand gently on her upper thigh, and though she recognized the touch was more reassuring than seductive, Dae was also acutely aware of how enjoyable the physical contact felt...and how much more enjoyable it could still be. Nasheta's sea-green eyes held her gaze steadily. "May I offer some advice?"

"If you'd like."

"Listen to your body, Dae. Heed its call, for it reveals the truth of your desires, and can guide you more reliably than your intellect in matters of the flesh." Nasheta's eyes ran hungrily over every exposed inch of her, and Dae could tell she would have loved nothing more than to let her idle hand caress the same path. "You do not yet realize the power you hold, little one...but you will."

"Power?"

"The power of innocent beauty, a body that men and women would do anything to possess. It is a gift—a powerful gift—you should not shy away from using." She squeezed gently with her fingers before withdrawing.

Dae smiled, still confused, but she arched an eyebrow in amusement at Nasheta's hand. "That was just an excuse to touch some skin, wasn't it?"

"Well." Nasheta gave her a playful wink. "Perhaps a little. But think about what I said, okay?"

"I will."

"Good." Nasheta clapped her hands, her whole demeanor changing in an instant from intriguingly seductive to childishly playful. "Come! Let us dive from the top of the fall." She began climbing the rocky cascade, finding easy handholds all the way.

Shivering despite the hot air, having just a little trouble dispelling the interesting tingling sensations that still raced over her skin, Dae hesitated only a moment before she followed.

Zafirah was striding purposefully toward the harem grounds when Falak caught up to her. The scout hesitated when she saw the expression of anticipation on the Scion's face, reluctant to spoil Zafirah's good mood after her recent tensions. But her mission was too important to wait.

"My Scion?"

Zafirah glanced at her, smiling, but didn't slow down. "Yes, Falak?"

"I have received urgent news; your attention is required."

"Not tonight, my friend. I have a prior commitment to Dae. Your news can wait until the morning—"

"With all respect, my Scion"—Falak bowed slightly as she walked—"it cannot wait. Indeed, events have grown more dire than we thought. Every moment now is precious."

Hearing the note of unease in Falak's tone, Zafirah stopped and turned her full attention to the scout. She read the grim expression on the dark-skinned woman's face, and reluctantly put thoughts of Dae aside. "You have received word from the scouts watching Shakir?"

Falak nodded. "Though not from the scouts themselves, Scion." She paused, then stated simply, "They were ambushed and slaughtered in the night; only one survived."

"Ambushed?" Zafirah's jaw dropped in surprise. Her scouts were fierce and stealthy warriors; their skills were legendary. "How? Was it Shakir?"

"It appears the Calif was behind the attack, yes."

"But—"

"The scout who survived wandered into the camp of the Herak. Her horse had fallen from wounds sustained in her escape, but she carried one of the weapons retrieved from the enemy. The Herak sent a swift-rider immediately to bring us news of her safety. He told me the device is unlike anything we have ever seen. It killed from a great distance and with tremendous accuracy."

"Where is the surviving scout now?" Zafirah asked.

"She is still being cared for by the Herak." Zafirah processed the information quickly, her agile mind working through to the inevitable, obvious conclusion. Still, Falak finished her train of thought before she could give it voice. "We must leave at once."

Zafirah considered a moment longer, wishing there was another way. But this news meant Shakir posed a greater threat than anticipated, and she needed to move fast before he attacked her people. No matter how enticing the prospect of a night alone with Dae might have been, Zafirah knew the lives under her protection came first. "Have Simhana saddled and an escort drawn from the barracks," she ordered quickly, her attitude shifting to that of a commander. "If we ride hard through the night and into the morning, we can reach the Herak before the sun forces us to stop." It would mean a brutal pace; the Herak lived near the deep-desert far to the south. "What of the swift-rider who brought us this news?"

"He is resting. His horse is near exhaustion but should recover with proper care."

Zafirah nodded, satisfied. "Make certain he does not leave El'Kasari before he is fully recovered. Draw provisions from the stores and equip another scouting party. Once we have learned more of this threat, I may need eyes in the deep desert once more."

Falak saluted smartly. "At once, Scion. We will be ready to leave before sundown."

"Excellent." The scout turned to leave. "Falak?"

"Yes, Scion?"

Zafirah's hard expression softened. "The survivor? Was it...?"

Falak smiled very slightly and nodded. "Bahira."

"I am pleased for you," Zafirah said. "I have seen how close the two of you have become."

"Thank you." Falak's eyes dropped. "In truth, I cannot help but feel ashamed of my relief. Ashamed that I am glad others died instead of her."

Zafirah offered her scout a comforting touch on the arm. Though she and Falak had shared pleasure with one another, she knew the bond her chief scout shared with Bahira ran deeper than the flesh. "Do not let such clouds darken the gift of her survival. It would anger the Goddess to see her mercy so ill-received."

Falak blinked back the moisture in her eyes and waved her hand at Zafirah. "Go. I suspect there is a young woman who will be greatly disappointed to hear she will not be enjoying your company this night. The least you can do is offer a proper apology."

"I will join you at the stables when I am done."

"Take whatever time you need. I will see to our escort."

The Scion nodded her thanks, then continued on to the harem grounds, the spring in her steps now noticeably subdued.

Entering the seraglio, Zafirah couldn't help but smile when she saw Dae lying on her back on a rock beside the waterfall, sunning herself. She had obviously been swimming recently; her clothes and hair were soaked. The brief outfit she wore was plastered to her body, almost transparent with moisture. Zafirah swallowed when Dae saw her and propped herself up on her elbows with a grin; she just knew the image of that lithe, ripe body was going to haunt her at every opportunity during the coming days.

*Damn you, Shakir,* she cursed silently. *You have no idea what your pathetic little rebellion is costing me!*

"*Ahlan,*" Dae greeted properly as Zafirah approached, demonstrating her recent efforts to learn the Jaharri language. "Was it unusually hot today, or should I adjust my scale again?"

"No, it…it was quite a hot day." *Just keep your eyes from wandering lower and perhaps you will escape the harem without ravishing her in front of everyone.* But the temptation to take advantage of this rare opportunity proved too great for the Scion to resist. Her eyes flicked rapidly down to take in the beauty of Dae's breasts through the sheer silk fabric. She could make out the outline of her areolas through the gauzy cloth, her nipples prominent, and almost moaned aloud at the sight. When she returned her eyes back to Dae's face, Zafirah could tell immediately her response had not been missed. Dae raised one eyebrow coyly but made no move to cover herself; she was clearly in a teasing mood. "So…what did you have in mind for us tonight?"

"Huh?" Zafirah struggled to keep her composure.

"Tonight? Remember, you offered to pose for me. Or have you forgotten the invitation so quickly?" The playful tone in Dae's voice complimented her flirtations well; it seemed she was learning quickly from the example of the other pleasure-servants.

"No, I was just…" Zafirah's gaze slipped helplessly back to the glory of Dae's body. For a moment, she forgot completely about Falak and the threat of Shakir, all thoughts driven far from her mind by the image before her—an image she had longed to behold for many months now. When she managed to tear her eyes away and focus once more on Dae's face, Zafirah saw the wicked glint in the young girl's emerald eyes and realized the whole display—from the moment she walked in—had been far from accidental. She guessed Dae had been lying in wait for her, setting a scene guaranteed to tempt her…and it was obvious she was enjoying the effect her display was having. Zafirah grit her teeth and asked for strength from the Goddess. *Why did this have to happen tonight of all nights?*

"You were just...what?"

Zafirah sighed and claimed the spot next to Dae, making certain her eyes didn't wander anywhere near the captivating blonde. "This is not fair," she said after a moment spent collecting her scattered thoughts.

"What's not fair?"

"There has been trouble among the southern tribes," Zafirah explained. "Warriors of the renegade nomads have banded together and attacked a party of my scouts. I must leave tonight so as to evaluate the threat they pose."

"Oh." Dae's playful expression vanished immediately, replaced by one of concern. "Are you... I mean, will you be okay? Will it be very dangerous?"

Dae's concern brought a warm feeling to Zafirah's heart. "The risk should not be great," she assured her quickly. "I will have a strong escort and have no intention of riding to battle before I understand my enemy. But I fear I must delay our appointment until I return."

"How long will it take?"

"I cannot know for certain, but I should not think more than a few days. We shall be riding to the camp of the Herak to talk with the scout who survived the attack; it will afford me an opportunity to visit with my mother. The ride out there will be fast and hard." The Scion gave her companion a wry smile. "Believe me when I say I would much prefer to entertain your company tonight than that of my horse, but—"

Dae held up hand. "No, that's okay. I understand. You have to take care of your people."

"I hope you are not offended."

"Why would I be offended?" Dae reached out and with only a slight moment of hesitation, shyly laid her hand on Zafirah's shoulder. Even this innocent contact seemed a promise of things to come, and the expression in Dae's eyes was reassuring. "We can spend some time together when you get back. I'm not going anywhere."

Zafirah accepted the contact hungrily. She would have liked to return the familiar touch but knew if her hands were given such leniency, they would most certainly misbehave. She glanced quickly at Dae's nearly naked body, then back to the garden. "I begin to feel as though I am cursed by Inshal," she remarked with a half-smile. "The thing I most desire in the entire world is dangled before my eyes, but each time I think it is within my grasp, something rises to snatch it away."

"Oh?" Dae leaned a little closer to her, batting her pale eyelashes coyly. "I thought you were doing pretty well, all things considered. Especially after last night." She looked down at her wet clothes and giggled. "I mean, I'm sitting here in see-through clothes just to give you something to look forward to. I think that should be evidence enough that your seduction is coming along quite nicely."

"You shall drive me to madness with such teasing, little Tahirah." Zafirah caught the younger woman's hand in her own and brought it to her lips, placing a delicate kiss on the palm. "I shall return as soon and as swiftly as I am able."

Dae tilted her head girlishly. "Promise?"

"Of course. I would never keep a beautiful woman waiting for pleasure."

"Psh!" Dae waved a hand playfully. "Best you be on your way, then. The sooner you leave, the sooner you'll be able to get back."

Zafirah reluctantly stood. Her sapphire eyes were soft and filled with deep affection as she gazed at Dae. "*Maasalama, aziza,*" she whispered. "I shall miss you every moment we are parted." Then, the Scion turned and walked from the seraglio quickly, before she decided to put her personal needs before the welfare of her people.

Dae watched Zafirah leave, her eyes wide with surprise at those parting words. She remembered the word *aziza*, having heard it from the lips of Johara and Hayam often enough during her time in the harem. But she had never expected to hear it from Zafirah, a woman who professed passion and lust, but never true love. A slow, sweet burning sensation clutched at her heart, and she felt unexpected tears prick at the corners of her eyes as she realized Nasheta had perhaps been correct.

Zafirah had called her "beloved."

"You allowed her to escape?"

The soldier paled at the cold, lethal edge in the voice asking the question. His fingers plucked nervously at the reins of the tall *mehari* standing behind him, and his throat constricted with visible fear. "W-we could not—I mean, sh-she was too fast for us. They charged straight into our line; there was nothing we could do to st—"

A single raised hand silenced the man. Shakir Al'Jadin regarded the others standing before him with an uncaring, malevolent stare. "A single scouting party, and you managed to lose five men in the battle." An ominous pause. "And one weapon." The Calif didn't care much about the loss of his men; what stirred his rage was the loss of the thunder-bow. Several dozen eyes hastily looked away, unable to meet the terrible scorn that was etched in every line of his face.

One of the braver members of the party spoke up. "*Effendi*, it is true one of the scouts escaped, but her horse was wounded. I myself fired into the beast, and my aim was true. El'Kasari is far from here; she will surely perish in the desert without her steed."

Shakir considered this, then scowled and shook his head. "And what if she is able to make it as far as the camp of the Herak? They will take her in and report at once to the Scion. Our greatest advantage right now is the element of surprise. The Whore knows nothing of the thunder-bows and so will be unprepared to counter them. And what have you done?" Shakir's face was dark with rage. "YOU HAVE GIVEN HER ONE OF THE WEAPONS!"

The soldiers flinched at the verbal lashing, but they all remained silent, knowing their words would only further enrage the Calif.

"No wonder El'Kasari has stood for so long, with fools and idiots like yourselves attacking it. We have been offered a chance to strike back at the people who have kept us cowed for so long, and your incompetence is bringing us to ruin!"

The first soldier stared straight ahead, his back stiff. "I apologize for allowing the scout to escape," he said.

Shakir regarded the man coldly, then, without a word, he drew a scimitar from the scabbard at his back and slashed out with the speed of a striking asp. The soldier's head fell to the sands; a few seconds later, his body joined it, and the camel he had been leading shied away the moment he dropped its reins. Shakir glanced at the body contemptuously. "Apology accepted."

His cold eyes shot to the other soldiers, who were staring at him in uncertain terror. "The rest of you take note: when I issue the order

'No survivors,' I mean precisely that. Let us have no more mishaps like this one, or I shall save the Scion the trouble of killing you by doing it myself." So saying, Shakir mounted his own lean warhorse and rode back to where the remainder of his army were waiting.

The loss wasn't critical, Shakir knew, but any failing at this point in his plans was utterly unacceptable to the ambitious young Calif. There had been no word from the trader who had promised to bring him more of the marvelous weapons from the western empire, and Shakir was beginning to realize he had erred in granting the foolish outlander his life. At the time, it had seemed an agreeable bargain, one that offered him his greatest opportunity to rise above the common dregs and pursue a meaningful conquest, but now...now he felt the threads of his plan fraying. Red-hot rage clouded the edges of his vision, and Shakir tried to steady his breathing.

All was not lost, he reminded himself. Perhaps his strategy would need some adjustment, but one did not survive in the deep desert long without learning the merits of improvisation. Shakir forced his lips into a thin smile as he approached the higher-ranked men in his army, not wanting any of them—Brak in particular—to sense anything amiss. It was only one weapon, after all. How much of an advantage could it really give the Scion?

# Chapter 14

THE DEEP FROWN ON ZAFIRAH'S face was hidden by the folds of her *haik*, but those around the Scion had no trouble reading her mood. She stood in the yurt of Jestart, leader of the Herak tribe, studying the object lying on the ground at her feet.

They had arrived nearer to midday than Zafirah might have liked, only pushing on through the rising heat because no shelter could be found on the stark sands. Once they reached the camp of the Herak, the retinue of fifty riders had seen immediately to their weary horses and made the proper, traditional exchange of greetings with their hosts, and then Zafirah was shown to the tent where Bahira lay, recovering from exposure and exhaustion. The scout offered her report to the Scion and Falak, concisely retelling the events of the ambush and how she had escaped when the other members of her party had fallen. Zafirah listened without interrupting, and when Bahira finished, she commended her for her efforts. Now, darkness was falling, and Zafirah joined Jestart in his yurt where she could see with her own eyes the instrument of death which had slain her scouts so effectively.

The weapon was long and slender, comprised of wood and steel. The renegade nomads had decorated it with the strings of beads and feathers typically favored among Jaharri tribes, but its overall design and workmanship were unmistakably foreign. Zafirah studied it in silence, puzzled by its seemingly benign appearance but respectful of the air of power it projected. When she reached out a hand to touch it, Jestart drew in a sharp breath.

"Be careful, Scion," he cautioned. "We are uncertain of how this device works exactly."

Zafirah nodded, but picked the weapon up anyway. It was heavy, and she hefted it cautiously.

"Bahira said she believed it worked much like a bow," she mused aloud. "It fires some kind of thunder that strikes the target dead from any range." The steel pipe that comprised most of the weapon's length seemed to gleam an ugly, menacing gray in the light of the *shamedan*. Zafirah drew back her *haik* with one hand and sniffed curiously; the weapon stank of sulfur and hellfire. "How did Shakir come by such a weapon?"

"More importantly," Falak said, "how many more of these does he have?"

"Bahira estimates his main camp comprises more than a hundred men, judging by the supplies he was receiving from the other tribes of his alliance. We must ensure he does not add to that number, or the threat he poses will become far greater." Zafirah puzzled with the weapon a few moments, then pulled the wooden part of it back to her shoulder. With her hands supporting its length, she lifted it to eye level, grunting when she saw how it was sighted. "If we learn how it works," she said, "we may be able to learn how to defeat it. Jestart?"

"Yes, Scion?"

"Have this weapon shown about the camp. It seems harmless now, but if any of your people can deduce its method we may stand a better chance against Shakir when he moves."

"As you wish, Scion."

Zafirah regarded the elder leader fondly. Jestart had led his tribe since the days of her father's rule, and Zafirah could not have held more respect and admiration for the man had they shared the same blood. She knew he would not appreciate her next order. "I regret that I must also request you move the camp closer to El'Kasari. I know this is not something you wish to do, but I will not allow you and your people to be slaughtered when the Calif of the Deharn attacks."

As expected, Jestart scowled, but at length he gave a slight bow of acceptance. "If you command it, Scion, it will be done."

"Thank you." Zafirah carefully placed the strange weapon back on the tent floor. "With your permission, my *spahi* and I shall remain here until Bahira is well enough to travel. We will take this devil-weapon with us to El'Kasari so the council may deliberate and study it. Falak, send the scouts we brought out into the southern desert. Do not attempt to draw near Shakir's camp; I only wish to know when he begins his advance."

"As you wish, Scion."

"For now…" Zafirah sighed and stretched, feeling her muscles ache from the hard ride. "There is little more we can do besides get some rest and prepare for tomorrow."

"We have prepared a yurt for you, Scion," Jestart said. "You are welcome to join our fire and even-meal. Your visit has stirred up much excitement among my people; I know many will be disappointed if they are not given a chance to meet with you."

Zafirah saw the twinkle in the older man's eyes and understood the hidden message in his words. Her skills in the bedroom were as legendary as her beauty, and doubtless many young women of the nomad tribe were eager to test the truth of her talents. "I would be much honored to join your meal but fear I must rest a little first. The ride through the night has taxed me overmuch, and my company will be of little worth until I regain some strength."

"Of course." Jestart bowed. "My people will show you to your yurt then. Join us when you are rested."

"My thanks."

Sometime later, Zafirah was jerked from a light but restorative slumber by the sound of rustling cloth and soft footsteps outside her yurt. She moved as swift and silent as a desert asp, her right hand straying to the hilt of a dagger that lay near her pallet. It had occurred to her that Shakir might risk sending one of his men to assassinate her during this visit. A figure hesitated, silhouetted against the light of the yurt door, then stepped inside. Zafirah relaxed in a heartbeat as soon as she made out the familiar features of her visitor.

"Rashida," she greeted with a slight smile, tossing the knife away. "I wondered when you would come see me."

The woman stepped closer, lighting one of the oil lamps that sat carefully on a small table near the center of the yurt. "'Rashida,' is it? How very formal." Her tone was amused. "You may be Scion now, Zafirah, but you will always be my little girl."

Zafirah sat up, crossing her legs beneath her. "'Mother', then." She opened her arms in invitation and cocked her head to the side. "Have you an embrace for your child?"

"Always." Rashida accepted the hug fondly, ruffling her hair when they parted. "My, it seems you grow taller and more beautiful each time I see you," she remarked with gentle pride, running her eyes over Zafirah. "A pity it takes the call of battle to bring you out here for a visit."

Zafirah looked away, properly shamed. "I know. And you have every right to think me a terrible daughter for not visiting more often, but…"

"But the city is your home, Zafirah, and you are Scion." Rashida smiled a quiet, slightly sad smile. "I understand."

Zafirah was grateful for her mother's acceptance; she knew her appointment as leader of the desert nation had not always been easy on her family. As her eyes adjusted fully to the low light she allowed herself a closer study of her mother. In her youth, Rashida had been a woman of great beauty, and the extra years and hard life she lived had done nothing more than add grace and dignity to her features. She had the same long, midnight-black hair and startling blue eyes as her daughter and was tall and willowy of frame. Zafirah noticed a new depth to the lines that creased the skin about her eyes and lips and a few more strands of gray in the dark tresses than she remembered, but she was pleased her mother still appeared strong and healthy. The Herak were a tough and willful tribe; they seemed almost to enjoy the punishing way the desert treated them, where every day was a challenge to be faced and overcome. It was that strength and pride which had first drawn Zafirah's father to Rashida, and time had done nothing to dilute it. "You look well," she said.

"Thank you." Rashida cupped her daughter's cheek with a callused hand and looked deep into her eyes, reading every emotion behind their crystal veil. "You have changed somewhat. You seem less abrasive than the last time I saw you."

"I was younger then; the extra year has made a considerable difference."

"So I see." Rashida gestured to the door. "I had expected to see you at the dinner. Jestart told me you were resting, which surprised me. I thought by now you would be prowling about the camp, searching for some young maiden to warm you through the night."

Zafirah waggled her eyebrows at her mother's teasing tone. "The night is young."

Rashida laughed lightly, but after a more careful look she shook her head. "Something has indeed changed in you, Zafirah," she said. "Your eyes are not the blazing furnaces they were a year ago. Their heat has taken on a softer quality." There was a long pause, then the older woman smiled. "Tell me about her."

Zafirah groaned. "Who told you?"

"Falak."

"Ah, I might have known. So my chief scout reports to you now, does she?"

"No." Rashida settled herself on a rug beside the coal-burner and assumed a knowing, wise air. "She simply respects that there are certain things a mother deserves to know about her child. So tell me, who is she, this woman who has captured your attention so?"

"I suspect Falak has told you all you could wish to know about her."

"She explained a few things, yes, but I would like to hear about her from your lips, little one."

The Scion considered, then shrugged and sat opposite her mother. "Her name is Dae," she started in a low, almost shy tone. "But I call her Tahirah, and I think she has grown to like it."

"And does she deserve such a name?"

"Oh yes, more so than I might desire. She swore when we met that she would never bed with me and has only recently admitted that her words were spoken in haste. She was captured by slavers in the eastern lands, and I rescued her and took her into the harem. While she has settled in well, it has taken some time for her to accept the ways of the Jaharri."

"She is beautiful?"

"More beautiful than the sparkle of a thousand stars," she whispered sincerely, her expression softening to a look of utter adoration. "Her hair is as golden as a flow of honey, and her eyes shine like wet emeralds. The vision of her in my mind has caused me many sleepless nights, but it has been worth the frustration." Zafirah was quiet under her mother's regard for a time, before she admitted sheepishly, "It is difficult for me, but…I am learning to temper my passions with patience."

"I hope she appreciates that."

Zafirah remembered very clearly the feel of Dae's body in her arms as she had held her the other night. "She is coming to understand such matters better."

"I am impressed. In truth, I had never expected to see this side of you, my daughter. I had never expected such a side existed. You have been a confident seductress since barely past your seventeenth year, when you stoutly claimed you would never give your heart to another completely. Now, it appears that boast has been proven wrong," Rashida said. "You love her?"

Zafirah shrugged and offered a nervous little half-smile. "It is difficult to believe, is it not? But she has made herself a place in my heart, though I am certain she did not intend to. And I cannot help but love her."

"She must be very special," Rashida said. "Perhaps you will bring her to visit me someday? I would very much like to meet the woman who could tame your wandering eye!"

Zafirah laughed. "My eye is as free to wander as it was a year ago, Mother. But my heart has been claimed beyond all doubt."

Rashida considered this, then shook her head. "You always were too easily ruled by your lusts, Zafirah. I hope this girl will not be hurt because of your appetites."

"I have never sought to conceal my nature from her, nor my opinions on the concept of monogamy. She has only ever seen me for who I am, and I hope she will respect me enough not to want to change me to better suit her own ideals."

"Mm." Rashida's lips thinned into a slightly disapproving line. "I will not argue the matter beyond a reminder that I have only ever loved one man in my life—your father—and I can assure you that such fidelity is not without its rewards. And even though he is dead, in my heart I shall remain ever true to him. But I know better than to debate this issue with his strong-willed daughter; it is an argument neither of us can win." After a pause, Rashida changed the subject. "Are you hungry? There is food and music to be found near the fire. You can tell me more about this young woman while we eat."

"Certainly. It was a long ride out here, and we only paused to eat when necessity demanded it." Standing, Zafirah offered her mother a hand. Rashida accepted, letting her daughter help her up, then they headed off together toward the sound of laughter and drums in comfortable, familiar silence.

In the yurt where Bahira lay recovering, the boisterous sounds of laughter and music were faint, muffled, and distant. Sitting beside the simple pallet where her lover rested, Falak felt a sense of relief at being separated from the revelry inspired by their visit to the isolated nomad encampment. In the low light of a single lamp she watched over Bahira, assessing the damage as she shivered feverishly and tossed about in her sleep. Bahira had been forced to walk many miles through the rising dawn heat after her horse collapsed from her injury, and Falak could guess her solitary journey had been one of pure heartache and sorrow. Worse than the dehydration was the grief she clearly felt for her fallen brothers and sisters and guilt over her inability to save them.

"Shakir will pay dearly for this," Falak whispered softly, seeing Bahira stir at her words. "I swear it."

Bahira regarded her lover and leader with a look of pain. "No price we might extract will return the fallen."

Falak heard the anguish in her voice and instantly sought to ease it, taking her lover's hand in her own and bringing it to her lips. She also felt the loss of her scouts keenly—she had personally recruited every member of the party, after all, and overseen most of their training—but the slaughter had clearly struck Bahira a deeper wound. This had been her first command, and it had ended in unprecedented tragedy. "This was not your fault, my love," Falak whispered fiercely, unable to bear the sight of tears in the younger woman's eyes. "There will always be losses in any battle; you did your duty under circumstances none of us could have anticipated. I could not ask for more from any soldier."

"Do not commend my actions," Bahira pleaded, the tears she had held back falling now in the face of Falak's compassion. "They are dead while I live on. Nasir was as a brother to me...and now he is gone, denied even the honor of a proper burial."

"They will be honored in the memory of those they left behind," Falak said. "And their loss shall be avenged when Shakir's army is destroyed."

"You will ride with the Scion when she faces him?"

Falak heard a new emotion surface in those words—fear. She would have sought to ease it had the responsibility of her position allowed it, but she could only nod. "We all must do our duty to defend the Peace."

"But these weapons…they are too powerful!" Bahira struggled to sit up on the pallet; she was clearly weak from her ordeal, but terror gave her strength. "You do not understand. You did not see the devastation they caused! We could not even strike back against Shakir's men…and if his army grows, you will be slaughtered—"

"A strategy is still being formulated," Falak interrupted. "The Scion will not risk the lives of her people in reckless battle, but neither will she allow the Calif of the Deharn to threaten the tribes of this alliance. Now lay back. You need your rest."

Bahira lay back at Falak's gentle insistence. "So you have sent others to watch the camp?"

Another nod. "We need to know the moment the enemy moves to strike. Do not fret," she added, "they will exercise all caution. We have a better understanding of the danger now, and they will not be seen."

"And the weapons… What have you learned?"

"Little more than what you have told us." It was obvious to Falak that her lover was still shaken by her experience and terrified by the power of the strange weapons. "When you are well enough to ride, we will return to El'Kasari. Perhaps the elders can tell us more." She watched Bahira's expression carefully, reading the storm of emotions that roiled behind her obvious grief. She was concerned that the loss of her fellows had shattered the young woman's confidence and scarred her deeply. "Will you ride with me when the time comes?"

Bahira turned her face away, unable to meet that penetrating gaze. "You would still have me fight by your side?" she asked quietly.

"Of course!" Falak gently but firmly forced her lover's eyes back to her. "Always."

"But after the massacre—"

"I told you, you are blameless for those deaths. Do not carry the burden any further." Leaning in, she placed a tender kiss on Bahira's forehead, hating Shakir for the pain he had caused to one she held so dear. "You stand as one of the finest scouts I have ever trained...and I say that without consideration of the love I feel for you."

A faint flicker of steel came to life in Bahira's eyes, still weak against the fresher anguish, but Falak was relieved to see it. She also welcomed the hard edge that crept into her voice. "Then I will ride with you." Clasping hands with Falak, she offered a slight, painful smile. "We will have our revenge...and Shakir will learn the folly of threatening the Peace."

"Excellent." Falak gently squeezed her lover's hand. "Now close your eyes, my love, and do not let fear mar your dreams. Rest will aid your recovery faster if it is given a proper chance to take root. Sleep." She was pleased when Bahira complied without argument and watched the rise and fall of her chest slow as the younger woman slipped peacefully into a deep slumber. Falak rested her head on the edge of the sleeping pallet, listening to the sounds of the camp at night and finding solace in the knowledge that the tribesmen would guard their sleep. She had a feeling they would need all their strength in the weeks to come.

Dae had heard the phrase "absence makes the heart grow fonder" many times in her life, but she was gaining a new appreciation of it now.

She had not expected to miss Zafirah and was surprised to find herself constantly glancing toward the entrance to the palace proper, always expecting—hoping—to see the familiar tall, dark-haired figure standing there watching her intently. She had grown so accustomed to Zafirah's visits that life seemed strange without her. Dae found herself longing for the Scion's return, wanting to indulge in more touches and kisses with the older woman, wanting an opportunity to explore the new dimensions to their connection.

A large part of Dae's longing no doubt stemmed from her growing acceptance of herself and her body as a sexual entity. She spent more and more of her time indulging in physical pleasure, and as she became more familiar with her own body, her touches grew bolder and more confident. Through long hours of practice, Dae found she could bring herself to climax very quickly, with just a few knowing caresses. Or, alternatively, she could prolong the ecstasy seemingly without end, teasing herself until the sheets of her bed were stained with sweat and her own juices, and the edges of her mind seemed to burn with the need to experience fulfillment. As she grew more knowledgeable and assured, Dae began wanting something more. She wanted to test these new skills on Zafirah, and perhaps learn a more refined level of expertise from the older, more experienced woman.

Of course, there were plenty of others in the harem who would have been more than happy to offer their assistance, and they made certain she was aware of their willingness. As the days went by, Dae noticed the behavior of the other pleasure-servants begin to change. It seemed that while they had respected her resistance to their advances before, now that she had expressed an interest and willingness to the Scion, Dae was once again fair game. Nasheta had been the first to proposition her that day in the pool, but the others weren't shy in following her example and set about expressing their own interest during Zafirah's absence.

At first, Dae thought the renewed attention was a result of her kiss with the Scion, but Inaya was quick to enlighten her.

"Little stays secret in a harem for long," she explained one day with an amused, seductive smile. "I doubt Johara and Hayam were able to keep their little 'educational session' with you to themselves. And also," she added with a wink, "you have been less than quiet in your room when you are practicing your new talents."

Dae's embarrassed reaction to this news seemed to entertain Inaya greatly.

At first, Dae quietly and bashfully rejected the advances of the other girls, but over time, something in her began to change. Inaya, watching with interest to see how her friend would handle herself, was overjoyed when the young blonde actually began to encourage the flirtations. Dae would often frolic in the pool with the other girls, making no effort whatsoever to maintain her modesty. In the evenings and at night she would join in the dancing, her technique improving quickly as she started using ever more daring and sexual movements. She would accept long, sensuous massages from the other pleasure-servants, who quickly made a game of seeing who could draw the most erotic-sounding moans from the delectable little blonde. The revealing, semi-transparent clothing that Dae had worn so self-consciously during her first months in the seraglio, she now wore with confidence and ease. She seemed to revel in the way her body drew the attention of all those around her, enjoying the hungry stares cast her way. Whenever someone approached her with an invitation of more intimate pleasures, Dae would offer a polite but flattered rejection, even as she allowed enticing, suggestive touches to linger over her flesh. Inaya noticed the girl had developed a new kind of smile, devilish yet playful, which seemed for some reason to be incredibly erotic. There was a new sparkle of mischief in her emerald eyes, and a new maturity to her movements and actions. Inaya was not the only one to recognize the change for what it was.

Dae was getting her first taste of sexual power...and she found the flavor very much to her liking!

Dae knew she was teasing the other girls, but the game was fun for her now. She knew no one would force her to do anything she didn't want to do, and this feeling of security made her bold. That little voice in the back of her mind—the one that had encouraged her not to cover up when she'd been swimming with Nasheta—grew stronger and louder as time passed. Although at times she was tempted to accept some of the invitations made by the other girls, Dae continued to hold back. Their flirtations were lighthearted and enjoyable; they excited her, yes, but not in the same way as Zafirah could. The Scion was magnetic and intense. When Dae lay on her bed each night, her hands running over slick, heated skin with lustful purpose, the image that always filled her senses was that of clear sapphire eyes and a crooked, seductive smile. And when she closed her eyes to go to sleep, her body warm and drowsy with satiation, she remembered the gentle expression of adoration and love on Zafirah's face before she'd left, and that single word, *aziza*, would cause a sweet ache to clutch at her heart. It was that memory more than anything else that stopped Dae from accepting the invitations made by her many admirers. Imagining what Zafirah might do to her, or what she might be allowed to do to Zafirah, had become Dae's new favorite way to pass the time. She couldn't wait for the Scion to return from her mission, eager to show off her new, more confident attitude.

Dae was lying beside the pool, letting the sun dry her clothes after having spent most of the morning in the cool waters, when a shadow fell across her. Sleepy eyelids parted to find Inaya standing over her, one eyebrow raised and a slight smile tugging at her full lips.

"*Salaam aleikum*, Dae." Dark eyes roved downwards, and Dae saw them pause quite deliberately to admire her breasts through the semi-transparent fabric of her gauzy top before they returned to her face. "May I join you?"

Dae waved a languid hand. "Sure. You should take a swim; the water's great." Now that she was more comfortable with her body and the attention she attracted, Dae found the pool offered a wonderful respite from the desert heat. With so much bare skin constantly on display in the seraglio, Dae had come to understand that it was a little silly to cling needlessly to the ideals of modesty she'd grown up with.

"Perhaps later." Inaya settled beside her. "I have spoken with the guards," she said. "They tell me Zafirah is expected to return to El'Kasari within a day, two at most."

Dae sighed, but didn't bother opening her eyes. "I hope everything went well for her."

"You have missed her, I think."

"Mmm…maybe I have. Though I'm sure I can think of a few ways to welcome her home."

Inaya laughed. "Such bold words from such an innocent mouth," she mocked playfully. "I have seen the changes in you these last few days, little one, but do not be too proud of your teasing games. You are but a babe in swaddling clothes compared to Zafirah when it comes to seduction."

"I know." Dae's grin remained unrepentant. "But I drove her to distraction before without even trying to; imagine what I could do if I put some effort into it."

Inaya was pleased that Dae was accepting her own desires at last, though a large part of her wished she could be there when the still-naïve girl got her first taste of real pleasure. In fact, a part of her wished to be responsible for providing that taste. And with all the other girls in the harem propositioning Dae, Inaya figured this to be as good a time as any to make her own offer. "You still have a great deal to learn, little one," she said in a husky tone.

Dipping a hand into the pool, Inaya wet her fingers, then held them above Dae's body, letting the water drip onto her stomach. The blonde chuckled, her abdominal muscles contracting in unconscious response. Inaya repeated her actions, this time letting the water drip a little higher. When Dae felt the sensation of the droplets falling onto her breasts a moment later, she opened both eyes fully and regarded Inaya with a raised eyebrow.

"Are you trying to get me wet?" Dae asked in a low burr, and from her playful expression it was clear she was fully aware her question had two layers.

"Is it working?" Inaya's eyes sparkled with amusement; she was no stranger to the game of seduction herself. In fact, it was her very favorite game, and one she had mastered long ago.

"Perhaps."

Inaya returned her hand to the pool. This time she ran her dripping fingers lightly over the skin of Dae's upper thigh and around her hip. Dae hitched in a sudden sharp breath at the erotic sensation of her touch.

"It feels nice?" Inaya asked very quietly.

"Very."

"Mm." Inaya licked her lips slowly as her touch crept higher, reveling in the shiver that raced over her friend's skin. "I wonder what else you might enjoy…"

Dae held perfectly still as Inaya continued to touch her, her expression one of divided arousal. Inaya had seen that look on many young women's faces; Dae clearly wanted the pleasure to continue but was worried her desire might be inappropriate. Her jaw worked soundlessly a few times but couldn't form words to ask Inaya to stop. "You know," Dae managed after a moment, "this isn't the way friends are supposed to touch each other."

"Oh?" Inaya hadn't missed the tremble in Dae's voice. "Did you learn that in your homeland?"

"Yes."

"No doubt from the same people who denied you knowledge of the pleasures you now exercise freely—and quite vocally—each night in your bedchamber, hmm?" Inaya smiled at the conflict in Dae's eyes. "Am I not desirable?" she asked with a slight pout.

Dae shivered. "I-it's not that—"

"I certainly find you extremely attractive."

"Yes, but—"

Inaya pressed a wet finger against Dae's lips, silencing her. "You are still trying to place boundaries on that which is limitless, my friend." Her voice was so soft it was almost ethereal, but Dae seemed hypnotized by her tone. "Pleasure and love are two different things; one feeds from the flesh, the other from the heart and soul. Do not confuse one with the other."

"But we're friends."

"And friendship is based upon trust, respect, and affection," Inaya agreed solemnly. "Qualities which can be deepened and made stronger through a sharing of intimacy and pleasure." She traced her long, delicate fingers down over Dae's collarbone, toying with her cleavage as she held her gaze intently. "You could share many things with me, Dae: fantasies, dreams, your deepest desires. Is it so wrong that a friend should want you to feel pleasure?"

"Well…" Dae was finding it difficult to argue with those deep, dark eyes gazing down at her so temptingly. Though she had grown accustomed to the others looking at her this way, it still seemed disconcerting when Inaya did it. Growing up, Dae's parents had allowed her few real friends. True, she had had the company of servants and her handmaidens, but her father had admonished her that as the daughter of a noble family, she should never become too familiar with the commoners. Dae valued the relationship she had formed with Inaya all the more because, like so many other things she had experienced since coming here, it was something she had never known before. The thought of deepening their friendship, of allowing it to grow intimate or carnal, was certainly not without its appeal. "I guess not, but—"

"If you would allow me, there are many things I could show you." Inaya's fingertips continued exploring the neckline of her damp top, and Dae struggled against the surge of arousal warming her blood. "Many paths of pleasure that could offer even greater insight into what you might share with the Scion when you feel yourself ready."

Dae almost moaned as a sudden image of herself and Inaya kissing and fondling one another sprang to life in her mind. Still, she rallied against the part of herself that wanted to simply give in to this seduction. "Others have made the same offer."

"And been rejected." Inaya cocked her head to the side, her light caresses growing still. "Will you reject me also?"

The forlorn expression on Inaya's face was almost too much for Dae to withstand, but she managed somehow. "For today, yes."

"For today?" Inaya's sultry smile returned immediately, her eyes hopeful. "And what of tomorrow?"

"I don't know. But anything is possible."

Inaya withdrew her hand to her side and sat back. "I can accept that."

There was silence for a while as the two friends sat, each lost in thoughts that were mostly licentious in nature. Then Inaya glanced at Dae curiously.

"Is this what you have told all the others who have propositioned you?"

Dae lay back on the warm rock, closing her eyes and grinning ear to ear. "Does it matter?"

Inaya considered a moment, and said, "I suppose not."

"Then don't bother asking the question."

The two exchanged amused looks, then burst into a fit of laughter.

# Chapter 15

Rumors of unrest among the renegade tribes wasted little time making their way through the city of El'Kasari. Zafirah's extended journey south seemed to give them credence, as did the perceptible tension among the *spahi*. Still, while such rumors might have driven a foreign city into a flurry of siege preparations and panic, the citizens of El'Kasari continued about their daily business without concern. They trusted their Scion implicitly; she had never failed them in protecting the Peace, and the army was stronger and more disciplined than it had been in decades. And if war did come, the people were ready to take up arms to defend their lives and their city.

Despite their calm, the people met Zafirah's return with at least some measure of relief, feeling better having their Scion back among them. In the cool of dusk many citizens gathered in the streets to welcome her home, and the tall, impressive woman touched her fingers to the hands of those who reached out to her as she rode past. Zafirah was careful to keep any trace of concern from her face. She was the very embodiment of strength and utter confidence—calm, beautiful, and self-assured. The people saw her and knew that whatever threat was manifesting in the deep desert, it could never hope to prevail against the might of their Scion.

They did not see the disquiet that marred Zafirah's normal expression of calm nor the tension stiffening her shoulders. They didn't notice the grim expressions on the faces of those riding escort for the Scion or the worried glances they cast toward the unassuming cloth-wrapped bundle tied to Simhana's saddle. When the soldiers disappeared behind the walls of the palace barracks, the people of El'Kasari returned to their own business happily, safe and secure in the knowledge that their beloved leader was back in their midst once more.

Striding through the hallways of the palace, Zafirah issued orders to the guards who fell into step beside her. "Assemble the council at once. Request the temple to send a representative to attend our meeting, preferably the High Priestess herself. We must learn more of Shakir's new army and the power it wields before we can counter it."

"Some of the council members are asleep, Scion—" began one of the guards hesitantly.

"Then wake them up!"

"A-at once, Scion." He hurried off on his mission.

Zafirah watched him leave, her sour mood only slightly mollified by being back in the familiar halls of her home. She wanted nothing more than to go immediately to the seraglio and see Dae but knew she couldn't let her other duties wait. Her trip south had made her realize just how deep her affection and need for Dae had become. Though she had taken pleasure with a few women from among the nomad tribe, Zafirah found their efforts only managed to appease her body; they could do little to settle her heart or mind. All the Scion wanted to do right now was take Dae in her arms and kiss her until she understood how much she was loved. The knowledge that she was going to have to wait an indeterminate length of time before she could see Dae only made Zafirah that much more irritable.

Continuing down the massive corridor, Zafirah glanced down at herself quickly, noting the damp sweatstains that darkened her vest and trousers. Her nose wrinkled. "I shall join the council as soon as I have had opportunity to change into something clean."

As expected, the meeting was little more than a waste of time. Zafirah informed the representatives of the various allied tribes of the danger mounting in the south, displaying the strange, alien weapon as evidence of their threat. Bahira, recovered from the exposure she'd suffered, recounted again the story of the ambush and requested Zafirah's permission to be among the first to ride against Shakir's forces. Recognizing the need for revenge in her eyes, Zafirah granted the request. The council members and the priests of Inshal all studied the weapon curiously, spending over an hour trying to deduce how it operated. In the end, they finally concluded that the device was beyond their wisdom; Zafirah was unsurprised. After another hour or so of heated debate, the council agreed that Shakir clearly intended to attack in short order, and that he and his allies should be stopped before they could cause any significant harm to the Scion Peace. Those tribes who were closest to El'Kasari would be called on to defend the Peace, offering their own warriors to complement the formidable elite *spahi*. Falak's scouts would report as soon as the renegade Calif left the sanctuary of the cliffs and encroached into the open; as soon as he was exposed, Zafirah intended to test his forces for herself.

By the time all these matters had been discussed and decided, the hour had grown late. Zafirah escaped as soon as the last member of the council left the chamber, heading as quickly as she could in the direction of her harem.

When she arrived she found few of her pleasure-servants still awake. The night air was chill and bitter. Zafirah scanned the gardens hastily, searching for and failing to find the face she most wanted to see. Sighing dejectedly, she was just about to leave when a soft voice from the shadows stopped her.

"She is sleeping."

Zafirah turned back to find Inaya standing nearby, the slender girl holding an unconsciously provocative pose. Dark eyes regarded her steadily, glittering as brightly as the stud in her navel. "She stayed awake late, hoping you would visit, but eventually succumbed to her weariness. Come, I doubt she would mind if you were to look in on her." Inaya gestured toward the sleeping chambers, and Zafirah fell into step behind her as she led the way out of the gardens.

They stopped outside the entrance to Dae's room. Within, bathed in the flickering light of a single low-burning oil lamp, Dae lay on her pallet in deep slumber. Zafirah sighed quietly, gazing for several long moments at Dae's unguarded, relaxed expression, just soaking in the sense of calm and peace that looking at the young blonde stirred in her. "I cannot believe how much I missed her presence these last few days," she whispered almost to herself.

"It may please you to know that the feeling was mutual."

Zafirah shifted her gaze to Inaya, surprised and hopeful. "She missed me?"

"Indeed. I think she had not realized how much she enjoyed your company until it was gone. And I believe you will find her eager to make up for the time you have been apart." Inaya paused, her gentle smile turning into a wicked grin. "She has changed a great deal in your absence, Scion—grown more aware of herself as a woman and as a creature deserving of pleasure."

Zafirah turned back to regard the slumbering figure. "She is so beautiful."

"And you are not the only one to appreciate that fact. Since the kiss she shared with you, Dae has become quite popular among the other girls."

"Hardly a surprise." A dark brow lifted curiously. "Has she succumbed to their advances?"

"Would you be jealous if I told you she had?" Inaya returned with equal interest.

Zafirah considered, then shook her head. "Envious, perhaps, though that is saying little. I am envious of the very clothes she wears, that they are able to touch her skin while I cannot. But it would make me happy to know she is experiencing pleasure and enjoyment."

It appeared from her quiet nod that this was the answer Inaya had expected to hear. "Well, while she has learned to enjoy the attention, Dae has refused all offers made to her...even my own." A slightly wry smile tugged at one corner of Inaya's mouth. "She has not admitted it, but I believe she wishes to save herself so that you may be the first to touch her intimately."

That statement sent a shiver across Zafirah's skin and caused heat to surge through her lower regions. She watched Dae shift in her sleep and heard a low, slightly erotic-sounding moan escape her. Her lips turned up in a sleepy smile, as though at a pleasant dream. *I wonder if she dreams of me*, the Scion mused, the thought warming her heart. "I shall see she is rewarded for her devotion," she said. "Tomorrow I shall spend as much time with her as I am able." As she watched the sleeping girl, Zafirah felt light hands begin to trace the contours of her back. Inaya leaned in against her, and she arched her back as the pleasure-servant's hands wandered confidently to her hips.

"Perhaps tonight," Inaya's husky voice suggested, "you might allow me the honor of welcoming you home properly, my Scion…?"

Zafirah chuckled, her body tired but still responsive. She turned around and looked down into deep, dark eyes filled with hungry promise. "It has been a long day, Inaya. I am weary from travel."

Inaya pouted up at her, her expression seductively tragic. "I could ease your muscles…relax you."

"I doubt what you have in mind would be relaxing."

"But fun." The slender girl pressed herself against Zafirah's taller frame, making certain her quarry was aware of every curve and hollow of her body. Eager hands wrapped themselves about a willing waist. Knowing fingers began to tease the sensitive area at the base of Zafirah's spine. "You could thank me for assisting with Dae's…'education'…"

Zafirah perked up immediately. "What are you talking about?"

Inaya's pearl-white teeth flashed in the dim light. She tugged at Zafirah's clothing with nimble, confident fingers. "Come to bed and I shall tell you," she said seductively, and Zafirah felt her resistance weakening. "Pleasure me well, and I shall describe in explicit detail the sounds your beloved makes each night while she explores herself, practicing skills she hopes to use on your body someday."

Zafirah groaned and allowed herself to be pulled along behind the slender temptress. *I can rest in the morning*, she decided, her fatigue quickly overcome with lust. They left Dae to her dreams, retiring to the Scion's bedchamber to "relax."

# Chapter 16

AFTER A MORNING SPENT TRAINING with the men and women of her army—dedicating extra time to the martial drills due to the imminent possibility of battle—Zafirah made her way quickly to the seraglio, eager to spend time with her favorite pleasure-servant. Dae greeted her with a kiss that, while brief, hinted at something far more carnal. When she asked about her trip and the rumors of danger rising, Zafirah hushed her immediately.

"I do not wish to think of such matters here," she whispered into a delicate ear. "Let the world outside fade away, I beg you. Just let me enjoy your company while I am able."

Dae agreed readily, obviously understanding that Zafirah needed respite from the responsibilities of her position. Taking hold of her smoothly muscled arm, she pulled Zafirah in the direction of the pool. Zafirah relished the affectionate, slightly possessive way Dae wrapped an arm about her waist, noticing but not questioning the warning glares Dae cast her fellow pleasure-servants. It was clear the girl wanted some time alone with her, and Zafirah felt a flash of pleasure race through her.

The two women spent all morning splashing about in the water and diving from the waterfall. Zafirah shed her regal stoicism and played enthusiastically with her pleasure-servants, though she found it almost impossible to keep her hands off Dae, who seemed to be flaunting her wet, nearly naked body about in a decidedly tempting fashion. Zafirah saw that Dae had indeed changed, just as Inaya had told her last night. And with the memory of what Inaya had whispered to her while she feasted upon her slick, honeyed flesh still burning in her mind, Zafirah found herself in a high state of arousal just being so near to Dae. A few times the urge to grab her and crush her against the edge of the pool where she could ravish her senseless became so strong that the Scion was forced to turn away, clenching her hands into fists and struggling to keep her breathing deep and even. *Tonight*, she counseled her raging libido. *Tonight, when you are alone with her, you may play. Not before.*

Dae, very much aware of how she was affecting Zafirah, displayed at least a little mercy to the enamored woman. She resisted the temptation to strip off her clothing completely and managed to keep her eager hands from exploring the parts of Zafirah's body that were calling stronger to her every day. From the look on Zafirah's face, Dae knew she would only be able to push her teasing so far before she would find herself laid out on a rock and devoured in front of the entire harem...which, she considered with a little shiver of delight and a quick lapse into fantasy, probably wouldn't be willing to remain spectators for long. And while the prospect of being devoured by two dozen extremely talented lovers held a certain level of appeal, Dae was determined to explore the world of erotic delights slowly, one step at a time. Laughing and splashing about in the waters, keeping one eye fixed on Zafirah at all times, Dae let herself just enjoy having the Scion back after her trip away. *Tonight*, she promised herself. *I'd wager anything she'll invite me to draw her tonight. And we'll see what happens once we're alone together.*

When they parted, as expected, Zafirah bent to whisper breathlessly into Dae's ear.

"Come visit me tonight in my bedchamber after even-meal. And bring your drawing materials."

Dae nodded, the smile on her face complementing the twinkle in her eyes. "I look forward to it, Scion."

As Dae walked away, she was extremely conscious of the admiring gaze lingering over the accentuated curves of her body.

Dae ate sparingly that evening, her stomach tied into knots with excitement and trepidation over what might happen when she was alone with Zafirah. Nervous but conscious of the subtle pull of arousal that had settled over her body, Dae left the seraglio with an escort of two harem guards. As she departed, the other girls whistled and offered a few extremely suggestive pieces of advice, laughing in delight at her colorful blush and clapping their enthusiastic encouragement. Dae clutched her pieces of parchment and sticks of sharpened lead to her chest, her mind filled with images of what she had been shown by Johara and Hayam, her senses remembering the scents and pleasures of what she had experienced of her own body.

Reaching their destination, Dae hesitantly entered Zafirah's bedchamber as the two guards offered her reassuring smiles before they disappeared. Looking around as she stepped into the chamber, she suddenly realized for the first time just how beautiful and comfortable Zafirah's room was. The air was filled with mixed but complementary perfumes of incense and oils, and numerous ornate *shamedan* bathed everything in a friendly light. There were several arched windows opening onto the terrace outside, and a coastal breeze served to cool the desert heat. What few pieces of art that decorated the room all portrayed the female figure in some fashion; Dae's attention was caught by an iron sculpture of two women locked in a passionate coupling. Stepping closer, she decided the artist had been working from life experience; the details of the piece were too intimate and explicit to suggest anything else. The enormous bed no longer struck her as a fearful thing. Rather, it seemed to hold a sense of mysterious promise, and Dae wondered if she would be appreciating the touch of those cool silk sheets and pillows against her naked skin later tonight.

"Welcome, *aziza*," whispered a familiar voice.

Dae turned, losing any words of response when she saw Zafirah standing in the corner of the room. She was wearing a midnight-blue robe, her long hair hanging free and wild about her shoulders. The robe was loosely tied at Zafirah's waist, exposing her cleavage and the inner curve of each breast, as well as everything else down to her navel. Dae couldn't help herself—she just stood there, mouth agape, staring in awe at the woman before her. The skin she could see was deeply tanned and muscular, and her fingers itched to pull that robe away completely to allow her a more comprehensive appreciation.

Zafirah grinned, pleased to see her efforts so well-received. She had deliberated all afternoon on how she should greet Dae's arrival, eventually rejecting the part of her that suggested she just throw the girl on the bed, tear her clothes away, and see how loudly she could make her scream in ecstasy. While less spectacular, the sheer robe certainly seemed to get Dae's attention quite nicely, and Zafirah let her stare for several minutes before she cleared her throat loudly. Dae shuddered and seemed to pull herself from a trance. Zafirah raised an eyebrow seductively. "See anything you like?"

Dae fumbled with her drawing materials, almost dropping the bundle as her arms lost all strength. "I-I-I...Y-You're very nice. I mean... beautiful..."

Zafirah stepped out of the corner, her hips swaying. "Thank you." She gestured to the parchment. "So, are you are ready to draw me?"

"Draw?" Dae stared stupidly for a moment, then shook her head as if dazed. "Oh, yes...draw. Of course, yes, um, where...I mean, how would you like me to...?"

"I thought I might pose on the bed," Zafirah suggested, her voice low and throaty. She indicated a plush, velvet-lined chair she had positioned earlier. "You may sit here if you like."

"Okay." Dae sat quickly and arranged a sheet of parchment across her lap, folding one leg underneath the other to support the paper.

"I know little of artistic matters," Zafirah said as she stepped up to the bed. "Will the light be sufficient for you? I could light more lamps if you require greater illumination."

"No, this...this should be fine, thank you."

"Excellent." She untied the slender sash that held her robe closed and tugged it loose. The silky material immediately fell from her shoulders, and she tossed it aside before arranging herself on the sheets of her bed.

She watched idly as Dae stared helplessly at her naked body, revealed in all its splendor in the flattering lamplight.

"W-what are you doing?" Dae managed to gasp.

Zafirah gave her feline smile. "I hoped you might draw me nude," she explained simply. "Why? Does this disturb you?"

"Well, no, not disturb, but I...I just thought you wanted me to draw you...dressed."

"Mm." Zafirah considered a moment, her head cocked to the side in contemplation. "If you insist upon clothing, I will comply, of course. However, I believe the female body is so perfectly suited for conversion into art and that to cover the full effect of its beauty is akin to the watering of wine—it saps the sweetness. But, if you prefer…"

"No!" Dae held up a hand as Zafirah began to reach for the robe. "This is fine. It just took me by surprise, that's all."

"Oh." Zafirah settled back down, lying on her side with one leg slightly raised, relaxing back against a pile of cushions with one arm draped across her belly while the other cradled her head. She smiled as Dae openly ran her eyes up and down her body, feeling tingles of arousal itch across her skin. "Will this be satisfactory?"

"Um…" Dae struggled to keep her mind on the task at hand, even as her libido insisted on pointing out the finer aspects of her study. *She's so firm; her breasts, her muscles, her skin…everything about her is perfect. And she would let you do anything to her that you like! ANYTHING! Think how smooth she'd feel under your fingers. Or better yet, your tongue…* Her eyes drifted to the elegantly shaved arrow of soft, dark curls that pointed between Zafirah's legs. She shivered and ordered herself to stay focused. "Could you pull your hair over your shoulder a little? And maybe bend your left knee more. Uh huh, that's good. Are you comfortable?"

"Eminently," Zafirah purred.

"Good, because you'll have to hold still while I do this." Dae set all lubricious thoughts firmly to one side for the moment and studied the figure lying before her critically. She analyzed the play of light over Zafirah's body, the angle of her limbs, and the lines of her form. Holding a stick of sharpened lead loosely in her right hand, Dae began to sketch out the first basic outline of her drawing.

Zafirah shifted on the bed to settle herself better. "I have never been drawn before," she said after a few minutes of silence. "Will it bother you if I talk while you work?"

"No, that's fine. Just try to stay still."

"Of course. Have you ever drawn a woman naked before?"

"Sort of. Husn fell asleep one evening after she'd been swimming and I sketched her. Her clothes were so transparent she might as well have been naked."

"And why did you choose to draw her at such a moment? Did you find her image pleasing?"

"She's very beautiful. All the girls in the harem are, which I suppose is a compliment to your taste in women." She offered Zafirah a quick grin. "Mostly I just draw people when I think they're going to stay still long enough for me to do a good job of them."

"Ah, I see. So the sight of her kindled no excitement in you?"

"Not at the time. A sleeping woman doesn't really offer much appeal to me."

Zafirah chuckled. "I see my line of questioning is going to be defeated." She paused. "And what about now?" she asked in a low voice. "Do you find me pleasing?"

Dae was no longer such a stranger to questions intended to seduce her. "You don't need me to tell you you're attractive, Zafirah. I've heard some of the poets who write about your beauty. They're not shy about offering praise where praise is due."

Zafirah pouted. "I know what others think. I am interested in your opinion. Be honest, Tahirah. Does the sight of me like this have no effect on you at all?"

Dae didn't stop her careful drawing, but she did let her eyes linger over Zafirah's more intimate attributes. "Honestly? I think you look ravishing. And I think you've seduced enough women in your life that you could hazard a guess as to how you're affecting me." She waggled her eyebrows, pleased to see how her blunt reply took Zafirah by surprise. She decided to press her advantage. "Were you planning on personally testing my level of excitement later on?"

Zafirah stared at her in astonishment, clearly taken aback. Seeing the amusement glittering in Dae's eyes, she laughed. "You have grown bold in my absence, little one," she said. "Do not think the change has gone unnoticed. I saw the way you were teasing me this morning. Do you realize how close I came to taking you right there in the pool?"

"I have a fairly good idea. But I didn't think you'd mind the show, and I liked the way you were responding to me."

"Oh, my body needs little incentive to respond to your presence, *aziza*, I assure you. Like right now, for instance..." Zafirah sighed as her left hand shifted subtly down her body, fingertips caressing her skin lightly. "I can feel your eyes on my body like a kiss of flame. Just being with you like this, naked, exposed...I cannot help but feel aroused."

Dae paused in her work to allow herself a moment just to look at Zafirah, and she suddenly noticed how stiff her nipples had become, how her breathing had grown shallower. It took her a moment to realize that Zafirah's left hand had ventured lower, and she gasped when she saw those long, slender fingers begin to stroke over glistening, intimate flesh. "Wh-what are you doing?"

Zafirah's eyes were smoky with pleasure as she fed off her own lust. "What does it look like I am doing?"

"I know what it looks like you're doing, but..." Dae trailed off. *She wouldn't, would she?*

Zafirah didn't hesitate to clear away any doubts. "I would very much enjoy letting you watch me," she purred. "It has been a long time since I last pleasured myself; your company would make it much more thrilling."

Dae sat very still for a few seconds, considering. *When am I going to get used to this*, she wondered vexedly? After all, it wasn't the first time someone had made her this offer. In fact, it wouldn't even be the first time she'd seen this act; the image of what Johara had done to herself was still vivid in Dae's mind. But with Zafirah, things like this always seemed to take on a whole new depth and intensity. Everything seemed a thousand times more erotic and spellbinding. Watching those long fingers play over tanned, toned flesh, Dae knew she didn't have the willpower to turn the offer down. "I-I can't really draw you if you're moving." It was the best protest she could come up with.

Zafirah's grin was pure wickedness. "Draw the parts of me that are still," she instructed, enjoying the game. "If you stop what you are doing, so will I."

Dae immediately returned to her work, struggling to divide her attention equally between her drawing and the far more compelling display being played out on the bed. "And when you finish...so will I."

Zafirah stroked herself languidly, not hurrying her pleasure but letting it build slowly under Dae's gaze. She moaned softly in contentment. "Talk to me."

Dae glanced up, her hand continuing to shade in Zafirah's muscles on the parchment. "What do you want me to say?"

"Anything. I like the sound of your voice. I like the way it feels against me." Zafirah bent her left leg a little more, allowing for better access to her center. "Perhaps you could tell me about what you did while I was away," she suggested. "I am greatly interested in hearing more about your new"—a dark eyebrow lifted knowingly—"activities…"

It took Dae only a moment to figure out what Zafirah was referring to. She groaned but couldn't stop the charming, embarrassed smile that stole across her face. "I guess nothing stays private in a harem, huh? Maybe I should learn to be quieter." She giggled, but decided there was little point in being self-conscious about her pre-bedtime ritual, not while she was sitting across from the most spectacularly gorgeous woman in the universe while she gave a very personal demonstration of "self-love." "How did you find out about that?"

"Inaya."

"Uh huh, predictably enough."

"So…" Zafirah again arched an eyebrow in invitation. "Tell me about it."

Dae shrugged awkwardly, feeling as though those blazing sapphire eyes could see right through her clothes, her flesh, all the way down to her soul. She felt naked under their gaze. "What's to tell? Johara and Hayam showed me how to do it, and it feels nice."

"How often do you indulge?"

"I don't know. Every night, I suppose…and most mornings."

Zafirah's voice dropped several octaves. "What do you do?"

Dae fixed her eyes firmly on her picture, taking a moment to accurately portray the details of Zafirah's face and using the time to compose herself. "You don't look like you need any lessons on the subject."

"No, but I would like to hear you describe how you touch yourself. In detail."

Dae noticed that Zafirah was now stroking herself with shorter, more purposeful motions. A slow smile spread across her lips as she realized how she was affecting the Scion and the power she held in this little game. She sat up straighter in her seat. "You want me to describe how I make myself come?" she asked, lowering the tone of her voice to what she hoped was something seductive.

"Yes."

Dae narrowed her eyes. "Will it make you wet, hearing how I slide my fingers down over the lips of my sex and let them dance in all that velvet heat?"

Zafirah's attentions were getting faster. "Gods, yessss!"

"How I like to go quicker and pinch my clitoris when I feel the first ripples of climax begin to wash through me...and how I scream out your name while my juices drip down my hand..."

"Gods, please! Yes!"

"Zafirah?"

"Mm."

"I've stopped drawing." Dae flashed an evil grin. "Aren't you supposed to stop too?"

"What?" Zafirah paused breathlessly, caught off guard by how suddenly the tables had been turned. "W-what are you...?"

"You said you'd stop if I did, so..." Dae held up her idle pencil, enjoying the thrill of knowing she was in control. She could see from Zafirah's expression that she would adhere to the rules she'd set for this little display. "Slow down. I'm not close to being done yet, which means neither are you."

Dae watched as Zafirah struggled to rein in her libido. It obviously hadn't occurred to her that such a young and supposedly inexperienced girl would take the initiative like this, and the thought thrilled Dae. Even as the Scion managed to drag herself out of a haze of arousal, Dae could tell she didn't want to discourage this development. She watched as Zafirah's fingers returned to her swollen, slick folds.

"All right," Zafirah gasped. "Please, may I ask you to continue?"

Dae considered the request carefully a moment, watching Zafirah rest her fingertips against her excitement in expectation. A brilliant shiver of pure desire rushed through her body with the realization that she was in command here; she would dictate the terms of Zafirah's pleasure and eventual climax. Dae had tasted a sample of sexual power in the harem, but this was so much stronger! She felt exhilarated and terrified at the same time, but no fear on earth was going to stop her from testing this new pleasure. She inclined her head slightly and touched the tip of her pencil to the parchment on her lap.

"Slowly," she ordered. "Or I'll stop again and make you wait all night for release."

Zafirah nodded obediently and resumed her caresses at a much more controlled pace.

Though more accustomed to taking an assertive role in the bedroom, Zafirah was no stranger to playing the submissive. There were few sexual practices she had not tested during the many years of her reign, and there were fewer she had not found enjoyable on at least some level. Seeing the look of excitement in Dae's eyes as she settled into her new position of authority, Zafirah felt herself grow even wetter. This was the perfect way to introduce Dae to more intimate pleasures; it gave her control and a sense of security, knowing that nothing would happen without her approval.

And besides, she thought as she saw a wicked gleam bloom in Dae's emerald eyes, there were few things as stimulating as the sight of an innocent girl taking up the reins of sexual power for the first time.

"Does it feel nice?"

"Huh?" Zafirah's attention, lust-dulled and fuzzy, focused quickly. "What did you say?"

"I asked if it felt nice?"

"Mmmm, yesss." Zafirah's fingers were coated with her arousal and slid smoothly along the petals of her swollen sex. "After your performance this morning, I am in urgent need of release." She moved two fingers lower and started to curl them inwards, but Dae's voice stopped her.

"No." She shook her head. "Don't go inside. Just stroke yourself slowly. I like that."

Zafirah whimpered, wanting deeper contact, but reluctantly obeyed Dae's command. "Is this how you touch yourself? Slowly, without penetration?"

Dae shrugged, splitting her focus between her art and her subject. "I'm still a virgin," she pointed out. "I can't touch myself like that yet. But it feels nice anyway. And no, I don't always go slowly." A wicked grin spread across her face as she saw her words excite Zafirah. "Sometimes I like to do it quickly, and I keep going until I get so dizzy and strained that I have to rest."

Zafirah's eyes squeezed shut, images of Dae pleasuring herself dancing across the insides of her lids. "Gods!" The muscles in her neck strained with the need to move. Her hips were desperate to pick up a rhythm against her fingers, but she fought to hold them still.

"You're speeding up again," Dae warned, thoroughly enamored with her new power. "And keep your eyes open. I want you to see me watching you while you do this."

Zafirah's gaze raked over Dae's figure hungrily, focusing on the swell of her breasts. She licked her lips. "It is difficult to control myself with you so close to me," she said breathlessly. "You are so beautiful."

"Thank you." There was a long pause while Dae concentrated on sketching. "Do you really find me so pleasing?"

"Of course."

"More so than the other girls?"

Zafirah's movements slowed as she considered the question seriously. "There are many forms of beauty, Tahirah, but I think I can say with honesty that yours appeals to me the greatest of all I have seen. There is something in you that stirs my heart as well as my loins in a way I have never experienced with any woman before you."

"And would it excite you to see more of me?"

Zafirah's breathing actually stopped entirely at the query so ingenuously posed. Her fingers came to a brief halt, then resumed their attentions with greater intensity. "Yes!" Her expression turned instantly pleading. "Please, let me look upon you!"

"Mm, I'm not sure. How do I know you'll behave yourself?"

"I promise," Zafirah assured quickly. "I shall do nothing more than look. Please, my Tahirah!"

The sly look in Dae's eyes was incredibly sexy. The seemingly innocent girl appeared to consider the matter as she worked. "I don't know that I can trust you—"

"You can! Please!"

"Wellll..." Dae chewed her lower lip thoughtfully; the tip of a pink tongue emerging briefly did nothing to cool Zafirah's ardor. "I suppose I could show you a little more of me, but I think I need some incentive first."

"Incentive?" Zafirah didn't like the look of mischief in those sparkling eyes one bit. "What would you have of me?"

"I don't really know." Skilled as she was in reading the desires of other women, Zafirah recognized that Dae was having difficulty sifting through the possibilities to find one she actually had the courage to voice. "Perhaps you could taste yourself," Dae suggested shyly after a long moment. "I thought that was very erotic when Johara did it."

"I think I should like to hear more of what my pleasure-servants have been showing you," Zafirah said. Still, the request was simple enough to fulfill, and she spent a long moment making certain her fingers were thoroughly soaked before bringing them to her lips. Maintaining eye contact, Zafirah ran her tongue slowly up each finger in turn, moaning at the familiar flavor of her arousal and enjoying the way Dae licked her lips unconsciously in reaction. She took her time, wanting to give a good show so she might earn her reward. The prospect of seeing Dae without the restrictions of clothing was making her dizzy with want.

When her task was completed, Zafirah returned her fingers lazily to their assignment between her legs. She lifted an eyebrow at Dae hopefully. "Is there anything else you wish to see?"

Dae, who looked dazed from the erotic display, struggled to respond. "I...can't think of anything right now."

Zafirah teased her fingers up the sensitive skin of her left thigh, then down again to where her heat was greatest. "So, may I see more?"

"Oh yes...more would be nice..." Dae murmured.

The Scion grinned and waved a hand at Dae to get her attention. "Tahirah?" When glassy emerald eyes managed to focus, Zafirah stared hungrily at Dae's top. "Please?"

"Oh...Right. Sorry." Dae laughed a little nervously but set her parchment and lead sticks to the side before reaching for the laces that held the cloth together over her breasts. Slowly, each lace was pulled free, revealing just a little more of her pale skin. Zafirah whimpered at the torture, wanting to hurry the girl along with a helping hand but not daring to move lest her reward be revoked. When the bejeweled cloth was eventually shrugged off and her breasts bared, Dae sat quietly and allowed Zafirah's eyes to explore her. Her nipples pebbled and grew hard under the hungry stare.

Zafirah stared for long minutes, her self-pleasuring pausing as she drank in Dae's beauty, committing every detail of that perfect body to memory.

Dae smiled a smile that was half-shy, half-brazen. "You like?"

"You are magnificent!" Zafirah breathed in awe. Though the Scion had seen countless women topless, somehow the sight of Dae became a new experience for her. It wasn't something she could define, but it felt like she was appreciating the beauty of the female form for the first time. "Divine perfection…"

"I think that might be going a little too far, but thank you." Dae gathered her drawing materials up again and resumed her work.

Zafirah's expression fell. "Wait, what…what about?" She gestured to the filmy trousers Dae still wore.

"Not tonight."

"But—"

A warning finger stopped her protest cold. "You promised you'd behave. We're taking this slowly, remember. After all, I'm still an innocent, naïve young maiden; my virtue won't be surrendered so easily." Dae's words were playful yet promising.

Zafirah settled back into her pose grudgingly. *Just enjoy what she is willing to share with you and do not press for more than she is ready to give,* she told herself sternly. "Very well. Though I would argue in the case of your naïveté; I think you know very well what you are doing to me, little one."

"True, but from the look of things, I'd say you have little to complain about." Dae glanced pointedly to where Zafirah's fingers were actively satisfying her body's need. After a long, lingering stare, she focused back on her drawing.

"I would very much like to see the rest of you, Tahirah." Zafirah stroked herself while gazing longingly at Dae's full breasts, imagining how they might feel and taste. "Tell me, are you proud of your beauty?"

"What do you mean?"

"Does your beauty please you? You possess exquisite form and features, Tahirah, beauty that others would admire and covet, and yet you display a notable lack of vanity for it. Do you consider such rare grace and splendor to be a blessing or a bane?"

Dae shrugged. "I guess I like the way I look. It hasn't ever really mattered much to me before, but...since I met you..." She trailed off with a shy smile.

"Your beauty is what brought you to my harem."

Dae regarded her naked breasts wryly, then the Scion. "Yeah, I'd guessed as much."

"But something deeper than your beauty stirs my passion for you," Zafirah said. Dae didn't respond, but Zafirah could see her words had had an effect. "Do you like watching me while I do this? Does it arouse you to see how deeply you affect me?"

Dae refused to raise her eyes, instead concentrating on her artwork. "It does. I think a person would have to be dead not to be affected by what you're doing."

"Mm." Zafirah could feel her need reaching a critical level. "How far are you from completion?"

"Not far. Why?" Dae asked. "Feeling anxious?"

"I will not last long with you teasing me this way."

"Then perhaps we should stop for a few minutes." Dae lifted her pencil threateningly. "Do you need some time to compose yourself?"

Zafirah growled, but stilled her fingers obediently. "Do not stop. Please, I want to finish."

Dae continued. "All right, then. I'll tell you when you can come."

Zafirah breathed a sigh of relief. "Thank you." As she caressed herself, she studied Dae curiously, noting the signs of arousal in her. "When you leave here and return to the seraglio, what will you do?"

"I don't know," she said with an exaggerated air of innocence. "I guess I might take a swim, if it's not too cold, and then go to sleep."

"Sleep?" Zafirah pouted, realizing she had been played again. "Will your body not require...satisfaction? A release of tensions after what I have shared with you?"

"Maybe."

"And?"

Dae shook her head with a little chuckle. "And what? I guess I'll do pretty much the same thing you're doing now, only without quite so much patience!"

"You will think of me as you pleasure yourself?"

"I usually do," Dae admitted.

"Will you be vocal?"

"You really like those details, don't you?"

"Your voice arouses me, as does the thought of you touching yourself."

"Maybe I should just show you so you don't have to wonder anymore." Scarlet raced across Dae's face almost as fast as an expression of excited approval spread across Zafirah's "I-I didn't mean that—"

"I would love to watch you! Please? We could do it together, feed off the other's image. It would be wonderful!"

"No."

"I would promise not to touch you! I would not even speak if you do not wish it!"

"I-I can't—"

"Why not?"

Dae opened her mouth to explain, but obviously couldn't find the right words. "I just…I can't, that's all. Not yet."

Zafirah's face fell, but she recognized that Dae's defenses would rise if she pushed the matter further. "Very well, *aziza,*" she said softly. "I will respect your wishes."

Silence descended for long minutes, broken only by the low scratching of Dae's pencil on parchment and the irregular, hard breaths of Zafirah. Eventually, Dae checked a shy glance at the Scion. "Zafirah?"

"Yes, little one?"

"I do like the idea."

Zafirah's expression softened. "When you are ready to share such intimacies with me," she said, "do not allow fear or embarrassment to stop you from letting me know it. I wish only for your pleasure."

"And I appreciate that." Dae paused, then added very quietly, "I really would like to let you watch me. The thought of it is extremely arousing." Dae's free hand went to her left breast and began to trail lightly over the sensitive flesh. "Johara and Hayam showed me how two women make love. I want to share those things with you."

"Mm, Inaya told me of your 'education.'"

Dae scowled without any malice. "That girl's tongue wags too easily."

*And with great talent!* Zafirah added silently, watching avidly as Dae caressed herself. "Do not be too hard on her. I extracted the information from her last night, along with many cries of passion. You would be surprised how effective pleasure can be for interrogation."

Seeing how fixed Zafirah's focus had become, Dae suddenly realized what she was doing and halted her touches. She cocked an eyebrow at the other woman's disappointed groan. "You like my breasts?"

"Very much."

"Mm." Dae's fingers circled the hard nub of her nipple, shivering at how sensitive she had become. "I like yours, too."

By now, Zafirah's entire body glistened under a film of sweat and she was trembling with the force of her need. "No more teasing, I beg of you! Finish your picture."

Dae realized Zafirah wouldn't last much longer, and that if pushed, her self-control would snap. Abandoning her breast, she began adding the final touches to her artwork. "You can go inside now," she allowed, seeing Zafirah's body trying to find a rhythm. "Don't touch your clitoris until I tell you to."

Zafirah released a heavenly sigh as she slid two fingers into her core. She thrust in and out slowly, eyes locked on Dae's upper body. The scent of sweat and sex filled the room with a familiar perfume.

Dae finished shading the last section of her picture and, after a moment spent contemplating her creation, calmly set the parchment and pencils aside. Folding her hands in her lap, she watched Zafirah expectantly. "All right…let me see you come."

The request itself, coupled with the expression on the young girl's face, was more than enough to throw Zafirah over the precipice of pleasure. Her body fell back against the pillows behind her as her legs splayed open fully. The muscles in her neck strained as her hand moved furiously against her sex. With a primal, joyous roar, Zafirah felt the waves of ecstasy roll through her with blinding force. When she felt them begin to ebb, she split two fingers along the shaft of her clitoris and squeezed gently while massaging with firm strokes. Almost instantly, the practiced, knowing ministrations sent the thrill of orgasm crashing through her again. Zafirah could feel her body pumping out fluids as she maintained her climax for several long, agonizingly sweet moments, only stopping when she hadn't strength enough to continue. Collapsing, exhausted, she dragged air into her lungs in desperate gasps.

Dae knew she was soaked with arousal as she watched Zafirah succumb to climax. It was a struggle just to keep her breathing steady as she stared at the other woman writhing on the bed before her, wanting desperately to join her and aid in her pleasure but lacking sufficient courage to do so. She squirmed a little in her seat, squeezing her legs together and enjoying the sensation of tense excitement that built in her center.

After several moments her eyes opened and Zafirah sat up, smiling languidly at her. Dae returned the smile. "You're loud," she remarked.

Zafirah laughed. "So, I hear, are you."

"Yeah, well..." Dae could feel the color spreading all the way down her chest. "It's hard not to get carried away."

"Indeed." Zafirah took a deep breath and exhaled slowly. "So, may I see your picture?"

"Of course." Dae reached over and picked up the parchment, collecting her top at the same time. Standing on somewhat weak legs, she handed the sketch to Zafirah before slipping the top back on, laughing at the disappointed groan as she covered her breasts.

Zafirah studied the drawing. Dae knew she had done a good job; while the art didn't portray what the Scion had actually been doing, it managed to capture her expression of fierce desire perfectly, along with the sexual tension that galvanized her body. The lighting gave a wonderful contrast over her muscular form.

"I am flattered by the attention you have paid to every detail. Your talent humbles me," she said.

Dae lowered her head modestly. "I'm glad you like it."

"You captured the moment well, though I think a few activities went unrecorded." Zafirah's eyes sparkled playfully.

"Yeah, well...I didn't quite feel comfortable drawing you exactly as you were."

"Mm." Zafirah studied the picture for a few moments longer. "May I keep this?"

"Of course. I drew it for you."

"Thank you. I shall treasure it always."

"You're welcome." Dae turned away from the longing in Zafirah's gaze, moving back a few paces to put some distance between them. Zafirah was dripping with animal sensuality at that moment, resplendent after her climax and smelling of sex and sweat. It was an intoxicating combination, and Dae knew it wouldn't take much for her to let lust consume her senses.

Seeming to recognize the effect she was having on her, Zafirah grabbed her discarded robe and donned it. "The night is yet young. Perhaps we could go for a walk through the palace?"

"Uh, I'd like that but not tonight." Dae paused, knowing it was foolish to feel self-conscious after the show Zafirah had given her. "I think I have some urgent needs that require immediate attention."

"Ah." Zafirah grinned unrepentantly. "I am pleased to have caused in you such a condition."

"I bet you are." Dae turned away from the other woman. Not really wanting to leave just yet, she wandered about the room curiously, recognizing aspects of Zafirah's nature everywhere. She paused in surprise at a table where a familiar object rested atop a velvet cloth. "Oh, wow! You have a rifle. I thought your people only used bows."

Zafirah glanced up sharply. When she saw what Dae was looking at, her eyes narrowed. "Rife-El?"

"Yeah." Dae reached out and ran a finger along the wooden stock of the weapon, smiling. "I guess you must trade with the western lands for them, right? This one doesn't look as ornate as the ones my people make."

The Scion strode over quickly and picked up the weapon. "You… you know what this is?"

"Of course." Dae studied the Scion wonderingly, seeing a tension in her that dispelled the languor of the previous hour. "You don't, though, do you?"

Zafirah shook her head.

"Then why do you have it?"

"Renegade tribes attacked a scouting party in the southern desert. They were armed with these weapons; only one of my scouts escaped the massacre. Their army will ride against my people probably within the week, and we know nothing of their weaknesses." Her eyes blazed fiercely, and Zafirah grabbed Dae by the shoulder. "This is a weapon of your land?"

"I-I guess so."

"Do you know how it works? Can you show me?"

Zafirah's grip on her was powerful, but Dae realized it was strength born of desperation, not anger toward her. "I don't know, maybe. My father had a rifle he used during the spring hunt. I saw him with it a few times but…"

Zafirah released her immediately. "You must tell me all you know."

"Okay…well, it's called a rifle for starters. It fires these small balls of lead that we call ballshot."

"From how great a distance can it kill?"

"I don't know, probably about twice as far as a bow. And my father said it was more accurate and powerful, too."

"So we have learned. How does it do this? Magic?"

Dae giggled a little and shook her head. "No, of course not. You pour black powder down into this tube—the barrel—and tap it firmly with a long stick. Then the ballshot goes in, and when you pull this lever here like this…" She curled a finger about the trigger and gave a sharp tug. The hammer snapped back and then immediately forward. Zafirah flinched as it struck a spark against a flint hidden at the base of the steel barrel. "That makes the powder explode, which fires the ballshot out here."

Zafirah nodded in understanding. "This powder? What is it?"

"We just call it black powder. I know it has coal dust in it, because my father had a big bin of it out in the barn. I don't know the other components, though."

Zafirah sniffed at the weapon distastefully. "It reeks of sulfur, the rock that burns. But what else?"

Dae shrugged helplessly. "I wish I could help you more."

"Mm." The Scion considered a long moment in silence, then asked, "Do you know any weaknesses of the weapon? How my people may defeat it?"

Dae thought about it. "Well, my father said the black powder wouldn't work if it got wet. I remember how disappointed he was when he had to cancel a hunt because it was raining too hard." Considering her words, she smiled ruefully. "I doubt that's much help to you, though, is it?"

"No, not much. Can we not shield ourselves from its fire?"

Dae shook her head. "Ballshot can penetrate all but the heaviest armor. You'd only weigh yourself down."

"Then what else?"

"Hm." Dae closed her eyes and tried to remember everything she'd ever heard about rifles and guns. The weapons were not commonly used in her homeland, at least not among the peasant classes, who could not be trusted with such deadly tools. Even among the armies of the nobility, firearms were used mostly to compliment the soldiers armed with longsword and shield, or in place of bow and arrow during their hunting contests. At last, she snapped her fingers. "They take time to reload, much longer than a bow. Once fired, they're useless for a time afterward."

"How long?"

"I guess it depends how well-trained the person reloading it is. But certainly long enough to attack them. Unless their army has another line of soldiers waiting to cover the others. My father's troops were trained that way, but it takes time and practice to master. I remember I used to love watching them in the fields... The way they moved was like a dance."

Zafirah hummed as she absorbed this information. "Anything else?"

Dae shrugged, wishing she knew more. "I-I suppose if they were carrying around barrels of the black powder with them, like in a wagon or on camels, you could blow them up with arrows soaked with oil. That would do a lot of damage, I know for sure. My father showed me what can happen with black powder so I wouldn't be tempted to play with it." Dae shuddered at the memory of that spectacular explosion that had forever stilled her curiosity about guns. "It's very dangerous if it catches on fire."

"Would you tell all this to my council?" Zafirah asked hopefully. "Anything at all you can remember would be useful."

"Of course, whatever I can do to help." Dae paused, observing the way Zafirah was regarding the rifle with caution and some fear. "This is why you went south, isn't it? Because your people were attacked with these?"

Zafirah nodded. "I must ride against the renegades as soon as they are exposed and cannot retreat."

A chill shiver ran up Dae's spine. "Y-you? Personally? Don't you have an army to fight for you?"

"I am their commander, Tahirah. It is a leader's place to lead, not to stay behind out of danger."

That wasn't the way most leaders in Dae's homeland viewed things, but she admired Zafirah's courage. "I'll do what I can to help you."

"I would be most grateful, as would my soldiers." Zafirah leaned down and placed a gentle kiss on Dae's forehead. "Tomorrow, I will assemble the council so you may share your knowledge."

"Okay." Dae smiled, still in a high state of arousal from Zafirah's display. "I guess I should get some sleep, then, huh?"

"Do you require an escort back to the harem?"

"No, I can manage." Dae laughed a little sheepishly. "The way I'm feeling right now, I'd probably end up inviting the guards back to my room with me!"

"Perhaps I should escort you personally then."

"Don't tempt me." A pause. "Any more than you already have, I mean."

Zafirah chuckled and patted her affectionately. "Then I shall bid you a pleasant night, *aziza*, and leave you to your dreams." She winked lecherously. "Do not exhaust yourself satisfying your needs, or you will be of no use as an advisor tomorrow."

Dae took her time wandering back to the harem, enjoying the beauty of the palace at night. A few guards gave her curious glances, knowing from her attire she was a pleasure-servant but not questioning her presence outside the seraglio. A few asked politely if they might be of assistance, but Dae assured them she was fine and was returning to her quarters for the evening. They accepted her words readily enough and wished her a pleasant night.

If Dae had hoped to find the other girls asleep, she was to be disappointed. As soon as she stepped back into the seraglio gardens she was met by at least a dozen of her fellow pleasure-servants, all of whom were eager to hear how her night with Zafirah had gone. Dae refused to go into any detail, which, quite naturally, led the girls to take up a guessing game of what delights the Scion might have shown her. Their graphic descriptions did nothing to cool her arousal, and she pleaded fatigue in order to escape. The girls laughed and let her go; they were all familiar with how a night spent in Zafirah's company could leave one in need of rest.

After stripping off her clothes, Dae crawled onto her sleeping pallet and extinguished the light. Closing her eyes, she let herself remember every detail of what she had shared with Zafirah that evening: every word spoken, every word she had wanted to speak. Fantasies of how she might have boldly ordered the dark-haired woman to stop her ministrations so she might see to her pleasure personally raced through Dae's mind as she let her arousal build. She didn't have the patience to drag this out, however, so her self-pleasuring was quick, almost frantic, and blisteringly intense. Only after three climaxes was Dae's body satisfied, and she took a moment to wash the sweat and juices from her body before closing her eyes once more and breathing a sigh of contentment.

The dreams that came and stole her away were vivid and erotic, alive with images of tanned skin and intense, crystalline eyes. Dae smiled in her sleep and murmured a single word filled with promise and warmth: "*Aziza…*"

# Chapter 17

"THIS IS FOLLY IN EXTREME, *Effendi*. We should wait!"

Shakir glanced from the ranks of his soldiers who were mobilizing to march and glared at Brak. Where others would have flinched to feel his burning gaze upon them, the grizzled elder remained impassive and unimpressed. He glared right back and repeated his protest. "You would set a hundred men against the Scion's legions? I had thought you were smarter than this!"

Shakir studied Brak a long moment in silence, then turned back to regard his troops. They were disciplined and well-organized, if not particularly numerous; even Brak could not deny that. Nevertheless, Shakir did not like the reminder that his plan for conquest was beginning to fray. In the last few weeks, his desire to strike against the Scion had deepened into a blind, consuming obsession, and in his frustration and rage, Shakir lashed out against his own men for even the slightest slip in discipline. He had felt the warriors watching him as he moved about the camp, nervous and wary, and despised them for the doubt he could see creeping into their eyes.

"Staying here is no longer an option, Brak," he finally spoke, his voice clear and certain. "Our outriders report the Herak have broken their camp and are moving closer to the city. The Scion Whore is alerted to danger; we must strike swiftly against the weaker tribes and cut them down before they can join her army and ride against us. If we do not, our enemy will crush us beneath sheer weight of numbers."

"But what of the extra weapons you promised?" Brak insisted angrily. "We should have five times our current number by now!"

"It is possible the trader has betrayed our pact," he admitted, keeping his face carefully expressionless to mask the growing fury he felt within. More than anything else, the treachery of the outlander merchant infuriated Shakir. In his darker musings he had concocted a lifetime of elaborate tortures he planned to inflict on the cursed outlander...if only the fates would see their paths intersect again. "If that is so, there is little we can do for the time being. We will complement the weapons with other warriors armed with spear, sword, and bow. We can still inflict damage on the Scion's forces."

"But no more than the stinging of a scorpion to bother a jackal." Brak snorted. "And when we are defeated, the vengeance of El'Kasari will be terrible! My people will suffer harshly for your failed promises of glory and retribution, Shakir!"

This time when Shakir pinned the elder with a piercing, angry glare, he was pleased to note a slight flicker of fear in the old man's eyes. Brak swallowed and glanced furtively away, and Shakir felt a vicious sense of satisfaction at seeing him cowed. He reveled in the full power of his zealotry, allowing the blind fury that drove him to burn brightly in his eyes.

"And so will you return to your camp in the desert?" the Calif asked in a mocking tone. "Will you run now, Brak, when battle calls you and your men? What will you tell your sons and daughters in the years to come when they ask why they must grovel in the sands while El'Kasari sits on the coast in defiance, fat and complacent? That you were too cowardly to seek a better life for them? That your fear of the enemy drove you back without even having lifted a blade against them?"

Brak's face flushed red with rage. "Bite your tongue, whelp!" he roared. His knuckles were white where he clutched the horn of his saddle as if he would have been happier to wrap his fingers about the Calif's neck. "My people do not run from battle! We will fight, and fight well!"

Shakir smiled thinly. "And the time to fight is now. We march north and east to smite the smaller tribes before the Scion can unite them under the banner of El'Kasari and retaliate."

Brak scowled darkly, and Shakir knew he still did not favor the improvised plan. "The Scion is no fool. Her scouts will know when we leave the cliffs."

"And when she comes to face us, we will be ready."

"How?"

Shakir held up his thunder-bow proudly. "These will level the field of battle. The Whore is a good fighter...but her skills will not avail her against our forces. She will ride at the head of her army, as she has always done in the past. We will pass the word through our people—a dozen of my tribe's finest horses will go to the one whose shot brings down the great Scion!" His smile dripped terrible malice. "When she has fallen...her army will crumble into chaos and we will tear them into pieces as they struggle to find order. Leaderless, their might will shatter easily."

Brak fell silent as he considered this, then he gave a reluctant but affirming grunt. The *spahi* were only as good as their leader; cut off the head, and the serpent would die. "True, if Zafirah were killed in battle—killed quickly and in view of her troops—morale would fail and confusion would be rampant."

"Then let us ride," Shakir said. "Northwards, gathering what men we can from the tribes of this alliance, and then on to the enemy." He smiled without humor as he surveyed his army, careful not to let his visage reveal any of the roiling emotions that plagued his mind and dug into his sanity. Shakir cared little for the fact that Brak was still studying him with a nervous eye or that his numbers were fewer than he had hoped for. If the life of every warrior he had assembled needed to be sacrificed in battle against the Scion, he would consider it a price well worth paying...so long as he could display Zafirah's head on a spear when the battle concluded.

He had only to contain his rage a little longer, to not give in to the zealous fire he could feel burning away at his mind, and he would have the opportunity to unleash that fury against the Scion's forces.

During the next week, Zafirah and Dae continued their romance at a more sedate pace. The Scion would spend what time she could away from her duties in the seraglio, more often than not favoring Dae's company over the more physically alluring temptations offered by the other pleasure-servants. Most nights they would walk together through the city or the palace halls and gardens, smiling and talking, hands clasped and shoulders frequently brushing. The various soldiers and servants about the palace would watch the couple as they strolled past, oblivious to all but the other, and would whisper between themselves how sweet the two seemed together.

Rumors that the Scion had initiated a courtship with the young outlander girl were quick to make their way out into the city, and the citizens of El'Kasari began making a point of offering Zafirah small tokens of devotion she might give to Dae whenever she walked among them. Knowing how little experience their beloved ruler had in affairs of the heart, most agreed the Scion could use all the help she could get in her quest to woo the charming girl.

When Dae mentioned how much she missed being able to read, Zafirah sent a contingent of traders to the docks to make enquiries among the foreign sailors. They returned with a vast assortment of scrolls and leather-bound books, written in many languages, but Dae was utterly delighted to find several works by familiar authors. Dae accepted all the love-tokens with demure blushes of pleasure, making certain Zafirah's kindness was rewarded with a lingering kiss every chance she got.

Indeed, the kisses and gentle touches exchanged between the two women grew more frequent as their bond strengthened—more frequent and less easily held in check. Though Zafirah was no stranger to the hungers of her sexual appetite, at times Dae found herself struggling to suppress urges and desires that surged within her like a rising tide. She would remember Inaya's words on the subject each night as she lay in bed, her body awash with longing despite her best efforts to appease it: *Sexual pleasure is about intimacy and passion. It is a hunger for the body of your lover that grows so great it consumes your every thought. A hunger so powerful it can never be fully satisfied, only calmed for a time.*

At the time, the explanation had seemed confusing; now, it was all too easily understood. Zafirah's body seemed like a magnet to her; it drew her to it with its intoxicating curves and an irresistible siren song of lust. Dae wanted to lose herself in Zafirah, wanted to drown her senses in white-hot ecstasies that promised a union and connection deeper and more terrifying than any she'd ever known. Her need for that consummation of the flesh grew stronger with the passing of each day, with every hour spent in Zafirah's company. And as much as she wanted to be sensible about the whole thing and to take her seduction and courtship one step at a time, Dae knew she didn't have the willpower to fight for restraint for long.

Thoughts of what delights she might share with Zafirah were rushing heedlessly through Dae's head as she returned to her bedchamber to prepare for another evening with her. That morning the Scion had asked if she might like to accompany her on a walk through the stables, and Dae, who had always been fond of horses despite never having learned to ride, had enthusiastically accepted the invitation. There was at least another hour before Zafirah would come collect her, time Dae planned on using to arrange her hair, clothing, and general appearance for her date. Those plans were overridden, however, when Dae reached the doorway to her room and heard something far more compelling: a low, extremely erotic-sounding moan originating from further down the corridor.

Dae stopped instantly, ears pricked. A moment later, a second breathless cry came, followed by the words, "Yes! *Nek ni*! Please, yes!"

A rush of blood flowed through her lower regions as those words cleared away any doubts as to what was inspiring the moaning, words she had learned from Johara and Hayam as part of her "education." Dae knew she had no business standing there listening to the continued noises, but her feet refused to obey all orders to carry her into her bedchamber...and instead, decided to take her further down the corridor toward the intriguing sounds. Shocked at the behavior of her uncooperative limbs, Dae tried to ignore the moans and whimpers as best she could while struggling to convince her body that its little rebellion was entirely inappropriate.

As she made her way down the corridor, it became apparent that the room from which these sounds were emanating was the one situated at the farthest end of the hallway. *That's Johara and Hayam's room*, Dae realized. This changed things a little for her; after all, the lovers had told her she was welcome to join them at any time, even if only to watch. Dae hesitated, considering. She was going to be spending time with Zafirah later. Did she really want to get herself all worked up by watching Johara and Hayam ravishing one another?

"Ah! Faster, please! Stop teasing me, I beg! *Nek ni*! Do it!"

Another voice—Hayam, she guessed from the exotic northern accent—replied. "Teasing you? I have barely begun to tease you. You will need to improve your begging if you hope to climax any time soon." A high-pitched squeak followed this statement, quickly making Dae's mind up for her. Steeling herself with a deep breath, she stepped into the doorway and cleared her throat.

The sight that greeted her was unexpected, and after her last visit to this room, Dae considered herself braced for pretty much anything. But when *three* pairs of eyes turned toward her, Dae could only stare, mouth agape, the witty and seductive introduction she had imagined herself using vanishing in a heartbeat.

Johara was reclining on the bed in the center of the room, only the briefest of undergarments keeping her from being completely naked. The lanky brunette had apparently been occupied watching her lover as she pleasured a third woman, a fellow harem inhabitant Dae didn't know very well named Suhayla, against the far wall. The scene itself might not have been so shocking to Dae—who, having lived in the harem for so long now, knew well enough that pleasure was shared as easily and as readily between three or more as between two—but for the fact that Suhayla was bound spread-eagled between a set of pillars by lengths of silken cord, her body glistening with sweat, eyes glazed with lust.

It took Dae only a moment to realize that Suhayla's bondage was quite voluntary. The eager, almost ravenous expression on her face was clear indication she was enjoying every moment of whatever Hayam had been doing to her.

Not expecting to find Johara and Hayam already entertaining a guest, Dae wasn't sure what she should do next. The etiquette of sexual liaisons among the pleasure-servants was still something of a mystery to her. "I-I'm sorry, I didn't...know you were..."

But Johara flashed a brilliant, pleased smile and shook her head. "Not at all, little Dae. You know you are welcome here any time." With the grace of a panther she rose from the bed and gestured for Dae to approach. "Please, do not be shy. Enter, and most welcome." Laughing gray eyes glanced toward Hayam and Suhayla, then back to Dae. "I am certain our guest will be delighted to entertain another spectator, right, Suhayla?"

The bound girl fixed hungry, hooded eyes on Dae, muscles strained with pleasure. "Oh yes. Delighted."

Johara grinned at her. "You see? We have been playing with Suhayla for over an hour now. Your interruption is far from unwanted. Please, will you not stay?"

Dae looked from Johara to Hayam, then to Suhayla, plucking at her trousers uncertainly. She hadn't spoken with Suhayla much during her time here; the girl was polite and quiet, born of the desert tribes and possessing the kind of beautiful, virtuous features one would never suspect could harbor immodest thoughts of any kind. She rarely danced with the other girls, rarely joined in their flirtatious behavior, and her sleeping patterns were such that Dae only saw her occasionally. Dae had wondered for a time if perhaps she simply didn't enjoy the attentions of other women as her fellow pleasure-servants did...a notion that had been shockingly corrected when Suhayla propositioned her one evening with suggestions so lurid in their detail that it seemed impossible they could have fallen from such seemingly innocent lips. Still, looking at her now, naked and bound, Dae acknowledged that the desert girl was ravishingly attractive. She took a cautious, wondering step closer, noticing for the first time that Hayam was wearing some kind of bizarre undergarment about her waist.

"What are you...?" She glanced to Johara for explanation. "Why is she tied up?"

Johara stepped behind Dae and gently guided her a few paces closer to the pair. "It is something Suhayla enjoys," she offered simply. "Suhayla comes to us several times each moon to be pleasured in such fashion." Gentle hands were laid upon Dae's shoulder, pressing her forward. "Come, it may interest you to see what Hayam is doing. This is yet another method of pleasure we did not have the opportunity to show you last time."

Hayam had turned back to her task, and Dae saw now that her hips were thrusting in an undulating manner against the bound Suhayla. When Johara guided her closer, she gasped in surprise. A strange shaft protruded from between Hayam's legs, pressing into Suhayla's womanhood on each forward thrust. The shaft seemed to be connected to Hayam by means of a leather harness strapped about her slender waist.

"It is a phallus," Johara explained when Dae turned to her in silent question. "They have many forms and designs and can be crafted from a variety of materials: leather, horn, wood, even stone. There are many different styles for different applications, but in general they are intended to substitute the male member."

Dae stared at the phallus as it disappeared into Suhayla slowly, the shaft gleaming with the juices her arousal as it slid in. The blush which ordinarily would have colored her cheeks was subdued by genuine intrigue at the device. "You mean a woman can make love like a man?" she asked, marveling at the concept.

"Not exactly. In my time as a body-slave, before I came to Zafirah, I experienced male lovers on occasion. None of them had quite the same technique as a woman in this style of passion, and certainly none of them possessed the same endurance!"

Suhayla was whimpering now, twisting slightly in her bonds. "Please, Hayam! Faster!"

Hayam just grinned and maintained her slow, teasing pace. Dae saw how she was controlling the rhythm of their motions by keeping firm hold of Suhayla's hips. When the captive girl tried to meet her thrusts, Hayam would pull back slightly, using her grip to steady their connection. Suhayla's whole body was rigid with need, her breathing shallow and desperate. But her pleas fell on deaf ears, for Hayam seemed to be enjoying her task too much to want to increase the speed of her thrusts anytime soon.

"Doesn't that hurt?" Dae asked, fascinated by the way the folds of Suhayla's sex seemed to cling to the phallus as it was withdrawn.

"For a virgin, yes, there is a moment of pain. But it is negligible compared to the pleasure of being filled by a lover so completely."

"Why does she like being tied up?" Dae wondered aloud. Warm hands rested on her shoulders a moment before gliding lower, over her arms and down to her hips, sparking fires in her sensitive skin all along the way. Johara shifted closer, and Dae felt her breath tickle her ear.

"Is it so difficult to understand the appeal?" Johara whispered, causing a tremble to wash through Dae as her touches became more intimate and suggestive. "Trust is such an important element of pleasure, little one, for without trust we can never truly be at ease. Suhayla enjoys the restraint because it sharpens her awareness of that trust element. To be naked and exposed…" Her hands shifted around to play along Dae's taut abdomen. "…helpless, entirely at our mercy…" Long fingers played idly with Dae's navel. "…yet to be comfortable in the knowledge that we will take that sacrifice of all control and reward it only with pleasure." Johara sighed as Dae sucked in a quick breath, squirming a little as the light touches stirred her arousal. "Can you not imagine how exciting that might feel if you were to give yourself to Zafirah is such a way? To demonstrate such absolute faith in her, to feed off of her arousal as she looks upon you, bound and helpless before her?" Her voice dropped to a seductive purr. "Might that not arouse you, little Dae?"

Dae could only nod slightly, her body brought to life by the sight of Hayam and Suhayla and the voice and touch of Johara.

"Or perhaps," Johara continued, "it would please you more to see the Scion tied to her bed, that magnificent body eagerly laid bare for whatever tender mercies you could devise?"

That image caused Dae to close her eyes and moan audibly. She offered no resistance as Johara's touch roamed up her front until her fingers were skirting along the edges of her top teasingly. "Yessss."

"Keep your eyes open, child," Johara instructed. "Watch Hayam work. She has been teasing Suhayla a long time now, denying her the fulfillment she craves. With such prolonged torment, her climax will be quite spectacular."

Dae did as she was bidden and opened her eyes, watching the way Suhayla was being taken and imagining how it might feel to be in her place. As it was, Johara's continued touches were enough to have caused her to soak her undergarments thoroughly, but she felt no shame for her excitement. Indeed, she was eager for more.

"Do you think Zafirah would really…let me tie her up?" she asked breathlessly, feeling Johara toy with the laces of her top.

"I cannot imagine the Scion denying you her body in any way you might claim it," came the husky reply. There was a playful pause. "Would it interest you to know that I have seen Zafirah in such a position before? Have pleasured her when she was bound?"

"Really?"

"Indeed. While it is not a style of passion she indulges in often, she is certainly no stranger to ropes and chains." Johara's voice was like a caress, lingering and sweet. "Oh, how she screamed when we finally allowed her to climax! Such bliss!" A sigh. "And for you, little one, she would offer up her very soul just to see you smile."

Dae stood unmoving, considering the validity of that claim seriously. "I suppose I'd do the same for her, too," she said.

Johara planted a light kiss on Dae's bare shoulder. "Love is a many-splendored thing." Looking down, Dae watched Johara's hands play against the silky, bejeweled material of her brief top. "Does my touch arouse you?" Johara teased. "Your nipples shall pierce cloth if they grow any stiffer."

Dae was all too aware of her body's response; she could feel her nipples straining against the gossamer material of her top, evidence of her mounting arousal. "Well, if you keep this up much longer—"

"It would be my greatest pleasure," Johara finished without hesitation, tugging suggestively at the laces of Dae's top. "If you would but grant permission for me to unlace this humble cord that hides your flesh from those who would admire you..."

Dae's breathing was ragged, but she was still in control of herself. Certainly she was in control enough to know she wanted this to continue. She gave a mental shrug. *What the hell. Let's see where this goes.* "All right, then. Slowly."

Johara's fingers stilled instantly, and Dae realized her offer had been playful, meant in jest. She hadn't expected Dae to take her up on it, and it was exciting for Dae to realize her bold response had taken the more experienced pleasure-servant by surprise. Even so, Johara didn't seem in any hurry to deny her invitation to take this further. With a gentle motion, she defeated the simple knot that held the cord tied. "I am honored," Johara whispered softly against her ear as she worked the laces out, and Dae was amused and pleased to feel that her hands—normally so confident and certain in matters of carnal delights—were trembling in anticipation. "You may ask me to stop any time you wish."

Dae arched her back a little, feeling very safe and at ease in Johara's arms. She shivered slightly as more of her smooth, pale skin was revealed with the parting of cloth. "I trust you."

"Were you not saving such intimacies for Zafirah?" Johara asked, the slight tremor in her voice revealing to Dae the depth of her excitement. "I have no desire to steal such opportunity from your love, no matter how tempting the prize."

"Some intimacies, yes," Dae said. "But things like this..." She sighed as Johara's touch scored close to her sensitive nipple. "Things like this I'm happy to share with you."

"As you wish, little one." Johara kissed, then licked along the pillar of Dae's neck, and Dae tilted her head to the side to allow her unrestricted access to her skin. "Perhaps you might care to assist in Suhayla's pleasure later? You could wear a phallus without risk to your physical virtue."

Dae shivered at the thought, then again as her top was pulled fully open and her breasts laid bare. "We'll see," she gasped. "I promised I'd meet Zafirah in the seraglio in an hour."

"Ooh, how wicked of you!" Johara teased lightheartedly. "Seeking a dalliance before your rendezvous with our beloved mistress."

"It's not like that," Dae protested weakly, pushing herself against Johara's hands as they caressed the curve of her breasts. "I heard a noise and thought...maybe I could watch..."

"And stir your passion before meeting with the Scion? You play with fire, little one, and I suspect you wish to get burned."

"Mm, maybe." Dae's legs almost gave out when Johara's fingers sought out her aroused nipples and began to twist them gently. Pleasure shot straight to her center, and she might have collapsed had the taller woman not moved to brace her up. She felt the length of Johara's body press against her back, aware of her feminine lines and the contact of her breasts. "This feels nice," she hummed, watching Hayam and Suhayla begin moving to a faster rhythm. The bound woman was gazing back at her hungrily while Hayam glanced back from time to time, smiling at her lover enviously.

"I think your mate is jealous," Dae observed with a slinky grin.

"Perhaps you might be willing to appease her another time."

Hayam threw her lover a quick smirk, then let her gaze linger over Dae's breasts a long moment before shifting her focus back to Suhayla.

"Well I wouldn't want you to have to fight over me," Dae said, quite enjoying the knowledge that she inspired such hunger in the others. "It seems only fair to include her."

"My sentiments exactly."

Suhayla's arms were straining desperately against the silken rope that held them spread. "Please," she sobbed, tendrils of her dark hair plastered to her face with sweat. "I cannot take much more, Hayam! Let me come!"

"Patience, lover," Hayam soothed. "I am in control of your pleasure for now and will decide when and how you climax." She moved her hips in a sharp and sudden thrust, fully embedding the phallus, then ground herself firmly against Suhayla. Suhayla's head lolled back, eyes rolling upward in their sockets. Hayam looked over to Dae as she withdrew from her captive, running a finger down Suhayla's cheek. "Such a deceptively innocent face she has, hmm? Much like you." She watched Johara's hands excite Dae's body with great interest. "Always the quiet ones who become demons in the bedroom."

Dae felt Johara's body shake against her as she chuckled. "What does she mean?"

Johara continued her attentive and experienced ministrations. "Nothing, little one. She refers to the fact that quiet and unassuming girls are often possessed of surprisingly intense, adventurous sexual natures."

"Really?"

"In my own experience, yes, though it is not a perfect truth by any means."

Dae considered this curiously as her senses were inflamed by Johara's touch. "What about Inaya? She's fairly quiet."

"Indeed she is, little one." Johara leaned closer and nibbled very lightly on Dae's ear before whispering, "But if you wish to learn more of her sexual tastes, you shall have to ask her directly. Her preferences are not so easily explained."

That statement intrigued Dae enormously, and she would have liked to pursue the subject further. However, Johara's attentions became suddenly more purposeful, effectively distracting her with pleasure. Dae gasped and grabbed at Johara's hands with her own, amazed by how sensitized her breasts had become and how the pleasure seemed to shoot straight down to her core. "Gods above!"

"You like?"

"Yes, but...how?"

The air in the room had grown thick with the mingled scents of their arousal, and when she felt Johara press her own center against her backside, Dae almost swooned at the erotic tension building fast between them. "Many years of experience, child, and a willing and enthusiastic soulmate with whom to practice." Johara's lips sucked at the hollow of Dae's neck, teeth scoring her pale skin. "You do not touch your breasts when you pleasure yourself?"

"I-I do but—GODS!" Dae uttered a shocked squeak of surprise as Johara tugged at her nipples. "They never felt like this before!"

"Perhaps you should spend more time attending to them," Johara suggested silkily. "They seem so delightfully sensitive..."

"Yesss!"

Dae's cries mingled with Suhayla's in an ecstatic orchestra as both women were pushed closer to climax. She felt Johara's hips begin grinding against her buttocks and flexed her muscles to encourage the stimulating movements. The sight of Hayam thrusting harder and faster into Suhayla, combined with the sensation of Johara's hands and the warmth of her body where it seemed to fuse with her own flesh, sent her pleasure spiraling ever higher. Dae struggled to hold her stance when she felt Johara's breath tickle the fine hairs at the nape of her neck and heard her husky whisper. "Will you come for me, little one? It would excite me greatly to feel you climax against me."

Dae didn't have breath to respond coherently, but her body had already decided the matter for her. Her sex was pulsing in time with her accelerated heartbeat, yearning for some kind of contact. But when she reached down to satisfy her need, Johara stopped her.

"No, Dae."

"But—"

"You need not touch yourself. Relax. Let me show you."

Whimpering, desperately wanting direct stimulation, Dae nevertheless allowed Johara to guide her hands back up to her breasts. "I can't—I mean…I want—"

"Release?" Johara's long fingers resumed their wonderful attentions. "You shall have it."

"But—"

"Trust me, little one. Pleasure lives in every part of your body, not just between your legs. Keep those emerald eyes of yours on Suhayla… and *feel* what I do."

Uncertain, but trusting in Johara's experience, Dae followed her instructions. She watched with rising excitement as Hayam claimed the bound girl with greater force and fervor, feeling blissful tingles arc between her grateful breasts and jealous sex. As Johara continued her artful ministrations, a familiar pressure built low in Dae's belly…a pressure she had learned could mean only one thing.

Her eyes widened in disbelief. Dae's legs weakened in expectation, her senses lust-addled and about to shatter. "I-I think…"

"I have you, little Dae. Let go."

Suhayla's cries were constant now, the hours of patient teasing her body had endured culminating in the dawn of inevitable climax. Dae felt her own sex tense in sympathy, then twitch and spasm. *This is impossible!*

"I can't—" she gasped.

But apparently, she could.

Dae screamed as her legs gave out, falling forward a little before Johara caught and steadied her. Waves of pleasure rushed through her in directionless patterns, her climax seeming to originate from every part of her body at once in an overwhelming tide. It was far more intense and shattering than anything she had experienced at her own hands, and Johara expertly kept her senses floating in a haze of swirling ecstasy for long moments. In some distant part of her mind, she heard and saw Suhayla succumb to her own orgasm, felt Johara rock her center firmly against her backside and hold the contact as she too was overwhelmed. When she started coming back to her senses, Dae was surprised to see Suhayla still caught in the thrashing grip of ultimate release. She hung limp and unresisting in her bondage, supported by a considerate Hayam, who continued to move against her until it became clear that she had lost consciousness.

Without knowing quite how it had happened, Dae found herself on the bed, cradled in Johara's lap as the tall woman stroked her hair gently and hummed a calming melody. When the final pulses of climax had dissipated, she looked around with a fuzzy expression. "Wh-what happened?"

"If you have cause to ask, perhaps I need to improve my technique."

Dae blushed and sat up, shifting on the bed to face Johara. "How did…? I mean, you never even touched me…there…" She glanced down, and her cheeks flushed hotter when she saw the dark patch at the crotch of her trousers where her climax had soaked the sheer silk.

Johara shushed her quietly. "No need to color so, little one. You were beautiful!"

Dae studied the pillows of the bed intently. "I didn't know that could happen like that."

"Experience is the highest form of education, and there is so very much you have yet to learn of these subjects."

Dae chuckled quietly at her own innocence. "And here I thought I was getting pretty good at it."

"No doubt you are, little one." Johara leaned down and placed a soft, chaste kiss on Dae's cheek, stroking her head fondly. "But there is far more to the world of pleasure than what your own hands can teach."

"So I see." Dae glanced over to where Hayam was wrestling with the knots that held Suhayla tied up. The desert girl was no help at all, unable to support her own weight due to her state of unconsciousness. "Will she be okay?"

"She will be fine," Johara assured her. "It is always this way with her; the intensity of such a climax steals her from us for a time, but she will recover soon enough to find herself tied to our bed, whereupon I shall have opportunity to ravish her while she thanks Hayam properly for giving her release."

Dae giggled and turned away, thinking. When she glanced at Johara again from beneath disheveled blonde locks, her eyes were playful yet shy. "You know, I still have a while before I'm supposed to meet with Zafirah. Would you maybe…like some help?"

Johara's white teeth flashed her a joyous smile. "Assistance is always appreciated." The two women made room on the bed for Hayam to lay her precious burden down, and Dae saw Johara grinning broadly at the unmasked expression of eager anticipation she couldn't hide. She managed a shy but excited smile, and Johara laughed and stroked her cheek affectionately.

"Always the quiet ones, indeed." Johara smiled...and given the circumstances, Dae didn't bother offering a protest.

Zafirah noticed that Dae was unusually subdued as they walked side by side through the palace hallways, but she politely kept her questions to herself. The way the young girl was stealing secretive, thoughtful glances at her, as well as the subtle scent of arousal that warred with the stronger perfume of jasmine and wild rose, gave the Scion at least a hint as to what was occupying Dae's thoughts. But as much as she would have liked to pursue the matter, Zafirah resisted. The news she had received from Falak's scouts less than an hour previous made her grateful for every moment she could enjoy with the lovely blonde.

When they reached the stables, Dae was surprised by the amount of activity going on all around. People—*spahi* riders, she surmised from their attire—hurried about the compound in orderly chaos while their captains issued orders in loud, serious voices. She looked curiously at Zafirah, able to meet the taller woman's gaze without blushing terribly for the first time that evening. "What's going on?"

Zafirah sighed. "The renegade tribes are on the move," she said. "They march toward the less-unified tribes of the Scion alliance, no doubt hoping to crush them quickly. We must ride out to face them on the desert sands."

Dae stared at her in shock for a moment, then spun back around the watch the soldiers. "You mean...war?"

"A battle, yes." Zafirah reached out to clasp Dae's hand reassuringly in her own. "Thanks to you, Tahirah, we at least ride with knowledge of our enemies and the power they wield. The information you gave the council about these Rife-El's will save many lives."

Dae shivered at the warmth of the Scion's hand, hoping Zafirah couldn't read her arousal too easily. Her time with Johara, Hayam, and Suhayla had left her in a highly responsive state, and her mind was still filled with images of naked, sweat-slicked flesh and writhing bodies. "I'm glad I could help you," she said. "Does this mean you'll be leaving tonight?"

"No, little one. Tonight and most of tomorrow will be spent organizing the army and preparing supply wagons and a route into the desert. We will leave when the sun begins to cool late tomorrow evening, marching through the night and camping through the day." Zafirah laid a hand on her shoulder and guided their footsteps through the busy stables. "I regret I must leave again so soon, but at least we shall have tonight together."

Dae returned the smile a little uncertainly; she wasn't convinced she could resist the urge to strip the older woman bare and demand a thorough ravishing before Zafirah left. Clearing her throat, she squeezed the larger hand clasped in her own. "You'll be in danger, won't you?"

"Some, perhaps, but I am as skilled in the warrior arts as I am in the arts of pleasure." Dark eyebrows waggled playfully. "Will you worry about me while I am gone?"

"Of course I will." Dae forced herself not to think about the possibility of Zafirah getting hurt, not liking the way it made her stomach churn with sickening dread. "But you'll be careful for me, I know."

"Have no fears, *aziza*. I shall return unscathed, and the foolish curs who threaten my people will flee back to the deep desert, tails between their legs!"

"Good." There was a pause then while they stopped to admire a group of *spahi* as they ran through a short, impressive series of equine acrobatics, Dae marveling at the sight in awe. When they continued on, Dae cast her taller companion a shy, wondering look. "Zafirah?"

"Hmm?"

"When...when you call me *aziza* like that...?"

"Yes?"

"Do you mean it? Is that what I am to you?"

Zafirah lifted a hand and tenderly ran her fingertips along Dae's cheek. She smiled, a warm, loving smile that caused Dae's heart to burn.

"I never speak words I do not mean, my Tahirah," she said, "that one least of all."

"Oh." Dae looked away, fearing she'd turn into a puddle if Zafirah continued looking at her like that. "Have you ever called anyone else that before?"

"No, only you." Soft lips brushed lightly against the crown of Dae's head, inspiring a sharp intake of breath. "You are my beloved. And I hope one day, you will consider me yours."

"I do!" Dae said quickly. "I-I definitely do, I just...wasn't sure..."

"Shush, I understand." Zafirah pulled Dae's shorter body to her, wrapping long arms about the girl's waist and resting her hands tentatively on her backside. "I do not make such things very clear, do I? Seeking pleasure with others so frequently?"

Dae breathed in the scent of spice and leather, wishing she could remain in this embrace all night. "Just part of your charm, Zafirah. And I really don't mind."

"Really?"

"Of course not. You've never forbade me to engage with the other girls in the harem. It would be hypocritical to ask you to restrain your desires, not to mention cruel, since we don't actually...you know? Together." A pause. "Yet."

"This is true." Zafirah soaked in the knowledge that Dae was willing to accept her completely, but soon enough, a wicked thought occurred. "So...have you?"

"Have I what?"

"Engaged with the other girls?" The way Dae instantly broke eye contact and let her hair fall forward to hide her face was all the answer Zafirah needed, and she raised an eyebrow curiously. "I know you spent some time with Johara and Hayam, but...?"

"I haven't done much," Dae defended modestly. "I want to share most things with you, at least for the first time. But..."

Zafirah's fingertips tickled Dae's side teasingly, making her giggle. "You must tell me more, my little temptress."

Dae escaped out of reach of the dark-haired woman's long arms, laughing playfully. "Well, I actually do have a few questions I'd like to ask you."

"Oh? Then consider my wisdom entirely at your disposal."

She glanced about the stable compound, noting the way several people were watching her and the Scion with amusement and interest. "Later, okay?"

Zafirah, more accustomed to life in the public eye, agreed it would be better to continue in private. "As you wish." She held out her hand for Dae to take, and together they continued their tour of the stables.

The evening was a pleasant one, passing quietly and without drama, for which Zafirah in particular was grateful. With the prospect of several days, possibly weeks, spent separated from El'Kasari and Dae, the Scion cherished every moment of this time spent in her gentle company. The coming battle would be an uncertain affair: she had only the cloudiest outline of a plan in mind to defeat Shakir and his renegade army, and the untested element of the foreign weapons added to the danger significantly. Still, Zafirah set thoughts of battle aside for now, content to enjoy the night and bask in Dae's affection.

It was late by the time they made their way back to the Scion's bedchamber, and Zafirah's body was humming with desire at the thought of what questions Dae might ask her and how she might be able to illustrate her answers. As Zafirah made her way around the room lighting oil lamps, Dae settled herself gingerly on the bed, hands folded demurely in her lap.

"So..." Zafirah glanced at the young blonde. "Questions?"

"Yes, umm..." Dae shifted, wondering if she had the courage to actually ask what she wanted, or where to even start. She took a steadying breath. "Well, before you came to the seraglio tonight, I paid a visit to Johara and Hayam."

"Indeed." Zafirah settled herself into a seat opposite from Dae, not wanting to tempt herself by sitting on the bed. "Were they...?" She raised an eyebrow meaningfully.

Dae couldn't stop the blood from rushing to her face and other, more southerly, places. "They were uh...occupied, yes." She paused. "With someone else."

"I see." Zafirah grinned, liking this tale very much already. "May I ask who?"

"Suhayla."

"Ah." Zafirah's grin grew wider, already suspecting where this conversation might be headed. "Let me guess; she was, shall we say... restrained?"

"How did you...?"

"Suhayla's preferences are well known to me, Tahirah. She is, after all, *my* pleasure-servant. I would consider myself remiss were I ignorant of what pleases her the most."

"Oh. Well, I...I suppose that makes sense."

"So, you wondered why she was bound?"

"No, Johara explained it to me so I understood." Dae tried to set her gaze anywhere else but Zafirah's face, but it wasn't easy; she could feel energy crackle between them, as though the air itself had become charged. "It seemed...interesting."

Zafirah made no comment, but her mind filled with images of Dae, naked and bound to her bed, pleading to be ravished at the point of her tongue. Her breathing became a little shallower.

"Anyway," Dae continued, "the thing I was wondering about... Hayam was using this thing on Suhayla. Johara called it a phallus." She glanced up. Zafirah nodded to show she understood what Dae was referring to. "Well, it definitely seemed like Suhayla was enjoying it, and I was curious about whether maybe...you...?" She left the question hanging.

Zafirah was silent a long while, amazed that the girl who once claimed she would never indulge in pleasure with another female was now asking whether she owned a phallus. After she shook away her initial lustful thoughts—which chiefly involved tying Dae up and introducing her to every sexual device in her collection in a very personal way—Zafirah stood and walked over to the intricately-carved wall cabinet mounted opposite her bed. She opened the double doors and gestured for Dae to come closer.

Curious, Dae moved to stand beside the taller woman, studying the contents of the cabinet with interest. Her lips pursed in consideration as she looked from one item to the next, estimating that there were at least a hundred individual pieces in the cabinet.

"What are they?" From the way they were displayed, she thought at first they were weapons of some kind, but if so, they were the strangest weapons she had ever seen.

Zafirah ran her fingers over the assorted items in an almost loving caress. "These are devices akin to the phallus you saw Hayam using— devices designed to bring pleasure to the female body."

Dae's eyes widened in awe as she regarded the cabinet with new respect. "*All* of them?"

"Yes, all of them."

She took a step closer, intrigued. "There are so many!"

"I have spent many years collecting them," Zafirah explained. "There are pieces here gathered from every corner of the known world. Even," she added with a smile, "from your own land."

"*My* land? But people don't use things like this in...my..." She trailed off as Zafirah regarded her with steady calm. "No—"

"The laws in your land may forbid women from lying with other women and men from lying with other men, but laws do not change the hearts of people, nor dictate the terms of love." Zafirah plucked an elegantly carved length of ivory from her collection and held it out. Dae saw it was a phallus, artistically carved to depict two women locked in an embrace. "This was made in the eastern lands especially for me. The woman who carved it most certainly did not agree with, nor adhere to, the laws that forbade her desires."

Dae was shocked by this revelation, even as a part of her found it strangely comforting. *Others in my land feel the same as I do.* In some absurd way, that idea made her feel not quite so confused or alone. She turned her attention back to the other sexual devices, trying to deduce how each one worked. Some were obvious, but others... She pointed to a string of what looked like glass beads. "What on earth do you do with those?"

Zafirah chuckled as she set the phallus back in its proper place. "I would be delighted to demonstrate their use, *aziza*."

"Some other time, perhaps." Dae let her eyes move over the amazing and varied tools of pleasure, awed by their number and diversity. "You've used all of these?"

"I have, at one time or another, tested each of them thoroughly, yes." Zafirah stepped closer and rested her hands on Dae's shoulders. "One day, perhaps you will be able to say the same."

The hours—weeks, more likely—of blistering pleasure that statement promised were enough to make Dae dizzy. "That might take a long time," she whispered hoarsely.

"I am a patient teacher."

"Then I could be a willing student." Dae turned about and surprised Zafirah with a searing kiss, standing on tiptoes to allow her tongue leverage to pierce the taller woman's lips and conquer her mouth. The Scion moaned and surrendered to the unusually aggressive assault, sucking at Dae's questing tongue hungrily and wrapping her in a tight embrace. When they eventually parted, both women were breathing hard.

Dae clutched at Zafirah greedily. "I wish you didn't have to leave. You have no idea how much I want to give you a proper goodbye."

Zafirah groaned and bent to suckle at Dae's neck, her lips unconsciously taking up the exact same position as Johara's had just hours earlier. "That would be wonderful."

"Mm." Dae pulled back and gazed up at the other woman with eyes ablaze with wicked passion. "But unfortunately for both of us, there's something I want even more."

"What?"

"To give you a proper welcome home when you return."

The excited light in Zafirah's eyes dimmed with the realization that once again, her lust would have to be leashed. "You are evil, my Tahirah," she moaned.

"Perhaps." Dae deliberately dragged her tongue along Zafirah's collarbone, feeling bold after her experiences with Johara, Hayam, and Suhayla. "But you have to admit, it makes an excellent incentive. You return to me safe and unharmed, and as a reward..." She sucked briefly at Zafirah's earlobe before whispering, "I let you show me how your tongue feels dancing over my most intimate and untouched treasures."

Zafirah mercifully pulled away. If their bodies remained in contact much longer, Dae knew she would be unable to control herself. Zafirah regarded her hungrily. "With such a promise in mind, Shakir and his dogs shall rue the day they thought to attack my people. But are you certain it is a promise you wish to keep?"

"Believe me, I'll be looking forward to it just as much as you." Dae shivered in memory. "It seemed so intense and erotic when Johara was feeding on Hayam. You have no idea how often I've imagined how it will feel letting you do that to me." She stepped closer, her expression predatory. "Or how you might taste when I do it to you..."

"Gods above, girl! Have some compassion!" Zafirah backed up a pace. "For such delicious reward, I would willingly take on a thousand warriors single-handed!"

"Really?" Dae's nose crinkled as a new thought occurred. "Then you won't mind if I add on an extra little condition, will you?"

Zafirah froze. "L-like what?"

"While you're away"—Dae smiled—"I want you to abstain from all sexual pleasure."

"*What?*"

"You heard me. No seducing the nomads' daughters. No 'motivating' the troops." Dae's voice dropped to a low purr. "When you get back to me, Zafirah, I want you so eager for my touch you'll explode the instant I lay hands upon your flesh."

Zafirah turned away, trembling, her eyes squeezed shut. "You cannot know what you ask of me."

"I do know," Dae said, reveling in the erotically charged atmosphere she'd created. "I understand how hard it is for you to deny yourself, but you can do it if you try. When we make love for the first time, I want it to be like it was when you took Nasheta. I want you dripping before I even touch you, delirious with want for me. I want to feel your love and desire in every way you can show it." She paused. "If you do this for me, *aziza*, I'll give you a welcome home you won't soon forget."

Zafirah considered the request seriously. True, it would be difficult to curb her appetites, but not impossible. After all, she could vent her energy somewhat on the battlefield and keep her mind occupied planning and refining her strategy against the renegade Calif. Slowly, a smile spread across her lips, and she turned back to face Dae. "Very well," she agreed. "But I have a condition of my own."

Sensing victory, Dae spread her hands in expectation. "Name it."

"You must adhere to the same rule."

Dae's smile vanished. "Me? But I don't—"

"While I am gone, my not-so-innocent little temptress, there will be no nightly forays into the world of self-induced ecstasies for you. As you lay in bed each night, your fingers will remain idle and well-behaved." Zafirah could tell from Dae's expression that this prospect held no appeal for the young woman. "When I return, I wish for you to hunger for me as greatly as I for you."

Dae pursed her lips in contemplation, then she gave a single firm nod. "I guess that's fair," she accepted grudgingly. "If you can behave yourself, I'm certain I can as well."

"Excellent." Zafirah clapped her hands. "And now, I fear the hour has grown late for us. There will be many matters requiring my attention tomorrow, and I will pay dearly for any lost sleep."

"I should probably get some rest too, I suppose," Dae said. She gave Zafirah a hopeful look. "Will you come visit me before you leave?"

"I promise, though I will not be able to give you as much of my time as I would wish." Steeling herself, Zafirah held out her arms and pulled Dae into a hug. "Once my people are safe and the enemy routed, I swear we will have all the time in the world to explore our affections, *aziza*. And I will show you such pleasure as you cannot imagine." She placed a light kiss on Dae's hair.

"Just be safe," she demanded in a fierce whisper. "Don't do something stupid like getting hurt, or you'll have wasted all this time you've spent seducing me."

Zafirah chuckled as she pulled away, her smile soft and filled with deep affection. "You have my word, Tahirah. I shall exercise all caution in the battle."

"Good."

The two parted after several more lingering kisses, neither looking forward to their separation, both already anxious to experience the bliss and heat of their reunion.

# Chapter 18

FROM ATOP SIMHANA, ZAFIRAH LOOKED out over the miles of featureless, open dunes that lay in every direction. Her experienced eyes perceived the subtle ridges and valleys that most foreign travelers were blind to. Out here, distances were deceptive; what looked like a single mile often proved to be ten or twenty. Behind her, she heard the quiet sounds of several hundred mounted horses following her lead in a great line. Outriders and Falak's scouts flanked the army in a swift-running cage of steel, making certain no surprises lurked in the hidden depressions of the dunes. The desert was bright with the light of a three-quarter moon, but there was little to see out here. The horizon stretched on forever, and it was all too easy to imagine that the whole world had been magically emptied of every rock and tree and now hung empty and barren under the stars. Looking out at the endless expanses of nothing, Zafirah felt an unusual sense of melancholy steal over her.

She had never felt so alone in all her life.

In the four days and nights since they had left El'Kasari, the army had covered good ground and they were now approaching their destination. Falak's scouts reported that Shakir and his ragtag accompaniment were close by, and the *spahi* were eager for battle. The numbers of the enemy were greater than they had anticipated, but no one seemed overly disconcerted by this news. The only thing that concerned them was the apparent low spirits of their beloved leader. Zafirah's mood couldn't help but affect her troops; they adored their ruler with religious intensity and utter devotion. Seeing her despondence as she rode along at the head of the column sent whispers through the ranks of the horsemen. It was clear to them that the Scion was suffering the pangs of lovesickness.

Zafirah was aware of their sidelong looks and knew it was petty to indulge her melancholia in light of the coming battle, but she couldn't seem to lift her spirits. She wasn't surprised when Falak, obviously responding to the pleading looks the soldiers were casting her, spurred her horse up to ride alongside Simhana. Zafirah glanced at her sullenly but remained silent.

"It is a quiet night," Falak observed conversationally. "If we ride till dawn without pause, we may be fortunate enough to meet up with Rehan and the Tek."

Zafirah grunted.

"My people report that Shakir and his army should move through the Ah'raf Pass before the sun rises a day hence. We shall have ample time to secure our position before he arrives, and a victory there would ensure the tribes beyond remain safe."

This time the Scion didn't bother making any sound.

Falak sighed. "Petulance is so unattractive on you, Zafirah," she said at last. "You are behaving like a child deprived of her sweets, and with a battle near at hand no less!"

That got Zafirah's attention. She stared at her scout in indignant shock. "I am *not* being petulant!"

"Yes, you are."

"Am not!" Zafirah turned away.

"And now you are sulking."

"Hmph!"

"Why do you fret so, my friend? Dae will be waiting for you when we return to the city."

"I know." Zafirah hadn't slept much these last few days, her mind filled with searing imaginings of what awaited her when Shakir was defeated and she could return to Dae. "I just miss her greatly."

The scout smiled fondly at her. "Being in love takes some getting used to, does it not?"

Zafirah nodded. "But my heart would not reject it for anything in the world."

"Perhaps you would benefit from some companionship," Falak suggested gently. "You have slept alone since we left El'Kasari; I know many are disappointed not to have opportunity to enjoy your talents."

"As tempting as that sounds, my friend, I cannot. Dae asked me to abstain from pleasure until such time as she can satisfy my desires personally."

Falak's jaw dropped in surprise. "And you agreed?"

A shrug. "The way she spoke, and the things she promised… Denial was not an option."

The scout shook her head, amazed. "I never thought to see you tamed by such an innocent creature as that girl."

Zafirah laughed, the sound echoing back to those riding behind her. "That girl is far less innocent than she appears, Falak. You guessed correctly when you told me she would learn the ways of pleasure and seduction from the others of my harem. Given time to fully embrace and understand her own longings, I suspect Dae will grow into a sexual force to be reckoned with." Her chuckle dissolved into a sigh of longing. "Now I must wait with great impatience till I can be with her again, and anticipate the intimacies we will share upon my return." There was a long period of silence before she glanced at her friend with an uncommonly shy expression. "To tell the truth, I am somewhat nervous. Is that not strange? I have pleasured countless women in my life, but the prospect of bedding this one girl makes my stomach churn and my hands shake."

"It is not so strange," Falak offered kindly. "Love is more than what the body shares, Zafirah. It is of the heart, as well."

Zafirah considered this, then nodded slowly. "I am learning this is true."

"But such thoughts have little place on the battlefield," Falak continued, her tone shifting to something more formal. "You need to focus, my Scion. When Shakir is defeated and the Peace maintained, there will be time to think of love and pleasure. For now, think only of battle and glory!"

Zafirah straightened in the saddle, properly recalled to her duty by Falak's words. "You are right, Falak, and I thank you for reminding me of my priorities."

The scout grinned, snapped a quick salute to her, then made her way back to her place in the column of riders. As she left, however, Zafirah's voice whispered quietly to the night.

"Yet I still miss her very much."

Inaya was walking past Dae's bedchamber on her way to search for food when a hand reached out and grabbed her by the arm. She gave a startled squeak as she was pulled into the room, her cry cut off by fingers pressed against her lips. Shrugging off the hand, Inaya spun about and glared at her accoster.

"Dae? What are you—"

"I need a favor," Dae said in a hushed voice, her eyes darting nervously to the corridor outside. "A…personal favor."

Seeing the charming blush spreading across her friend's face, Inaya's mood changed from indignant to intrigued in the blink of an eye. "From me?"

"I didn't know who else to ask. It's kind of a private thing, you know?"

"Of course. I understand the value of discretion."

Dae snorted reproachfully and gave her a glare. "Yeah, Zafirah told me how little it took to get you to part with explicit details about my personal habits."

"Little? On the contrary, my friend, I assure you I made the Scion work very hard for every scrap of information she gleaned." Inaya winked saucily and clapped her hands together softly. "So, what assistance did you require that inspired you to drag me into your bedchamber?"

Dae turned away, unable to look her in the eye. Her response, combined with her awkward expression, led Inaya to guess her request would likely involve furthering her erotic education. "I was hoping to surprise Zafirah when she returns with something…sexy. Something she'll appreciate."

"Drape yourself naked upon her bed," Inaya advised without hesitation. "Her appreciation shall be readily apparent."

"No, I had something else in mind." Dae paused and took a deep, steadying breath. "I wanted you to help sh-shave me."

Inaya's eyes narrowed uncertainly. "Pardon me? Shave? But your hair is radiant, little one, why would you—"

"Not my head, I mean my..." Dae gestured vaguely in the direction of her thighs. Her voice dropped to a more conspiratorial volume. "You know, like Johara."

Sudden understanding dawned in Inaya's face and her eyes widened appropriately. "Ah, I see." *Try not to look too eager*, she told herself firmly, all thoughts of food vanishing as she wondered if the opportunity had finally come for her to dine on rarer, sweeter fruits. "Are you certain? Once done, such grooming must be maintained or it will cause you much discomfort."

"I know, but I'd like to do it. If you think Zafirah would be pleased?"

"Oh, little one, I think she would find you delicious no matter what you do. But certainly, this could be fun, if nothing else." Inaya let her eyes roam appreciatively over Dae's figure. "So what exactly were you hoping I could do for you?"

"Well, I don't really uh...know how to go about something like this, you know. And I figured maybe you...did."

Inaya appeared to consider this. "You wish me to shave you?"

"Yes." Dae seemed thoroughly embarrassed making the request, but equally determined to follow through on her plan.

"Hm. I suppose I could. In the interests of friendship, of course." Inaya gestured Dae toward the bed. "You wait here. I must retrieve some things from my room." As she turned to leave, she glanced back and gave her friend's skimpy outfit a disapproving look. "While I am gone, please remove your trousers and underwear."

Dae shook her head, and Inaya remained a brief moment longer to watch her fidgeting hands begin unfastening the waistband of her shimmering pantaloons. Leaving the room, Inaya heard the girl muttering behind her, "I can't believe I'm doing this," and couldn't help but smile.

Returning to her own room to gather the requisite supplies, Inaya tried to keep from getting overly excited. Dae was too inexperienced to appreciate that her request wasn't actually an uncommon one...at least, not in the palace harem, where most of the girls practiced this type of grooming. For many among them, mutual grooming sessions often served as a precursor to more intimate play, and Inaya was certainly not above taking advantage of the opportunity should she find Dae receptive. Inaya wasn't the only one to notice that Dae's bedchamber had grown rather quiet of late, and many had speculated whether the girl had taken to stuffing a gag in her mouth to stifle the sounds of her enthusiastic self-pleasuring to avoid their teasing, or if she was simply no longer indulging her rapidly burgeoning sexual desires. Whatever the cause, Inaya was supremely confident in her own skills as a seductress... and Dae was far too beautiful a young woman not to stir her carnal appetite.

When she again entered Dae's bedchamber Inaya was holding a wide, shallow dish filled with gently steaming water in both hands, along with a folded length of blue-dyed cloth. The instant she saw Dae, bare-bottomed and blushing adorably, she paused to spend a lengthy moment admiring the girl's more intimate beauties. She whistled low. "Very nice, little one," she said, setting the bowl on a table and crawling onto the bed beside her friend, letting her appreciation show. "Very nice indeed. Now..." Spreading open the cloth, she revealed an ivory-handled razor, a small glass vial, and a velvet pouch. She picked up the pouch first and sprinkled a fine white powder into the bowl. "This is a mixture made from dried and crushed soap berries," she explained to her nervously watching friend. "It is mixed with perfumes and oils to help soothe your skin." Inaya made a slight waving gesture. "If you would spread your legs for me, please...?"

Her face so red it was almost aglow, Dae did as she requested, hesitantly parting her legs a few inches. Clucking under her breath, Inaya reached over and pulled the younger girl's legs apart brashly. "No cause to be shy, little one. I have seen more than my share of naked women in my life, and you need not hide your charms," she said, dipping her hands into the bowl and rubbing her fingers together. A thick, sweet-smelling foam lathered almost immediately. Looking her friend in the eye, Inaya held up a soapy hand. "Are you ready?"

"I-I guess." Dae's emerald eyes were wide, and she swallowed loudly. She looked to be on the verge of changing her mind, and Inaya quickly reassured her.

"Just relax. I shall be very gentle."

Dae nodded, watching Inaya's fingers advance and wondering if she might not have been better served at least attempting to do this on her own. This idea had been running through her mind ever since she had watched Johara and Hayam together, and every time she revisited the experience in her fantasies she found her focus fixating on how beautiful the sight of Johara's bare sex had seemed. There was something about it that struck her as extremely appealing, something that had more to do with aesthetics than anything else...and since Zafirah was similarly groomed, Dae figured the Scion shared the same view. Although, Dae could admit privately, the thought of how much she might be able to more fully appreciate the sensation of Zafirah's tongue against her naked center certainly contributed to her decision to go ahead with her plan. Steeling her resolve, trying hard not to let the modesty of her upbringing spoil her decision with guilt or shame, Dae held still as Inaya's fingers approached her.

The next thing she knew, her friend was running those long, slippery fingers between her legs, touching places no one had ever touched before...except herself, of course. She tensed in shock at first, a guilty thrill of pleasure coursing through her body as Inaya rubbed her gently and lathered the concoction over her soft blonde curls. The fingers withdrew after several rather delightful moments, than Dae heard the sound of steel snapping. Her eyes widened as she watched Inaya stroke the edge of the gleaming razor. "Uh..."

Her trepidation must have been obvious, for Inaya offered her a look of reassurance. "Do not fear, little one. This is a common practice among body-slaves and pleasure-servants. I have done this many times, both for myself and others, and I have never drawn so much as a single drop of blood." Dae watched Inaya lower her face closer to the crux of her thighs, one soft, warm hand pressing her left leg back gently to hold her steady. Inaya's dark eyes settled on her center, and Dae tried to keep her heartbeat from racing. She felt exposed, vulnerable...but stronger still was a sense of daring excitement. She felt Inaya's warm breath wash over her sensitive skin. "Just try to hold still for me and do not tense up."

"Okay." Dae clutched at the silk sheets beneath her and mentally urged herself to calm down. Seeing how intently Inaya was studying the exposed petals of her sex didn't make it easy, and feeling the cool kiss of sharpened steel against her sensitive skin made it harder still. Against her will, Dae found herself succumbing to the first flushes of arousal. It was impossible not to; after resisting the desire to touch herself for so many days, her body was extremely receptive to the stimulation—however innocent—it was receiving. Squeezing her eyes shut tight, she tried to concentrate on keeping her breathing deep and even, conscious of the growing tension between her legs and hoping Inaya wouldn't notice her excitement.

Inaya, of course, was trying very hard not to notice...no easy task, for she thought the girl's sex looked just as adorably sweet and irresistible as the rest of her body. As she carefully and gently drew the edge of the razor across Dae's skin, leaving her satin-smooth and glistening, Inaya couldn't help but gaze adoringly at the rising blush that colored the girl's labia a charming shade of coral pink. Shaving the fine blonde curls from the crown of Dae's center, she heard a stifled gasp and smiled, letting her fingers deliberately—but not overtly—tease against the hood of her friend's clitoris while she pulled the skin taut. Inaya could feel herself growing wet from touching Dae as she had long dreamed of doing, but she kept her focus tuned to the task at hand. "Would you like me to remove it all, or shall I leave a design?" she asked calmly.

"Huh?" Dae's eyes snapped open and Inaya grinned up at her, amused by how quickly the girl had gotten lost in sensation. A light blush brought color to her cheeks, and Inaya, reading her expression and body language with a knowing eye, sensed that Dae would have happily allowed her caresses to bring her to the edge without further interruption. "Oh, um...I suppose a design would be good. Maybe something like Johara has."

"As you wish." Inaya continued with her task, humming quietly as she worked and trying not to enjoy herself too much.

Dae was doing very much the same thing. *She's your friend!* she berated herself sternly. *Stop getting carried away!* Still, the feel of Inaya's long, delicate fingers brushing against her most intimate flesh, combined with the sensation of the cool blade against her bare skin and the overall eroticism of the situation, resulted in one very stimulated and aroused little blonde. Balling her fingers into fists and squeezing her eyes shut,

Dae tried to think about anything except how nice this was making her feel.

At last, Inaya seemed to have finished the task and, dipping the cloth she'd brought into the water, began to clean away the remaining lather. After running her fingers over the smooth skin, touching up those few places that had escaped her diligent grooming, she patted Dae's thigh happily. "It is done."

Dae opened her eyes and looked curiously down at herself. The soft tangle of hairs between her legs had been tamed, and now her sex was completely bare except for a short, elegant arrow that tapered down toward her center. The sight was every bit as attractive as she had hoped it would be, and she reached down to touch herself. "It's so smooth!" she marveled with a delighted smile.

"And you must keep it that way, or you will soon regret asking me to do this."

Dae watched Inaya pick up the small glass vial that sat beside the pouch of crushed soap berries and flick the stopper off with her thumb. "This is the oil of the *sarangura* bush. It will soothe your skin further and slow the growth of your hair." Shooing Dae's hands away, Inaya poured a few drops of the oil onto her sex and began rubbing it slowly over the naked skin. Dae lay back once more, eyes closed and teeth worrying at her lower lip. After a while, she sensed Inaya's ministrations grow more tender and intent. A low, barely audible whimper escaped her, and she struggled against her rising—and increasingly obvious—arousal.

"I can feel you growing wet," she heard Inaya's voice whisper seductively, "even with the oil."

Dae's eyelids parted, hearing something carnal and ravenous in her friend's tone, and she tried halfheartedly to close her legs. Inaya gently stopped her, smiling at her silent protest. "Relax, little one. It is not unusual to become aroused during such grooming. Indeed, your body will likely be extremely responsive and sensitized now that everything is so naked." Languid fingers slid over the hood of Dae's clit, causing her thighs to tremble. "You feel so wonderfully smooth. I could touch you like this for hours."

"No." Dae tensed and shook her head, bolstering her resistance to Inaya's tempting overtures by remembering her promise to Zafirah. "I can't."

"Why not? I can see it in your eyes that you want this…can feel it in the tremble of your body." Inaya pouted, her fingers aiding her persuasion. "You need not be shy, my friend. Let me pleasure you—"

"I-I can't. I'm sorry." Despite her words, Dae did nothing to halt Inaya's extremely welcome caresses. She was fighting a losing battle, discovering just how hard it was to say no to a fully-wakened libido. Dae simply hadn't the heart to end the pleasurable caresses. "I want to, but—"

"But what? You are in need, and I am only too willing to satisfy you."

"I promised Zafirah I wouldn't."

"Zafirah?" Inaya's beguiling smile turned to a throaty chuckle. "The Scion would never wish to deny you pleasure. Surely you realize that by now."

"No, you don't understand. We made a deal to abstain." Her words sounded weak even in her own ears, and she doubted they would dissuade Inaya. "We wanted to…you know…when she gets back, I mean—"

"Ah, say no more, little one, I believe I understand. You wish to sweeten the moment of your union by building the anticipation, no?"

"Something like that."

"Mm." Inaya didn't cease her gentle touches as she considered this dilemma. She was determined to pleasure the beautiful little blonde; she just needed the right argument. Looking up at Dae's conflicted expression, she batted her eyelashes and affected her most disappointed but hopeful pout. "Is there no way I could convince you to stray from the path of your arrangement with the Scion?"

"I-I don't…think so—Oh, yes!"

Inaya flashed her friend a wicked grin. "Nice, hm?" She stroked firmly against the hardened nub of flesh that still hid behind its protective hood. "You know, when Zafirah sees you like this, I think she will be willing to forgive any lapse in self-control. Indeed, for the chance to lay between your thighs, I have little doubt she would forgive you anything!"

"W-we need to stop." Dae was almost panting now, her legs splayed unresistingly to Inaya's attentions. "We have to— Ahh! Gods, *PLEASE!*"

"Please what?" teased Inaya, sensing her capitulation. "Do you mean, please do this?"

Dae's hips shot forward. "Yes, that!"

"But I thought we were stopping." Long, skilled fingers halted menacingly. "Hm?"

"No. No stopping, please!"

Inaya accepted her triumph graciously. Her fingers resumed their lazy caresses, in no hurry to end their play now that victory had been secured. "As you wish, little one." As she worked, Inaya shifted to better position herself between her friend's legs. "It has been my most ardent desire to pleasure you for a long time now," she admitted quietly. "You shall not be disappointed by my efforts."

"Yessss!" Dae was dizzy with need and in no condition to fend off her friend's seduction. Abandoning herself to the inevitable, she relaxed and resigned her senses to the pleasure she was receiving from those talented fingers stroking her ever so gently. Propping herself up on her elbows, she stared hungrily at Inaya's body. When her friend leaned closer to her, full lips parted in anticipation, Dae didn't hesitate to meet her kiss passionately, her tongue demanding and eager as it dueled for space in Inaya's mouth. There was a different edge to this kiss than the ones she'd shared with Zafirah; it was filled with fire and desire, yes, but there wasn't the same soul-shattering, toe-curling emotional force that there was when she locked lips with the Scion. Still, Dae moaned when Inaya nibbled aggressively at her slippery tongue, feeling her arousal rise a few notches further.

Dae wasn't the only one in need of satisfaction, however, and Inaya pulled herself closer against her body and grabbed for Dae's hand, guiding it to the beaded sash that circled her slender waist and held her skirt together. "Will you pleasure me, too?" she asked hopefully, never stopping her caresses. "Please, I want to feel you touching me."

Caught in the heat of the moment, Dae didn't hesitate. Inaya was undeniably beautiful, and Dae had entertained numerous fantasies of sharing pleasure with her since she had voiced her own interest. Her eager fingers clawed at the simple knot in the sash and eventually released it. Inaya's skirt, which was really little more than a few scraps of silk draped with intricate strings of swaying glass beads, fell away, revealing her firm, dusky body to Dae's appreciative gaze. Her eyes devoured the planes of smooth, olive-dark skin, traveling lower quickly, then widening when they noticed something unexpected. Dae froze, shocked and surprised. "Wh-what's that?"

"Hm?" Inaya withdrew slightly from her when she saw what had caught her attention. She spread her legs to better display her hidden treasures. "You mean this?" With her free hand, she spread herself open and languidly stroked the metal stud that ran through the hood of her clitoris. "It is just more jewelry, like the one in my navel. Do you like it?"

"I-I-I don't...I mean, how..? Didn't it hurt?" Dae said, staring in amazement. Even with all the things she had been exposed to during her time in the harem, she could never have imagined such a bold form of bodily ornamentation.

"Of course, a little. But the pleasure was equally intense." Inaya slowed her ministrations when she saw Dae's lingering distraction over the intimate jewelry.

"Why would you want jewelry...there?"

"It heightens the sensitivity of my clitoris and increases my pleasure," Inaya explained matter-of-factly. "My nipples are also pierced for much the same reason. See?" She casually unlaced her top and exposed her breasts, showing off a pair of elegant silver rings set with sparkling diamonds.

Dae winced, even as a part of her admitted the jewelry was rather beautiful, in a barbaric yet extremely erotic fashion. She moved a little closer, genuinely intrigued. "It doesn't hurt when you touch them?"

"On the contrary; the sensation goes directly to my center. Besides, I find that a little pain mixes very nicely with pleasure. It can sharpen the senses, make things so much more intense and exciting." Dark eyes hooded. "I enjoy the darker elements of passion, little one, and you will find my jewelry makes me extremely responsive. I can be brought to climax with ease and frequency, as I would be happy to demonstrate. Please...?" She reached for Dae's hand and guided it to her glistening sex. "You may touch it."

Curious despite herself, Dae fingered the steel bar gently. The contrast between the hard metal of the stud and the silken, smooth skin surrounding it was interesting, and it wasn't long before Dae's touches grew bolder and more inquisitive. When Inaya gasped and uttered a low-pitched cry, Dae immediately stopped her exploring caresses and looked up, concerned. "Did I hurt you?"

"No, little one. It feels wonderful."

Reassured, Dae returned her fingers to their task, sighing when she felt Inaya do the same. Soon, the two were settled into a comfortable position lying side by side on the bed, half facing each other as their fingers caressed and their lips joined in increasingly breathless kisses.

Inaya was delighted to find Dae just as vocal now as when she was indulging alone. Many nights she had lain in her bed listening to the muffled cries of self-induced ecstasy coming from Dae's room, and more often than not the sounds would incite her to touch herself as well. Now, feeling the liquid heat of her beautiful friend against her fingers, breathing in the sweet, musky scent of her arousal while she listened to those little squeaks of pleasure, Inaya was realizing a fantasy that had been swimming about in her head since Dae first arrived in the harem. She was determined to make the moment a memorable one for the girl, if only to secure her desire to repeat the experience.

"You feel so good, little one," she whispered heatedly when Dae broke from another long kiss, knowing how arousing words could be. "So wet...so hot. Will you come for me? I want to feel you climax against my fingers."

As intended, the request shot Dae's lust into overload. The young girl seemed to be having a hard time continuing her task of pleasuring Inaya, the flashes of ecstasy burning away her concentration and urging her focus to the center of her own body. When Inaya felt Dae's touch lose its rhythm, she immediately redoubled her own efforts.

"Are you close, little one? Come for me."

Dae collapsed onto her back, thighs trembling as Inaya's practiced fingers spurred her on. The breathless sobs escaping her throat turned to full-fledged, pleading cries as her senses began to take flight. Inaya recognized the signs of impending climax and increased the speed of her attentions, focusing on the now not-so-shy bud of Dae's clitoris as it peeked out from its secretive hood. Her efforts were rewarded with a sudden increase in liquid flowing from the girl's sex, and as much as she wanted to lower her lips to sample Dae's sweetness, Inaya didn't want to do anything that might startle the innocent girl. Instead she dipped her face down to suck and lick along Dae's collarbone, reveling in the little spasms she could feel rippling against her fingers as the girl squirmed in delicious rapture.

Dae's orgasm was quick, sharp, and intense. And, Inaya noted with private amusement, *very* loud. She suspected the poor girl would be teased mercilessly by the other pleasure-servants when she next visited the seraglio. Still, watching her recover her wits after the final spasms had passed, Inaya felt only pride in her actions. Dae was a stunning, desirable young woman, and by Inaya's reckoning, she had a good deal of catching up to do when it came to carnal exploits.

When Dae felt her breathing had returned to normal and her senses were grounded once more, she sat up a little and was immediately greeted by the sight of Inaya happily licking her fingers clean of her essence. Her cheeks instantly burned with furious heat. Inaya threw her a rakish grin. "Did you like that?"

Dae fought a wave of self-consciousness in the wake of her spent passion, not really knowing what to say. "It was nice." A pause. "Thank you."

"Not at all, little one. I am always happy to assist a friend. Especially one who makes such delightful noises at the height of passion!"

Dae's blush wasn't getting much opportunity to subside. "I'm not that loud," she protested weakly.

"Then why do your cries still ring in my ears, hm?" Inaya sucked the last of the clear nectar from her fingers and licked her lips. "You taste as sweet as you look," she declared cheerfully. "Perhaps next time, you would allow me the honor of sampling your flavor directly from the source..?"

"Um...I-I suppose. If you wanted to." *Next time?* Dae felt her insides stir a little. *No wonder Zafirah can't control her desires. Who could, with gorgeous women like Inaya ready to fulfill your every fantasy?* She ran her eyes over Inaya's sanguine form, admiring how her dark hair shimmered with blue highlights in the flickering lamplight, and felt her energy return. "In the meantime, though, I think I should finish what I was working on when you distracted me."

"Oh?" Inaya promptly lay back on the bedsheets and spread her legs, brazenly showing off her bejeweled and glistening sex. "Then my body is yours to claim, my friend."

"Hussy," Dae scolded, moving closer with an eager expression on her face. Settling between Inaya's legs, she ran her fingers along the tanned skin toward the gleaming metal bar that pierced the girl's clitoris. She teased the silken petals of Inaya's labia for a few minutes before turning her attention to the delicate little stud, her fingers stroking against it cautiously. Inaya's hips bucked and she cried out breathlessly. "Harder, little one!"

Dae flicked the metal gently, intrigued. Inaya growled and cupped her breasts, her fingers tugging at the rings that pierced each nipple. "Again! Please, keep doing that…Harder!"

She repeated her actions, watching as her friend mauled her own breasts and finding the sight enormously erotic. When she slid two fingers over the sensitive shaft of Inaya's clit and pinched gently, the raven-haired girl threw her head back and wildly screamed out her climax. Dae continued her ministrations, knowing from her own experiences how nice it felt to hold the moment of release as long as possible. She rubbed her fingers quickly and firmly across the full length of Inaya's dripping sex, enjoying the tremors she could feel beneath her touch.

Only when Inaya's body finally had no more to give and her muscles went limp did Dae withdraw her hand and, after making certain her friend was still too dazed to be paying attention, hesitantly brought her wet fingers to her lips. Dae had tasted herself only once before, her curiosity eventually growing stronger than her uncertainty, and she had found the taste actually quite pleasing. Inaya's flavor was similar to her own, only sharper and not so sweet. She quickly licked herself clean when she saw Inaya begin to stir and sit up.

Inaya gave a deep, languid sigh. "Thank you, Dae. That was wonderful! Every bit as wonderful as I have often imagined it would be." Inaya's normally immaculate hair was now rather disheveled, but her smile was as radiant as ever. "You have learned the ways of pleasing a woman well."

Dae shrugged modestly. "I've had good teachers."

"Mm." Inaya blew an errant strand of blue-black hair from her face and sat up on the bed. "Would you like to practice some more? I would be willing to contribute my body to your further studies."

Dae giggled and looked away. "Thanks, but I think I'd rather wait for Zafirah to get back. Though I appreciate the offer very much."

"As you wish."

"I can't believe how easily I got carried away," Dae said, recalling her promise to the Scion and feeling a little guilty now that her passion had been appeased. "I just hope Zafirah isn't upset about it. I mean, I asked her to deny herself while she was away, and then I go and get all naked and sweaty with you."

"Well, if you feel any guilt over this little escapade, just think how much fun you could have apologizing to Zafirah." Inaya reached out and ran a finger lazily down Dae's arm until their fingers were brushing against each other. "Or perhaps, if she will not forgive you so easily, think how much fun she could have devising an appropriate punishment for you!"

Dae's eyes hooded as a few ideas sprang immediately to mind. "Yeah...I've been very, very wicked, haven't I?"

"Mmhm." Inaya purred and licked her lips, one hand wandering down to toy idly with her lower jewelry. "Such a naughty girl."

"But I'd be willing to do anything if she'd forgive me..."

"Anything."

"Yeah." Dae smiled a sexy, sensuous smile. "And she'd probably like hearing about what we did, too. I bet she'd find it extremely exciting."

"Then we should make it a tale worth the retelling," Inaya suggested, stroking herself wantonly now.

Hearing her friend-cum-lover starting to breathe more harshly, Dae returned her focus to the reclining girl. She froze at the sight of Inaya openly fondling herself. *She's got stamina, I'll give her that.* "What are you doing?"

Inaya flashed a playful, unrepentant grin. "Contributing to your story."

Dae's desire surged anew. She shifted on the bed, reaching for the laces that still held her top closed. Inaya, already naked, watched her avidly as she slipped out of the last of her clothing. Dae noted the way Inaya's fingers moved with greater purpose as she stared hungrily at her breasts and decided there was little sense in wasting this opportunity to explore further with her friend after everything they had already shared. "Well, I'd hate for Zafirah to get bored when I tell her what we got up to."

"Indeed."

"Are you still willing to let me practice my…technique…on you?"

Inaya pulled her hands away from her weeping sex. "Always."

"Excellent." Dae dove right in eagerly, claiming Inaya's lips with a fierce, almost bruising kiss and moaning when fingers already slick with arousal sought her breasts. As her senses were further intoxicated by the combined scents of perfume and arousal, Dae spared a moment to wonder if Zafirah was managing to behave herself any better than she was.

# Chapter 19

THE AH'RAF PASS WAS A well-known landmark for those seeking passage across the Jaharri desert unscathed. In times past, before the Scion Peace, traders avoided the deceptively inviting path that ran between two great stretches of sharp-edged sandstone escarpment, knowing that bandits favored the many caves and hollows as places from which to launch surprise attacks. In more recent times, however, the pass was as useful and important to foreigners and the desert nomads as to the Kah-hari oasis. It offered protected shelter to weary travelers in the numerous wind-carved caves that pockmarked the cliffs, and more importantly, it was a safe route that was largely shielded from the vicious and unpredictable dust storms that could rise up without warning on the barren dunes. There was little doubt in Zafirah's mind that Shakir would use the pass to reach the tribes beyond.

Which made it the perfect site to prepare and execute an ambush.

Of course there were murmurings of concern from among the Scion's commanders and advisers. The Ah'raf Pass was highly exposed and devoid of any dips or gullies; it was hardly ideal terrain in which to hide an army nearly three-hundred strong. Also, the pass itself was too narrow to mount an effective cavalry charge, which would deprive the *spahi* of their most valuable asset: speed. But Zafirah ignored the whispered remarks, ordering her troops with a confident smile to take up their positions. By the time all was in readiness, the hour had grown late, and the Scion raised a questioning eyebrow at her head scout.

Falak consulted with her outriders before reporting to Zafirah. "Shakir and his men are approaching the pass. They shall be here before full dark."

"How many?"

A hesitant pause. "My scouts estimate their numbers somewhere between four and five hundred."

Zafirah appeared unconcerned. "Wagons?"

"Three, and heavily laden, by the depth of their tracks."

"Excellent."

Falak's face was serious as she studied her leader. "This plan of yours involves much risk, my Scion. From what my people saw, Shakir is keeping those armed with these devil-weapons in the center of his line. They ride *mehari* and will be able to retreat quickly if the trap is sprung too soon."

Zafirah looked off into the distance, her expression masked by her *haik*. "Or so he thinks," she said. "The young Calif has a great deal to learn of battle. I will ensure he is educated before the night is through." She regarded her chief scout intently. "Your people know what to do?"

"I have issued your orders. They shall wait for your signal to attack."

"Excellent. Remember, Falak, full quarter and full mercy. We are not here to deprive families of their providers, only to stop Shakir's crusade and maintain the Peace." With a flick of the reins, Zafirah urged Simhana up the rocky path that led to the top of the escarpment, a climb that would have been impossible for any other horse but the desert-bred mare. There, she was pleased to find a group of thirty scouts armed with their powerful bows waiting for her. Several barrels had been stacked along the edge of the precipice, just as she had ordered. Another thirty scouts were perched atop the cliff on the other side of the Pass, similarly supplied. The scouts nodded in greeting to the Scion, then gestured wordlessly to the southwest.

Shielding her eyes from the last rays of the setting sun, Zafirah saw a cloud of dust rising out along the dunes: Shakir's army. She fingered the hilt of her sword, looking forward to the coming confrontation. After so many days without any kind of sexual release, the Scion was eager to vent some of her pent-up energy in the heat of battle. She watched the dust cloud move closer, then saw distant figures emerge from the desert and halt a few miles from the pass. "The young jackal is cautious," she muttered beneath her *haik*, smiling without humor. "Bold, but certainly not stupid."

She could only wait and see if the Calif of the Deharn would favor his caution over ambition and hatred.

Out on the shifting sands, Shakir studied the looming pass shrewdly, sensing something amiss. During the days of travel across the desert, the young Calif had slipped deeper into his madness. He drove his men hard, punishing even the slightest slip in discipline with savage brutality. The zealous fire in his eyes now burned brighter with the added fuel of insanity, and he cared little that his troops were following him more out of fear than genuine respect. Looking at the Ah'raf Pass, Shakir felt a subtle shifting in the air around him...the tense calm that preceded glorious battle. He knew Zafirah would not wait long to attack him, but surely she was not so foolish as to choose the pass for a battle! Her *spahi* would be useless. No, more likely she was waiting for him on the other side, some miles from the cliffs where the open terrain would better suit her horsemen. Shakir grinned, caressing the length of his thunder-bow lovingly. The Scion Whore was in for a rude surprise.

Still, Shakir was not foolish enough to question his warrior instincts. He pointed out two of his *mehari* riders and gestured toward the pass. "Go! See that our way is clear!"

The two immediately rode off to scout ahead, returning after several minutes. "The pass is clear," was their report.

"And the sands beyond?"

"Nothing. Not so much as a single scout or outrider."

Shakir considered this, then waved the two men back into position, apparently satisfied. "We ride through the night, then. If we make good time we will fall upon the Sakaran tribe before the break of dawn. Move forward!"

The procession rolled on, slow but tireless. Shakir led the way, along with a group of maybe a hundred troops mostly mounted on horses and armed with spears and javelins. These riders formed a forward defense for the true core of the army: those armed with the thunder-bows. Their job would be to hold back any frontal assault and enable those behind them the time they needed to fire and reload without hindrance. Behind them rolled three heavy wagons, each bearing a burden of several large barrels filled with the magical powder that fueled the foreign weapons, as well as ammunition, spare weapons, and camping supplies. Bringing up the rear came the reserve troops, men and women recruited from the renegade tribes, most riding mangy camels and armed with dented swords and a few bows. Though not the most experienced fighters, this final group was numerous and provided useful additional muscle to Shakir's force.

This was the army that rode into the Ah'raf Pass as the sun departed the skies.

Zafirah looked down from the cliff top to the line of riders below. The scouts watched her eagerly, arrows nocked, waiting for the signal to attack. As the first of Shakir's men exited the far end of the pass, a few of the scouts shifted nervously, uncertain what was going on. Were they just going to let the enemy get away? But Zafirah ignored them, waiting patiently until the forward third of the army below was clear of the cliffs, leaving a long line of men still in the pass and the rest straggling behind. She trusted her instincts, waiting until she felt the low, excited bubble burst within her, the one that told her the perfect moment had come. Then, tilting her head back, the Scion let loose a shattering, ululating war cry that echoed down into the canyon, gaining strength as it reverberated through the caves and crevices. The scouts joined in with cries of their own, and most began to fire arrows into the panicked enemy below. Those near the barrels positioned at the far ends of the escarpment, however, watched until the Scion waved her hand to them, then pushed the giant containers over the edge.

Zafirah watched, exultant, as the barrels hit the ground and shattered, spraying liquid everywhere and soaking the entrance and exit of the pass. She heard several sudden claps of thunder boom through the canyon and realized the enemy was trying to fight back. She smiled thinly. It was already too late. At her gesture, the scouts lit the tips of special arrows that had been soaked in oil and took aim at the barrels below.

"Fire!"

The blazing shafts cut like lightning through the dusk. A moment later Zafirah grinned as they ignited the lamp oil that had filled each barrel, creating two walls of roaring fire below and illuminating the targets in the darkness. Those men who were trying to retreat or push forward milled about, growing ever more panicked as they realized they were trapped.

It was a strategy untested in the desert lands, one Zafirah had learned from ambassadors from the west. It was more commonly used in the defense of castles than open land, and she was pleased to see it work so effectively. Now Shakir's army was split into thirds, with the most dangerous section—the men armed with the foreign weapons—trapped in the center of the pass, easy prey for the scouts raining arrows down upon them. Those who had already made it through the pass turned about but couldn't help their fellows on the other side of the fire. The largest group at the rear milled about uncertainly, searching for an enemy to fight but finding none. They could only watch in horror as their comrades were slaughtered. Many turned to flee, and Zafirah's orders were that her army would not pursue. Full quarter, full mercy...

But those in the canyon had brought their own doom with them.

Zafirah's cold gaze turned to the three wagons, currently abandoned in the center of the pass while horses and camels reared about in a disorganized panic.

"There." She pointed to the wagons. "Burn them!" Five scouts took up oil-soaked fire-arrows and loosed them without hesitation into the wagons.

Zafirah had been warned by Dae that the black powder was highly volatile, but she had no true understanding of explosives or their effects. The ensuing blast shook the ground, deafening those perched high above on the cliff top and knocking most of them backward. Zafirah's jaw dropped in awe and she staggered, almost losing her footing as a ball of fire, smoke, and debris tore through the pass in a wave of death, choking the air and causing a dozen small avalanches along the rock wall. The sheer force of the shockwave was more powerful and murderous than she could ever have imagined, amplified by the high, close walls of the cliffs.

Whispering a brief prayer to the Goddess, Zafirah found her feet again and looked down, stunned, as the sounds below grew ominously silent in the wake of the blast. When the smoke had cleared, she and the other scouts squinted against the smoke rising from below.

Nothing moved in the Ah'raf Pass except the flames.

Zafirah swallowed, her hands trembling a little at the unexpectedly powerful force of the blast. Then she turned to her equally stunned scouts, her eyes wide but resolute. "Such is the fate of those who would bring death into our lands." Turning away, she gestured for the others to follow. "Come. This day's work is not yet over."

Casting nervous glances at the rising smoke that twisted through the still evening air, the scouts followed her back down the path and onto the plains below.

Still shaken by the devastation of the explosion, Zafirah was nonetheless thrilled to see her strategy work so utterly well. The *spahi* and their well-trained mounts had been lying flat against the ground, looking like nothing more than a patch of rocky terrain in the light of dusk, but now they rose and sped against the remains of Shakir's army. Whooping and hollering, the Scion spurred Simhana to a gallop, eager to take her share of the fighting. Her curved scimitar dipped and rose in fluid, unrelenting arcs, each time cutting an enemy down. Her attacks were not lethal, however. Where she could she simply disabled her foes, cutting a path through their ranks and screaming out her war cry as she rode.

As one of the first to make it through the pass, Shakir now stood staring at the charred remains of his precious army through the wall of flame that had dropped from out of the heavens. He heard the cries of his men struck by the lethal shower of arrows, but could only watch, impotent with rage, as those around him tried to rally a defense against an enemy they couldn't see. Shakir's fingers clenched into fists and he felt a blinding, insane rage build within him. Hearing a dull roaring sound behind him, he turned and finally saw the enemy. Hundreds of *spahi* riders had risen like ghosts from the desert sands, their position masked by the cover of dark. Shakir realized too late that the cunning *spahi* had laid their well-trained mounts on the ground, concealing them in the few shallow depressions so they would not be silhouetted against the skyline. Now they raced toward the burning pass, their numbers overwhelming. Still, Shakir felt no fear, only the rage. He clasped his thunder-bow tightly and scanned the approaching tide carefully while the men around him wheeled to face the horde.

He had only one shot, but he planned to make it count. The Scion Whore would pay for this treacherous ambush with her life.

Shakir watched his men fall through a red mist of rage. He had never seen Zafirah before, but when he saw the tall figure—obviously a woman by the curves of her form—mounted on the most magnificent white warhorse he had ever beheld, slashing through his army without effort or concern, his lips twisted into a savage, trembling grin. That figure could only be the mighty Scion, and with tremulous hands he raised his thunder-bow, sighting along its shaft and willing his breathe to steady. When his quarry paused in the battle briefly, her sharp gaze looking all around, Shakir's finger tightened on the trigger. The Scion was perfectly aligned in his sights.

"NO!"

A black-robed figure crashed into the Calif just as he fired, the thunder-bow jolted to the side by the impact. Shakir was knocked from his horse, speechless with fury. He gained his feet and looked immediately to the Scion, laughing when he saw his shot had not been thwarted completely. The mounted woman clutched at her shoulder, barely maintaining a grip on her sword. Shakir drew his own weapon and turned to face the one who had spoiled his shot. The woman—a scout from her attire—had launched herself from a stone outcropping and was struggling to get her feet back under her. Still, she glared at him with raw, furious hatred, holding her sword before her with grim purpose.

"You shall die, bitch!" he spat, almost foaming at the mouth with frenzied rage.

"A long time after you," Bahira replied, exultant in her moment of vengeance. "You slaughtered my friends, my brothers and sisters! For that, your life is forfeit."

Shakir wiped at his face with the back of his arm, his once handsome face warped by his madness, his charismatic grin now distorted and inhuman. He waved his scimitar in a gesture of invitation. "Then come. Your Whore Scion will follow close at your heels into the hereafter!"

With a flash of light and a clash of steel, the two combatants locked blades.

Zafirah was stunned by the roar of thunder and the sudden lancing pain that speared through her chest. She clutched at the injury with her free hand even as she tightened her grip on her sword, mindful of how exposed she was, how injured and still stuck in the thickest fighting. Blood welled between her fingers as she looked down to study the damage. The shot had taken her in the upper chest, a finger's width below her right collarbone. The pain was terrible, but Zafirah was no stranger to injury. One of the renegades charged her with an enthusiastic cry, seeing her distracted, and Zafirah barely got her scimitar up in time to deflect a spear thrust that would have skewered her through the belly. Grunting away the pain, she managed to put enough strength behind her backswing to slice the razor edge of her sword across her assailant's neck, opening his throat. The man dropped his spear and grabbed at the mortal wound, stumbling and falling back to the ground.

Zafirah stubbornly ignored the flashing white spots of light behind her eyes and the nausea that tightened in her gut, trying to assess the damage. The wound itself wouldn't kill her, but if she didn't stop the flow of blood quickly, she could lose consciousness. If that happened, she would be an easy target for the enemy still fighting desperately against her *spahi* in a losing battle. Squeezing Simhana's flanks, Zafirah ordered the mare to carry her from the fight to safety; she needed to attend to her injury before she bled to death. That thought brought to mind the promise she'd made to Dae, her beloved, that she would return unharmed to her. A painful smile pulled at her lips.

"I hope you will forgive me, my Tahirah. Such promises are not easily kept."

Bahira was a skilled fighter, but she couldn't match the zealous, furious strength of the renegade Calif. Shakir was tireless and enraged;

he rained blow after blow upon the young scout until her arms ached from the shattering force of his attacks. Stumbling, but still determined, Bahira struggled to keep her sword up, unable to find an opening between Shakir's relentless assault. Her hand and arm were numb, and with one final, smashing strike from the Calif, her sword flew from her almost dead grasp. Bahira fell to the sand, breathing hard, stormy eyes glaring up at her enemy without fear.

Shakir laughed at her courage and lifted his sword high. "Join your fellows in hell!" he snarled.

Bahira didn't flinch as she saw the firelight gleam brightly off the edge of the curved steel, determined to meet her fate with head held high. But the final blow never came. Shakir's smile suddenly turned into an expression of pained shock. His eyes widened. His mouth dropped in a silent scream. The sword fell from his hand and he clutched at his back frantically for a moment, then pitched headfirst into the sand.

A raven-fletched arrow stuck out of his back, directly over his heart.

Bahira looked about and saw the familiar dark face of Falak grinning at her from nearby. Tension left her body in a sudden wave of relief, and she laughed and waved to her lover. Falak returned the wave. Bahira glanced at Shakir's body, nudging it with her foot to ensure he was really dead. Then she stood up, collected her sword, and wiped her brow in exaggerated relief. Falak laughed heartily even as she nocked a new arrow and fired into the subdued ranks of the enemy.

The battle didn't last much longer. When the men of Shakir's army began to kneel, holding their weapons above their heads in poses of submission, Falak looked around for Zafirah. She grew worried when she found no sign of her in the slowly calming tide of battle and stepped up onto a boulder to address the enemy, whistling sharply to get their attention.

"Your leader is fallen!" she shouted, her voice carrying through the canyon to those still milling about on the other side, uncertain what was happening. "You are defeated! We do not wish this to be a slaughter, to deprive your families of their loved ones here. Return to your tribes now and we will let you go in peace. But remember the lesson you have learned this night: the Scion Peace will be defended at all costs. Do not come upon us in anger again!"

After a few minutes, the men and women of Shakir's army began to struggle to their feet and pick themselves up. There were few dead among their number, but many limped or clutched at bleeding wounds. They helped one another walk back into the canyon, past the fires which had died away as their fuel was consumed. The charred and blasted remains of those who had been trapped in the pass made a powerful impression, and most resolved never to challenge the might of the Scion ever again.

Within an hour, the broken army was making its way back to the deep desert. Falak figured it would be many years before they would be strong enough to begin their raids again. When the last of the enemy had withdrawn from the field, Falak looked about curiously, seeing many others doing the same. Where was Zafirah? A murmuring of concern rose among the riders. Falak waved a hand. "Find her!"

It wasn't long before a cry alerted the chief scout that the Scion had been located. Pushing her way through the *spahi* who gathered around the rocky base of the cliffs, Falak willed her heart to be steady and refused to think the worst. "Let me through! Where is sh—" Her eyes widened. "Holy Inshal!"

Zafirah lay in the arms of the *spahi* who had found her, looking around with a dazed expression. Nearby, several other warriors were trying to calm Simhana, cautiously keeping clear of the warhorse's sharp, kicking hooves as she sought to defend her fallen mistress. The right side of Zafirah's upper torso was stained dark with blood. A nasty wound on her forehead bled sluggishly down her face, and her hair was a mess. Still, she managed a pained smile when she saw Falak approaching.

Kneeling beside the Scion, Falak shook her head. "Oh, Zafirah. What happened?"

Zafirah grimaced and tried to sit up, only to find the task beyond her ability. "I fear I found some ill on the battlefield," she said sheepishly.

Falak reached out to inspect Zafirah's wounds, drawing a hiss of pain despite her gentle touch. The gash on her head was ugly but not life-threatening, yet the small hole in the Scion's chest continued to bleed. Falak pressed the cloth of Zafirah's *haik* into the wound. "We must get you back to El'Kasari," she said, looking back to those gathered behind her. "Go! Make a litter for your Scion. And the rest of you, see to the others who are injured! We must be on the move within the hour." The men hurried off to gather spear shafts and cloth to form a litter. The scout stroked Zafirah's hair soothingly. "You are fortunate the Calif's aim did not hold true, my friend."

"Shakir?" Zafirah looked around her. "Is he..?"

"Dead? Yes."

"His army?"

"Returning from whence they came. Now we must see to our own injured. But your wounds require the attention of the healers in the city." Falak touched the torn edges of the gash on Zafirah's forehead, wincing sympathetically. "This was not done by a blade."

The Scion scowled. "I fell from Simhana and struck my head on a rock," she admitted. "Is it bad?"

"It will scar." Falak gave a dramatic, lamenting sigh. "Alas, I fear your beauty is ruined forever. What woman will bed you now that you are so hideously disfigured?"

Zafirah's scowl deepened, but she found at least some measure of relief in the joking, knowing her wounds couldn't be too serious if Falak was teasing her. "It is more than my appearance that lures so many to my bed," she boasted weakly. "My tongue is still in fine working order!" She waggled the muscle in question at the scout to demonstrate.

Falak laughed. "And let us hope it stays that way, lest your little Dae be deprived of the opportunity to sample its expertise!"

Zafirah would have chuckled but she felt too dizzy and weak. Lying back in the gentle arms of the *spahi* holding her up, she relaxed and tried to keep her eyes open. It was dangerous to fall asleep after a head wound, she knew, and so Zafirah concentrated on the activity of those around her. The right side of her body ached and throbbed, and her head felt hot, but she wasn't in mortal danger yet. The ride back to El'Kasari would not be easy, and neither would facing the ministrations of the healers. Zafirah was fairly sure the small ball of lead that had caused her this pain was still embedded in her flesh; she wasn't looking forward to having it removed. Forcing her eyelids to stay open, the Scion pushed past thoughts of the unpleasantness ahead of her and concentrated instead on thoughts of how Dae might be willing to "assist" in her recuperation.

# Chapter 20

"I want to see her!"

With eyes wet with tears, Dae glared at the two guards barring the entrance to Zafirah's bedchamber as if she could remove them from out of her path with the sheer force of her anguish. The two female guards exchanged uncertain glances, but refused to stand aside.

"Argh!" Dae lunged between them, only to be held back by a second set of guards who had escorted her from the harem. "Let me go! I want to see her!" In desperation she wiggled and squirmed, slapping at the hands that held her firmly. Dae's struggles diminished, and a sob shook her slender frame as she collapsed weakly to the floor.

"What is going on here?" came a new voice, commanding and stern. "Guards? Who is—"

Dae looked up to find a strange woman standing over her—tall, with skin like polished ebony and eyes almost as intense as Zafirah's. She snuffled and sat up a little. "I want to see Zafirah."

The woman looked down at her, her expression softening. "The Scion is resting," she explained gently. "Our healers have removed the missile from her chest, but she is still sedated. It will take time for her to recover, and there is little you can do for her while she sleeps."

"S-she's going to be all right, then?"

"Yes, little one. She will be fine once she has had opportunity to heal."

Dae felt a tremendous surge of relief wash through her, releasing the sickening tension that had been her constant companion since word arrived two days ago that Zafirah had been severely wounded in the battle against the renegades. When she heard the Scion had returned to the palace, Dae had alternately threatened and pleaded with the harem guards until they agreed to escort her to Zafirah's bedchamber. Their compliance came mostly from a realization that the girl would make herself sick with worry if her need for reassurance went unanswered. Now, finally, Dae felt the heavy grip that had tightened around her heart ease a little, though her eyes were still shiny with unshed tears. "Thank the Gods!" she breathed fervently.

"Indeed." The dark-skinned woman waved the guards back and offered her hand to Dae, helping her to her feet. "The return trek through the desert taxed Zafirah's strength despite our best efforts to ward off the heat. She developed a mild fever, but it has broken and her sleep is untroubled now. Despite suffering from exposure and blood loss, our healers have advised me her condition should improve quickly."

"Can I at least see her?"

The woman considered her request gravely. "I suppose there would be no harm in permitting a visit. A *brief* visit. Come."

Dae practically flew past the guards as they parted to allow her through to Zafirah's chamber, rushing over to the bed where the Scion lay sleeping. She stopped, hands covering her mouth, when she saw how pale the injured woman was, and moaned aloud when she caught sight of the neatly sutured cut on Zafirah's forehead.

"It is not as bad as it looks," the dark-skinned woman assured her, stepping closer and brushing a strand of hair from Zafirah's face. "The Scion heals quickly. Given a year, the scars of this battle will be as faded as the memory of the fight itself. Do not look so horrified, little Dae. These wounds are badges of honor for a warrior like Zafirah."

Dae looked up at the strange woman, surprised. "You know who I am?"

"Of course. I was with Zafirah when she first rescued you from the slavers in the desert, though you were in no condition to remember my face. I am Falak, leader of the Scion's scouts." She paused, then added, "She and I have been friends for many years."

"Friends?" Dae looked the taller woman up and down shrewdly, wondering if Zafirah had bedded her. *Probably*. She took in the slender, graceful body and full, sensuous lips with a critical eye. *Definitely*. Still,

Falak possessed a pleasant and calm demeanor that set Dae quickly at ease, and she found herself a little curious. Zafirah held the devotion and love of her people, but few of them could honestly claim her as a friend. Dae sidled closer to the scout. "So...has she ever talked to you about me?"

"She has said enough that her affection and love for you are obvious," Falak replied. "In truth, I recognized the depth of her feelings some time before she did. I believe Zafirah fell in love with you almost from the first moment she laid eyes upon you in the desert."

"Really?"

"It seemed that way to me, yes."

Dae's nose crinkled in pleasure at this little insight. She turned back to the unconscious woman, her expression soft and loving. "I guess it was a bit like that for me, too," she whispered almost to herself. "She made me feel so many new things when we first met, things I didn't understand. Didn't *want* to understand. But now..." She trailed off. "This isn't how I imagined welcoming her home."

"I do not doubt the truth of that, little one, but unfortunately for both of you, Zafirah will need to regain her strength before she is ready to entertain your desire for a proper reunion." The scout shook her head fondly and sighed. "She will not be pleased to hear that her passion for you must continue to be held in check."

Dae looked away at the knowing glint in Falak's eyes. "Yes, well...I'm not too thrilled about it myself."

Falak laughed and patted her on the shoulder. "Patience has its own rewards, Dae. Let Zafirah heal before you start tempting her with carnal delights."

"Mm." Dae was tired from the lack of sleep wrought by two nights of constant worry, and now that she had seen Zafirah and been reassured she was alive and in no danger of dying, those hours of tension were catching up to her. "When will she wake up?"

"Perhaps by nightfall, though the longer she sleeps the better. She will be weak for many days to come, however."

"Can I come see her tomorrow?"

"If you like." Falak's lips pursed seriously. "I have little doubt Zafirah would find solace in your company, but I warn you now to be mindful of her condition. Do not let her seduce you with assurances that she is feeling well, and try not to tease her further. She will be feeling considerable frustration after so long without pleasure, but will only do herself more harm by spending her energy in bed sports."

Dae suppressed a cheeky grin and nodded sincerely at the dark scout. "I'll make sure she behaves herself."

"Be certain you behave yourself as well, child," Falak said sternly. "I can see beyond that virtuous facade of yours. Keep your visits brief and innocent until she has healed and is well."

"I'll be good." Leaning down, Dae placed a tender kiss on Zafirah's forehead, careful of the sutured cut. "She's really not going to like this, is she?"

"After living so many months in anticipation? No, little one, and I cannot say I blame her." Falak held out a hand to Dae. "Come. I will see you back to the seraglio. The other pleasure-servants must surely be concerned for their Scion as well."

Dae accepted the hand and let Falak lead her from the chamber, casting a glance back over her shoulder to Zafirah and promising silently that this delay would be as short-lived as she could possibly make it.

As promised, Dae returned to visit the next morning, pleased to find Zafirah awake and already looking much improved. Her naturally olive skin still seemed a shade too pale, but her eyes had regained their bright sparkle and she smiled in obvious delight as soon as Dae entered her room.

"*Ahlan, aziza,*" she greeted, propping herself up on her elbows. "Have you come to take advantage of me in my weakened condition?"

Dae chuckled, further relieved to see the Scion in good humor. "Oh, I'd love to," she teased, "but sadly I don't think you could handle me right now."

Zafirah raised an eyebrow and sat up a little straighter, visibly struggling not to wince at the stiff pain in her shoulder and chest. "A challenge, hm? Oh, but how this wound debilitates me! I fear I am far too weak to offer much resistance. Indeed, I am quite thoroughly at your mercy, my Tahirah."

"I can see that." Dae sat gingerly on the edge of the bed, out of Zafirah's reach. She knew if the Scion managed to add her hands to the invitation she would never be able to resist, which would doubtless lead to much pleasure for herself and possible death for Zafirah. So she folded her hands primly in her lap and regarded the recovering woman apologetically. "But you know we can't do any of that stuff yet," she said. "I'm sure Falak gave you the same warnings she gave me."

"Falak, bah! She underestimates the recuperative power of sexual pleasure." The sapphire gaze became pleading. "Would you not like to make me feel better?"

Dae groaned. "You know I would, but I'm not going to risk your health by exhausting your energy in lovemaking when you should be resting." She reached out and laid her hand on Zafirah's shoulder. "Once you're healed, I promise you can introduce me to every erotic thing you've been dreaming of these last few months. But until then, we're both going to behave ourselves. Understand?"

Zafirah pouted. "Would you not even allow me to touch you a little? I could bring you pleasure without moving much at all."

"Oh? And I can trust you not to get carried away, right?"

"Of course!"

Dae shook her head. "When we make love, Zafirah, I *want* you to get carried away. I want us both to get carried away." She sighed at the thwarted expression on the Scion's face. "Hey, come on. Don't look like that. It's a few more days, maybe a week or two at most. Aren't I worth the wait?" It was a low blow, but Dae needed Zafirah's compliance.

As expected, Zafirah immediately hung her head and looked properly chastised. "I just want you so much," she whispered fiercely, unable to meet Dae's eyes.

"I know. But for now, let's just concentrate on letting your body heal." Her gaze fell to the bandages that wrapped about Zafirah's upper torso. "Does it hurt much?"

"Some," Zafirah admitted. "Like a dull throbbing. My muscles ache and it hurts to stretch them, and my chest feels rather heavy."

"You were shot, right?"

"Yes."

Dae shuddered. "Then you were very lucky," she said quietly, running the fingers of her right hand over the edges of the bandage. "A hair's breadth to the left and…" she trailed off, not wanting to finish that thought. "You promised to return unharmed."

"I did. And I wish with all my heart that I had kept that promise. My heart, and every other part of me also." That comment brought a slight smile to Dae's face, and she wiped a few tears from her eyes before they could fall.

"Does this mean I have not earned my reward?" Zafirah asked.

"No, but you'll have to wait for it a little longer now."

"A dire enough punishment as is, I think."

Dae cleared her throat at the heat in Zafirah's eyes. *Gods, she arouses me so easily! How can it be possible to want something this badly?* She decided to change the subject, thinking it would be wise not to linger on such topics. "Can I get you anything? Maybe something to drink?"

Zafirah licked her lips salaciously, obviously not willing to be so easily detoured. "Something sweet, perhaps?" she purred hopefully.

"Don't make this harder than it has to be for us."

A long sigh, then the heat in her sapphire eyes reluctantly dissipated. "I apologize. And water would be wonderful, thank you."

Dae poured Zafirah a drink from a nearby urn and handed it to her. "So, aside from you being shot, how did the battle go? Did you win?"

"Of course." Zafirah affected a playfully insulted expression that she would even doubt the outcome of the battle. "In the Jaharri tongue, Zafirah means 'victorious,' and I would never shame my father by dishonoring the name he gave me. I believe many years will pass before the renegade tribes find the courage to start their raids again."

"I'm glad." A pause. "Were many people hurt?"

"Some, but not half so many as might have been had we not known the strengths of our enemy. Your advice on the foreign weapons was extremely valuable to me." Zafirah finished off her water and handed the ornate cup back to Dae. "And what of you, *aziza*? How did you pass the time in my absence?"

Dae focused quickly on the embroidered silk cushions on the bed, a thin blade of excitement lancing through her groin at the memory of her experience with Inaya. "Um, you know, I-I just…did the normal stuff, I guess. Nothing too exciting. There was a magician who came and visited us. He was…pretty good, I guess."

"I see." Zafirah sat up straighter, clearly intrigued by her response. "And his illusions were such that they make you blush to remember them, hm?"

Dae willed herself to calm down. "No."

"Then why do you color so? What happened?"

"Nothing."

"You are a terrible liar," Zafirah said. "Tell me, please. I beg of you."

"I…I can't."

"Why not?" Zafirah's voice dropped to a sexy rumble. "Is it something so wicked that you cannot give it voice?"

"No, it's just…it's meant to be a surprise for you, that's all." Dae realized that was the wrong thing to say when Zafirah's interest immediately seemed to double.

"For me? Hm. And why can I not have it now?" Curious sapphire eyes studied her face, and Dae knew she was doing a terrible job concealing her emotions. "Is it something…sexual?"

A slight nod.

"Will you tell me if I guess?"

"No."

"A hint?"

"Uh uh."

Zafirah lay back on her bed and pouted. "You are too cruel to me, Tahirah," she scolded, though her tone was playful. "Now my thoughts shall be plagued with libidinous ponderings for days!"

"Well it serves you right for asking me about it," Dae defended primly. "Now let's talk about something else."

Dae remained with the Scion until it became clear Zafirah needed to rest, then she left with a promise to return later that night. Over the next week she continued in this fashion, spending at least a few hours each day with the Scion as she recovered from her injuries, mostly just talking and helping to ease her boredom, but occasionally indulging in a few kisses and lingering touches. It was obvious Zafirah wasn't accustomed to inactivity; she chafed against the pain of her wounds, wanting to move about and resume her normal routine as soon as possible. Thankfully, once she'd recovered from her fever, she was able to leave her bed and walk around the palace once more, her arm strapped tightly across her chest to keep it still. Dae often joined her, enjoying the company and learning more about the woman who had claimed her heart.

A week and four days passed before Dae began to seriously consider consummating her relationship with Zafirah. She wanted to be certain she wasn't making light of the other woman's condition in order to appease her own desires, but even the most discriminating of her observations couldn't argue with the fact that Zafirah had made a rapid recovery. The Scion's right arm was still stiff and only allowed for a limited range of motion, but her strength had returned in full, and she no longer complained of pain when she breathed deeply. And with her return to health, of course, Zafirah's playful, hopeful seduction resumed. Her dark sapphire eyes burned with need every minute they spent together, and Dae felt her own body growing ever more anxious to sample the ecstasies she had been promised for so long. All her fears were gone now, and when she saw that Zafirah was feeling better, she started planning for what she hoped would be one of the greatest experiences of her life.

It was time for their dreams and desires to be fulfilled.

# Chapter 21

HER PALMS WERE DAMP WITH sweat. Butterflies fluttered about chaotically in her stomach. She sucked on her lower lip in a nervous habit as she strode down the palace hallways, flanked on either side by a harem guard, shoulders squared and eyes alight with excitement and daring. She was aware of the two female guards exchanging amused smiles with one another, neither of them requiring any explanation as to what was motivating her visit to Zafirah's room tonight.

Dae stopped at the entrance to the Scion's bedchamber and waited for the guard to announce her. As soon as she heard Zafirah's welcome she marched brashly into the room and over to the bed, not even glancing at the woman who rose to greet her. Her escort remained standing at attention outside the doorway.

"Dismiss the guards," she said quietly, not trying to conceal the hunger in her voice.

In the pregnant silence that followed her command, Dae heard Zafirah take a sharp breath, clearly recognizing her intent. She waved a hand vaguely to the guards. "Return to your duties," she ordered.

As soon as the sound of the guards retreating footsteps had faded, Dae took a deep breath and reached for the laces of her top. Her back was turned to Zafirah, but she could feel those smoldering eyes burning into her as she quickly stripped off her brief clothing, pleased to find her fingers only trembled slightly. Her trousers and undergarments slid down her legs and pooled around her ankles on the cool marble floor, and she heard Zafirah's breathing hitch suddenly as her form was revealed. Dae glanced over her shoulder and flashed her admirer a sexy smile.

"Are you feeling strong enough," she asked in a seductive purr, "or should I come back later?"

Zafirah's jaw worked up and down a few times before she managed to argue her tongue into forming words. "In truth, I am stricken with a sudden weakness. But I shall endure."

"Excellent." Dae turned around and faced the Scion, feeling a rush of arousal burn through her body as she watched dark sapphire eyes consume every inch of her naked form. She had expected to feel uneasy at this moment, exposed, but instead there was only a sense of excitement and comfort. She trusted Zafirah completely and was eager to get this thing underway, despite her inexperience.

Zafirah's eyes roamed down the girl's body, pausing at her breasts before continuing on to admire her flat stomach and the flare of her hips. Dae rested her right hand on her hip in a languid pose when Zafirah's gaze settled on her bare center, widening her stance slightly to better reveal herself.

"You like it?" Dae asked, running the fingers of her left hand through the neatly trimmed blonde curls and along the smooth flesh of her sex. "I wanted to surprise you with something special, something I knew you'd enjoy."

Zafirah's heart was beating double time trying to keep up with the rush of blood that shot straight to her suddenly needful groin, and for a moment she could only stare in mute astonishment at the erotic sight of Dae's freshly groomed nether regions. This wasn't something she'd been expecting, but it certainly had a powerful effect. *This is it,* she thought exultantly. *The most beautiful woman in the world is standing naked before me, wanting me to make love to her!* "Y-You did this…" Her voice cracked and she cleared her throat. "You did this for me?"

"Uh huh." Dae continued stroking herself with a single fingertip. "What do you think?"

"I think I should like to appreciate your efforts in as intimate a fashion as possible."

Dae's eyes danced merrily. "That's exactly what I was hoping for."

Zafirah started to recover some of her equilibrium at seeing the playful expression on Dae's face. "How did..?"

"Inaya helped me the first time." Emerald eyes lowered for a moment sheepishly. "She was, uh, eager to make it a...pleasing...experience for me. And I have to confess I didn't do much to fight her off."

Zafirah's eyes widened. "She pleasured you?"

Dae nodded. "I'm sorry. I know I agreed to behave myself if you did, but I...I couldn't help it. I've never had to deal with these sorts of feelings before. I guess I got carried away. But..." Green eyes glanced up shyly through blonde bangs. "I was hoping you might be willing to forgive my lack of self control, if I forgive you for getting yourself injured."

Under the circumstances, Zafirah thought she would have forgiven Dae for bedding her entire harem. And probably half the army, too! "You are young, Tahirah. It is understandable that you are eager to explore the wonders of sexual pleasure, and I would imagine self-control will come with experience."

"I thought you'd understand." Dae took a few steps toward her, her voice dropping to a lower pitch. "And you know, I'm going to try very hard to make up for my little indiscretion."

Zafirah's nostrils flared as the girl approached. She was amazed she hadn't just thrown Dae onto the bed and begun ravishing her by now. But she wanted this to be as wonderful an experience for her *aziza* as she could make it, which would require patience and reserve. Still, imaginings of what Dae and Inaya might have done to one another skipped through her mind tauntingly, exciting her further. "This indiscretion..?"

Dae paused, one blonde brow raised curiously. "What about it?"

"I should very much like to hear more of it."

Dae didn't seem at all surprised by her request; in fact by the look on her face it appeared she had expected nothing less. She glanced down the length of her own naked body, then at Zafirah, who was still clad in a flowing silk *chador*. "You're way overdressed," she stated, closing the distance between them further, almost daring the Scion to give in and take her. "If you stand very still and behave yourself while I rectify that situation, I'll describe exactly what Inaya and I did."

Zafirah straightened herself slightly and closed her eyes, thinking it would be easier to endure being disrobed by the girl if she didn't have to look at the glory of her unveiled body. Dae accepted this as an invitation to continue and reached out to begin unraveling the folds of silk cloth. As her fingers worked to free Zafirah of her clothes, Dae began relating the tale of her experience with Inaya. Though she spoke softly, Zafirah could sense her partner's rising desire and enjoyed the caress of a light coastal breeze against her bare skin. With her eyes closed, she had no trouble conjuring to mind pictures to illustrate the story being told to her. *Perhaps in the future, Dae and I might share our pleasure with Inaya… and maybe many others.* Zafirah recalled the look on Dae's face when she had spoken of her experiences with Johara, Hayam, and Suhayla. *Yes, I think she would find that notion very appealing. Perhaps the whole harem…* Zafirah groaned audibly, a slight tremble running through her at the images that sprang to mind.

Dae had actually rehearsed her story in anticipation of Zafirah's desire to hear it, and having overheard a number of the more risque tales told by the other pleasure-servants, she knew just how to paint a veiled and tempting picture for her lover-to-be. Watching her expression of restrained but rising excitement, thoroughly enjoying the effect her words were having, Dae admired each new area of skin as it was revealed. Undressing Zafirah was something she'd imagined doing countless times in her daydreams, but the task was far more erotic than even her most lurid and adventurous fantasies had allowed for.

*It's like unwrapping a birthday present,* she thought, licking her lips and admiring every newly revealed section of olive-tanned skin as she peeled off the *chador. A tall, amazingly gorgeous birthday present with bright blue eyes and*—more cloth fell away, causing Dae's mouth to go dry as all the moisture in her body was called to a more urgent appointment in the south—*Oh my! Very nice, very tasty-looking breasts, on a woman who's going to let me do anything I want with her!* Caught up in her licentious musings, Dae forgot where she was in her story and stammered slightly. She shook her head to clear it, choosing to ignore Zafirah's slightly amused smile, then continued.

When at last Dae had completed her task, she stepped back a few paces to fully admire Zafirah's body, tossing aside the length of gilt-edged silk that made up the *chador*. The Scion's right arm and shoulder were still wrapped in bandages, so Dae wasn't willing to disturb the still-tender injury any more than she needed to. Besides, there was plenty to look at besides that small covered area, and Dae was no longer shy about staring. So much flesh. So much soft muscle. It was difficult to know where to begin.

Glinting eyes opened and regarded her steadily, waiting for her next move. Dae remained still for long moments, and Zafirah made no move to hurry her, seemingly content to just allow her the opportunity to once again enjoy the sight of her body. When Dae had concluded her appreciative inspection, she looked up into Zafirah's eyes shyly. "I'm not really sure how to start."

"How would you like to start?"

Dae gave a half-shrug.

"Well, I would be happy to lead this dance if you so desire. Or"—Zafirah bowed humbly—"perhaps you might be more at ease having me as your most willing and enthusiastic servant, attentive to your every whim…?"

Dae considered those options seriously, grateful to Zafirah for giving her the choice. Of course both scenarios were intriguing, but for their first time together, Dae decided she'd be more comfortable being in control of what happened. She squared her shoulders and pointed to the bed. "Lie down on your stomach." A breath. "Please."

Zafirah recognized the same sudden excitement at having control light up Dae's eyes as she had seen when she'd posed for the girl many weeks ago. She bowed slightly and did as instructed, settling herself facedown on the silk sheets of her bed, taking just a moment to make certain her stiff arm wouldn't cause her any pain. She waited, feeling Dae's eyes exploring her backside and thighs, hearing silence, then the clink of glass from somewhere to her right. A moment later she felt the weight of the girl's body shift the mattress slightly as Dae joined her on the bed. Something warm and liquid was poured onto her sensitized skin, then delicate hands began to roam over her muscles slowly, exploring with only a slight degree of hesitance. Zafirah moaned low and deep, applauding the girl's chosen course. When Dae spoke, her smile was almost audible.

"This is something I learned from the other girls. I think they enjoyed massaging me almost as much I enjoyed letting them, although"— a soft giggle—"I'm pretty sure they were just trying to get me worked up so I'd let them do other things to me. Things I wanted to share with you…at least for the first time." Soft hands slick with scented oil spread like dragonfly wings over Zafirah's shoulder blades, firmly kneading the muscle before journeying lower. "Do you like it?"

"Mmmm." Zafirah's eyes were closed with pleasure as she hummed contentedly. "Very much."

"Am I doing it right? I've never—"

"Perfectly, my Tahirah. I do not think you could touch me in any style other than absolute perfection."

Dae's touches quickly gained confidence as she acquainted herself more intimately with Zafirah's body. "I always got really…wet…when I let the others do this to me," she admitted quietly. "And when they told me all the other things they wanted to do…all the pleasures they wanted to share with me…it wasn't easy resisting the temptations they offered."

"And how do you find being the provider of such pleasure? Does it arouse you also?"

"Yes." Zafirah felt Dae shift on the bed, kneeling beside her and settling the length of her thigh against her hip as her hands drifted down to her buttocks. Zafirah's breath caught in her throat when the girl boldly pressed her fingers between her thighs, stroking against the wet heat of her core. "As it does you, I see."

Zafirah growled when the fingers were withdrawn.

"Everything about you arouses me, Zafirah," Dae continued. "Your body. Your eyes. The sound of your voice. The way you look at me. And especially the way you kiss me." Her hands were now working on the firm muscles of Zafirah's upper thigh. "You know what I'd like to do right now?"

"Uh…no."

Dae's tone turned purely wicked, teasing, and playful. "I'd like to straddle you and rub myself against your…" She gave Zafirah's butt a light smack.

Zafirah groaned, feeling the molten river between her legs flow stronger. Gods, the girl was going to kill her if she kept up her game!

"You'd feel so slippery and hot against me." Dae's voice dropped a full octave. "It'd be so easy to just ride you till I came!"

"By the Gods!" After such an extended period without pleasure, Zafirah's body was quickly pushed to the edge by Dae's words. Her breathing accelerated and every muscle in her body tensed as the pressure built within her. As much as she wanted to allow Dae to bask in this foreplay, she knew it wouldn't take much more from the girl to send her soaring.

Dae's hands paused. "You're close already, aren't you?"

Zafirah nodded, trying to concentrate on the hands massaging her and not on the sensation of lust-fueled pressure building within her.

"You're not used to going so long without release, right?"

Another nod. Zafirah tried to keep herself still, wanting to allow Dae to move at her own pace. There was a long moment of silence, and she could sense the young girl considering her next course of action carefully. When she spoke, her voice was steady and determined.

"Could you spread your legs a little for me, please?"

Zafirah almost sobbed with relief at the request, complying quickly and without comment. She needed this. Oh, how she needed this! Her body froze completely when she felt Dae slide two oil-slicked fingers between her legs to stroke her sex from behind, and she fought against the first rolling waves of ecstasy for as long as she could. But Dae's fingers found an instinctive rhythm quickly, and feeling the innocence and awe in her touch was more than Zafirah could endure. After only a few moments the sensations overwhelmed her, and she squirmed in breathless, ecstatic release, the climax so sudden and powerful that it tore a cry from her throat. As the fingers continued to gently fondle her spasming sex, Zafirah dimly heard Dae's voice speaking calmly over the roar of her passion. "This is just to take the edge off. There are so many things I want us to do tonight, but I can see you're a bit impatient so…" Zafirah didn't hear any more, her senses listening only to those wonderful fingers working their magic on her raging core.

When at last the pulses of ecstasy had run their course, Zafirah collapsed limply on the bedsheets. Her heart—which moments ago seemed ready to burst—adopted a less critical rhythm, and her breathing slowly returned to normal. She felt Dae's fingers withdraw from her sensitive sex and casually resume their task of massaging her legs. Zafirah hummed happily, enjoying the lingering tingles in her blood, feeling relaxed for the first time in weeks. "Thank you so much, *aziza*," she said, glancing over her shoulder at the obviously pleased blonde. "My body responds so readily to you, to your touch, your words…I could restrain my need no longer."

Dae's nose crinkled delightedly. "You're very welcome." Watching and hearing Zafirah climax had been an incredible and extremely arousing experience—more so than last time, because now Dae had known she was the one directly responsible for that pleasure. There was a certain sense of pride that came from providing such pleasure. As she finished rubbing oil into the last part of Zafirah's legs, the urge to return her fingers to that velvet heat grew stronger, and Dae imagined loving the older woman as she had seen Hayam love Johara, burying her fingers deep within her sex. She drew back a little to give Zafirah room. "Could you turn over now, please? I'd like to do your front."

As soon as Zafirah had settled herself again, Dae spent a few minutes just letting her eyes admire the feast of flesh before her, conscious of those startlingly clear sapphire gems watching her avidly. Her hands trembled slightly as she poured more oil over the Scion's body, running a line down the valley of her cleavage, along the taut muscles of her abdomen, and finally down to her already slick mound. Setting aside the small glass vial, Dae leaned forward and claimed Zafirah's lips. The two dueled softly with their tongues for long minutes, Dae making good use of the control her position afforded her to guide and control the kiss. She boldly nibbled on Zafirah's lower lip, then licked along her jawline before suckling at her neck, excited by the clean scent of the woman's dark hair and the readiness of her body for more pleasure. She continued laying kisses over Zafirah's face, occasionally returning to dance with her mouth and tongue. Dae slid her hands between their bodies tentatively and cupped her full breasts. It was amazing, but she could almost taste the change in the Scion's skin. When her fingers sought out the stiff points of Zafirah's nipples, Dae was rewarded with an enthusiastic, "Yes, Tahirah! Touch me!" She tore her mouth away from Zafirah's neck, wanting to watch what she was doing.

Zafirah's breasts were smaller than her own, firm yet soft, and infinitely touchable. Dae's fingers dipped into the river of oil running through her cleavage, then began gently covering every inch of bronzed skin with the glistening liquid. She took her time, knowing from her experiences with Johara just how wonderful it could feel to have one's breasts thoroughly attended to, and wanting to demonstrate everything she'd learned for Zafirah's pleasure. "Your skin is so soft," she said quietly. "Are your breasts very sensitive?"

Zafirah's jaw clenched tight as Dae lovingly fondled her. "Very."

"I can tell. And I want to learn everything that pleases you, Zafirah. Everything about your body; every muscle...every aching nerve...and every way I might consume you."

The Scion applauded her words with a throaty groan.

When she felt satisfied with her manual efforts, Dae let her hands drift lower to Zafirah's rippling abdomen. Her fingers traced over several old battle scars. She hesitated only a moment to wonder if the oil were safe to consume, then decided she didn't really care if it wasn't and dipped her head down to lavish those glorious breasts with her lips, teeth, and tongue. Zafirah clutched at the silk sheets desperately, staring up at the ceiling with passion-glazed eyes as Dae hungrily ravished her.

"Oh Gods! YESSSS!"

The oil tasted slightly bitter, but Zafirah's flesh was intoxicating. Dae ran the tip of her tongue in tight circles around the nub of a hard nipple, then tugged it between her teeth, grinning at her lover's responses. But as much as she would have liked to spend the rest of the night devoting her attention solely to Zafirah's breasts, Dae's fingers were itching to do some more exploring further south—explorations which would require her eyes to act as overseers. Reluctantly she pulled herself away from her banquet so she could guide her touches with more confidence down to toy with the neatly-groomed dark curls that seemed to point her toward the even more intriguing mound of Zafirah's sex.

She heard Zafirah's breathing turn ragged the moment she realized where her attention had shifted. Without hesitation the tall woman spread her legs, inviting Dae's eyes to roam where they would. Though she'd climaxed just minutes ago, Zafirah seemed more than ready to soar again, but she made no move to hasten Dae's explorations.

Dae gazed at the swollen lips of Zafirah's sex, seeing them glistening more from her previous orgasm than from the scented oil she'd been applying. Her fingers played over the hollow of Zafirah's hip, delaying the moment of contact while she sorted through exactly what she intended to do here. *I could taste her*, she considered, imagining how it might feel to lower her lips and feast on that slick flesh just as she had feasted on her breasts. But she was very uncertain of herself in that field yet, conscious of her inexperience now more than ever. *I want to taste her, but I don't really know how. I mean, I've seen Johara and Hayam together, and Suhayla, but I still have only a vague idea of what to do. Maybe I should let her show me first before I try that.* Dae didn't let herself dwell too long on the shortcomings of her naïveté; there were many other things she could explore for the time being.

Dae looked back to Zafirah, who had been watching her intently. She smiled, inching her fingers closer to the heat she could feel radiating from her lover's center. "I want to be inside you," she said. "Would you like that?"

"Please. I need you now!"

Dae let her fingers lightly stroke Zafirah's labia, exploring and learning. She watched the older woman's eyes squeeze shut and her body tense eagerly, then very gently sent two fingers in search of deeper heat.

"Oh yes!" Zafirah's back arched, and she struggled visibly to steady her breathing and maintain control as Dae felt her fingers gripped by desperate muscles.

Dae watched her fingers disappear into Zafirah's core, amazed by what she was feeling. *I'm inside her!* The realization of such intimacy was beautifully terrifying, and Dae was surprised to feel tears in her eyes as she slipped deeper into her new lover. "I can feel you all around me," she whispered in awe. "I can feel your muscles pulling me into you. You feel sssooo soft...so wet."

"For you," Zafirah gasped, her focus devoted wholly on the sensation of Dae's fingers within her. "Please, more. I want to feel more of you!"

Dae responded by adding a third finger to the two already inside the Scion, instinct and intuition guiding her now to find a slow rhythm as she thrust in and out of Zafirah. After a moment, she twisted her hand around a little and found she could use her thumb to stimulate her lover's clitoris as she worked. This discovery prompted some rather vocal praise from the writhing Scion.

"Yes Tahirah! *Katha ath nan!*"

Dae paused, uncertain of the Jaharri words. "What?"

"Keep going! Touch me more, please! Never stop."

Dae cheerfully resumed, exhilarated as much by the desperate lust in Zafirah's expression as she was by the readiness of her body's response. Zafirah's cries of passion sounded like music to her ears, and she was especially pleased when her ministrations earned an enthusiastic "*Nek ni!*" from her lover. She was even more gratified when she felt the muscles around her fingers begin to tighten, warning of an impending climax. Dae sped up, watching Zafirah tense and delighting in the sound of her name being cried out as a sudden flood of liquid soaked her hand. The tremors continued to wrack Zafirah's body for long moments, squeezing Dae's fingers gently until they eased. When she finally withdrew, Dae moved so she could gather her spent lover in her arms while she recovered, feeling very pleased with herself despite how overwhelming the experience had been.

Wrapped in the warm and gentle embrace as she caught her breath, Zafirah couldn't have imagined a more blissful union. Dae's fingers combed lovingly through her long dark hair, and she gave a low sigh of utter contentment. When the roaring fire in her blood had settled back to a simmering heat, Zafirah wriggled around so she could look up into her young lover's grinning face, taking the opportunity to press as much of her naked body against Dae as possible. "You are amazing."

"Really?"

Zafirah nodded sincerely.

"Hm." Dae bent down and kissed her softly. "I wasn't really sure what I was doing. I mean, that's the first time I ever…"

"I understand."

Dae looked faintly embarrassed. "I know I'm not as…experienced, as the other girls, but—"

Zafirah immediately pressed a finger to her lips to quiet her insecurities. "Shh, speak no more of such things. Experience comes with time, and matters far less than a desire to learn. Do not be troubled by fears that I find you in any way unsatisfying, my Tahirah. You inflame my passion more than any woman I have ever known, and feeling you touch me even innocently sends shivers straight to my core."

"Well, I am a pleasure-servant, after all."

"Indeed you are...and so much more." Zafirah's gaze slipped helplessly down Dae's neckline to her cleavage, and she felt that simmering flame within her burn stronger. "But now, I wonder how best I might show my gratitude for the joy you have bestowed upon me." She eyed Dae's naked breasts and licked her lips. "Tell me, *aziza*, how would you have me pleasure you?"

Emerald eyes darted away momentarily, but when they looked back at her Zafirah could plainly tell by the excitement in her expression that Dae had had her answer prepared for a good long while. Resting her weight on her elbows, Dae reclined back on the colorful silken sheets of Zafirah's bed, spreading her legs and gazing directly into her eyes. It appeared any sense of guilt or embarrassment she might normally have felt was being drowned in a rising tide of lust, and Zafirah suspected Dae was actually reveling in this chance to act with complete wantonness. As her thighs parted, Dae let one hand trace the inner curve of her breasts, down her stomach to caress her bare sex; Zafirah's eyes obediently followed the same path. "Lick me," Dae ordered confidently. "I want to feel the acclaimed magic of your tongue."

Zafirah's eyelids hooded as she gazed upon the glistening, naked folds of Dae's sex, her mouth watering at the thought of tasting her lover's most intimate flesh. While she wanted to explore Dae's body slowly and thoroughly, learning every inch of her alabaster skin, she knew there would be time enough for that later. For now, there was only that simple command to obey. "Your wish is my most fervent desire, Tahirah." She moved eagerly to lie between the blonde's legs, smiling at the obvious anticipation in Dae's watchful eyes. When she licked teasingly at the girl's upper thigh, Dae giggled. Zafirah took a deep breath, the scent of her lover's arousal only whetting her appetite. "I hope you enjoy this as much as me," she said, before dipping her head down and taking her first taste of Dae's desire.

Dae cried out at the initial contact, then mewed in rapture as Zafirah flicked her tongue sinuously around her clitoris and between the lips of her sex. Zafirah paused to savor the taste of the girl, humming low in her throat at the sweetness of her essence. She ran a finger teasingly over Dae's blushing labia, grinning up into the watching emerald eyes staring down at her. "Mm...your desire flows like honey from a hive, *aziza*," she whispered, blowing cool air across Dae's heated core and admiring the resulting tremor that shook her thighs. "I could drink from you for days and need no other nourishment."

Zafirah's tongue roamed everywhere, diligent and merciless in its mission of pleasure. The taste of Dae's arousal was more intoxicating than the headiest wine, and Zafirah was thrilled by how responsive she was to her every attention. With her nimble tongue she explored every fold and delicious crevice of Dae's sex, occasionally pausing to suck gently at her clit and savor the honeyed nectar that flowed so abundantly from her core. Zafirah applied her legendary skill to the task of bringing her young lover's body to the edge, if only so she could do it again and again until Dae either begged her to stop or faded from consciousness.

Dae was utterly stunned by the way her body responded. Though she had pondered long on the various devices of pleasure she'd seen in the Scion's collection, and on the many pleasures offered by the beguiling pleasure-servants, this was certainly the act which had occupied Dae's bedtime thoughts more than any other these last few weeks. Zafirah's tongue explored her slowly at first, expertly teasing her passion higher till her senses reeled in a haze of lust. She clutched at the Scion's head, driven by raw need to tangle her fingers in that dark mane and pull her tighter against her desperate center. The sensation defied description. Dae had thought herself no longer a stranger to pleasure, but now realized her experiences were woefully lacking. Nothing that her fingers nor the fingers of those few others who had touched her had ever done came close to the experience of Zafirah's mouth and tongue. Blistering, burning, shattering sparks of exquisite pleasure pounded through her body, coloring her vision in rainbows and reducing her verbal skills to squeaks and screams of joy and encouragement. She felt her climax building like a roaring inferno in the back of her mind and rallied against it valiantly, wanting this feeling to go on and on.

But Dae couldn't hold out against her orgasm for long. She had heard a good deal of talk among the other girls in the harem praising Zafirah's skills as a lover, and could not deny that her reputation was well-earned. She screamed Zafirah's name as her spirit seemed to burst into a thousand glittering shards that rained down from the heavens. But just as her climax reached its peak and began to subside, Zafirah's mouth suddenly clamped down on her swollen clit and suckled forcefully, laving the stiff bundle of nerves firmly with her tongue. Immediately Dae was overwhelmed by a second stunning wave of ecstasy, unable to find breath to scream anew. She managed a slight whimper and a gasp, her body weakening even as her more ethereal senses were cresting higher and higher in a seemingly endless spiral. For a moment the whole world seemed to fall away into blackness beneath her, along with her awareness of what she was experiencing, but when she came back to herself, her body was already in the grip of a third climax, brought on by Zafirah's expert ministrations. She writhed weakly under Zafirah's oral devotions, lightheaded and dizzy as her lungs struggled to find new air. Tangling her fingers in Zafirah's midnight tresses, she managed to drag her lover's lips away from their feast.

"No more," she croaked hoarsely, gasping for breath. "Please...I can't take anymore! I need to catch my breath."

Zafirah withdrew, grinning up at her with lips wet with her release. "As you wish, *aziza*," she agreed cheerfully. "Though I trust we are far from finished with this night's festivities?"

"Sure, just...give me a moment to recover. Gods, you could kill a girl with that tongue!" Dae was grateful for the reprieve from such astonishingly intense pleasure, though half of her wished it could continue without cessation.

Zafirah slid her uninjured arm around Dae and pulled her onto her lap, tangling their legs together and stroking her long golden hair softly. "Was that to your liking?" she inquired playfully.

"Oh yeah." Dae laughed shakily, enjoying the slight friction of the oil covering Zafirah's skin against her body. "Even though I think you nearly killed me!"

"There is a great deal more I plan to show you," Zafirah promised. "I wish to hear more of those delightful cries of pleasure you make just before climax robs you of all reason and abashment."

"I'm not that loud."

The Scion chuckled, not bothering to argue. Instead she began running the fingers of her left hand down over Dae's body, lightly toying with her sensitive breasts and teasing the fires of her passion back to wakefulness.

Dae shivered, content just to lie back and let her lover touch her gently. Zafirah was arousing her, but it wasn't rushed or hurried now. She sighed, feeling fabulously decadent and not minding one bit. "Zafirah?"

"Mm?"

"Can I choose something from the cabinet?"

Zafirah's hands stilled a moment, looking down at her curiously. "Another time, perhaps," she said. "There is the matter of your virginity yet to be dealt with, and I would not have that honor bestowed upon any but my own fingers."

Dae's expression turned thoughtful. "Have you ever...?"

"Deflowered a maiden? Yes, though it has been some time."

"Will it hu...hurt much?"

Zafirah heard the slight quaver in her voice that Dae could not quite suppress and leaned forward to place a soothing kiss on her forehead. "Have no fear, little one," she assured. "I shall be gentle, and any pain you feel will be so overwhelmed by pleasure that your mind will scarcely recognize it."

Dae relaxed a little, feeling an aura of comfort envelope her as she lay in Zafirah's embrace. "I trust you."

Zafirah was quiet for a minute, just letting her touches roam aimlessly over Dae's body, feeling quiet awe at the beauty before her. "When you feel ready, I would be more than happy to demonstrate any device in my collection. Or, if you are taken by an adventurous spirit, perhaps you could test something yourself. On me, or on your own self, if you would prefer to explore your limits in private to better learn what you will find pleasing."

Dae grinned wickedly and rolled an emerald eye up to regard her desert lover. "I think I like the sound of that." A second later she squealed as Zafirah lightly pinched her right nipple.

"I thought you might."

Knowing fingers continued to excite and explore, and Dae closed her eyes and gave herself over to sensation. The way Zafirah touched her was incredible. She felt almost like a goddess, sensing a reverent air to the Scion's attention, as though she were doing more than simply making love to her… She was worshiping something sacred. It was, she admitted privately, enormously flattering to have such a powerful, beautiful woman pay her such intimate attention, and she gave a little moan of encouragement as Zafirah's touches became more intense and purposeful.

Zafirah held herself in check for as long as she could, but Dae was so responsive to her that the need to do more soon grew too powerful. Very gently, she laid the girl down on the sheets once more before beginning a slow journey down her body with hands, lips, and tongue. Her long, dark hair fanned out to cover the pale skin of Dae's torso and abdomen, making the ticklish girl wriggle and laugh. Zafirah smiled when her hand dipped between her silken thighs and Dae spread her legs in eager accommodation, clearly ready for more pleasuring.

This time, Zafirah was more patient and gentle, wanting to be certain Dae was properly relaxed and fully aroused before she went further. Dae was still very sensitive from her previous ravishing, so Zafirah used only the lightest of caresses, shifting her attention constantly from one point to another, never giving direct stimulation to the throbbing, needful bud of her clitoris. Her fingers spread the nectar of Dae's arousal all over her slick sex, teasing her until at last she begged for firmer contact.

"Please, Zafirah, stop teasing me!"

"Relax, Tahirah. Good things reward those with patience to wait."

Dae growled and bucked her hips fiercely. "Well, I'm not really in the mood to be patient right now."

Zafirah chuckled, thinking that for such an innocent maiden, Dae displayed a healthy enthusiasm. "Trust me, my *aziza*. Just relax. Let me love you." Dae's hips thrust forward again, and Zafirah replied with a quick, appeasing lick to the girl's clit. "If you cannot behave yourself, perhaps I should tie you up, hm?"

Emerald eyes looked down sharply, filled with prurient hunger. "Ooh, yes! Yes, do it!"

Zafirah could only shake her head, surprised by how eager Dae had become to experience such carnal delights. "It was intended as a threat, not an incentive. Perhaps another time. Please, lie still for me."

Dae gave her a pouty frown but lay back compliantly. While Zafirah resumed her patient ministrations, she cupped her own breasts and began to play with her nipples, doubtless hoping the extra stimulation might let her reach the edge sooner.

Zafirah knew the best way to take a virgin's maidenhead without pain was to distract her with pleasure, to beguile the senses so all feelings merged into ecstasy. She artfully manipulated Dae's passion, keeping her poised at the brink of release but never quite giving her enough to send her flying. She ignored the pleas and threats directed her way from the frustrated girl, but eventually slid two fingers into the tight, untouched heat of her core. Dae was more than ready, she sensed, feeling the muscles clamp down around her immediately. Pushing forward, Zafirah came to the thin barrier of Dae's maidenhead. She withdrew, massaging the inner walls of her lover's sex gently; at the same time she finally dipped her head down and began lavishing attention on the neglected bundle of nerves that throbbed in time with Dae's rising pulse.

Dae felt it coming and her body tensed in anticipation. She was aware that Zafirah was inside her, touching places she hadn't dared touch herself, and though she dimly feared the pain she knew was coming, she wanted to feel her lover as deep within her as she could possibly get her. This climax came on slowly, the first waves crashing upon her with subtle, lingering force, but followed quickly by a more intense, stunning surge of pleasure. Dae screamed out loud as she felt heat suddenly tear inwards between her legs and was dimly aware that Zafirah had penetrated her completely, forever erasing any trace of her virginity and laying claim to her body in the most deeply intimate way. But the swift stab of pain was only slight, far less traumatic than she had feared, and seemed to push her climax to a higher level. Soon, all she felt were those fingers inside her—stroking her, loving her, keeping her cresting on a wave of ecstasy she prayed would never end.

As if in answer to her unspoken supplication, Zafirah's fingers curled slightly within her, touching some deep, secretive spot inside that her own self-explorations had never sought. The wracking waves of climax intensified, and Dae wondered for half a moment if Zafirah intended to keep her locked in this state of relentless ecstasy forever. When at last the tremors began to subside, Zafirah skilfully slowed her ministrations and allowed her to come back to herself. When she finally withdrew her fingers from their snug nest, she placed a last, lingering kiss to Dae's sex before shifting round so she could hold her tenderly while she recovered.

Dae sighed blissfully as the Scion wrapped her in a calming embrace. She became aware of a slight feeling of dull pain between her legs now that the pleasure had faded, but smiled anyway with the knowledge that she had crossed that final line and had given herself fully to Zafirah.

"How do you feel?" the Scion asked quietly.

Dae snaked her arms around her lover's waist and pulled her tight against her. "I feel wonderful."

"Then I am pleased." Long, graceful fingers twisted fondly through Dae's long hair. "You may be a little sore for a few days to come, but when your body has recovered in full there will be many new pleasures to discover."

"Mm." Dae felt a slight wave of drowsiness steal over her as it so often did in the wake of a climax, but she fought against it, wanting to continue. Looking around Zafirah's room, her eyes fell on a small, intricate bronze statue of two women caught in the throes of passion. Her lips pursed in speculation. "Zafirah?"

"Yes, *aziza*?"

She pointed. "Have you ever done that?"

Zafirah glanced where she indicated, then grinned mischievously. "Indeed I have. Among Jaharri women, the act is known as 'kissing petals.'"

"Oh." Silence. Then, "Can we try it now?"

The Scion chuckled, shaking her head in amusement. "My, such a voracious appetite for one so new to these pleasures." Still, she wasted no time repositioning their bodies on the bed, straddling Dae's left leg and sliding forward so her center pressed against her mound. "Nevertheless, it is an excellent idea."

Dae's eyes rolled back in their sockets as Zafirah began moving against her, the slippery, silken touch of her bare sex against her own providing the most deliciously wet friction. Lying back, she relaxed and let the older woman take the lead, half her mind focused on the sensations between her legs, the other half already planning what they might do next.

She hoped Zafirah wasn't expecting to get much sleep tonight.

# *Epilogue*

The glare of the sun woke Dae late the next morning. Through the slits of her eyes she glared at the windows irritably. Groaning quietly, she stirred and took mental stock of her position. She was lying on Zafirah's bed, the taller woman's body spooned against her own, long, tanned arms wrapped possessively about her middle. She could feel warm breath tickle the back of her neck, and the sensuous sensation of naked skin pressed all along her frame. Dae was a little stiff and sore from the night's activities, but she smiled at the scent of sex that clung to the silk sheets, remembering everything they'd done…and everything Zafirah had promised her they would do in the future.

Closing her eyes against the light, Dae snuggled back against the warm body behind her and let her sleepy thoughts ponder that future and reflect on the months she'd lived in the palace. Since she'd come of age and her parents had begun their reluctant search to find her a husband, Dae had often contemplated the life she would live away from her family. She had imagined a man, handsome and strong, who would treat her with gentlemanly affection. There would be a house with servants and, one day, children, and she would be happy and cared for all her life. She had hoped to find the kind of love she saw every day between her parents, but there had always been something missing from her musings; they had lacked some essential element without which they could never feel real for her. Now, with her recent emotional maturity, Dae recognized those fantasies as those of an innocent child, pale and confused, lacking any trace of passion or desire. Certainly they were a far cry from the fantasies she now entertained with delicious abandon.

Absently twining her fingers with those of her new lover, basking in the aftermath of their first night together, Dae knew that the relationship she had found here with Zafirah—and indeed the friendships she had forged with all the girls of the harem—was more complete and fulfilling than any she could have found in her homeland.

Teeth nipped at her shoulder, drawing her from drowsy musings back to the present, and Dae giggled as Zafirah squeezed her lightly and stretched. That familiar, deep yet feminine voice whispered in her ear. "It is early yet."

"The sun woke me." Dae wriggled around until she was facing her partner. She gazed adoringly into those clear sapphire eyes, reaching out to lightly run her fingers over the contours of the older woman's face. "Good morning."

"A very good morning indeed, that it finds you naked in my arms."

Dae uttered a throaty gasp when she traced her fingertip over Zafirah's lips and she took her finger into her mouth and sucked it briefly. "Inaya told me you prefer to sleep alone after you've finished with your pleasure. Is that true?" she managed to ask.

"It is." A pause. "But it seems every rule has exceptions, and I would never send you back to the seraglio after we make love."

"Mm." Dae regarded Zafirah seriously. "So, where do we go from here?"

"Wherever you wish to go, *aziza*." She gave Dae a cautious, hesitant look. "I love you, Dae. Never doubt that. But it is not within me to resist the temptations of the flesh."

Dae silenced her lover with a kiss, understanding what Zafirah was saying, and what she feared her response might be. "I'm not asking you to give away the harem, Zafirah, or the other girls. I knew all this when I fell in love with you, and long before we made love."

Zafirah was visibly relieved by Dae's understanding. "I would be happy for you to share my quarters," she offered. "In truth, I never thought I would have a Consort, but..."

"You want me to move out of the harem?"

"If you would like."

Dae considered the offer seriously, looking around the room and trying to envision herself living here. At length, she sighed. "I like it in the seraglio. And you're there a lot anyway, right? Almost all the time when you're not busy being Scion. Maybe, for the time being, I could just stay there."

Zafirah's expression fell slightly. "If that is what you would prefer."

"Don't look like that. I'll spend the nights here with you, after all. Although I doubt we'll be doing a lot of sleeping." She reached down and caressed Zafirah's breasts teasingly. "I just enjoy being around the other girls, that's all. They're my friends."

Zafirah's smile returned at the mention of Dae sleeping there. "I understand. And besides,"—she waggled her eyebrows rakishly—"my entire harem would scream for my blood if I deprived them of the opportunity to seduce you!"

Dae laughed, but she could not deny a shiver of anticipation at the thought of improving her skills under the talented instruction of the other pleasure-servants. Inaya had told her the jewel of pleasure held many facets; she longed to at least sample each and every one of the many avenues of pleasure available to her. Thoughts of what new talents she might learn from the other girls sent shivers of anticipation running down her spine.

"W-would that be okay?" Dae asked shyly. "If I let them…do things with me?"

"Do you really need to ask?" Zafirah kissed her soundly. "I am happy for you to share yourself with others, little one…especially if you tell me all the details afterward."

"Or better yet, invite you to join in, right?"

"Of course." Zafirah's eyes burned bright.

"Hmm. Maybe we could see if Inaya would like to join us some time," Dae suggested, thinking it would be extremely exciting to watch Zafirah and her friend together, and to join in when she felt like it. *Four hands*, she thought. *Two tongues. And so many fingers…!* "Or maybe Johara and Hayam. We could be just like them, sharing our love."

"Indeed." Zafirah was silent for a long moment, an odd trace of vulnerability creeping into her normally steady gaze before she said in a carefully casual tone, "I would be much honored if you would agree to consecrate our love in the eyes of the Goddess."

Dae froze, her mind taking several seconds to process Zafirah's words and to realize that she had just been proposed to. "Y-you mean like...a mar— I mean, a joining?"

Zafirah looked away. "If you would prefer not to, I understand completely, but...yes, a joining."

Tears welled suddenly in Dae's eyes. "I'd love that. Very much."

Zafirah's grin was pure delight and relief. "Really?"

"Of course!" Stunned, beyond excited, Dae felt her love and desire for this woman double. She pushed Zafirah down and straddled her belly. "Does this mean I'd be your wife?"

"You would be my Consort...and wife, I suppose."

Dae smiled at the title, liking the way it sounded. Looking down at Zafirah, feeling her hands move around the curve of her hip and up her body to cover her breasts, Dae felt aroused. Zafirah flexed her stomach muscles and grinned up at her when she moaned. "There would be a ceremony and an exchange of vows and tokens. In the eyes of the Jaharri people, we would be as one, unified and unbroken."

"I really like the sound of that." Dae rocked her hips, enjoying the firm muscles pressed against her moistening core. "How about you give me a taste of what I can expect from our wedding night?"

Dae knew the term "wedding" wasn't part of Jaharri vocabulary, but Zafirah seemed to have no difficulty interpreting its intent from her undulating movements. "As you wish, my Tahirah," she said, letting her hands fall away from Dae's breasts so she could help guide the motion of her hips. "As you wish."

Outside in the palace halls, screams of joy and words of lust echoed through the corridors. The marble walls carried the sound clearly over long distances. Guards and servants alike paused to exchange amused grins, shaking their heads and marveling at the endurance and enthusiasm of the little foreign blonde, before they went about their business with the kind of selective deafness that comes only after years of practice.

# Glossary

**Ahlan:** Hello.

**Aseau:** Sunset.

**Aziza:** Beloved.

**Chador:** An article of women's clothing.

**Dohar:** Mid-afternoon.

**Effendi:** A term of respect and honor.

**Haik:** A desert head-dress, consisting of a length of cloth wrapped about the head and face.

**Harem:** 'The forbidden;' The sphere of women in a usually polygynous household and their quarters.

**Hauze:** An artificial water pond.

**Katha ath nan:** Caress my sex.

**Nek ni:** Fuck me.

**Salaam aleikum:** 'Peace be with you.' A polite greeting of respect.

**Seraglio:** The quarters designated to the harem.

**Shamedan:** Candelabra.

**Sirocco:** Summer windstorm.

**Souk:** Market

**Spahi:** Desert cavalry troops

**Maasalama:** Farewell.

**Mehari:** Racing camel.

**Tsharraafna:** I am pleased to meet you.

When writing erotica, every reader is like a light in a darkened room...
Let me know if I turned you on.
:)
Amber.

# About Amber Jacobs

Amber Jacobs was born in Adelaide, South Australia. She grew up in Victoria, spending most of her adolescent years living on a wildlife shelter and helping to care for a motley menagerie of orphaned and injured native animals. Since graduating from University with a BA in Communication, Amber has worked in a variety of jobs but has always nurtured her creative energy through writing and art. She is always working on new stories and ideas that usually incorporate her passion for animals, medieval history, and lesbian romance.

## CONNECT WITH AMBER:
Facebook: www.facebook.com/people/
Amber-Jacobs/100010392061669

E-Mail: amberj8@hotmail.com

# Other Books from Ylva Publishing

www.ylva-publishing.com

# Heart's Surrender
**Emma Weimann**

ISBN: 978-3-95533-183-2
Length: 305 pages (63,000 words)

Neither Samantha Freedman nor Gillian Jennings are looking for a relationship when they begin a no-strings-attached affair. But soon simple attraction turns into something more. What happens when the worlds of a handywoman and a pampered housewife collide? Can nights of hot, erotic fun lead to love, or will these two very different women go their separate ways?


# Hearts and Flowers Border
(2nd revised edition)
**L.T. Smith**

ISBN: 978-3-95533-179-5
Length: 291 pages (71,000 words)

A visitor from her past jolts Laura Stewart into memories—some funny, some heart-wrenching. Thirteen years ago, Laura buried those memories so deeply she never believed they would resurface. Still, the pain of first love mars Laura's present life and might even destroy her chance of happiness with the beautiful, yet seemingly unobtainable Emma Jenkins. Can Laura let go of the past?

# Hot Line
**Alison Grey**

ISBN: 978-3-95533-048-4
Length: 114 pages (27,000 words)

Two women from different worlds. Linda, a successful psychologist, uses her work to distance herself from her loneliness. Christina works for a sex hotline to make ends meet. Their worlds collide when Linda calls Christina's sex line. Instead of wanting phone sex, Linda makes an unexpected proposition. Does Christina dare accept the offer that will change both their lives?

# Don't Be Shy
**Jae and Astrid Ohletz [Ed.]**

ISBN: 978-3-95533-383-6
Length: 350 pages (139,000 words)

From kinky phone sex to unexpected, steamy encounters with the new neighbor. Fun with a love swing and unexpected relaxation techniques. This anthology has it all.

Twenty-five authors of lesbian fiction bring you short stories that focus on the sensual, red-hot delights of sex between women and the celebration of the female form in all its diverse hedonism.

Are you in the mood for something spicy?

# Coming from Ylva Publishing

www.ylva-publishing.com

# The Club

**A.L. Brooks**

Welcome to The Club—leave your inhibitions and your everyday cares at the door, and indulge yourself in an evening of anonymous, no-strings, woman-on-woman action. For many visitors to The Club, this is exactly what they are looking for, and what they get. For others, however, the emotions run high, and one night of sex changes their lives in ways they couldn't have imagined.

*Nights of Silk and Sapphire*
© 2016 by Amber Jacobs

ISBN: 978-3-95533-511-3

Also available as e-book.

Published by Ylva Publishing, legal entity of Ylva Verlag, e.Kfr.

Ylva Verlag, e.Kfr.
Owner: Astrid Ohletz
Am Kirschgarten 2
65830 Kriftel
Germany

www.ylva-publishing.com

First edition: 2016

Credits
Edited by Gill McKnight and Therese Arkenberg
Cover Design and Print Layout by Streetlight Graphics

Printed in Great Britain
by Amazon